Lavender Morning

BOOKS BY JUDE DEVERAUX

The Velvet Promise
Highland Velvet
Velvet Song
Velvet Angel
Sweetbriar
Counterfeit Lady
Lost Lady
River Lady
Twin of Fire
Twin of Ice
The Temptress
The Raider
The Princess
The Awakening
The Maiden
The Taming
The Conquest
A Knight in Shining Armor
Holly
Wishes
Mountain Laurel
The Duchess
Eternity

JUDE DEVERAUX

Lavender Morning

ATRIA BOOKS

New York London Toronto Sydney

ATRIA BOOKS

A Division of Simon & Schuster, Inc.
1230 Avenue of the Americas
New York, NY 10020

This Atria Books hardcover edition May 2009

ATRIA BOOKS and colophon are trademarks
of Simon & Schuster, Inc.

For information about special discounts for bulk purchases,
please contact Simon & Schuster Special Sales at 1-866-506-1949
or business@simonandschuster.com

Designed by Davina Mock-Maniscalco

Manufactured in the United States of America

1   3   5   7   9   10   8   6   4   2

Library of Congress Cataloging-in-Publication Data
Deveraux, Jude.
Lavender morning / Jude Deveraux
1. Inheritance and succession—Fiction. 2. Self-actualization
(Psychology)—Fiction.
I. Title.
PS3554.E9273L38   2009
813'.54—dc22   2008023637

ISBN-13: 978-1-4165-9175-7
ISBN-10:   1-4165-9175-3

Prologue

"HELEN?" ASKED THE person on the other end of the line. "Helen Aldredge?"

If anyone had asked her, Helen would have said that it had been so long since she'd heard Edilean Harcourt's voice that she wouldn't have recognized it. But she did. She'd heard those elegant, patrician tones only a few times, but each time had been significant. Because of who the caller was, Helen didn't point out that her married name was Connor. "Miss Edi? Is that you?"

"What a good memory you have."

Helen visualized the woman as she remembered her: tall, thin, perfect posture, her dark hair never out of place. Her clothes were always of the finest quality and of a timeless style. She had to be close to ninety now—Helen's father David's age. "I had good ancestors," Helen said, then wanted to bite her tongue. Her father and Miss Edi had once been engaged to marry, but when Edilean returned from World War II, her beloved David was married to Helen's mother, Mary Alice Welsch. The trauma had been so great that Miss Edi turned the big, old house her family had owned for generations over to her wastrel of a brother, left the town named for her ancestress, and never married. Even today, some of the older people in Edilean spoke of the Great Tragedy—and they still looked at Helen's mother with cool eyes. What David and Mary Alice had done caused the end of the direct line of the Harcourt family—the founding family. Since Edilean, Virginia, was so near Colonial Williamsburg, losing direct descendants of people who had hobnobbed with George Washington and Thomas Jefferson was a major blow to them.

"Yes, you do have good ancestry," Miss Edi said without hesitation. "In fact, I'm so sure of your capabilities that I decided to ask **you** to help me."

"Help you?" Helen asked cautiously. All her life she'd been told of the feuds and anger that had come about because of what happened in her father's lifetime. She wasn't supposed to have heard about it, because everything was talked about in whispers, but Helen had always been a curious person. She'd sat to one side of the porch, played with her dolls, and listened.

"Yes, dear, help," Miss Edi said in a patronizing way that made Helen blush. "I'm not going to ask you to bake a hundred cookies for the church sale, so you can get that out of your mind."

"I wasn't—" Helen started to defend herself, then stopped. She was at the kitchen sink and she could see her husband, James, outside struggling with the new bird feeder. Someone should outlaw retirement for men, she thought for the thousandth time. Without a doubt, James would come in angry about the feeder and she'd have to listen to his tirade. He used to manage hundreds of employees across several states, but now all he had was his wife and grown son to boss around. More than once Helen had gone running to wherever Luke was and asked if she could spend the afternoon with him. Luke would give her that amused look of his and set her to weeding.

"All right," Helen said, "what can I help you with?" Never mind that she hadn't spoken to this woman in what? Twenty years?

"I've been told that I have less than a year to live and—" She cut off at a sound from Helen. "Please, no sympathy. No one has ever wanted to leave this earth more than I do. I've been here much too long. But being told I have a full year left has made me think about what I still need to do in my life."

At that, Helen smiled. Miss Edi might no longer live in the town named after her great-something grandmother, but she'd made an impact on it. That the town still existed was due to Miss Edi. "You've done a lot for Edilean. You've—"

"Yes, dear, I know I've paid for things and written letters and raised a ruckus when people wanted to take away our homes. I've done all that, but that was easy. It just took money and noise. What I haven't done is right some wrongs that happened when I was a young woman."

Helen nearly groaned aloud. Here it comes, she thought. The Story. The one about how her mother, Mary Alice, stole Miss Edi's boyfriend at the end of World War II. Poor Miss Edi. Rotten ol' Mary Alice. She'd heard it all before. "Yes, I know—"

"No, no," Miss Edi said, yet again cutting Helen off. "I'm not talking about what your parents did back when the dinosaurs roamed the earth. That's done with. I'm talking about now, today. What happened then has changed today."

Frowning, Helen turned away from the sight of her husband kicking the bird feeder, which he couldn't get to stand upright. "You mean that if my father had married **you,** quite a few lives would be different," she said slowly.

"Perhaps," Miss Edi said, but she sounded amused. "What do you know about the fourteenth of November, 1941?"

"That it was just before the attack on Pearl Harbor?" Helen asked cautiously.

"Then I take it that your eavesdropping when you were a little girl didn't let you hear everything, did it?"

In spite of herself, Helen laughed. "No, it didn't. Miss Edi, would you please tell me what this is about? My husband is about to come in for lunch, so I don't have much time."

"I want you to come here to Florida to visit me. Think you can bear to be away from your husband for that long?"

"The man is retired. I may move in with you."

Miss Edi gave a dry little laugh. "All right, but you can't tell anyone where you're going or who you're seeing. I have some things to talk to you about, and we have to figure out how you're going to do what has to be done. I will, of course, pay for everything. Unless you're not interested, that is."

"A free trip? Secrets revealed? I'm very interested. How do we arrange this?"

"I'll send all the travel information to my house and you can pick it up there. How's that handsome son of yours?"

Helen hesitated. Should she give the stock answer she gave to everyone else? Hardly anyone knew the full extent of what Luke had been through in the last few years, but Helen thought that, somehow, Miss Edi knew. "He's recovering slowly. Mostly he hides out in the gardens around town and digs holes. He doesn't want to talk to anyone about his problems, not even me."

"How about if I change his life?"

"For good or bad?" Helen asked, but she stood up straighter. Her only child, her son, was in pain, and she didn't know how to help him.

"For good," Miss Edi said. "All right, you better go give your husband lunch. Remember that you're not to tell anyone about me. The tickets should be there tomorrow by ten, so pick them up at the house, then call me. When you get here, I'll have someone meet you at the airport."

"All right," Helen said as the back door opened.

"Damned thing!" she heard James muttering. "I should write the attorney general's office about that worthless piece of garbage."

Helen rolled her eyes. "Will do," she whispered. "I have to go."

Miss Edi hung up, sat by the telephone, looked at it for a moment, then she used the two canes to get out of the chair. Her legs were causing her so much pain today that she wanted to lie down and never get up. She hobbled to the big box that sat on top of the piano bench and thought of the photos inside and of the full stories of what had happened to all of them so very long ago.

She picked up the thin green book that was their high school senior yearbook. Class of 1937. She didn't need to open it because she could see all of them in her mind, and she was glad she hadn't been to Edilean, Virginia, in the last few years. She missed the place, missed the trees and the changing seasons, but what she didn't like was seeing the aging faces of her friends. Or seeing their names on gravestones. Who would have believed that the last remaining people alive would be her and David and Mary Alice? And Pru—but she didn't count. Nearly all the others had died, some of them recently, some a ways back. Poor Sara died back in . . . Edi couldn't remember the date, but she knew it was a long time ago.

She put the book down and looked at the little box that contained photos of all of them, but she didn't open it. She was feeling worse than usual today, and she was sure the doctor was wrong. She didn't have a year left, but she was glad of that. The pain in her old, scarred legs was getting worse. On the days when she did get out of bed, she had to force herself. And when she couldn't make herself get up, she had that annoyingly cheerful little nurse get her laptop computer, and she spent her whole day on it. What a glorious thing the Internet was! And how very much she could find out through it.

She'd even looked up David's family and seen that his eldest brother had made it through the war. He'd lived to make a success of a business. Several times she'd come close to calling the family, but the pain she knew she'd feel stopped her. Besides, she doubted if they'd ever heard of her. David was killed just weeks after they met.

As Edi walked toward the kitchen, she thought of Jocelyn. As always, just the thought of the young woman made her pain ease and her mind relax.

It had been Alexander McDowell, the man whose life was at the center of all the secrets and heartache, who'd put Edi together with the young girl.

"Her grandparents, the Scovills, were dear, dear friends of mine," Alex said, his voice raspy from a lifetime of cigarettes. "Their beautiful daughter Claire was sent to the best schools. At her coming-out party, she had eleven marriage proposals. But she didn't marry until she was thirty-three, and then she chose the country club's handyman."

Miss Edi had been through too much in her life to be a snob. "What was he like as a person?"

"Good to her. Lazy, barely literate, but good to her. They had a daughter named Jocelyn, and just a few years later, beautiful Claire died."

Maybe it was the name "Claire" or maybe it was that at that time Edi had been at a crossroads in her life. She'd spent her working life traveling with Dr. Brenner. His family's fortune gave him the freedom to work unpaid, so he'd traveled around the world, helping wherever he was needed. It was said that if a bomb was dropped, Dr. Brenner booked his flight before it exploded. The truth was that Edi did the booking, and she was always with the doctor.

But when he retired, that meant Edi did also. Should she go back to Edilean to live in that big house with her brother, who bored her to death? Or should she live quietly on her pension and savings and maybe write her memoirs—yet another boring prospect?

When Alex McDowell, a man she'd known since they were babies together, offered her a job managing charity funds and looking after the young granddaughter of his friends, Edi accepted.

"I don't know what the child is like," Alex said those many years ago. "For all I know, she could have the brains of her father. What I do know is that after her mother died, she lived with her grandparents. After they died, Jocelyn—that's the girl's name—was left in the full custody of her father."

"He doesn't harm her, does he?" Miss Edi asked quickly.

"No, I've had PIs looking in on her, and I've had no reports of anything like that, but her father has reverted."

"Reverted? To what?" Miss Edi asked sharply.

Alex chuckled. "Worse than what you're imagining. He remarried to a woman with identical twin daughters, and they ride motorcycles together."

For a second, Miss Edi closed her eyes. The name "Clare" and the image of motorcycles filled her mind.

". . . Boca Raton," Alex was saying.

"Sorry, but I didn't hear all that."

"I have a house in the same gated community where young Jocelyn lives with her father and the Steps, as she calls them. One of my detectives talked to her."

"She talked to a stranger?" Miss Edi snapped.

Again, Alex chuckled. "You haven't changed, have you? I can assure you that the meeting was well chaperoned. They were at a NASCAR race."

"A what?"

"Just trust me on this: You'd hate the thing. Edi, what I'm asking is if you'd mind living in Boca Raton. You'd be three houses from Claire's daughter and watching out for her while you work for me."

If it had been anyone else, Edi would have checked her enthusiasm, but Alex was an old, trusted friend. "I would love to," she said. "Truly love to."

"I thought the warmth of Florida would be good for your legs."

"Not moving back to Edilean and being looked at with pity for being an old maid will be the best thing for my legs."

"You, an old maid," Alex said. "I will always see you as twenty-three and the most beautiful woman in—"

"Stop that or I'll tell Lissie on you."

"She loves you as much as I do," Alex said quickly. "So give me your address and I'll send you all the particulars."

"Thank you," Edi said. "Thank you very much."

"No," Alex said, "the thanks are always to you. If it weren't for you . . ."

"I know. Give kisses to everyone for me," she said, then hung up. It was a full moment before her smile nearly cracked her face. She was a great believer in doors opening and closing. The door with Dr. Brenner had closed and a new one had opened.

Now, so many years later, Jocelyn Minton was the love of Miss Edi's life. The child she didn't have. The heart of the home she'd missed out on.

Whenever Jocelyn could escape her duties at that little college that worked her half to death but paid her little, she jumped in her car and drove home. After the obligatory visit to her father and stepmother, she'd head straight to Edi's house. The two of them would embrace, thoroughly glad to see each other. Jocelyn was the only person who wasn't intimidated by Edi's stern appearance. She'd hug Edi just as she'd done when she was a child. "My lifesaver," she called Edi. "Without you I don't know how I would have survived my child-hood."

Edi knew it was an exaggeration; after all, people didn't die from a lack of books. They didn't actually die from being stuck in a house with a fa-ther, stepmother, and two stepsisters who thought truck rallies were high society. But there were different ways to die.

The truth was that their meeting had been the best thing that ever happened to both of them. Edi had only lived in the lovely house Alex had bought for four months when she first saw the child with her family. The house they lived in had belonged to Jocelyn's grandparents, and after her mother's death it had been willed to the granddaughter. It hadn't taken much work to find out that what money had been left had been quickly spent.

Miss Edi saw the parents in their leather clothes, their two overly tall twin daughters wearing as little as was legally allowable, then Jocelyn straggling behind them. She usually had a book in her hand and her dishwater blonde hair covering her face, but the first time Edi got a good look at her, she saw intelligence in the girl's deep blue eyes. She wasn't the beauty that her mother had been—Miss Edi had seen photos—but there was something about her that drew Edi to the child. Maybe it was her square chin with just the tiniest hint of a cleft in it. It reminded her of another square chin that she'd once loved with all her heart. Or maybe it was the way the child seemed to know that she was different from the people she lived with.

At the beginning Miss Edi had twice arranged it so she could speak to the girl. One time was at the library, and they spent thirty minutes discussing the Narnia books, and just as they parted, they introduced themselves. The second time, Miss Edi decided to take a walk that went past the child's house. She was outside on her bicycle, riding around and around on it. "When I was a child we played hopscotch," Miss Edi said.

"What's that?"

"If you have some chalk I'll show you."

Miss Edi waited while Jocelyn went inside and got the chalk. Back then, Miss Edi had only needed to use one cane for walking. But all those years of standing up while she took care of Dr. Brenner and his team had further damaged the muscles in her legs, and she knew that it wouldn't be long before she was forced to use two canes, then a walker, then . . . She didn't like to think about those things.

She felt someone watching her and turned to see Jocelyn's father. He was wearing what she'd known as a "skivvy shirt," something men in her generation kept covered. He seemed to have tattoos all over his body and he hadn't shaved for days. He was working on a blue motorcycle and constantly turning the handle to make it sound louder. The neighbors had quit complaining, but not because he was a homeowner in the restricted community. If that was all he was, they would have thrown him out. But Gary Minton was still the handyman, the one who came in the middle of the night when the toilet overflowed and flooded the bathroom. He'd also pulled a child off the bottom of a swimming pool, and climbed a tree to get a terrified little boy down. All in all, the noise of a few motorcycles was easy to put up with.

But he was watching Miss Edi as though trying to assess her, to see if it was all right for his daughter to be with her. Miss Edi turned away. Better to ask if the child should be with **him.**

It was only minutes before Jocelyn returned with the chalk, and Miss Edi showed her how to draw the hopscotch chart on the concrete driveway, throw the rock, then follow it on one foot. She'd been delighted by the game.

A few days later, when Edi opened her front door and saw the scrawny, poorly clad little girl, her blonde hair covering her face, sitting on her front steps and crying, she wasn't surprised.

"I'm sorry," the girl said as she jumped up. "I didn't mean to . . ." She didn't seem to know what to say.

Edi saw the corner of a plastic suitcase behind a

hibiscus bush and figured the child was running away from home.

That first day, Edi purposefully kept the child at her house for nearly three hours. They talked of books and a science project she was making at school. What Edi wanted to do was teach that father of hers a lesson; she wanted to make him worry. He should pay more attention to where his child was.

While Edi walked Jocelyn back to her house, she was thinking that when the relieved parents came to the door, she would give them a piece of her mind. But to Edi's shock, her father and stepmother hadn't been aware that the girl had run away. Worse, when they were told, they weren't worried or surprised. Their attitude was that Jocelyn did what she wanted to and they had no idea what that was.

That night, Edi called Alex and told him the child's situation was worse than he'd thought. "She's extremely intelligent and loves learning and culture. You should have seen her face when I played Vivaldi! It's as if Shakespeare were living with the town morons. Did I tell you about those two repulsive stepsisters of hers?"

"Yes," Alex said, "but tell me again."

The next weekend, as Edi hoped she would,

the girl showed up on the sidewalk, trying to look as though she were just passing by. Edi asked the child in, then called her father and asked if she might be allowed to help Edi with a project she was working on. That he didn't ask what the project was or inquire about the length of the stay solidified her bad impression of him. "Yeah," her father said on the phone, "I heard about you and I know where you live. Sure, Joce can stay there. If you gotta lotta books Joce'll be happy. She's just like her momma."

"Then she may stay here for the afternoon?" Edi asked, sounding even more stiff than she usually did. She was trying to conceal a growing dislike for the man.

"Sure. Let her stay. We're gonna go to a rally so we'll be home late. Hey! You wanta keep her overnight, you can do that. I bet Joce'd like that."

"Perhaps I shall," Edi said, then hung up.

Jocelyn had spent the night. In fact, they enjoyed each other's company so much that the child didn't leave until Sunday evening. As she started to go, she turned back, ran to Edi, and threw her arms around her waist. "You are the nicest, smartest, most wonderful person I've ever met."

Edi tried to remain aloof, but she couldn't help hugging the girl back.

After that, Jocelyn spent weekends at Edi's house and most of the holidays. They were two lonely people who needed each other and were thrilled to have found one another. They made a life together, with outings on Saturdays, church on Sundays, and time to be quiet and sit in the garden.

As for her father, for all that Edi had at first judged him to be uncaring, she found out that he loved his daughter as much as he'd loved her mother, and all he wanted was for Jocelyn to be happy. "I can't give her what she woulda had if her mother had lived," he told Edi, "but maybe you can. Joce can go to your house all she wants to, and if you need anything from me, you just let me know." He glanced at his wife and twin step-daughters waiting for him in the car. "They're like me and we fit together, but Joce is . . . different."

Edi knew what it felt like to be different, and Jocelyn was as out of place in her home as Edi had been at times in her life.

The years with Jocelyn had been the happiest of Edi's life. It had been wonderful to teach a young mind, and to show her the world. When her family went to Disney World, Edi took Jocelyn to New York to the Metropolitan Opera. When her step-sisters were wearing short shorts to show off their long legs, Jocelyn was wearing Edi's pearls with a twin set.

The summer Joce turned sixteen, she and Miss Edi went to London, Paris, and Rome together. The traveling had been difficult on Miss Edi. Between her legs and her age, she didn't have much energy. But Jocelyn had spent the days wandering about the cities and photographing them. In the evenings she shared her new stories with Miss Edi's old ones.

In London Edi had shown Joce where she'd met David—no last name given—the man she'd loved and lost. "There was only one man for me, and he was it," she said as she looked at the big white marble building where they'd met.

By that time, Jocelyn had heard the story a dozen times but she never tired of it. "One love." "A love for all time." "A forever love." These were terms she'd heard many times. "Hold out for it," Miss Edi said. "Wait for that kind of love," she advised, and Jocelyn had always agreed. One true love.

Besides the pleasure of the time they spent together, as she grew older, Jocelyn often aided Miss Edi with the charities she administered. Joce did research and sometimes even traveled to see them. Three times she discovered frauds and as a result, she developed friendships with a couple of men in the local police department.

But what Miss Edi never told was that the money she gave away wasn't hers. She carefully concealed the fact that the money came from Alexander McDowell of Edilean, Virginia. In all their years of friendship, neither his name nor the town's was ever mentioned.

When Jocelyn started going to a small college not too far away, Edi had been lost without her. At first, Jocelyn had been so busy with her weekend job and all she'd had to do to put herself through school, she couldn't even call. They e-mailed and texted often—Miss Edi loved any new technology that came out—but it wasn't the same.

After six months of college, Miss Edi started paying Jocelyn's tuition so she wouldn't have to spend all her time at the school. This was done without the knowledge of her father or the "Steps," as they called the two skinny, blonde twins. Edi didn't think her father would object, but she didn't want to risk it. And she especially didn't want to risk that the stepdaughters would hit her up for money. Although people often spoke of how beautiful the girls were, Edi didn't find them so. Several times they'd shown up at Edi's house when Jocelyn wasn't there, and they'd looked around her house as though they were trying to guess the value of everything. Edi disliked them as much as she loved Jocelyn.

Jocelyn graduated from college with a degree in English literature and got part-time work at the same school as a teaching assistant. And through a friend of Miss Edi's, she got freelance employment helping authors research the biographies they were trying to write. Joce was excellent at both jobs, and she especially loved spending her days in libraries, buried in old files.

When Edi realized that the little pains in her chest were more than just aging, she started thinking about Jocelyn's future. If Edi died and left everything to Jocelyn, as she planned to do, she had no doubt that the Steps would do what they could to take it from her.

Edi wanted to leave Jocelyn with a great deal more than just her possessions. She wanted to leave her with a future. No. What she really wanted was to leave her a **family.** Jocelyn had spent most of her life living with old people, first her grandparents, then Miss Edi. Edi had taken everything she knew about Jocelyn into consideration, then she'd spent a long time and done a lot of work to figure out how to give Jocelyn what she needed.

Now, she closed the lid on the book of memorabilia and slowly made her way to the kitchen. What dreadful thing had the little nurse left her for dinner? Probably something with the word **taco** in the title. When she heard the overnight delivery truck pull into the drive to pick up the package for Helen, she smiled.

As Edi opened the refrigerator, she thought that the best thing about all this was that she wasn't going to be around when Jocelyn found out that Edi had . . . Well, not really lied, but she'd omitted an awful lot about herself. Since Jocelyn loved to ask Edi about her long life, it hadn't been easy to skip years and brush over the whole truth, but Edi had managed it.

She pulled out the big salad that had been left for her and put it on the table. Jocelyn wasn't going to be happy when she was told certain things, but Edi had faith that Jocelyn would search to find the answers to everything.

Smiling, Edi thought how her life plan for Jocelyn excluded those too-tall, too-skinny stepsisters who paraded around with next to no clothes on. That those girls had become "famous"—a term Miss Edi detested—said much too much about the modern world.

Jocelyn didn't think Edi knew it, but the young woman had given up a great deal to look after an old woman, and Edi wanted to make it up to her. What Edi wanted to give Jocelyn was the **truth.** But she wasn't just going to **tell** her everything, she was going to make Jocelyn search it out, work for it, something she was so very good at doing.

"And please forgive me," Edi whispered. That was her most fervent hope, that Jocelyn would forgive her for so many secrets kept for so very long. "I made a promise, a vow," she whispered, "and I honored it."

In her mind, she began composing the letter she was going to leave with her will.

1

Jocelyn glanced at herself in the hotel mirror for the last time. This is it, she thought. This is the moment. Her instinct was to put her nightgown back on and climb back into bed. Wonder what was on HBO during the day? Did this hotel have HBO? Maybe she should look for a hotel that did.

She took a deep breath, looked back at the mirror, and straightened her shoulders. What would Miss Edi say if she saw her slumping like this? At the thought of Miss Edi, tears again came to her eyes, but she blinked them away. It had been four months since the funeral, but she still missed her friend so much she sometimes didn't know how to function. Every day she wanted to call Miss Edi and tell her something that had happened, but each day she discovered afresh that she was gone.

"I can do this," Joce said as she looked in the mirror. "I really and truly can do this." She was dressed conservatively, in a skirt and an ironed, white cotton blouse, just the way Miss Edi had taught her. Her shoulder-length, dark blonde hair was pulled back with a headband, and she had on very little makeup. All she knew about the town of Edilean, Virginia, was that Miss Edi had grown up there, so Jocelyn didn't want to arrive in jeans and a tube top and shock the locals.

She picked up her car keys, grabbed the handle of her big black suitcase, and rolled it to the door. Tonight she'd be sleeping in her own house. It was a house she'd never seen, never even heard about until a lawyer told Joce she'd inherited it, but it was still hers.

Just days ago, she'd sat in the lawyer's office in Boca Raton, Florida, dressed all in black and wearing the pearls Miss Edi had given her. It was months after Miss Edi's funeral, but her will stated that it was to be read on the first day of May after she died. If she'd died on June the first, that would have meant waiting eleven months. But she'd died in her sleep just into the new year, so Jocelyn had had time to grieve before facing the ordeal of hearing what was in the will.

Beside her sat her father, his wife beside him, and next to her were the Steps, Belinda and Ashley. But now they were better known as Bell and Ash. Due to their mother's indefatigable efforts, they'd become models—and the media had loved the idea of there being two of them. In the last ten years they'd been on the covers of all the top magazines. They'd traveled all over the world and modeled the clothes of every designer. When they walked through a mall, teenage girls followed them, their mouths open in awe. And males of every age looked at them with lust.

But for all their fame, to Jocelyn's mind, the Steps hadn't changed since they were all kids together. As children, the twins loved to make up things they said Joce had done to them, then tell their mother. Louisa used to glare at her stepdaughter and say, "Wait 'til your father gets home." But when Gary Minton returned, he'd just shake his head and do whatever he could to stay out of the turmoil. His objective in life was to have a good time, not to referee his three children. He'd retreat to his garage workshop, his wife and his tall stepdaughters trailing behind him. Jocelyn would leave and go to Miss Edi.

"So what did the old witch leave you?" Bell asked as she stretched her long neck to see Jocelyn at the far end of the row of chairs.

For Joce, it had never been difficult to tell the twins apart. Bell was the smarter of the two, the leader, while Ash was quieter and did whatever her sister wanted her to. Since that usually meant saying something nasty to gain a laugh, Ash was often the one to stay away from.

"Her love," Jocelyn said, refusing to look at her stepsister. Bell was on her third husband now, and her mother was hinting that that marriage was about to fail. "Poor thing," her mother said. "Those men just don't understand my darling baby."

"They don't understand her belief that she can have affairs even if she's married," Joce muttered under her breath.

"What was that?" Louisa asked sharply, sounding as though she were about to say "Wait 'til your father gets home." The woman couldn't seem to understand that her "babies" would turn thirty this year and that their fifteen minutes of fame was already on the downward spiral. Just last week Joce had read that two eighteen-year-old girls were "the new Bell and Ash."

Jocelyn didn't begrudge the Steps their fame—

or the fortune that they seemed to have spent. To her, they were just the same: always bad tempered, jealous of everyone, and disdainful of anyone who wasn't in the gossip rags every week. When they were kids, they'd been extremely envious of Jocelyn because she spent so much time at "that rich old bat's house." They refused to believe that Miss Edi didn't give Joce bags full of money every week. "If she doesn't give you things, then why do you go over there?"

"Because I **like** her!" Joce said again and again. "No. I love her."

"Ahhhh," they would say in that tone that was meant to say they knew everything.

Joce would just shut the door to her bedroom in their faces, or, better yet, she'd go to Miss Edi's house.

But now Miss Edi was gone forever, and Jocelyn was requested to be at the reading of the will. The lawyer, a man who looked to be older than Miss Edi, came in a side door and seemed startled at the sight of the five of them. "I was told it would just be Miss Jocelyn," he said, glancing at her, then looking at her father as though demanding an explanation.

"I, uh . . . ," Gary Minton started. The years had been kind to him, and he was still a handsome man. With his dark hair with just a touch of gray at the temples, and his dark brows, he looked much younger than he was.

"We take care of our own," said his wife from beside him. It was as though the years Gary's face didn't carry were etched on his wife's. Sun, cigarettes, and wind had weathered her skin so she looked like a dried-up mummy.

"You don't mind if we're here, do you?" Bell said in a purring voice to the lawyer. Both twins were wearing micro-miniskirts, their famous long legs stretched out until they nearly touched his desk. The little tops they wore were open almost to the waist.

Mr. Johnson glanced at them over his half glasses and gave a bit of a frown. He seemed to want to tell them to put their clothes on. He looked back at Jocelyn, noted her plain black suit with the crisp white blouse under it, the pearls around her neck, and gave a little smile. "If Miss Jocelyn approves, you may remain."

"Oh, la tee da," Ash said. "**Miss** Jocelyn. Miss college-educated Jocelyn. Will you read a book to us?"

"I'm sure someone will have to," Jocelyn said without taking her eyes off the lawyer. "They can stay. They'll find out everything anyway."

"All right then." He looked down at the papers.

"Basically, Edilean Harcourt left you, Jocelyn Minton, everything."

"And how much is that?" Bell asked quickly.

Mr. Johnson turned to her. "It's not my business to tell anything more. Whatever Miss Jocelyn tells you is her concern, but I will say nothing. Now, if you'll excuse me, I have work to do." He picked up a brown paper, string-tied folder and handed it across the desk to Jocelyn. "All the information is in there, and you may look through the documents in your own time."

When he remained standing, Joce also stood. "Thank you," she said as she took the portfolio. "I'll read it later."

"I would suggest that you read it when you're alone. In privacy. Edilean wrote some things that I think she meant only for you to see."

"Everything to her?" Ash asked, at last understanding what had been said. "But what about us? We used to visit the old woman all the time."

Mr. Johnson's old face moved into a bit of a smile. "How could I have forgotten?" He took a key out of his pocket, and unlocked a drawer in his desk. "She left these for you."

He held out two small, blue satin bags, and the contents looked to be bumpy, as though they contained jewels.

"Oooooh," Bell and Ash said in unison. "For us? Why that darling. She shouldn't have. We really didn't expect anything."

With their much-photographed faces alight, they opened the bags, then looked up at the lawyer in consternation. "What are these?"

Ash dumped the contents of her bag into the palm of her hand. There were about twenty small black objects, some of which had been emerald cut, some in the round diamond shape. "What are they? I've never seen stones like these before."

"Are they black diamonds?" Bell asked.

"In a way, they are," Mr. Johnson said, then, still smiling, he started for the door, but he paused with his hand on the knob. Turning just a bit, he gave Jocelyn a wink, then he left the room.

Joce had to work to keep a straight face. The "black diamonds" that Miss Edi had left for the stepsisters were actually pieces of coal.

She didn't say a word as they left the offices. She sat in the back of the car on the drive home and listened as Bell and Ash, sitting beside her, held the pieces of coal up to the light and exclaimed over their beauty and discussed how they were going to have them set.

Joce looked out the window to hide her smile. The joke that Miss Edi had left her jealous, greedy stepsisters lumps of coal made her miss her friend with a painful longing. Miss Edi had been mother, grandmother, friend, and mentor all in one.

Joce glanced up and saw her father frowning at her in the rearview mirror. She could see that he knew what the "stones" were and he was dreading the coming fury when the Steps found out. But she didn't mind. She planned to be gone long before the Steps discovered what the black stones were. Her bags were packed and in the back of her car, and as soon as they got home, she was going back to her job at the university.

Only when Jocelyn was back at school and in her tiny apartment did she open the packet that contained Miss Edi's will. She'd tried to steel herself for what she'd find, but nothing prepared her to see an envelope with that beloved handwriting on it.

TO MY JOCELYN it said on the envelope.

With trembling hands, she opened it, pulled out the letter, and began to read.

My dear, dear Jocelyn,

I promise I won't be maudlin. I don't know if it's been days or months since my demise, but knowing your soft heart, you're probably still grieving. I know all

too well what it is to lose people you love. I've had to stand by and watch most of the people I loved die. I was very nearly the last one left.

Now, to business. The house in Boca is not mine, nor is most of the furniture. By now I'm sure the contents have been moved out and put up for auction. But don't worry, my dear, the best of what I owned, meaning everything that I took from Edilean Manor, will go back to where it came from.

Jocelyn put the letter down. "Edilean Manor?" she said aloud. She'd never heard of the place. After her initial confusion, a feeling of betrayal ran through her. She'd spent a great deal of her life with Miss Edi, had traveled with her, met many people from her past, and had heard hundreds of stories about her time with Dr. Brenner. But Miss Edi had never mentioned Edilean Manor. It must have been important, as it was named for Miss Edi—or she was named for it.

Jocelyn looked back at the letter.

I know, dear, you're angry and hurt. I can see that frown of yours. I told you so

much about my life, but I never mentioned Edilean, Virginia. As you can guess from the unusual name, the town "belonged" to my family—or at least we thought it did. Centuries ago, my ancestor came from Scotland with an elegant wife and a wagonload of gold. He bought a thousand acres outside Williamsburg, Virginia, laid out a town square, then named the place after his young wife. The legend in my family is that his wife was of a much higher class than he was, but when her father refused to let his daughter marry the stable lad, he ran off with the girl and a great deal of her father's money. No one ever knew if she was abducted or if she went willingly.

I'm sure the truth is much less romantic than that, but Angus Harcourt did build a big brick house in about 1770, and my family lived in it until I broke the tradition. My father left the house to me alone because my brother, Bertrand, couldn't manage money. If he had a dime, he'd buy something that cost a quarter.

I grew up sure that I'd live in Edilean Manor with David Aldredge, the man I

was engaged to, and raise a strong, healthy, handsome family. But, alas, fate has a way of changing our lives. In this case, it was a war that changed everything and everyone. When I left Edilean, I let my brother live in the house, but I kept strict watch over him. Bertrand died a long time ago, and for years now the house has been empty.

Dear Jocelyn, I'm leaving you a house you've never heard of in a town I carefully never mentioned.

Jocelyn put the letter down and stared into space for a moment. A house built in 1770? And outside beautiful Williamsburg? She looked around her drab little apartment. It had been the best she could afford on her tiny salary. But an entire house! An old one!

She looked back down at the letter.

There's something else I want to tell you. Remember how good I was at knowing who at church would make a good couple and who wouldn't last six months? If you'll remember, I was always right. I'm sure you also remember that I

**learned from experience not to interfere
in your personal life—after you were old
enough to have one, that is. But now I
can no longer see your wrath, so I'm
going to tell you something. The perfect
man for you lives in Edilean. He's the
grandson of two friends with whom I
went to high school, Alex and Lissie Mc-
Dowell. They're gone now, but their
grandson looks so much like Alex that I
thought he'd never aged. On one of my
trips to Edilean—yes, dear, I went in secret—I told Alex that, and he laughed
hard. It was good to see him laugh again,
as there were days in the past when he
found nothing to amuse him. His wife,
Lissie, was a saint for what she did. I
look forward to seeing them both again
in a Better Place.**

Jocelyn looked up. A man for her? The
thought made her want to smile and cry at the
same time. Twice, Miss Edi had tried to match
her up with young men from church, but both
times she'd refused to so much as go out to dinner with them. They were boring young men,
and she doubted if either of them had ever had a

creative thought in his life. She hadn't given her reasons for turning the men down, but Miss Edi had known what was going on. "Beer drinking does not qualify as an Olympic sport," she'd said quietly, then walked away. Joce's face had turned three shades of red. Two weeks before, Miss Edi had driven by Jocelyn's house when she'd been standing outside with two young men on motor-cycles and downing a can of beer. For all that Joce loved the ballet, she was sometimes drawn to the life her family led.

"Like my mother," she said aloud, then looked back down at the letter.

His name is Ramsey McDowell and he's an attorney. But I can assure you that he's more than that. My last request of you is that you give the young man a chance to show you that he's right for you. And, re-member: I am never wrong about these things.

As for the house, there's some furniture in it, but not much, and there are some tenants in the wings. They are both young women from families I've known for many years. Sara grew up in Edilean, so she can help you find whatever you need. Tess is

new to the area, but I knew her grandmother better than I wanted to.

That's all, my dear. I know you'll make
the best of all that I leave you. I apologize
that my housekeeper won't be there, but
the poor dear was older than I am. I have
a gardener, so maybe he can help you
with whatever else you need.

I wish you all the luck in the world, and
please remember that I'll be watching
over you every minute of your life.

It took Jocelyn the rest of the evening to recover
from the letter. It sounded so much like Miss Edi
that it was almost as though she were in the room
with her. She slept with the letter curled up in her
hands.

The next morning, her mind was so full of all
that she'd learned in the last twenty-four hours that
she could barely concentrate. Her job as teaching
assistant had become uncomfortable because she'd
had a year-long affair with one of the other assis-
tants. When they had to work together, he scowled
at her across the table and she found it very unpleasant.

He'd been the third man in a row who had been
perfectly suitable for her, but in the end, she'd not

wanted to go on with any of them. Jocelyn knew it was all Miss Edi's fault. She'd told Jocelyn about the man she'd been in love with who'd been killed in World War II—a true love, and that's what Joce wanted.

"He was my all to me," Miss Edi said in the voice that she used only when she spoke of him. She had only one small photo of him in his uniform, which was inside a folding picture frame she kept by her bed. He was an extraordinarily good-looking young man, with dark blond hair, and a strong chin. The frame was oval, and on the other side was a photo of Miss Edi in her army uniform. She was so young, so beautiful. Beneath David's photo was a tiny braid of hair, her dark intertwined with his blond. Miss Edi would hold the frame, say, "David," then her eyes would glaze over.

Over the years, Joce had pressed her for details, but Miss Edi would just say he was a young man from her war experience—which had been brutal and she had the scars to prove it.

But at last Jocelyn had found out something about him. His name was David Aldredge, and he and Miss Edi had been engaged to be married in Edilean, Virginia. But David's death in the war had ended that.

"No wonder she couldn't bear to mention Edilean," Jocelyn whispered.

To Jocelyn, Miss Edi's love for the man had become a legend. It epitomized the love that she wanted. But so far, Joce hadn't been able to find it. Miss Edi never knew it, but Joce had twice lived with young men, and she'd been quite happy with the arrangement. It was nice to have someone to go home to, to tell about her day, and to laugh with about what had gone on. But when the men started talking about rings and mortgages and babies, Jocelyn ran. She didn't know what it was that was missing from her relationships, but it wasn't there—and she was going to hold out until it was.

And now Miss Edi had given her a way to change everything. That evening, she looked through the legal papers, read them carefully, and held the key that was in the package. All the legal work was being handled by the firm of McDowell, Aldredge, and Welsch in Edilean, Virginia.

The name of "Aldredge" made her pause for a moment before she could go on. Did descendants of Miss Edi's David still live there?

A letter was included saying that when she got to Edilean, she should stop by the office and she'd be told about the financial arrangements. The letter was signed by Ramsey McDowell.

Jocelyn shook her head at Miss Edi's letter. "You never give up, do you?" she said, her eyes raised upward. But the truth was that Miss Edi **was** always right about the couples at church. Many times Jocelyn had caught Miss Edi staring at a young couple who were more interested in each other than what the pastor had to say. Afterward, she'd tell Jocelyn—and only her—what she thought of them. "True love," she'd sometimes say, but not very often. "Pure sex," she said once and made Joce laugh. She was right both times.

"Ramsey McDowell," Jocelyn said, then looked back at the letter. He'd put his home phone number on there. It was only seven. On impulse, she picked up her cell, called him, and he answered on the third ring.

"Hello?"

His voice was nice, deep and smooth. Like chocolate, she thought. "Is this Mr. McDowell?"

"I think of that as being my father, but I guess I qualify. Is this Miss Minton?"

She hesitated. How had he known that? "Caller ID."

"Can't live without it," he said. "You know how

we lawyers are. We must fight off the masses because of our underhanded dealings. Are you going
to be here soon?"

"I don't know," Joce said, smiling at his sense of
humor. "This is all quite new to me. I'd never
heard of Edilean, Virginia, until I saw the will, so
I'm still in a bit of shock."

"Never heard of us? I'll have you know we're the
biggest small town in Virginia. Or is that the smallest big town? I never can remember what our
mayor says we are. Ask me what you need to know
and I'll tell you everything. Oh! Wait! I need to
fasten a diaper. There, that's done. Now, what can
I tell you about us?"

"Diaper? You're married?" Her shocked tone
told too much, and when he hesitated before answering, she grimaced.

"Nephew. I have a very fertile sister who pops
them out like corn over a grill. She just stuck her
tongue out at me, but then the baby kicked. The
one inside her, that is. And the one on her hip. Ex-
cuse me, Miss Minton, but I have to take the
phone to another room before my sister throws
something at me."

Joce was smiling as she waited, hearing foot-
steps, then a door close and, finally, quiet.

"There now, I'm in what passes for a library in my house and I'm all yours. Figuratively speaking that is. Now tell me what I can do for you."

"I don't really know. I didn't know Miss Edi owned a house, much less a town."

"Actually, she had to give us our freedom in 1864, and—"

"Three," Joce said before she thought, then wished she hadn't. "Sorry, you were saying?"

"I see . . . 1863. Emancipation Proclamation. Can you tell me the day?"

"January the first," she said cautiously, not sure if this would get her labeled as a know-it-all or worse.

"January the first, 1863. Well, Miss Minton, I can see that you and I are going to get along quite well." There was a change in his voice as he went from teasing banter to more serious. "What can I tell you?"

"I don't know where to begin. I want to know about the house, the town, about the people. Everything."

"It would take much too much time to talk about all of this over the phone," he said. "My suggestion is that you come here to Edilean and we sit down and talk about everything in person. How about if we have dinner and discuss this at length? Shall we say Saturday next at eight?"

She drew in her breath. That was just eight days away. "I don't know if I can get there by then."

"Shall I send a car?"

"I, uh, no, that won't be necessary. I have a car. How do I keep the roof repaired?" she blurted.

"A practical woman," Ramsey said. "I like that. I'm not at liberty to say the exact extent of what Miss Edi left you, but I can assure you that you'll be able to keep the roof in **great** repair."

She smiled at that. She didn't relish the idea of having the responsibility of the care of a very old house and no way to support it.

"Miss Minton, what is your hesitation? The beautiful town of Edilean is awaiting you, plus a magnificent old house, and Colonial Williamsburg is right next door. What more could you want?"

She started to say "Time," but didn't. Suddenly, she had one of those moments that rarely happen in a lifetime. In an instant, she knew what she was going to do: She was going to change her life. Since Miss Edi's death, Jocelyn hadn't made a single change. She had the same job she no longer liked, the same routine, the same dull, dark apartment. Her friends now looked at her with sadness because Joce was no longer part of a couple. They were already talking about fixing her up with blind dates. The real difference in Jocelyn's life was that her best friend was gone. Now, if she went "home" it was to her father's house, to motorcycles outside, NASCAR on the TV inside, and the pitying looks of her stepmother. Poor Jocelyn, she had nothing and no one.

This was Friday, and if she quit her job tomorrow morning, then she'd have days to sort out all the things she needed to do, like turn off the water, and—

"Could I wire you some money?" he asked, seeming to think her silence had to do with expenses. "No, wait, that's no good. You'd have to give me your bank account numbers and you shouldn't do that. For all you know I'm a . . ." He hesitated.

"A lawyer?"

"That's right. Scum of the earth. We spend years in school learning how to rip people off. How about if I overnight you a check?"

"I have enough to do what I need to," she said. "It's just that this is a big step."

"If you know the date of the Emancipation Proclamation, then you love history. So how can you wait to see a house that was built in the eighteenth century? No velvet ropes anywhere. You can explore all you want. Did you know that the stables were recently rebuilt? And there's a cellar that's intact. And I believe the attic is full of trunks of old clothes and diaries."

"Mr. McDowell, I think you missed your calling. You should be traveling around the country on a covered wagon and selling snake oil."

"No, no snake oil. I sell Miss Edi's Golden Elixir. It's made from rainbows and flecked with gold dust from the leprechauns' pots. Guaranteed to cure anything that ails you. You have a boyfriend?"

"And what will the elixir do to him?" she asked, smiling.

"No," he said, seriously, "do you have a boyfriend?"

"Not since he asked me to marry him and I ran away screaming."

"Ah," he said.

Joce wished she could take back her comment. "I mean, it wasn't actually like that. He's very nice and I'm not adverse to marriage, but—"

"No explanation needed. My last girlfriend led me into a jewelry store and they had to take me away in an ambulance."

"A kindred soul."

"Sounds like it. Now, what about dinner?"

"Maybe you shouldn't make reservations yet," she said cautiously. "In case I don't make it out of here in time."

"Who said anything about reservations? I was thinking about wine and pasta served on a table-cloth on the floor of your new eighteenth-century house. By candlelight. With strawberries dipped in warm chocolate for dessert."

"Oh, my goodness," she said. "You are going to be a problem, aren't you?"

"I hope so. I like a girl who knows her history. And I like this photo of you that Miss Edi sent me last year. You still have this red bikini?"

Jocelyn couldn't contain her laugh. "She passed that thing around to half the men at our church. When I had my twenty-sixth birthday and still wasn't married, I thought she was going to staple it to the trees and leave a phone number."

"When was this photo taken?" he asked, and there was a touch of fear in his voice. She could almost hear the unasked question of, How many birthdays ago was that?

"Actually, it was quite a while ago," she said mischievously. "So, shall I see you at the end of the week?"

"I'll be there," he said, but his voice was no longer so buoyant.

Jocelyn hung up and mentally began a list that started with "go to the gym every day this week."

The photo of her in the bikini had been taken just last summer, but who knew what had happened under her clothes during the winter?

So that was Ramsey McDowell, she thought as she got up and began to look through her closet. Tomorrow she'd stop by her professor's office and resign. She knew he wouldn't be bothered; there were four applicants for every job on campus.

She paused with her hand on the clothes. Maybe now she could write her own book. Something nonfiction, historical. Maybe she could write the history of the town of Edilean. She'd start with the Scotsman who stole a man's gold and his beautiful daughter, then ran off to the wild country of America. What was Edilean like in 1770? For that matter, what was it like now?

Ten minutes later, she'd Googled the town. The history of the town was much what Miss Edi had written. It had been started by a Scotsman named Angus Harcourt, who'd built a large house for his beautiful wife, then set about putting in acres of crops. But his wife, Edilean, had been lonely, so she'd designed the streets of a tiny town that had eight small areas of parkland in it. Smack in the middle she'd planted an oak tree from an acorn she'd taken from her father's estate. Over the centuries, the tree had been replaced three times, but each time the transplant had been a scion of the original tree.

Jocelyn went on to read that in the 1950s, her Edilean Harcourt had led a four-year-long court battle when the state of Virginia tried to evict the residents, as over five thousand acres of the surrounding land was being turned into a nature preserve. "It was because Miss Edi—as she is called by everyone"—Joce read—"won the battle that the tiny town of Edilean survives today. No new houses are allowed to be built, but the ones that are there are preserved so that it's almost like stepping back into time.

"The town has several upscale shops that draw tourists from Williamsburg, but the crowning jewel is Edilean Manor, built by Angus Harcourt in 1770, and lived in by the same family since then. Unfortunately, the house and grounds are not open to the public."

"I'm glad of that," Jocelyn said, then moved closer to the screen to see the photos and thought she could see a sign in front of one of the pretty white houses. Was that Ramsey's office? Did he live in the same building where he worked? He'd asked her if she had a boyfriend, but did he have a girlfriend?

She clicked on the button that said EDILEAN MANOR, and there it was. Jocelyn stared at it with wide eyes. The façade was perfectly symmetrical: two stories, five windows wide, all brick. On both sides were single-story wings with little porches on them. "I guess that's where my tenants live," she said, marveling at the idea that she now owned this wonderful old house.

Five minutes later, she was tearing through her closet like a leaf blower. She was going to get rid of all the things that she no longer wore, then see what was left. Fifteen minutes later, she looked at her nearly bare closet and said, "I'm going shopping."

The next few days had been a blur of activity as she hurried to get ready to leave, to go to her brand-new life.

And now, she was in Williamsburg, it was 11 A.M. Saturday morning, hotel checkout time, everything she owned was stuffed into her little Mini Cooper, and she was about to see "her house" for the first time. She didn't know if she was elated or scared to death. New town, new state even, and all new people—one of whom she had a sort of date with tonight.

"You **can** do this," she said again and opened the hotel door.

2

S**HE CLUTCHED THE** MapQuest printout in her
hand as she drove. The directions were simple:
leave Williamsburg on Highway 5, the one that led
to all the plantations, and just a few miles out she'd
come to McTern Road. Three miles later, she was to
take a right onto Edilean Road, then drive through
the town until she ended up at her new/old house.

McTern Road was easy to find, but she thought
there was a mistake because it meandered through
forest that seemed to have been there since the
earth began. She'd read that Edilean was in the
middle of a nature preserve, but she hadn't expected it to be this close to primordial forest.

She moved to one side as a couple of men in a
big black truck pulling a fishing boat with two mo-

tors on the back rushed past her. They waved their thanks for giving them the right of way.

Edilean Road was clearly marked and she was glad to see that the surface was well maintained. She'd been a little concerned that it would be a gravel road with weeds down the center.

About a mile before she reached the town, the wild-looking forest gave way to specimen oaks and beeches and big sycamores. She didn't have to be told that she had entered land that at one time had been part of a rich plantation.

When she reached the center of Edilean, she paused for a moment to look at it. The Web site had been only partially right. The town was half as big as it seemed in the photos, but it was twice as charming. Big willow trees hung over the street so that all the parking was in the shade. There wasn't a new building anywhere, and the old structures had been maintained beautifully.

The church was on her left, and on impulse, she turned right so she'd go through the heart of the place. She wanted to see the "parklike" areas that the original Edilean had designed, and she wanted to see that oak tree.

Another left took her to the main street, Lairdton. Joce had seen that nearly all the street names were of Scottish origin and the road through the middle was Lairdton. Since "ton" was an old way to shorten "town," that meant that Angus Harcourt had named the street Laird's Town. She guessed that back in the eighteenth century, the stable lad, Angus Harcourt, had raised himself to being the laird of a clan and wanted people to know that he owned all of it.

Jocelyn saw an ice cream parlor that looked like something off a movie set and a store of used books. "Gold mine!" she said aloud. Out-of-print books were some of her favorite things in life.

She saw a little grocery with produce in a bin in front, and a woman wearing a long skirt with a tasseled belt. There was a bandana tied around her head and her shirt had been tie-dyed. "Wonder if she went to Woodstock?" Jocelyn muttered.

There was the usual store full of old furniture and some other businesses.

And in the middle, on a big, grassy circle, was an enormous oak tree. There were half a dozen benches under its shade and two teenagers were kissing, while some younger kids were laughing at them.

The last two houses before the road disappeared into overhanging trees were the ones in the photos on the Internet. They were big, white, and looked inviting. In front of one a woman was sweeping the porch, and as though she knew who Jocelyn was, she halted her broom and stared.

Jocelyn was so absorbed in looking back at the woman that she almost missed the turn at the end of Lairdton. One block down was a sign that said TAM WAY. She glanced in her rearview mirror and saw that the woman was no longer on the porch. She probably went inside to start the gossip line. What would they say? That the outsider is here to take over our beloved Miss Edi's house?

Jocelyn drove slowly down the country road. There were only three houses along the way, and unless she missed her guess, they'd once been part of the plantation of Edilean Manor. She could see that there were old sections on the houses, but they'd been remodeled and expanded over the years.

When she came to some stone columns that were nearly hidden by vines, she knew she'd reached it. There was a little marble plaque in one of them and she could see enough letters to know what it said.

This is it, she thought, and pulled into the drive. There were so many huge trees that she could see nothing, and it occurred to her that maybe what she'd seen were photos of the house before it was torn down. She knew from the research she'd done at school that you had to read the fine print under the pictures to see if the house still existed.

Suddenly, the trees parted and she saw the house, and it was exactly like the photos. Because she'd visited many old houses in her life, she immediately saw that the house was in pristine condition. There were houses less than a year old that weren't as well kept as this one was. Every window, shutter, and rain gutter was perfect.

On each side of the house was a wing with its own little porch, and for a moment Joce thought about knocking on the doors and asking permission to go inside. But that was ridiculous.

With her eyes on the house, looking at every inch of it, she got out, opened the back of the car, and took out her suitcase. She pulled it behind her as she climbed the wooden steps up to the small porch in front of the door.

She took the key out of her jacket pocket, inserted it into the old lock, and when it turned, her heart began to beat quickly.

"Hello? Anybody here?" Jocelyn called as she opened the old door. From the look of it, the door was original to the house, which made it over two hundred years old. She left her big black suitcase by the door and slowly walked farther inside, her heels echoing on the bare wooden floor.

She was in the entrance hall, and as she'd hoped, it went all the way through the house. To her right were two closed doors and to her left on either side of the staircase were two more closed doors. She hoped the house hadn't been altered and that behind the doors were big rooms and not little cubicles that had been cut up by centuries of owners.

The staircase was magnificent, and she felt sure that the banister was one piece of mahogany. Turning, she looked up to the top of the stairs and saw more closed doors—and, just like in the hallway, there wasn't a stick of furniture to be seen.

She walked to the far end of the big, bare hallway and looked through the window. Outside were giant trees that might be as old as the house. She wanted to walk under them and sit on one of the little white-painted iron chairs.

As she watched, a young woman walked from the right side of the house with what looked like a dress wrapped in a towel and a sewing basket in her hand. Joce blinked a few times, thinking she'd walked into a time warp. Who sewed today? Who carried a big basket with what looked to be a pincushion top? Had Miss Edi sent Joce into a place where time stood still?

She smiled at the idea, then, instantly, the smile was gone. Even though it had been months since her friend died, Joce still wasn't ready to let her go. No more funny e-mails, no more telephone chats that could go on for hours. No Miss Edi to run home to whenever she had a chance. No more sitting together over a steaming pot of tea and confiding all her worries, fears, and triumphs. Never again would she hear those familiar words, "Of course it's none of my business, but if I were in your place, I would—"

Joce blinked back tears and gave a glance at the closed doors leading off the big hallway, then back at the woman sitting under the shade tree. There were rooms to explore and she should see about groceries and whether there was a bed for the night. But she looked back at the woman—and she won.

Joce had to use her key to unlock the back door, then she went out into the fresh spring air and toward the woman. She was so absorbed in her sewing that she didn't seem to hear anyone approach, so Joce had time to look at her. She was quite young, early twenties, and she looked like a poster child for Innocence. Her face was a perfect oval and her skin like porcelain. Her brown hair had golden highlights that looked natural, and she wore a dress that could have come out of a Kate Greenaway drawing.

Joce didn't want to startle her so she said, "Hello" from several feet away, but the young woman went on sewing and didn't look up. It wasn't until Joce was just an arm's length away that she saw the woman was wearing earbuds. Smiling, Joce pulled out the chair on the other side of the table and sat down.

"Hello," the woman said, not at all startled. She pulled the earbuds off and turned off her iPod.

"Let me guess," Joce said. "Enya."

The pretty young woman blinked, then smiled. "Oh, I see. I look like I've never seen a dirty movie in my life, so I must play angelic music." She pulled the earphone peg out and turned it back on. Out blasted ZZ Top. "I have a hippie mother," she said. "My father's a doctor and as conservative as they come, but my mother likes hard rock and plays it as loud as she can—when my father's not home, that is."

"The neighbors don't complain?"

"One of them did, but my mom poured her a margarita, and when my dad got home they were dancing together. There haven't been any complaints since."

Joce laughed, still looking at the pretty young

woman. "Do you get your face from your mother or your father?"

"My Great-aunt Lissie. Or so I've been told. She used her looks to snare the richest man in town, had half a dozen kids, then proceeded to spend all her husband's money."

Jocelyn didn't let her face show her recognition of the name "Lissie," the woman Miss Edi had mentioned in her letter. Instead, she said, "My kind of woman. Is that your dress you're sewing?"

"Heavens no! I couldn't afford something like this." She held up the garment to show Joce. It was midnight blue and had an intricate pattern of beads and crystals across the bodice, but several lines of beads were hanging loose. "I told her to be careful. I told her there were to be no trysts in the moonlight, and no fumbling in the backseat of the car. This dress cost thousands, and I said it had to be treated with care. But did she listen to me? Of course not."

"From the look of it, she did a lot of fumbling."

"I think so, and since she was banging on my door at six this morning telling me I **had** to fix it by tonight, it's my guess that she did **not** fumble with her husband."

Joce laughed. "Are you my tenant?"

"Oh! Sorry. I didn't introduce myself. I'm Sara Shaw," she said. "I live in that side and Tess Newland lives over there."

"I'm—"

"The entire town knows who you are. Everyone's been waiting for you since the crack of dawn."

"The woman at the grocery store stared at me."

"My mother," Sara said. "She's already called and told me you were on your way."

"And the woman on the porch with the broom?"

"My aunt Helen. She called Mom and got a busy signal because Mom was calling me. I would imagine that by now the sheriff has looked up your license plate number."

Jocelyn didn't know what to say to that, so she just blinked.

"Would you like some iced tea?" Sara asked. "I just made a pitcher."

"I'd love some, but—" She hesitated.

"Only if it's not half sugar?" Sara asked as she stood up, carefully rolled the dress in the big towel, then put it on the little white table.

Joce could feel her face flushing red.

"Don't worry about it. We're used to Yankees down here."

"I'm far from being a Yankee. I'm from Florida," Joce said as she followed Sara toward the big brick house. "That's south of here."

"Mm-hmm," she said over her shoulder. "I think maybe Southern is a state of mind as much as a place. And haven't such a lot of people moved from up North down to Florida?"

Joce couldn't help smiling. They'd reached the screen door of the east wing, and yet again she paused to look up at the house. There were no oddly shaped windows, no rooms that jutted out, nothing that in modern terms made a house "interesting." Edilean Manor was as plain and therefore as beautiful as a house could be.

Sara stepped into the coolness of her side of the house, Joce behind her. They were in a kitchen that looked like it had been put in in about 1965, and although it had been maintained, it certainly hadn't been renovated. "Is that Formica? And is that . . . ?"

"Avocado," Sara said, looking at the drab green refrigerator. "Personally, I think the Smithsonian would be interested in this place. They should move it just as it is into a museum."

Joce looked at the big, white enamel sink under the window and agreed. The kitchen wasn't old enough to be charming. It was just ugly.

"I think I'll complain to my landlord," Sara said.

"You should," Joce said, looking at the old stove. It matched the refrigerator. Her head came up. "Oh! Wait. I'm your landlord."

Sara laughed as she went to the refrigerator and got out a big pitcher of iced tea. "Took you long enough."

"This whole idea of owning a house hasn't sunk in yet. I haven't even seen the inside."

"You'll have time to explore. There are some old buildings outside too, but maybe you know that." Sara nodded toward the little chrome table against the wall. It had a red surface and matching chrome chairs with red seats and backs.

Joce sat down and watched as Sara poured two glasses of tea and put what looked to be home-made cookies on a plate.

"I know very little. All of this is new to me," Joce said. "I'm still recovering from . . . from . . ."

"Miss Edi's death?" Sara asked softly.

Joce nodded. "Did you know her?"

"No, I never met her. But I've certainly heard enough about her."

"Have you?" Joce drank deeply of the tea. She hadn't realized she was thirsty, then she ate a cookie in two bites. When she started on the second one, she looked at Sara's wide eyes. "Sorry. I've been driving for days and I guess I forgot to eat." The truth was that she'd been so nervous last night she couldn't eat her dinner, and this morning she'd skipped breakfast.

"Now that is true concentration!" Sara didn't say anything else, but went to the refrigerator, took out a bowl of something, then got some lettuce, mayonnaise, and bread. She put it all on the counter, then held up the bread. "Look! It's Yankee bread. No Wonder Bread allowed in my house."

"Does it have pineapple in it?"

Sara looked confused.

"No pineapple, no bread. At home in Florida we put pineapple in everything. Or coconut."

It was Sara's turn to laugh. "Okay, I'll stop stereotyping. It's just that Edilean is so near Williamsburg that we get more than our share of tourists. They think we fry everything."

"You don't?"

"Not since we heard the word **cholesterol.**"

As Joce took the sandwich on a plate, she said, "You don't have to do this. Really. I can feed myself."

"You have a lot to learn about us Southerners. We feed people. I think it's in our DNA," Sara said. "Do you mind if we take this outside so I can finish that dress?"

"Gladly," Joce said as she carried her glass and plate and followed Sara out to the table. When they were seated, Sara with the dress across her lap, needle in hand, Joce took a bite. "Did you make this?" It was chicken salad and had sliced grapes and apples in it. It was delicious, like something from an expensive deli.

"No, my mother did. She's sure I'm going to starve living alone. Or worse, that I'll eat something that isn't homegrown and organic. She raised those chickens, and the apples are from our trees."

Joce looked at the sandwich in doubt. "You knew this chicken?"

Sara shrugged. "By the time I was three I learned not to name any living thing around our house. Except my sisters. I named them, but they still didn't end up in a pot."

Joce nearly choked. "Don't get me started! Whatever sister story you have, I can top it."

"Think so? **Both** my sisters graduated from Tulane with cum laude degrees. Both of them got married the week after they graduated—to doctors, of course. And both of them got pregnant the week after they married. And they were virgins on their wedding nights."

Joce took a drink, then gave Sara a smug look. "No competition. My sisters are Steps. They're identical twins, beautiful, naturally blonde, and are five feet eleven inches tall. You know what they call me? Cindy."

"Cindy?" Sara's eyes widened. "Not . . ."

"Right. Short for Cinderella."

Sara didn't want to concede the title just yet. "I have four utterly perfect nieces and nephews, two of each. They never, ever forget to say please and thank you."

"Ever hear of Bell and Ash?"

"The models? Sure. Last week they were on the cover of— No!" Sara gasped. "You can't be telling the truth. They're your . . . ?"

"Stepsisters," Jocelyn said.

"You win. Or lose, I don't know which. I think I'll call my sisters and tell them I'm glad they're mine." She looked at Joce in speculation. "How do you stand it?"

"I get by," she said, shrugging as she looked at Sara. "I don't think I would have made it if it weren't for Miss Edi. She was the one who saved me." She looked down at her sandwich. "Speaking of Miss Edi, she said you'd lived here all your life."

"In the town, not in this house."

"Sure," Joce said cautiously, then chewed while

she tried to think of a polite way to bring up what she wanted to talk about. "Do you know a man named Ramsey McDowell?"

"Of course," Sara said, but she didn't look up.

"What's he like?"

"Beautiful, brilliant, sophisticated. What exactly do you want to know about him?"

"I take it then that he's a heartbreaker."

Sara took a while to answer and when she did, there was caution in her voice. "He's broken some hearts, yes."

"But he's never had his broken?"

Sara looked up from the dress. "I think I should tell you that Ramsey is my cousin, so there's family loyalty there. I'd have to know you a lot better than I do now before I say much about him."

"It's just that he's coming here tonight for dinner, and I'd like to know more about him than just the one conversation we had. He seems to be—"

"Rams is coming here? Tonight? What did you do to rate that?" Sara looked impressed.

"Nothing that I know of," Joce said. "He's handling all the paperwork for the house, so I guess—"

"That's work, and he does that at his office. What did you do to get him to come to your house?"

"I . . . I don't know, except that I knew the date the Emancipation Proclamation was issued."

"That would do it. Rams loves smart people, and he loves history." Sara took a spool of thread from the box and rethreaded her needle. "That's where the girls make their mistakes with my cousin."

"What do you mean?"

"They think Rams is like all the other men and goes for low-cut dresses. He likes those but he likes brains more. Besides, Tess erased the dress theory forever. As for what else he likes, you can ask Tess about women or food or whatever. She knows him better than we do."

"Tess? Oh, yes. The other tenant. What does she have to do with Ramsey . . . Rams?"

"She runs his life." When Joce raised her eyebrows, Sara shook her head. "No, not in that way. Tess runs his law office and she's so good at it, she tends to run his life as well. If you get flowers on your birthday from Rams, they were probably chosen and sent by Tess."

"Ah, one of **those** secretaries. Dotes on him, half in love with him? That sort of thing?"

Sara smiled. "She says she can't stand him, and she frequently lets him know it."

"So why does she work for him? Why does she live here in Edilean?"

Sara shrugged. "I have no idea. Tess is a mystery to me, and I know she's a mystery to Rams. But she lets him know when he does something she doesn't like."

"So what does she have to do with a low-cut dress?"

"You'll have to get Rams to tell you **that** story."

"You know, I think I read in some book that when you go on a first date with a man, you do not ask him what his secretary and a low-cut dress have in common."

Sara laughed. "I'm sure you're right, but Rams has always been able to laugh at himself. Listen, this is just a warning, but when you meet Tess, don't call her a secretary, and do **not** ask her about that dress. She's sick of the story."

"All right," Jocelyn said as she pushed her empty plate away. Already she was beginning to feel a bit overwhelmed with all she had to learn.

Sara seemed to know what she was thinking. "You'll do fine. Everyone is just curious, that's all. But I do warn you that everyone in this town— who actually lives here, that is—is going to want you to tell them about Miss Edi."

"I can understand that," Joce said. "The towns-people must have loved her very much."

"Loved her?" Sara said. "The truth is that there

are few people still alive who really knew her. Except for Aunt Mary Alice, that is, but she can't very well love her, now can she?"

"I don't know," Joce said. "Why couldn't your aunt Mary Alice love Miss Edi?"

"I thought you two were friends. Surely you must know Miss Edi's tragic love story?"

Joce gave a sigh. "Until a few days ago I would have said I knew nearly everything about her, but I'm learning that I didn't know that much. She never mentioned Edilean, Virginia, or this house. I do know that she was once deeply in love with a young man from here who was killed in World War II."

"Killed!" Sara said. "Killed by feisty little Mary Alice Welsch getting herself pregnant by him and making him marry her. When Miss Edi came home from the war there was the man she loved, married to someone else."

Once again Jocelyn had that feeling of betrayal. This wasn't the story she'd been told. All the love that Miss Edi had told her about, her great, deep love for David Aldredge, hadn't ended in death. It had ended in a shotgun wedding. No wonder Miss Edi never mentioned Edilean and no wonder she lied about her beloved's death. Better death than betrayal!

Joce tried to compose herself so Sara couldn't see what she was feeling. "Didn't all this happen a long, long time ago?" Joce asked. "You make it sound like it happened yesterday."

"This is Virginia and we remember things. My grandmother used to tell me stories about the War Between the States. She knew who loved whom and who was jilted. So now I tell stories from another war. Whatever, I've heard Miss Edi's story a thousand times. The Harcourt family started the town, owned the biggest house, laid out the town square, all that. Even after they lost most of their money, they were still the most important family. By World War II, the McDowells were far richer, but they didn't have the cachet the Harcourts did."

As Joce finished her tea, she tried to put the real story together. "So Miss Edi came home from World War II, her legs a mass of burn scars, and she found out that the man she loved had married someone else?"

"That's right."

"So what did she do?" Joce asked.

"The house and what money the family had left was in Miss Edi's name, but she turned the house over to her younger brother. I don't know about the money. My Great-aunt Lissie used to say that Bertrand wasn't much of a man."

"What does that mean? That he didn't ride horses up the staircase at midnight?"

"Now, now, don't let the Yankee in you come to the surface."

"Sorry," Joce said, but she was smiling. "I've read too many romantic novels."

"Haven't we all? As I was saying, Miss Edi came back, saw her man had been stolen from her, so she gave the house to her lazy brother and left town. But not before she had MAW draw up a forty-five-page contract for her brother to sign. She may have been hurt, but she wasn't stupid."

"MAW?" Joce asked.

"The local law firm. McDowell, Aldredge, and Welsch."

"Aldredge," Jocelyn said under her breath, then louder, "always the same names. Tell me, do you people ever move away from your hometown like the rest of the U.S. does?"

"**They** do, but **we** stay."

Joce nodded. "Right. The tourists. The outsiders. They come and go, but yawl stay."

"You didn't say it correctly, so you might as well quit trying. You have to be at least third-generation Southern to be able to say 'you all' correctly."

"I'll keep that in mind. What happened to Miss Edi's brother?"

"Died in his sleep years ago. Aunt Lissie said he was a man who could do absolutely nothing and make himself believe it was work."

"I think I may have met him," Joce said. "I might even have dated him."

"I knew the moment we met that you and I had a lot in common."

They smiled at each other, two women in mutual understanding, then they sat in silence for a while and Joce looked out over the grounds. She still wasn't used to the idea that she was now a property owner. She glanced back at the house, at the sheer, perfect beauty of it, and felt cold chills come over her arms.

Nor had she reconciled herself to the fact that the woman who'd practically been her mother had either left out a lot about her life, or had outright lied to her. Jocelyn had lived with the idea of the "perfect love" Miss Edi'd had for a fallen soldier since she first heard it when she was a child. In fact, the image of that love had been her guide, her yardstick that she'd measured her every relationship against. When a man got serious, Jocelyn asked herself if this was a man she loved with the passion that Miss Edi had felt for her David. No man, no feelings Joce had ever had, had come close to the picture of "true love" that Miss Edi planted there.

But now Jocelyn was finding out that Miss Edi's great love was just a tawdry affair. The man had jilted her for another woman.

"So what are you going to do with the house?" Sara asked, bringing Joce out of reverie. "Sell it? Make it into apartments?"

Joce wasn't fooled by her tone of not caring, of seeming to just be asking a question. So this is why the welcome carpet was rolled out so lavishly, she thought. Had someone told Sara to do whatever she needed to to find out what Miss Edi's heir was planning to do with the old house? "How much do you think I could get for all those old bricks?"

She waited for Sara to laugh, but she didn't. She kept her head down as she sewed on the beads.

"Sara," Joce said, "I'm a lover of history. Since I got out of school I've made my living by helping people research the past."

Sara looked at her with cool eyes. "It would make a wonderful B and B."

Joce groaned. "That's not me. I'm more of an introvert. I can talk with one person at a time, but put me among crowds of strangers and I crawl into my shell."

Sara kept looking at her, obviously waiting for something she could tell the townspeople. Joce had a vision of the telephones lines becoming so busy they caught fire. Or maybe the overuse of cell phones would make the TVs go out.

Joce couldn't hold out under Sara's unblinking stare. "I don't know what I'm going to do. I really don't. Miss Edi left me the house and I assume some money, but I have no idea how much." Suddenly, Jocelyn didn't want to tell more about herself than she already had. There were too many things going on inside her mind that were confusing for her to think clearly—and she certainly wasn't about to tell anyone of her ideas of writing about Miss Edi. "You know of any job openings?"

"Tess got the last good job in town."

Joce glanced toward the far side of the house at the other wing. The doors were closed and the windows shut. "By the way, what do you do? Other than repair dresses, that is."

"That's what I do," Sara said as she cut the thread. "Mostly, I tailor dresses for ladies who buy a size six, then can't get into it on the night they're supposed to wear it."

"You can make a living at that?" Joce asked.

Sara gave a shrug.

Joce was sure there was more to what she did for a living, but she didn't seem to want to tell what it was. All Joce hoped was that it wasn't something illegal. She hoped Sara wasn't growing marijuana in a back bedroom. At that thought, she wondered if all landlords felt like this. What would she do if the bathtubs started leaking? What about termites? Miss Edi mentioned a gardener. What was his salary?

Joce glanced at the house and wondered where she was to sleep tonight. Was there a bed in the house?

Sara pulled a cell phone out of her sewing box, opened it, and looked at the time. "I have to go. This dress has to be back to its owner before hubby gets home." Hurriedly, she rolled the dress in the towel and gathered it in her arms. "Would you take those things in for me?" She nodded to the dishes and sewing box.

"Sure," Joce said. "If you trust me."

"I not only trust you, I think it's possible that I like you. See you soon," she called as she ran back toward the house.

Jocelyn sat where she was, looking at the house and trying to make some sense of all that she'd heard since walking into the lawyer's office. One time when Joce was sixteen she'd come home from school to find that all the Steps, mother and sisters, were gone and the house was quiet. Her father was alone in the garage, working on one of his bikes. She'd stood in the doorway, watching him for a moment. They rarely had time together, as his "new family," as Joce always thought of them, took all of his time and energy.

"Off to Miss Edi's?" he asked.

"Sure. We're reading Thomas Hardy." As she knew, he had nothing to say about that. Gary Minton wasn't given to contemplation.

"Honey?" he said as she walked past him. "I hope you don't give her all of your life. I hope you save some for yourself."

She liked that he called her "honey" but she didn't pay attention to his words. As always, her only thought had been to get away before the Steps returned and took over. Their noise and demands ruled the house, her father, everything. Sometimes it seemed that when her stepsisters were around, they controlled the universe.

Now, she glanced at her watch. She had hours before Ramsey McDowell was to arrive, but she wanted to see the house and take her time getting ready. She'd bought a dress that was perfect for a picnic in an old house.

Her house, she thought, and smiled up at it.

3

L UKE WATCHED AS she—the new owner of
Edilean Manor—left the house and strolled
across the lawn to sit with Sara. He knew how she
felt. Sara was a magnet for people and had been
since they were children. Sara always cared, and always had time to listen to other people's problems.
He well knew that half of the reason women called
her to repair their clothes was because they wanted
to talk to Sara.

Last summer he and some of the cousins, Charlie, Rams, and Sara, were having dinner in Williamsburg when Charlie said she should put out a
shingle and get paid for all her hours of listening
to people about their problems.

"I couldn't stand all those years in school," she said.

"Who said anything about school?" Rams asked. "Just put up the shingle. Luke here will carve it or paint it or whatever for you."

"And you'll draw up a contract and charge her more than she makes in a year," Luke shot back.

"If you two start going at each other tonight I'll walk out," Sara warned. "I want a nice, quiet dinner without you two playing one- upmanship."

When all three men were quiet and looking as though they planned to stay that way, Sara shook her head. "All right, go to it. Tear each other up for all I care. Charlie, order me another one of these drinks."

"You sure?" Charlie asked. "You've never been one to hold your liquor."

"Then one of you will have to hold my hair while I throw up, and another one will have to carry me to the car."

Luke pulled a quarter from his pocket and looked at Ramsey. "Heads and I get the hair. Tails and you get the rest of her. She's put on too much weight for me."

"You two are disgusting," Sara said, but she was laughing.

Now, Luke sharpened the blades of the lawn mower on the whetstone as he looked out through the little round window in the brick wall. He was in what used to be the stables of the old house, but most of it had fallen down long ago. While old Bertrand lived there, the house had been taken care of, as per Miss Edi's instructions, but the out-buildings had been allowed to fall into ruin.

"You didn't put the care of them in the con-tract?" Luke asked Ramsey. "You just took care of the house and not the grounds?"

"Are you implying that **I** made out the contract in 1946?"

"Okay, then your dad."

"He was one year old."

"Whoever, whenever, it is **your** job to look after the place," Luke said when he'd returned to Edilean and seen the state of the outbuildings.

"Maybe you should have stayed here and taken care of them," Ramsey said, unperturbed by his cousin's anger. "Maybe you shouldn't have run off to the far ends of the earth and done whatever it is that's made you so damned angry."

Luke opened his mouth to say something, but closed it. "Go away. Go do whatever you do in your little office and let me take care of this."

It had taken Luke months to restore the old

buildings. He only rebuilt part of the stables, but he used materials from the time the house was built. He dug old bricks out of the ground, even dug up a well that had been filled in with bricks that had been handmade and fired when Edilean Manor was the center of a plantation.

It had been hard, physical labor, something that Luke needed at the time, and he'd enjoyed the solitude of working alone. No one was living in the house then, as old Bertrand had died. There was a housekeeper who came every day, but she was so old she could hardly climb the stairs. When Luke saw her hobbling about, too feeble to accomplish much, he'd taken over. He got her a fat chair and a radio, and he set her up in the living room. When Ramsey, as the lawyer in charge of Miss Edi's estate, saw what he'd done, he said he'd write Miss Edi and tell her the housekeeper should be put out to pasture. But Rams looked hard at Luke as he said it. They both knew the woman's family needed the money, so she was kept on, and Luke did the work. He kept the house in repair, and when the furniture arrived, it was Luke who saw to its placement. One Saturday with cousins and beer and pizza got the larger pieces up the stairs.

Except for the tenants, in essence, the house had been Luke's for the past few years. He was the one who repaired the roof and got the dead pigeon out of the wall. And he rebuilt the top of the chimney when it was hit by lightning.

When he was told that Miss Edi had died and left the house to some girl who'd never seen the place, Luke had an urge to burn it down. Better that than let someone who didn't appreciate it have it.

"Maybe she's a historian," Ramsey said. "Or maybe she's an architect—or even a building contractor. We don't know what she is."

Luke didn't like the way his cousin was defending this unknown woman who was going to take over what most people thought of as the heart of Edilean. All his life he'd heard people say that if Edilean Manor was destroyed, the town wouldn't live a year.

But Ramsey had been so happy about the new inheritor that Luke knew he was up to something. One day after work he went to Tess. She answered his knock but didn't invite him in. "What's he up to about this new owner?" Luke asked, not bothering with preliminaries. And there was no need to explain who "he" was.

Tess was a woman of few words. "Edilean Harcourt sent him a photo of her. In a bikini."

Luke understood immediately. If he knew his

cousin, Rams planned to make a play for her. He loved Edilean Manor almost as much as Luke did. "Got it," Luke said.

Tess stepped to the side and opened the screen door wider. "You want a beer?"

"Love one."

Now, "she" had arrived, and Luke watched her as she sat and talked with Sara. She was pretty, but not strikingly so. She was a little above average height, and her hair looked like the girls' used to get in the summer. It would turn from brown to sun-streaked over the months, and he wondered if hers was natural or if she spent hours in a salon.

She was dressed as old-fashioned as Sara, and that made him smile. Sara loved to wear dresses with long sleeves even in the heat of summer. But then she knew they looked good on her. She was as pretty and as delicate as a flower, and when she wore something like a bright red tank top and jeans she looked almost odd.

Luke thought that if he had a camera with him he would have taken their photo. There was Sara in her prim little dress, her sewing on her lap, and across from her was this new woman wearing something like in an illustration in **Alice in Wonderland.** He thought the headband was an especially perfect touch.

A priss and a prude, he thought. That's who Miss Edi had left the house to. A woman heading toward spinsterhood who would probably dedicate her entire life to the house. No doubt she'd work hard to find furniture of exactly the right time period and within a few months she'd make Edilean Manor into a museum.

He'd made up his mind about her within minutes of first seeing her, and if it hadn't been for his mother, he would have told her he quit. Let Ramsey have her, he thought. Let him ooze charm all over her and have her fall for him. Of course he'd probably do what he always did and find some little thing wrong with her, then dump her. But maybe it would backfire and she'd be so heartbroken she'd put the house up for sale.

Yeah, he thought, smiling to himself. Maybe she'd sell the place.

But his mother's voice was in his head, so he stayed where he was in the old stables and watched Sara and the new owner.

He knew something was up when his mother appeared at his door at six this morning with a covered plate of blueberry pancakes. Luke smiled. "So what's Dad done this time that you're bringing me his breakfast?" Luke's father had retired a year ago, and since then he'd nearly driven his wife insane with his puttering around the house.

"Nothing. I talked him into going to a tractor show."

"Without you?"

"In case he asks, I have the worst headache you've ever seen. That's enough about me. Miss Edi's girl comes today and I want you to promise that you'll be nice to her." While she talked, she was heating up the pancakes for her son and cleaning his kitchen as she moved about his house.

Luke groaned. "What is it you want me to do this time? Take her out to dinner? Show her the sights? It's too early for the water parks, so do I have to take her to some fife and drum concert?"

"I want you to leave her alone. She belongs to Ramsey."

Luke's eyes widened.

"No, you don't," Helen said as she put the pancakes in front of him. "You're not going to take this as a challenge. She's already talked to Rams and she likes him."

"Didn't waste any time, did he? But then I hear there was a bikini shot of her that he liked before he ever talked to her."

"Men are like that," Helen said in dismissal.

"Are we?" Luke's mouth was full.

"Do you understand me? Be nice and stay away from her. Keep to the gardening."

"What if **I** like her?" He told himself he was a grown man and it didn't matter that his own mother was taking the side of his cousin, but he couldn't help feeling betrayed.

"You won't. She was trained by Miss Edi, which means she likes men in tuxedos, not in . . ." She glared at his tattered jeans and dirty T-shirt. "Do we have everything clear between us?"

"Sure," Luke said. The last thing he wanted was female trouble. "Let Ramsey have her. Let them move into Edilean Manor and raise a dozen kids. What do I care?"

But now, Luke kept watching Sara and the woman . . . What was her name? Jocelyn. An old-fashioned name that suited her. As he watched the two of them, he was beginning to change his opinion of her. She laughed easily and often. And whatever she was saying was interesting to Sara. In fact, Sara was doing most of the talking, which was unusual. Usually, Sara was the listener.

Twice, Luke saw her . . . Jocelyn, look at the house with a mixture of love and disbelief, as though she were shocked that it could be hers. But that couldn't be, could it? Surely Miss Edi had told her she was leaving the place to her.

When the lawn mower blade was so sharp he could have sliced salami with it, he still stayed in the stables and watched them. He opened a bottle of water and drank it while leaning against the wall and looking out the little window. If he left, they'd see him, and he didn't want that. Sara knew he was there, but she hadn't called to him to come meet the new owner. That meant they were having some serious girl talk.

Suddenly, Sara jumped up, grabbed the dress she was working on, and ran into her house. That she left her precious sewing box in the care of this stranger told Luke a lot. Sara liked her.

The woman sat there for a while, then she picked up the dishes they'd used and the sewing box, and took them back to her own part of the house. As far as Luke knew, she hadn't so much as walked through the house. He knew that upstairs was a bed that had been made up for her with clean sheets and new pillows. His mother had done that yesterday. After she left, Luke went up there and looked at the pretty little soaps his mother had put out for her, and the new, freshly washed towels. If royalty had visited Edilean, there couldn't have been more of a fuss made.

Luke didn't know why it all made him feel angry, but it did. What did they know about this woman? Except what she looked like in a bikini, that is.

When she was inside the house, Luke left the stables and cleared away his tools. His truck was parked in back and he tossed shovels and loppers in with a bang. If she came out and had something to say about . . . about anything, he'd tell her he was quitting.

He got in the truck, started it, and drove to the road that went out the back of the property, the servants' exit. But on impulse, he turned toward the front of the house.

Just as he got to the gate, Ramsey pulled in in his black Mercedes sedan and blocked the exit. Luke just wanted to leave, but he could see that Rams wasn't about to let him pass. When his cousin put his window down, Luke stuck his head out the truck window.

"Have you seen her yet?"

"Who?" Luke asked.

"Miss Edi's ghost. You know who I mean. Have you seen her?"

"Maybe."

"So what's she look like?"

"Bad. Real bad. She's so ugly I had to use a mirror to look at her," Luke said.

"That good, huh?" Ramsey said. "I was hoping so. I was a little worried about . . . Nothing. I wasn't worried at all."

"Would you move that gas guzzler of yours and let me by?"

"I need your help," Ramsey said. "Aunt Ellie said Sara's with Jocelyn, so I want you to get Sara to keep Jocelyn busy for twenty minutes while I set up."

"Set up?" Luke asked. "What are you talking about? Are you planning fireworks?"

"Maybe," Ramsey said with a grin. "She knows I'm coming and I'm bringing dinner, but I don't want her to see me lugging this stuff out of the car and hauling it into the house. Hey! I know. I'll go talk to Jocelyn and **you** set up for me. You know how to chill champagne, don't you?"

"Put it in the creek with the beer," Luke said as he backed up his truck. What the hell was up with this whole town? he wondered. First his mother tells him to stay away from this woman, then Ramsey wants him to play butler.

When they got to the wide, graveled area in front of the house, they parked their vehicles by

Jocelyn's silver Mini Cooper and got out. Ramsey was in black trousers, white shirt, and blue tie. He pulled the tie off and tossed it onto the front seat of the car. "What a day! I planned to be here an hour ago, but old man Segal nearly drove me crazy. He and his son had another fight, so the old man changed his will again."

Ramsey opened the back car door, pulled out a huge picnic basket, then looked up at the windows of the house. "You don't think she's watching, do you?"

"Why are you asking me? You obviously know more about her than I do."

"What's wrong with you?" Ramsey asked. "You have a falling-out with your latest girl?"

"Never has happened, never will. Can you tell me why you're so interested in this woman?"

"I think she may be the one."

"Not again," Luke said with a groan.

"This girl spent most of her life with Miss Edi. She spent her weekends at the ballet. She can play the piano and dance a waltz. And she has a brain."

"So that means she's someone you can show off at the country club and at those benefits they give over in Williamsburg."

"If by that you mean I'd like to meet someone

with an education, who also happens to be beautiful, yes."

Luke glanced up at the windows. "Sounds like I **should** get to know her."

Ramsey snorted. "You'd probably scare her to death. Or she'd faint at the smell of you."

"A lot of those girls like bad boys."

"Don't flatter yourself. Bad boy. Give me a break. Just go to Sara's, knock on the door, and tell her to keep Jocelyn busy for about twenty minutes. I'll ring the bell when I'm ready. Think you can do that?"

Luke started to tell him that Sara wasn't home, and that Jocelyn was in her own house, but he didn't. His mother had asked him to be nice to the new owner. She didn't say anything about driving Ramsey crazy. In fact, annoying his cousin was Luke's favorite game in the world.

"Sure," Luke said, trying to look grumpy, but he was smiling on the inside.

ᕦᕤ

Jocelyn looked at the little clock on the bedside table and saw she still had thirty minutes until Ramsey was to arrive. She was already so nervous she felt like a teenager going on her first date. After Sara left, she'd made a quick run-through of the house and seen that the rooms had not been altered. As she'd been told, what little furniture there was in the rooms was from Miss Edi's house in Florida. There were no knickknacks, just empty cabinets and shelves. Three of the rooms contained a rug and four or five good pieces of antique furniture, but nothing else. The kitchen was still in the 1950s, a bit better than Sara's, but not much. She liked the huge sink and the big pine table, but thought the stove would benefit by being turned on its back and having flowers planted in its belly.

After her cursory look through the house, she wrestled her suitcase up the stairs and began to get ready for her date.

She'd been delighted when she saw the bed with its clean linens and the bathroom that was filled with towels and beautiful soaps. She didn't know who had prepared this welcome, but she certainly wanted to thank them.

She took a long shower, washed her hair, then blow-dried it. She got out her new white cotton dress with the Battenberg lace along the bottom of the skirt and knew it would be perfect for tonight. While still in her robe, she heated her little travel iron, then set about ironing every wrinkle out of the cotton. Miss Edi had been a stickler for well-ironed clothes. She didn't believe in permanent press or even knitwear. "You can tell a lady by the quality of her clothing and how well it's maintained," she'd said many times.

When Jocelyn finished dressing, she thought, Now what do I do? Her only thought was to see if Sara had come home. She'd left Sara's dishes and sewing box in her own hall, so maybe she should take them back now.

Minutes later, she was in Sara's apartment—she'd left the back door unlocked—but she wasn't home. Just as Jocelyn put the dishes down, there was a knock on the front door. She wasn't sure she should answer it. After all, it was Sara's house. But then it was also her own house.

Jocelyn opened the door to see a tall, dark-haired man standing there. He had on jeans and a dirty T-shirt, and he hadn't shaved in days, but these things didn't detract from his beauty. He had dark green eyes above a nose that could only be described as patrician, and his full lips were finely chiseled above a well-formed chin. Sara had said he was "beautiful" and he was.

"You're the new owner." It was a statement, not a question.

His voice was deep and rich, just as it had been on the telephone, and she was sure she'd never seen a man she was more attracted to. "Yes, I am. And you're Ramsey."

"Ramsey? Lord no! He's a lawyer. Do I look like a lawyer?"

"Oh," she said, disappointed. She looked away to try to conceal her attraction to him. "No, I guess you don't look like a lawyer. You're here to see Sara, aren't you? She's not here."

"I know. I saw her leave."

She turned back to look at him, still standing in the doorway. "If you know she's not here, why did you knock on the door?"

"I'm your gardener, Luke Connor." He was watching her closely, as though he was trying to figure her out.

Before she could reply, she heard a noise outside, to her right, then he leaned back, looked toward the front of the house, and waved his hand, as though to tell someone to go away. In the next second, he pushed his way past her and into the house.

"Would you mind!" Jocelyn said. "You can't come barging in here like this and—"

"Don't get your pin feathers ruffled," he said as he shut the front door behind him.

"This isn't my place and I don't think you should be in here."

"Yes it is."

"Is what?"

"Your house."

"Yes, technically, it is, but this part is rented to Sara Shaw. She—"

"She's my cousin," he said over his shoulder as he went to the kitchen.

Jocelyn was close behind him. "If you're Sara's cousin, does that mean you're Ramsey's brother?"

He opened the refrigerator and pulled out a beer. As he leaned back against the counter, he looked her up and down in a way that Jocelyn had never liked. It was the way all men who knew they were good-looking looked at women, as though they knew the women belonged to them—if they wanted them.

"What is it with you and ol' Cousin Rams? You two have something going already?"

She took a step back from him. Her first attraction to him was fading. "Not that it's any of your business, but I've never met him. Sara told me he was her cousin, and if you're also her cousin, then I assumed you were related to Ramsey."

"I am. But then, we're all cousins. Sara, Rams, Charlie, Ken, and me. We have the same great-grandparents."

There was something about his attitude that she didn't like. He was laughing at her, but she had no idea what she was doing to amuse him. As far as she could tell, the entire town seemed to be related to one another. "What about Ramsey's sister? Is she a cousin too?"

He looked puzzled. "Of course she is. She's . . ." He stopped because he realized she was teasing him. He'd left some people off the list of cousins. He often found that people not from the South laughed when relatives were mentioned. "Are you a—"

"So help me, if you ask me if I'm a Yankee, I'll—"

"You'll what?" he asked, his eyebrows raised in interest.

"I'll cut the heads off the roses. I don't know. How do you punish a gardener?"

He gave her a look that almost made her blush. "That's the most interesting question I've been asked all day."

She was quickly developing a dislike of the man. Jocelyn looked at her watch. "I have to go. I'm meeting someone."

"Yeah, Rams. He's over there working up a sweat to make a fairyland for you two."

"That was nasty of you to ruin the surprise."

"Waste of time, if you ask me."

She gave him a look up and down that she hoped was full of contempt. "But then I suppose your idea of a date is a six-pack and a bag of potato chips."

"Corn chips," he said. "I like corn chips. I especially like those blue ones. She shows up with blue corn chips and a six of Samuel Adams and she just might get lucky."

"I guess that's supposed to be funny."

"Just being honest."

"You're like so many men I've met—and never want to meet again." She went to the back door to open it and leave, but he blocked her way.

"You can't leave yet. Rams said he'd ring the bell when he's ready."

"He sent **you** over here to detain me?"

"He's not **that** dumb. He sent me to tell Sara to keep you busy, but he forgot to ask me if Sara was here. Why don't you sit down and be still so you don't wrinkle your pretty new dress? I'm going to make myself a sandwich. I'd offer you one, but Rams has enough food for half the town over there, so you better not eat now."

She was standing at the end of Sara's Formica-clad counter and considering what to do next. Stay here and have this vain man laugh at her for things she didn't understand, or leave and spoil Ramsey's surprise? All in all, she thought that she'd rather see Ramsey than stay here with this man.

Jocelyn turned just as Luke went to put his sandwich ingredients on the counter. Her arm hit his hand, and the plastic mustard dispenser squirted on her. Bright yellow mustard went down the front of her white dress.

"You did that on purpose," she said. "You meant to do that."

"No I didn't," he said, and sounded truly contrite. "Honest, I didn't." Gone was the attitude and the half smirk he'd worn since he'd pushed his way into the apartment. "I am sorry. Really."

Turning, he grabbed a clean dishcloth off the rack over the sink and wet it. "Here," he said, "let me help you."

She held her blouse out from her chest as she thought about how she could slip back into the house and change without seeing Ramsey. But he said he was going to set up the picnic on the floor. If that meant the hall, there was no way she could get past him—which meant she was going to meet him with her front covered in mustard.

"What the hell are you doing?"

Jocelyn and Luke turned toward the back door and there stood a man she was sure was Ramsey. He was an inch or two shorter than Luke and a bit heavier, but he had the same dark hair and green eyes, and almost the same nose and chin. They were two truly gorgeous men.

Jocelyn looked from Ramsey to Luke and saw that he was hovering over the front of her with a wet cloth. Instantly, she stepped out of his reach. "He threw mustard on me," she said, her eyes on Ramsey.

Ramsey looked at Luke with a threat in his eyes.

Luke threw up his hands. "Accident. I swear. She's yours." With his hands still up, he backed out of the room, and she heard the front door open and close.

"Are you all right?" Ramsey asked.

"Fine. Really, I am, but I look awful. I wanted to at least be presentable when we met."

"You look great!" Ramsey said with such enthusiasm that she smiled back.

"You're very kind."

"No I'm not. I'm a lawyer, remember? How about if we go to your house, the main part of it, that is, and have something to eat? Are you hungry?"

"Starving."

He went down the hall to the front door and opened it for her, and when she was beside him, he said, "I apologize for my cousin. Luke is . . ." He gave a shrug, as though there were no words to describe the man.

"That's all right," Jocelyn said. "We all have relatives."

"Unfortunately, I have more than most."

As they stepped outside, she saw Luke speed away in a beat-up old truck that reminded her of the vehicles she'd seen around her father's house when she was growing up. As far as she could tell, Luke Connor was the kind of man Miss Edi had warned her against. Worse, he was the kind of man Jocelyn's sweet, elegant, educated mother had fallen so hard for. After they were married, Gary Minton had done what he could to be what his refined little wife's family wanted him to be, but a month after she died, he was back in leathers, whiskers on his face, and straddling a Harley.

"Are you sure you're all right?" Ramsey asked. "Did Luke upset you that bad?"

"Of course not," Jocelyn said, smiling as she came back to the present. "Let me change my clothes and I'll be fine."

"Tonight your smallest wish is my command," Ramsey said and gave her a half bow.

"Then, kind sir, lead me to yon castle that I might prepare myself for thee."

Ramsey grinned, held out his arm to her, and they walked together to the front door of Edilean Manor.

4

"THIS IS TRULY beautiful," Jocelyn said and meant it. Ramsey had gone to a lot of trouble with the dinner, and she appreciated it. There was an old, white, trapuntoed quilt on the floor of the hallway and two huge pillows on each side. The meal was angel hair pasta in a light sauce of sautéed tomatoes and basil, with bread and salad.

"Did you get the vegetables from Sara's mother?" she asked.

"Of course. If I bought tomatoes that didn't come from her I think she might picket my office."

The dishes were Limoges in one of her favorite patterns, and the wineglasses had to have come from Colonial Williamsburg. They were hand-blown in an eighteenth-century design.

Ramsey was stretched out on the pillow opposite her, and in the candlelight he looked even more handsome than he did when she first met him. The truth was that he made her a bit nervous. There was something about the absolute perfection of him that made her wish she were more perfect.

"Why is there so little furniture in the house?" Joce asked. She was sitting upright on the opposite side of the quilt. "I don't mean to sound greedy, but it seems strange that a house that's been lived in for so many generations would have so little in it. If I'd guessed, I would have said it was packed to the gills with at least a lot of Victorian ornaments."

"In a word, Bertrand," Ramsey said. He'd finished his pasta and was sipping the white wine. "I don't really know too much about it, as my father personally handled Miss Edi, but Dad always muttered things under his breath whenever ol' Bertrand's name was mentioned. I think he had a problem with the horses."

"Your father gambled?" Joce asked.

Ramsey looked at her to see if she was kidding.

"Sorry. My sense of humor," she said. "So Bertrand had a gambling problem."

Ramsey looked at her over the wineglass. "He had some kind of problem. At least I think he did.

I never really knew Miss Edi, but from what I heard of her, it always struck me as odd that she let him sell off most everything that was in this house. I remember when I was a kid and a huge truck pulled up in front of the house."

"It got through those narrow gates?"

"Good eye!" he said. "No, no truck can get through those pillars. Luke's pickup has been scraped on them more than once."

Ramsey took a drink of wine, then got up to begin clearing away the remnants of the pasta and salad. When Joce started to help him, he told her to sit still. She waited while he carried the plates into the kitchen, and when he returned, he had a little machine that looked like a fondue pot. "My sister assures me that this thing is perfect for melting chocolate. She says her second child was conceived the night they bought it." He looked at her. "Sorry. Bad story for a first date."

"You're forgiven, but only if you tell me about the moving van."

"Oh, yes. They had to park it in the road, and a smaller truck carried furniture out to it. It was a Saturday and all of us kids nearly drove the movers crazy. We were in the truck, in the house, even hiding inside cabinets that they had to carry. They were ready to throw us all into the pond."

"What did your parents say? Wasn't that dangerous?"

"They were right there, watching everything, and the adults who couldn't be there to watch paid us to run to their house every hour and tell them what was going on. Sara was the fastest on her bike, so she delivered the messages. You know, I still think she didn't split the money fairly. I think she kept most of it for herself."

"The cousins," Joce said, smiling. "All for one; one for all."

He broke pieces of chocolate into the little pot that he'd plugged in, and was now stirring them around. "I guess. I think it was fun when we were kids, but now I find it more than a little confining. Like today. I really apologize about what—"

Joce didn't want to hear another word about Luke and the mustard. "What did they take away in the van?"

"The good stuff."

"The yellow couch, the end tables, the big armoire, the four chairs in the dining room," Joce said. "It was all in Miss Edi's house in Florida. I believe she sold what she didn't send back here at auction."

"I know she did."

"And the money . . . ?"

"Nope," Ramsey said. "I'm not saying a word about business tonight. Which means that you have to come to my office first thing Monday morning so I can tell you everything."

"I bet there are contingencies concerning the house, aren't there?"

Ramsey shook his head at her. "Don't try to get 'round me. I'm not saying a word."

"All right," she said, sipping her wine. "So Miss Edi took the good furniture and left the bad stuff for her brother to sell to pay his gambling debts."

"My mother said she thought Miss Edi used her brother to run a big yard sale. It saved her money and gave him something to do."

"That sounds like her."

"There!" Ramsey said. "The pot is ready. Take one of these." He held out a little box full of long forks. "And spear one of these." He opened a container of fat, perfectly ripe strawberries. "Then dip."

She did so. "Delicious. Really wonderful. I feel pregnant already." When he didn't say anything, she looked at him. "Yet again, my dumb sense of humor."

"No, I like it. It's just that I'm not used to beautiful girls who can make jokes."

"They don't have to. They just sit there, and that's enough."

"I meant . . . ," he began, then smiled. "I'm coming off as a moron. It's just that I want this night to succeed."

Jocelyn wiped chocolate off her chin. "It's succeeding with me. Hey! Thanks for fixing the bedroom for me."

"The bedroom?"

"You know, linens, soap, that sort of thing. I would have had to spend the night elsewhere if you hadn't done that. You did do it, didn't you?"

"'Fraid not. Probably some of the ladies from the church."

"Speaking of which, I saw a church when I drove in. Miss Edi and I went every Sunday, and I miss it."

"Church," Ramsey said, as though he'd never heard of the place before. "If you show up in church on Sunday my mother is going to think you're so perfect that she's going to go out and buy us wedding rings."

"That bad, huh?"

"Are you kidding? I'm thirty-two and haven't produced a kid."

"What about your sister and your other siblings?"

"It's just the two of us," Ramsey said, "and my

mother isn't content with the brood that Viv produces. She wants kids from me too."

From the way he was looking at her, Jocelyn didn't know whether to fall into his arms or push him out the door and bolt it. "I wear a size five ring, and I want a four-carat, emerald-cut, pink diamond."

This time Ramsey groaned. "You tell her that and I'm a goner."

"Does Sara make wedding dresses? If she does, I have some ideas about mine."

Ramsey laughed.

"No, really. You think Sara's mom could get enough white roses together for me that I could fill the church?"

"Stop it!" he said, laughing. "Really, we can't talk about this or my mother will somehow hear it and show up at the door. If you had any idea what I go through—" He cut himself off. "What I want to hear about is you and Miss Edi."

"We were kindred souls," Jocelyn said. She opened her mouth to start telling him her life story, but she stopped herself. If she told everything tonight, what would they talk about on the second date? And she truly hoped there would be a second date because she liked him.

"Okay," Ramsey said, "keep your secrets. But I'll get them out of you."

As she watched, he got up off the pillows, and standing up, he stretched. His shirt clung to the muscles in his chest and arms, and Joce couldn't pry her eyes away. When he caught her looking, she quickly turned away, but it wasn't fast enough to keep her from being embarrassed.

"Do you play golf?" he asked.

"What?"

"Golf? Do you play?"

"No."

"Tennis?" he asked.

"Sorry. No tennis. And before you ask, I don't swim very well, and I don't play bridge, and I'm not good at clubs."

"So what do you like to do?" he asked. "No, wait, don't tell me. Let me find out. You must do something besides dream about your wedding."

"Not much."

Smiling, he began to clear up the dishes, but this time Joce helped. "So what do you imagine the groom looking like?"

"Blond, blue eyed," she said instantly, and Ramsey laughed.

"I deserved that." He put the dishes on the big

kitchen table and looked around him. "You must want to redo this kitchen."

There were three naked lightbulbs hanging from the ceiling, and the light glared off everything, making it almost eerie in the room. "How could you even think of changing this room?" she said in mock horror.

"How about a marble-topped island instead of this table?" he asked, looking at her. "And a new sink, of course."

She looked at the sink and felt a pang at the thought of its going. It was huge and on legs, with two enormous bowls with a tall porcelain back, and drain boards on both sides. She looked away from it. "Are you asking me if I can cook?" Before he could answer, she said, "I can't. Miss Edi had a woman who'd worked for her for over twenty years, and she cooked wonderful meals. Meanwhile, at my parents' house . . . Well, the less said about there the better. But I can make cupcakes."

"Cupcakes?"

"It was a project I did in school, and Miss Edi let me use her kitchen. I can even use a pastry tube."

"That's good," he said, but his voice sounded

dubious, and for a while there was a silence between them, and Jocelyn suppressed a yawn. It had been a very long day.

"Look, I think I better go," he said. "It's getting late. Shall I pick you up for church tomorrow?"

"If you and I walked into church together, we would be mated for life." She was making a joke, but he didn't smile.

"I've heard of worse things."

"Yeah, me too," she said, but she didn't meet his eyes. "How about if I meet you there? Ten A.M., right?"

"If you miss Sunday School, it is, and I usually do."

"Late sleeper?"

"Late worker," he said. "I have about three hours of paperwork to do tonight."

"Really?"

"Yes," he said.

"Could I help?"

For a moment he looked puzzled, as though he were trying to figure out if she was again joking. "Thanks, but no. We're handling a big divorce case and I'm trying to find some missing money. How could a man afford to pay cash for a three-million-dollar house if he only makes sixty grand a year? At least that's the question his wife wants to know."

"I'm not good on money," she said, "but I could . . . I've done a lot of research, so if you ever need help on that, let me know."

"And cupcakes," he said, smiling. "We can't forget the cupcakes."

"I never forget the cupcakes," she said, but her smile was forced. When he reached for a plate, she said, "Just leave everything and I'll clean up tomorrow. You need to go to work and get as much done as possible so you can go to church in the morning."

"Thanks," he said, then seemed not to know what else to say. "So I'll see you in church then?"

"If you can pull yourself out of bed," she said.

He started toward the front door, and she followed him. He opened it, then paused, and for a moment she thought he was going to kiss her, but then he stepped onto the little porch.

"Thank you for everything," she said. "I really enjoyed it."

"Yeah," he said as he went down the steps. "Me too."

Jocelyn closed the door and leaned against it. What in the world was wrong with her? She'd had a very romantic date with **the** man, the one Miss Edi said was to be the love of her life. But somehow, she'd ruined it. She didn't know how, but she had. Of course her lame jokes about marriage didn't help. It's a wonder he didn't run out the door. What was it he'd said on the phone? That the last time a woman talked to him about marriage they'd had to call an ambulance.

She looked at her watch. It was only nine-thirty. So much for her "date." In spite of the early hour, she yawned. Maybe the problem was that she was exhausted. Meeting new people, seeing the house, having a date all in one day was too much for anyone.

She left the dirty dishes on the table, flipped the switch to turn out the awful kitchen lights, then started toward the stairs to go to bed. It was when she passed the back door and heard it click that her heart leaped into her throat. Someone was at the door! And he was trying to break in!

Jocelyn's mind raced as she tried to remember where her cell phone was. Upstairs. Or was it downstairs? She couldn't remember. Had a land-line been hooked up? In the busyness of the day, she'd never even looked for a telephone.

Someone pulled on the door, and she plastered herself against the wall, her heart beating hard. Bending, she moved under the window by the door so the intruder couldn't see her as she crawled past. If she could get to the front door before he did, she could get out.

As she got past the door, she saw a shadow, then the moonlight showed her a figure. He was big. He had dark hair. He . . .

She stood up straight. It was Ramsey. He must have forgotten something. She grabbed the door-knob and pulled it inward—and came face-to-face with Luke.

"What are you doing?"

He looked more surprised to see her than she did him. "Checking the doors," he said. "I thought you might forget to lock them, so I—"

"Sara leaves her door unlocked. I thought this was one of those towns where no one locks their doors."

"Don't kid yourself," he said, then took a step back. "Look, I'm sorry. There weren't any lights on, so I thought you'd gone to bed."

"Were you watching the house?"

"That's what I do," he said. "That's my job, re-member? Weren't you told about me? Or are you still mad about the mustard?"

She dropped her hostility. "No, I know that was an accident. Would you like to come in and have some tea?"

"With you and Ramsey?"

"Like you don't know that he left ten minutes ago," she said.

He gave her a crooked smile, then stepped inside. The quilt and the candlesticks were still on the floor, along with the chocolate pot and some strawberries. "So did you kick him out?"

"No, I did not kick him out. He had to go home to work."

Bending over, he ran his finger inside the still warm pot, then put his chocolate-covered finger in his mouth. "That makes sense. I guess that's why he went to Tess after he left you."

Joce stopped walking and turned to look at him. He had the pot in his hands and was running a strawberry through it. "He did what?"

"Went to see his assistant, Tess. She lives next door. She runs his life."

"I've already been told that. But he's there now?"

"Sure," Luke said, raising his eyes to hers. "Who told you about Tess? Not Rams, that's for sure."

"What does that mean?" She started for the kitchen again. "Come on," she said over her shoulder, "and bring that if you want."

"Thanks," he said as he followed her, the cord to the pot dragging across the floor. "I thought that maybe tomorrow you and I could talk about what you want to do with the garden."

"I don't know anything about gardening." She was opening cabinet doors, looking for a teapot or tea bags, something.

"This tea is too much trouble for you. Really, I didn't mean to bother you. I'll get something to eat on the way home. They have a few fast-food places over in Williamsburg. Off the highway. It's not too far away. Couple of hours, that's all."

She couldn't help laughing. "All right, sit down," she said, and he did. She took the container of leftover pasta out of the old refrigerator and stuck it in an ancient microwave.

"What makes you think that Rams didn't tell me about his secretary?" She tried to seem as though she didn't care, and she used his nickname to sound closer to him.

"I take it you haven't met Tess," Luke said as he got up, went to the cabinets, then reached over her head to get a plate. He took a knife and fork out of a drawer.

Jocelyn hadn't looked in the cabinets, so she didn't know where anything was. "No, I haven't met her, but I've heard about her."

"From Sara? She tell you about the red dress?"

"What is it with this woman and a low-cut,

red dress?" Joce asked as she opened the microwave.

"Sure you want to hear?"

"I'm all grown up. I think I can stand it. What
happened with the secretary and a dress?"

Luke took the bowl of pasta from her, dumped it
on the plate, and put it on the table. "Want some?"

"No, thank you. I ate earlier. With Ramsey, remember?"

"Oh, yeah. You were together such a short time
that I nearly forgot about that date. It **was** a date,
wasn't it?"

Joce didn't bother to answer him but poured
some wine into a glass and took a sip. "Sorry, but
that's the last of it," she said, but her tone let Luke
know she wasn't sorry at all. What was it about this
man that put her in the worst possible mood? Or
was her mood caused by the fact that Ramsey had
made her think they were on the way to becoming
an item, then he'd gone next door to another
woman?

Luke got up, opened the refrigerator, and got
out a beer.

"You certainly have made yourself at home in
my house."

"I'm here a lot, so you better get used to me."
He tasted the pasta. "This is pretty good. Did

Rams make it? He always was a good cook. He can even make worm pies. You should get him to tell you about them."

"Before or after you tell me about the red dress?"

"Oh, that," Luke said, his mouth full. "Tess doesn't take well to being given orders. The way she sees it, she does her job and that's all that's required of her. Anything else is her own business."

"Don't we all feel that way?" Joce asked. She sat down in a chair across from him.

"Not to the extent Tess does, but Rams always was a bit of what we call down here persnickety."

"I see," Jocelyn said with a cool smile. "He can cook and now he's persnickety. What will you tell me next? He used to be a female?"

"Not that I know of," Luke said innocently. "Did he tell you he wanted to be? I hear there are some really good clinics for that kind of thing nowadays. Not that **I** know anything about them, but I bet ol' Rams knows a lot."

Joce couldn't keep from laughing. "You're horrible. Just tell me the story."

Luke ate a few more bites, then said, "It was simple really. Rams told Tess he didn't like what she was wearing."

"She didn't take it off, did she?"

"Is that what the secretaries do in law offices in Florida? If so, I'm in the wrong state."

She narrowed her eyes at him.

"No, she didn't remove anything. It was just after she started working at MAW. That's—"

"I know what it is. Go on."

"You certainly have picked up on a lot around here. So, anyway, Tess had only been there about six weeks, but already she'd straightened out the whole office. She'd fired two secretaries and made the two she kept actually work. It was a true revelation to my cousin Rams. A woman who did some work to earn what she was paid."

"Does he know you talk about him like this?"

"Did he tell you about **me**?"

"I am happy to say that we never spoke a single word about you all night."

"Hour and a half." Luke waved his fork around. "I mean, technically speaking, it wasn't really a whole night. It was just an hour and a half. Pretty short date, wasn't it? Now if it had been me taking a woman out—"

"Yeah, I know. You would have made love on the blue corn chips. Get on with the story about Ramsey."

"To make love on a bed of blue corn chips.

Now, there's something I haven't tried. Do you know about this from experience?"

"My experience is none of your business. What did Ramsey do?"

"He didn't **do** anything. He's more of a talker than a doer. Now me . . . Okay, stop looking at me like that. Anyway, all the men in the office were pleased with Tess in every way. I mean, she's smart and sassy, and did whoever told you about her tell you that she's drop-dead gorgeous?"

"No," Jocelyn said but didn't elaborate.

"She is. A real knockout. Sometimes when she walks across the lawn I have to shut off the mower and just sit there and watch her. But, anyway, Rams wasn't happy with what he had. As usual with him, he wanted **more.** Always more. He called her into his office for what he said was an 'evaluation' and told her that her work was excellent, but he wasn't too pleased with what she wore. He didn't like her jeans and shirt and he hated the cowboy boots. He told her that he wanted her to start wearing dresses to work. No more trousers."

Jocelyn leaned back in the chair, her eyes wide. "What in the world did she do?"

"Wore a dress. Any more of that garlic bread left?"

Jocelyn got up and handed him the basket.

"Sara said 'low-cut' and you said 'red.' So what was the dress like?"

"I wasn't in town that day so I didn't get to see it, but . . . Hang on a minute." He leaned back in his chair and pulled his cell phone out of the little case on his hip. "I have to keep this with me at all times because I'm a volunteer with the fire department." He pushed a few buttons. "Ah, here it is. This is what my cousin Ken sent me. He's the **W** in MAW."

Jocelyn took the phone and looked at the photo. It was of a woman in a red dress, except that there was very little to the garment. It was shorter than the Steps' shortest, and the sides were open to the waist, as was the front. The woman's face was turned away so she couldn't see it, but her long, auburn hair fell in fat curls past her shoulders. And her body was magnificent.

"I see," Joce said as she handed the phone back to him.

"Yeah, that's what everyone said that day. 'I see.' The worst thing is that Rams had some of those blue bloods coming in from Williamsburg that day, and they saw Tess in her dress. But Ken said they took it pretty well. When their mouths hung open, Tess told them that Ramsey didn't like her usual attire, so he'd told her to wear a dress and she did. After that, Rams was the butt of a lot of jokes."

"And now I guess Tess wears whatever she wants to."

"Tess does what she wants to do, and no one ever even makes a suggestion that she should do otherwise."

"And that's where Ramsey went after he left me."

"He usually does," Luke said. He held up the cord to the chocolate pot. "You wouldn't mind plugging this in, would you?"

She looked for an outlet, but when she couldn't find one, he got an extension cord out of a drawer and plugged it into the overhead light. The dangling cord was ugly, but it worked.

"Join me?" he asked as he dipped a strawberry into the chocolate, but she shook her head no. She wondered what Ramsey was doing next door.

"Thinking about ol' Rams?" Luke asked. When she didn't answer, he said, "So what's the deal with you and my cousin? Are you one of those women who's set her cap for him and you plan to be Mrs. McDowell by the end of the year?"

"No, I haven't 'set my cap' for him. What an old-fashioned phrase. Have you finished those strawberries yet? It's late, and I'd like to go to bed. I'm going to church tomorrow."

"Rams picking you up?"

Suddenly, Jocelyn didn't like what was going on. She didn't want to walk into church tomorrow and have people looking at her as though they knew she'd had visits from two men in one night. More important, she didn't want to become embroiled in whatever was going on between these two cousins. It was obvious that Luke's only interest in her was Ramsey's attention.

"You know, I think I've said more than enough about my personal life. I think that if you continue to work here, you and I should get some things straight. From now on, I'll check my own locks, so you don't have to skulk around my house late at night."

"This is late to you?"

She ignored his question. "Second, I'd like you to keep your nose out of my life. This is a small town and if you and I start . . ." She waved her hand to the whole scene of the two of them in her almost-dark kitchen. "I just don't think it's good for this to happen again."

"Sure," he said as he swung his long legs out of the chair. "Sorry to have bothered you."

Jocelyn hadn't meant to be so cold, and she certainly didn't want to alienate someone who worked for her, someone she was going to see daily, but at the same time she thought it was better to not start any gossip.

She followed him to the back door, ready to lock it after he left. He paused on the doorstep.

"Tell me, Miss Minton," he said formally, "you had a date with my cousin tonight, but I wonder what you would say if **I** asked you out."

She took a step farther back into the house. "Luke, you seem like a nice man, and from what little I saw of the garden, you do good work, but I don't think that you and I . . . Well, I mean . . . We're not . . ."

"I understand," he said, then tugged on the front lock of his hair and bent his head to her in an old-fashioned, subservient way. "Good night, Miss Minton," he said, then went down the stairs and disappeared into the night.

Jocelyn shut the door, locked it, then leaned against it. What a day! she thought. Too much, too fast.

She went up the stairs to her bedroom and once again smiled at the clean bed. Tomorrow at church she'd have to find out who'd made this welcome for her and thank them.

She tried to keep herself from doing it, but she

looked out the window to the driveway below. Ramsey's car was still there, so he was still with Tess. The drop-dead gorgeous Tess.

Jocelyn washed her face, slathered on moisturizer, put on her nightgown, and climbed into bed. Her first thought was of Luke. She wasn't naive enough not to know that everything he'd done tonight was one of those male competitions over a female. Luke made her feel like a female deer, with two rutting stags fighting over her. From what she could piece together, Ramsey and Luke had been competing over everything their entire lives.

So now she was the new trophy. Brand-new in town, knew nothing and no one, new owner of the "big house." Yes sirree Bob, she was the prize to beat all prizes.

She knew Luke was part of the contest, but the question was whether Ramsey was or not. Of the two men, she certainly liked Ramsey better. He'd gone to a great deal of trouble to prepare a meal for her and create a romantic setting in her barren, lonely house.

On the other hand, Luke had lied about locks needing to be checked so he could gain entry into her house late at night. Then he'd pretty much helped himself to the meal Ramsey had prepared.

As far as she could tell, Ramsey was a giver and Luke a taker.

All in all, as she started to go to sleep, she thought about what Luke had said as he was leaving. Not that Luke had seriously asked her out. She had a vision of him in a bar, laughing with his fifty or so other cousins about how he'd taken Ramsey's girl away from him. "Ol' Rams didn't even see me coming," she could almost hear him say. "I just swooped in and stole her right from under Rams's nose."

The vision was so unsettling that she hit the pillows with her fist and stared up at the ceiling. If Ramsey "won" her, would he do the same thing at a cocktail party? She could see Ramsey at a country club, raising his glass of single malt as he said to a group of men, "And here's to yet again trumping my cousin."

When Joce heard Ramsey's car start, then drive away, she thought, And there's another problem. This Tess sounded much too close to Ramsey for her liking. Tonight when Luke showed her Tess's photo Jocelyn had felt downright jealous. Jealous! What a truly absurd emotion. Jealous of what? A man she'd met just that night? A man who may or may not have been using her in some stupid contest with his cousin?

When the car was gone, Joce felt her body relax—and that made her even more angry. She'd been tense because a man she'd just met had been in the apartment of another woman?

Okay, Jocelyn, she told herself, you need to get a life. Before you even so much as think about a man, you need to get a **life.**

The room was quiet and she eventually drifted off to sleep.

5

"I BLEW IT," RAMSEY said as soon as Tess opened her door. "I nearly killed myself to make a good first impression, but I blew it. She made jokes and I just sat there and stared at her. It was like I didn't even know what she was saying."

"I'm charging you for this," Tess said. "Time and a half."

"Whatever," he said as he sat down in the big chair in her living room. "Wine, chocolate-covered strawberries. I did it all because I really wanted to make her think . . . I don't know what I hoped to accomplish, but I didn't pull it off."

"You wanted to make her think that even though you live in this two-bit hick town you are a

man of the world. So who got the whole thing together for you?"

"My mom and Viv." He looked up at her.
"What makes you think I didn't do it myself?"

"You can barely feed yourself. Did you make
that pasta thing for her?"

"Sure. What else was I going to make? It's the
only thing I know how to cook." He looked back
at her again. "What the hell do you have on?"

"What I sleep in," Tess said, glancing down at
her white silk nightgown with the matching lace-
trimmed robe.

"Well, put some clothes on."

"If I'm turning you on and it's too much for
you, then I suggest you never again barge into my
place in the middle of the night."

"Am I going to be billed extra for getting turned
on?" Ramsey asked sullenly.

"No, but that's a thought."

"You have anything to drink?"

"Lots," she said, "but you're not getting any.
You have to drive home, remember? Besides, I'm
expecting company later."

"Who?" he shot at her.

"One of your cousins."

"So help me, if it's Luke, I'll—"

"What?" she asked. "Forbid me to see him?

Luke is better looking than you and he isn't developing a spare tire around his middle from sitting at a desk all day. And I'm beginning to think he's smarter than you are."

Ramsey just stared at the floor. "So marry him. I wish you would." He paused. "I like this woman."

"Which one?" Tess asked as she sat down across from him. She had a whiskey in her hand, and she sipped it while she looked at him.

"You know which one," he said. "Jocelyn. Miss Edi's protégée."

"Ah, that one. Is it her or her house you like? It would certainly look good to the men in Colonial Williamsburg if you lived in a house that looked like a Founding Father built it. They might even give you more of their legal work. It would mean more money for you."

"You can be really funny sometimes. Ha ha. I'm laughing my head off." He got up and went to the cabinet on the far wall. "Don't say anything, I'm just having some tonic water. You have any ice?"

"You know where the kitchen is."

"You certainly know how to make a man feel welcome."

"If he's invited, I do," she called after him as he disappeared into her kitchen.

Moments later, he reappeared with a bowl full

of ice. "I hate your kitchen," he said. "It's worse than Sara's. Worse than Joce's."

"So put in a new one for me," she said, brushing her long hair out of her eyes.

"And what? Write it off on expenses? Maybe if you were my mistress . . ." He looked at her over his drink. He'd never before seen her in her nightclothes and she was better looking than usual—if that was possible. Her almond eyes were heavily darkened and her lips reddened.

"You keep looking at me like that and I'll throw you out. In fact, why don't you go home right now?"

Ramsey sat back down in the chair and looked away from her. "I know her."

"What?"

"I know her. Jocelyn. I never told anybody this, but Granddad used to let me read the letters he and Miss Edi exchanged."

"Wasn't there one of those Southern feuds or secrets or some such rubbish involved with your mother and the rest of them?"

"My mother came from Oregon," Ramsey said. "And, no, there was no feud concerning my parents' generation. Whatever happened involved my grandparents. As always with you, you have things in this town mixed up."

"I'm charging you an extra hour for that re-mark. So what's the problem? And remember, the clock is ticking. You read some old letters, then what?"

"Miss Edi was a consummate letter writer. I think she corresponded with people all over the world, and my grandfather was one of them. He visited her several times, and I think my grand-mother was a bit jealous. She said he used any ex-cuse he could come up with to fly down to Florida and spend a few days with Miss Edi."

"And?" Tess said quickly. "Could you please hurry up with this story? I told you, I have a date."

"It's ten o'clock at night, everything is closed, and, besides, you're in your nightgown. For what reason could you be meeting—" He paused, his eyes wide. "Oh."

"You know, I think you should sit down with your sister and let her tell you how babies are made. Or at least how people practice to make them."

"I'm trying to tell you something that's impor-tant to me, something I've never told anyone else, and you're making fun of me."

"Did I **ask** you to come over here at night and tell me all about your bad date with little Miss Prim and Proper?"

"Did you meet her?"

"No, but I saw her, and Luke told me about her."

"Is he who you're waiting for?"

"I'm waiting for the local high school football team."

"You know, Tess, you could use a little of Jocelyn's ladylike manners."

"If I had them, I wouldn't have let you in here tonight to bellyache about your new girlfriend."

"That's the problem! She isn't my girlfriend, and if I don't do something better than what I did tonight, she never will be."

Tess refilled her glass, then sat back down across from him. "I take it that I can't get rid of you until you cry enough in your beer to get it all out."

"Beer? That's a good idea. You have any?"

"Luke keeps a six-pack in my refrigerator."

Ramsey raised his hands as though in frustration, then got up and went to the kitchen. When he didn't come back to the living room, she went to him.

"What are you doing in my refrigerator? There's nothing in there for you to eat."

"You have eggs."

"Only because Sara gave them to me. They have blue shells," she added in wonder.

"Ameraucanas."

"What?"

"Ameraucanas are the breed of chickens Sara's family raises, and they lay blue and green eggs," Ramsey said patiently as he took the bowl of eggs from the refrigerator and a container of butter. It was labeled SHAW FARMS, as was the loaf of bread. "I'm starving. Want some toast and scrambled eggs?"

"I thought you could only cook that pasta dish of yours."

"I don't think scrambled eggs count as cooking."

"If I could scramble an egg I'd go on TV as a cook."

Ramsey glanced at her as he pulled a skillet from a cabinet. Last Christmas he'd bought her a complete set of pots and pans. A month later, when she still hadn't opened them, he took them out, washed them, and put them away. Whereas the other men in the office gave Tess gifts of considerable value in gratitude for all she did for them, Ramsey gave her things he knew she needed. But then, he was the only one who'd seen the inside of her apartment and knew what she didn't have. For the most part, his gifts had stayed to the kitchen, as he gave her knives, dishes, glassware, and small appliances. Luke said it gave Ramsey a reason to go to Tess's apartment and unpack everything, but that wasn't true. He wanted her to be comfortable, and also, he wanted her to stay in tiny Edilean. Since she'd arrived, his life had run much smoother—and best was that she was a friend he could talk to. A real friend, not a blood relative. One thing about Tess was that whatever she heard, it stayed with her. He could tell her the most intimate things about his life and he knew she'd never tell anyone.

"So?" he asked. "You want some eggs or not?"

"Will it get rid of you faster if I eat something?"

"Yeah," he said, giving her a one-sided grin. "What's your date going to think when he arrives and I'm here?"

"That you want some work done," she said as she took a seat at the little table against the wall.

"Okay, so don't tell me," he said as he broke eggs into a bowl, mixed them with a fork, then dropped them into the hot skillet.

"One thing about you is that your ego is always intact. No matter what I say, you still think that I want to be with you."

"Tess, whether you like it or not, you and I are friends." He paused as he searched through a drawer for a spatula. "You need some pot holders and some new dishtowels. I'll pick some up for you at Williams-Sonoma."

Tess shook her head at him. "What am I? Your maiden aunt who you have to take care of? Would you please tell me what you have to say, then leave? I have—"

"Yeah, I know, a mysterious date who hasn't shown up yet even though it's after ten." He divided the eggs, put them on two plates, and set one in front of her. "Eat," he ordered. "I think you're losing weight."

"Sex burns a lot of calories. Speaking of which, I take it you didn't score with your little Alice."

"Alice?"

"Luke said she dresses like **Alice in Wonderland.**"

"When did you see him?"

"A couple of hours ago. Jealous?"

Ramsey snorted in derision. "Of Luke? You must be kidding. Anyway, as I was saying, my grandfather let me read Miss Edi's letters when I was growing up. She wrote a lot about this little girl, Jocelyn Minton, who she was half-raising."

"Let me guess, you fell in love with her through the letters and now you want to make her your wife and live happily ever after. Good! Now that that's done, you can leave."

"Finish your eggs," Ramsey said when she stood up. "I don't know why you have to be so cynical about everything."

"Maybe it comes from spending my days with lawyers. It makes me see the world as one long lawsuit."

"The way I see it, I help people."

"Yeah, like with the Berners' divorce? You and I both know that man hid his income to keep his wife from spending him blind. He bought her that big house he couldn't afford just to try to please her, but all she does is nag him. If you had any conscience, you'd tell her she gets nothing and has to earn her own living. But no, thanks to your cleverness, she's going to walk away with it all, and he's going to get the debt. He'll be seventy before he's back on his feet again."

"So maybe that isn't a good example of my helping people."

"So what is?"

"How about Miss Edi?" he asked.

"Rich old woman who paid your firm a fortune. What a hero you are! Are you here tonight to ask me to help you get closer to this house's new owner? For what? Marriage? A hot affair?"

"What is your hostility toward her?"

Tess pushed her empty plate away. "I don't

know, maybe it has to do with having two—not one but **two**—men come to me today to go on and on about her. What is her secret? I saw her, and she's not a great beauty. I haven't heard that she's brilliant, so what's the hold she has over you men?"

Ramsey was looking at her with his mouth open. "You're jealous of Jocelyn, aren't you?"

Tess threw her hands into the air and stood up. "That's it. I want you to leave now. And for your information, I am **not** jealous of her or anyone else. If I wanted either you or Luke I could have you."

Ramsey snorted. "I know you too well to feel romantic about you. Is that what your problem is? That a man comes over late at night and isn't dizzy with the beauty of you?"

"You're sick, you know that?" She practically stomped to the front door and opened it. "Go home. Now."

"All right," Ramsey said. "I apologize. I thought it was going to be a great night with Jocelyn, but . . ."

"But what?" she asked impatiently, holding the screen door wide.

"We ran out of things to talk about."

At that, all the anger left Tess. If there was one

thing Ramsey McDowell could do, it was talk. She couldn't help smiling. "Did you ask her what she planned to do with her life now that she's a stranger in a town where everyone not only knows one another but they're related? Your cousins have to marry from outside here or they'll give birth to morons. Did you ask her about her plans for the future?"

"No," Ramsey said. "I guess I didn't think of it that way. Edilean is home to me, so I . . ." His head came up. "She likes to make cupcakes."

"Cupcakes. You had a first date with her and that's all you found out about her? That she likes to make cupcakes?"

"I'm not a complete idiot. We talked about other things."

"Like what?"

"For your information, we talked about marriage."

Closing her eyes, Tess shook her head. "I don't know how you got through law school. You have no brain."

He was standing in her doorway, and she knew that her apartment was filling with mosquitoes, but she also knew that if she didn't give him some advice he'd never leave. "Create a cupcake emergency."

"A what?"

"Make up something where cupcakes are needed immediately and she's the only one who can make them."

"How can cupcakes be an emergency?"

"I don't know. Talk to your sister. Kids and cupcakes go together. Let Viv work it out. And from now on, talk to anyone but **me** about your love problems. Got it?"

"Yeah, maybe," he said.

Tess could see that she'd given him something to think about, so she pushed him out the door and closed it behind him.

Saturday night, she thought. This is what Saturday night in a small town was like. While she was pretending to wait for some man who didn't show up, she'd had to deal with a lovesick boss who didn't know what to say to his new girlfriend. "What does he expect me to do?" Tess mumbled. "Hold his hand and listen, then give him advice on how to win the woman?"

And how was she supposed to do that? Tess had no idea what this woman Jocelyn Minton was like. Sara liked her and Luke seemed to be mesmerized by her, but that didn't tell much.

The truth was, that as far as Tess could tell, she didn't like the woman. Or maybe it was as Ramsey said, and she was jealous. But not jealous as he thought she was. Tess had read the legal papers in Ramsey's office and she knew that Jocelyn had been given everything all her life. As a child she'd been befriended by a rich old woman who'd died and left her everything. It was straight out of Dickens.

If Tess was jealous it was because Jocelyn had been given so much while nothing had been given to Tess. Her parents died when she was young, and she'd been raised by a grandmother who treated hate as one of the four food groups—and she insisted on full servings of it daily. "They ruined my life," her grandmother used to say. "Edilean Harcourt and all of them took my life from me. I could have done something, been somebody, but that town destroyed everything I had. If it weren't for what they did to me, you and I would be rich now. Living in luxury. McDowell and Harcourt. They're the ones who stole everything."

Tess had to shake her head to clear it of the angry old woman's voice. She was paying her grandmother back for all she'd received, meaning food, clothing, and shelter, so why wouldn't the old woman's voice leave her?

Tess put the dishes in the washer, turned off the glaring overhead light, and went to her bedroom. She took off the itchy white silk gown and robe, and put on the big T-shirt she usually slept in. She'd only put on the new gown when she'd seen Ramsey drive up. From what Luke told her today, she'd guessed that Jocelyn and Ramsey wouldn't hit it off well.

While Ramsey was having his picnic with the new owner, Luke had returned and visited Tess. "He's never any good when he's nervous," Luke said as he put his long legs on her coffee table and drank beer from the bottle. Luke had never given her oh-so-practical gifts as Ramsey did. In fact, Luke had never given her anything. Tess had a feeling that when and if Luke Connor gave a woman so much as a daisy it would mean a lot.

After Luke left, she wondered if he'd been warning her that Ramsey's date probably wouldn't go well—and if it didn't, they both knew he'd show up at Tess's apartment afterward. Disappointment coupled with the proximity of Tess would be more than Ramsey could withstand.

So Tess had, in her own way, prepared for Ramsey's arrival. She put on the white peignoir set that had cost her a week's salary and some makeup.

She still didn't know what had made her do that. Was it because before Jocelyn's arrival, she was all anyone in town could talk about? Tess had pretended she didn't know how Ramsay arranged the dinner, but the truth was that three women had told her in detail what Ramsey was doing. "His mother borrowed my quilt," she heard. "Viv borrowed my best candlesticks. You know, the ones my mother left me."

By the time Saturday came, she knew in detail what Ramsey was planning for that night. All for some woman he'd never met.

That afternoon Tess had been in the back garden, looking at it with regret because it was no longer going to belong to just her and Sara and Luke. The three of them were a good group, meaning that no one stepped on another's toes. They knew how to give each other privacy. But now that was all over because the new owner was going to take over the garden as well as the house, and everything would change.

When Tess turned back to the house, she saw "her" for the first time. She was walking across the grass to Sara's apartment and she had Sara's sewing basket in her hand. That Sara trusted the woman with her precious sewing basket was another strike against her. Sara certainly never trusted Tess with the thing! But then, to be fair, it was quite possible, even likely, that there would be an emergency at MAW—something catastrophic, such as Ken not being able to find his notes for court or the copier jamming—and Tess would have to go running. Sara's sewing basket might get left in the rain.

Minutes later, Luke left the workshop and was obviously in such a bad mood that he didn't even see Tess standing just a few feet away. She watched him get in his truck, then instead of going out the back as he usually did, he turned left and went to the front of the house.

Tess stood still and watched as Jocelyn walked across the lawn. She had on a white dress that a nun could have worn with impunity, and there wasn't a crease in it. Does she ever sit down? Tess wondered.

Tess couldn't help herself as she scurried around the house toward the front to see what was going on. Luke and Ramsey were in the driveway, and as usual, they were having a confrontation. When Tess first arrived in Edilean, she'd disliked the way the two of them seemed to spend their lives trying to outdo the other, but she was used to it now. She couldn't hear them, but she didn't need to. She knew that one was telling the other what to do and the other one was saying no.

When Luke went to Sara's apartment and knocked on the door, Tess was surprised. He must know that Sara wasn't there.

Tess stood under the trees and watched as Luke talked to the new owner, then practically pushed his way into the apartment. If he'd tried that with Tess, she would have pushed him back out. Interesting, she thought.

Minutes later, Ramsey rang the little bell that hung on the side of the house. Its function had long ago been replaced by a doorbell, but the family seemed to like anything that was old-fashioned, so they used the bell whenever possible.

When there was no response, Ramsey went into the big house, and Tess stepped farther back into the trees. She heard the back door to the house and figured Ramsey had gone to Sara's apartment to get Jocelyn. Tess didn't have to wait long. When Luke came storming out of the apartment, he looked to be genuinely furious. Everyone knew Luke had a short fuse, but she'd never seen him angry with Ramsey. True, they played at their little games and loved to pretend to be mad, but they weren't. But Luke was truly angry as he got in his truck and sped away.

Ramsey left Sara's apartment with his arm around Jocelyn's shoulders, and her pristine white dress was stained with what looked to be mustard. Tess wondered if Luke had done that. Good for him! she thought.

When Ramsey and Jocelyn were inside the house, Tess went to her own apartment. About thirty minutes later, Luke showed up at her door for the second time that day. His handsome face was still angry. "He still in there?" he asked, as usual, not bothering to say who "he" was.

"Far as I know," Tess said as she motioned to the couch and he sat down while she got him a beer. "If you like her so much, why didn't **you** ask her out?"

"I've been told that she belongs to Ramsey."

"Why would anyone say that?" When Luke just sat there in sullen silence, she put up her hand. "So don't tell me. I don't want to know anyway. It's my guess that that old woman everyone talks about—Edi—is behind—"

"Miss Edi," Luke said. "Show some respect for your elders."

After that, she hadn't talked much, but Luke had.

At first he talked about the garden, saying he wanted to put in an herb bed because that was in keeping with the house. "But I don't know if she'll like it or not."

As Luke talked, telling her everything about Jocelyn, from the way she dressed to her hair color, Tess had to grit her teeth. Was this yet another one of those competitions with his cousin, or was it more?

Tess put a bowl of blue corn chips in front of him.

Luke left after about a half hour, and Tess's instinct told her that Ramsey would stop by her apartment after he left Jocelyn—whatever time that was.

Now, Tess creamed the makeup off her face and checked her skin in the 4X mirror. Satisfied that she saw nothing worse than yesterday, she moisturized, then went to bed. What an idiot Ramsey was! How could she have men over at night without the town knowing? Or at least men other than the two who had been in her apartment. But then, they were part of "the family," as it was known in town. Sometimes Tess felt like she worked for the Mafia.

Good! Tess thought. Let them concentrate on someone other than her. Let them put their attention on this Jocelyn and not see what Tess was doing.

As she fell asleep, she wondered if this Jocelyn woman knew that her date had gone to Tess's apartment afterward. Did she know that Luke had been there that afternoon?

She punched at the pillow in anger. Jocelyn inherited the house while Tess got . . . What? She still hadn't figured that out yet.

Just before she went to sleep she thought, cupcakes! Did you ever hear anything so lame in your life? Maybe she and Ramsey deserved each other.

6

T EN MINUTES AFTER she arrived at church, Jocelyn wanted to throw her clothes in her little car and leave town. Everyone was so very nice to her, but she could hear the unspoken questions as loud as though they were shouting them.

The big one seemed to be **What are you going to do?** They meant do to their precious house. It was as though they feared a wrecking crew would show up on Monday morning.

The little church was packed, with every seat filled. When she heard the pastor make a comment about the Lord using whatever He could to get people into church, Jocelyn tried to will her face not to blush, but she couldn't control it. She well knew that so many people had shown up today just to see **her.**

She took a seat in the middle, on the left side of the aisle, and when Sara sat down by her, she nearly hugged her. "Don't worry, it will only get worse," Sara said when the sixth couple walked down the aisle and stared at Jocelyn.

"Don't make me laugh." Joce tried to see if she recognized anyone. The woman from the grocery waved to Sara.

"Your mother, right?"

"Very good. I told her that if she sat down by you and asked you what you thought of organic produce I'd buy some insecticide and spray something with it."

"Your cruelty amazes me." When Jocelyn saw another woman she recognized, she leaned closer to Sara. "I saw her on the porch with the broom."

"She's Luke's mother, and she fixed your bedroom for you."

"I thought Ramsey did it," Joce said. "I even thanked him for it."

"He didn't take credit, did he?" Sara asked sharply.

"No, he was honest. He said he thought the ladies from church did it. I'll have to thank her."

"And Luke. He carried the bed and mattresses upstairs, and he helped arrange everything."

Jocelyn wasn't sure how she felt knowing that Luke had been the one to prepare her bed for her. "I can't tell if Luke likes me or hates me—or if he's just using me to play some game with Ramsey."

"Probably all of them," Sara said as she nodded toward people filing into the church. "I know he's worried that you'll not care about the house. Your house means a lot to the town. People kind of think of it as their own, and they're worried what you'll do with it."

"Sell it for bricks, you mean."

"You do know that you can't really do that, don't you? Even if you sell it, you have to offer it first to the National Register of Historic Places."

Jocelyn wanted to make a sarcastic remark to that, but she didn't. None of these people knew her, but she reassured herself that Miss Edi had known her well, and that's why she'd left the house to Jocelyn. She decided to change the subject. "Is Tess here?"

"Tess in church?" Sara gave a little laugh. "The roof would probably fly off the building."

"I don't know if I want to meet her or not."

"She can be . . . acerbic, I think that might be the word."

"A pure bitch?" Jocelyn said, then lowered her voice. "I think I may have just talked my way out of heaven."

"You were talking about hunting dogs, weren't you?" Sara asked, her eyes wide in innocence, making Joce smile. The music was starting and she picked up her hymnal.

Ramsey slid into the pew beside Jocelyn. "Sorry I was almost late. What page?"

Jocelyn showed him and expected him to get his own hymnal, but he took one side of hers and shared. His voice was nice and from the way he sang, he knew the words well.

"Get your work done?" she whispered when they sat back down.

"Most of it."

"Tess help you?" she asked, as though it were an unimportant question.

"Not with the work. I talked to her about you."

With that disarming statement, he turned his attention to the pastor.

After the service, Jocelyn was separated from Sara and Ramsey, and pulled into a sea of people who all had something to say to her.

She received many invitations to dinners and barbecues, and to join clubs, and to just visit. She was caught on the church steps by three women from Colonial Williamsburg who were talking to her about joining some committees for historic preservation when Sara whispered, "Give me your purse."

Joce kept her face on the women while slipping her small handbag to Sara. Minutes later, she looked up, and Sara was in Joce's car, the passenger door open, and waving to her. "I'm sorry, but I have to go," Jocelyn said. "It's important or I'd stay longer."

"Let us give you our cards and you can call us," one woman said.

Joce took the three cards, then hurried across the sidewalk and the lawn to get to the car.

"Shut the door quick!" Sara said as she skidded out of the parking lot in a hail of gravel. "We're going to pave next month," she said. "Peeling out won't be nearly as satisfying."

Joce took off her hat as she pulled bobby pins from her hair and let it hang down about her neck. "That was an ordeal. Animals in zoos aren't stared at as much as I was."

"Mothers have sons, and people need jobs, and charities need volunteers and money. You are open season."

"No, no," Joce said, her head back. "Tell me this isn't so."

"Yup, it is. You hungry?"

"Yes," Joce said. "Can we go to a grocery and get something? I have nothing in my house to eat. I don't even have a skillet to cook it in."

"I don't think that food will be a problem, at least not for a few days."

"What do you mean?"

"You'll see," Sara said cryptically as she pulled into the drive in front of Edilean Manor. "Uh oh."

"What?"

"It's Tess. They woke her up."

Standing in the driveway was the gorgeous Tess, and the phone photo hadn't done her justice. She was tall and beautiful, and right now she looked angry.

Sara parked Joce's car and got out. "How bad was it?" she asked Tess.

"What time did she leave for church?" Tess nodded toward Joce, who still sat in the car.

"Early," Sara said without asking Jocelyn.

Joce got out of the car and went to stand beside Sara. Neither woman looked at her.

"They started coming at eight," Tess said. "They knew the damned door was unlocked, but nothing would do but for them to pound on **my** door and make me tell them the door was unlocked. After that I left the main door wide open, but it wasn't

enough for them. They still banged on **my** door."
Tess turned to look at Jocelyn. "I can't imagine that
you're worth all this bother." Her almond eyes
were narrowed and her lips curved into a sneer.

"And you must be Tess," Joce said, forcing a
smile. "I'm—"

"Everyone knows who you are," Tess snapped.
"Here and in Williamsburg, they know who you
are. You're rich and you own a big house. Yeah, I'd
say you're the hit of the county."

"Tess, please," Sara said, her voice pleading.

"Please, what?" Tess asked. "Just because she
sucked up to some old woman and got her money,
does that mean I have to be pulled out of bed on a
Sunday morning to get her food?"

"Tess," Sara said. "Please be nice. You haven't
even met Jocelyn."

Tess looked Joce up and down and obviously
found her wanting. "Now that you're so rich,
maybe you can afford to do something with yourself."

Sara's eyes widened, but she was silent. Tess's
anger-filled remark seemed to be more than she
could handle.

Joce gave a little smile. "You're beautiful but I'm
nice and I won the prize. Says something about
what people value, doesn't it?"

For a moment, both Sara and Tess stared at her.

"Is that all you have?" Joce asked, her voice calm. "Come on, you can do better than that. An old woman left me money and a house, so I must have done something bad to earn it. You could make a lot out of that. Or can't you?"

Sara looked like she might faint from what she was hearing. Would the women attack each other? Was she going to have to deal with hair pulling and scratching?

Tess gave Jocelyn a look of interest. "Where'd you learn to give it back like that?"

"Her sisters are—" Sara began, but Joce put her hand up to stop her.

"I listen; I learn," Joce said, then she looked at Sara, dismissing Tess. "What were you talking about when you mentioned food?"

"Everyone in town wanted to welcome you, so they brought food," Sara said, as though it were a custom everywhere. "Aunt Martha—that's Ramsey's mother—told people to stay away yesterday, so they hit this morning. But you weren't here before church."

"I went—" Jocelyn cut herself off. She wasn't going to start the habit of telling people where she was every minute of every day. "No, I wasn't here. I left early."

"So they knocked on my door to ask **my** permission to enter the 'big house,'" Tess said as she looked Jocelyn up and down, as though wondering who and what she was.

"Come on," Sara said, "let's see what they left you." When Tess stayed in the driveway, Sara turned to her. "You coming?"

Jocelyn looked at Tess in the sunlight, that fabulous auburn hair glistening, and she was tempted to tell her to stay outside. Tess reminded Joce too much of the world of the Steps. "Come on," she said. "Maybe Sara and I can do your roots later."

"It's natural," Tess said before she thought.

"So's mine," Joce shot back.

"Well, mine isn't," Sara said. "If you two are going to get in a catfight, I need to call some cousins to watch. They'll never forgive me if they miss it."

Joce stepped back to let Tess know she was welcome in the house. This woman is going to take some work to like, she thought, looking at Sara with longing. Why couldn't there have been another Sara in the other apartment? On second thought, maybe she could find Tess an apartment somewhere else. In a men's locker room, maybe. From the look of her, she'd probably love that!

Jocelyn wasn't prepared for what she saw in the

kitchen. The table and the countertops were covered with what looked to be a hundred containers of food.

Sara opened the refrigerator. Inside were more dishes and foil-wrapped parcels.

There were casseroles, chicken prepared in many ways, a ham, baskets full of baked goods, cakes, pies, and bags of early produce from home gardens.

"I can't eat all this," Jocelyn whispered, in awe at the sheer quantity of food.

Tess stood to one side and watched the two women circle around the table and countertops. They didn't seem to have even one thought of what to do about that much perishable food. The situation reminded her of MAW. Half the time those men didn't have a clue as to what should be done. But all her life Tess had had the ability to "see" what should be done in a situation. The lawyers said she had a true gift, a rare talent.

Sara stopped walking and looked at Tess. "What should we do?"

Jocelyn didn't look up but assumed that because it was her house the question was for her. "I'm to see Ramsey tomorrow and maybe if I get some money, I'll go get a freezer, and—" She broke off when she saw that Sara was looking at Tess.

Jocelyn looked at her too. "You have any different ideas?" She couldn't keep the hostility out of her voice. Was it always going to be a fight with this woman?

"My suggestion is that we eat all we want, then we put as much as we can in a car and give it away. You'll have to keep the plates and containers, as the women will want them back, but we can give away the food, and I know where to take it." She looked at Joce. "If you can bear to part with any of it, that is."

Sara looked at Joce to make a decision.

"I like it," Jocelyn said. "I like the idea very much." As she looked at Sara, she opened the cabinet where Luke got a plate last night. It was empty. She knew there was a plate in the dishwasher, but they needed more. "Do either of you know if I have any plates?"

"Luke's outside, he knows," Tess said.

"Invite him and have to listen about Ramsey?" Jocelyn asked.

"You catch on fast," Tess said, sounding surprised.

"I vote that we don't invite anyone. Let's have a feast by ourselves. Women only," Sara said as she opened a cabinet on the far wall and took out three plates. "There's not much left that Bertrand didn't sell. My mother bought a gorgeous set of Wedg-wood from him."

"She'll give it to you when you get married," Tess said.

Jocelyn looked at Sara with interest.

"And where am I going to find someone?" Sara asked. "I never leave this town except to deliver a dress to some woman."

"They have any sons?" Jocelyn asked.

"Not any that I'd have."

"Sara is known around town to be the pickiest woman in the state," Tess said. "Look at her, she's a man's dream. Beautiful and virginal."

"Not hardly," Sara said.

"It's the look of the package that matters," Tess said as she heaped a plate full of food. "You look innocent, and I look like I've done everything."

"And everyone," Joce added as she filled her plate. "Sorry, I was just agreeing with you. So what about me? I'm not either one of those things."

"Wife," Tess said. "You look like a wife and mother. So how come you don't have a husband and three kids?"

"Tess . . . ," Sara said in warning.

"I had responsibilities," Joce said as she made a place on the table and sat down. "I couldn't go far away from . . . what was going on in my life."

"The old woman," Tess said.

Jocelyn shrugged but said nothing. She didn't want to tell this woman more about her life than she already knew.

The three of them sat down at the table, the food all around them, and for a while they didn't speak.

"I hear you bake cupcakes," Tess said in a way that made it sound like an accusation—and frivolous.

Joce looked at Sara. "Is it me or is everything she says touched with a nasty edge to it?"

"It's her," Sara said, then looked at Tess. "Sorry, but it's true. Usually, Tess, you save your hatefulness for the men you work for, so what's made you get it in for Jocelyn?"

Tess just looked about the kitchen.

"Ah," Sara said.

"What does that mean?" Joce asked. "Did I miss something?"

"You inherited this house. You inherited . . . What is it, Tess? Millions?"

"I'm not allowed to say."

Both women looked at her, not blinking, and waited.

Tess shrugged as she bit into a chicken leg. "You

tell Rams I told you and I'll burn the house down with you in it."

"Sounds fair to me," Joce said.

"The money stays with the house. If you stay here, you control it all, but if you leave, both the house and the money go to some foundation."

"The Great Sin," Jocelyn said. "If I leave, strangers will come into Edilean. How will the townspeople stand it?"

"They have to have strangers to breed with," Tess said. "To give variety to the gene pool."

"Cut it out," Sara said. "I'll have you know that Edilean is a very nice place to live."

"It is since they put in the outlet mall in Williamsburg," Tess said.

"Outlet mall?" Joce said. "Why did no one tell me that oh-so-vital piece of information?"

"Because you've spent all your time with the best-looking men in this one-horse town," Tess said.

"Meow," Sara said.

"You're just jealous because we can have the men here and you can't. They're all your relatives."

"So what's with you and Ramsey?" Joce asked Tess. "I saw the photo of you in the red dress."

Tess gave a little smile. "That was a day! I was in

the best shape of my life, and here was this jerk telling me I was to dress more conservatively. Did he think I didn't know that all those men were watching every step I took? If I started wearing dresses, they'd do the John Candy."

Joce looked at her in question.

"Drop something on the floor, then look up as they pick it up?"

"I hope you're exaggerating," Joce said. "Surely they wouldn't . . ."

"Maybe not, but they'd think about it. That was more than I wanted."

"Okay, so men are men. You certainly showed them, though."

Tess shrugged. "Maybe. I paid the price by having photos of me posted all over the Internet. Ken wanted to put the picture on a brochure about the law office, but his wife wouldn't let him."

"Where did he get his wife?" Joce asked.

"Massachusetts," Tess said quickly. "Mail order."

"You two are bad," Sara said. "You'd think you didn't like this town."

"What do I know?" Joce said. "I just got here. So far I've had a lawyer make me a very romantic picnic on the floor, but he left after only an hour and a half. And I have a surly gardener who likes to show up and make me feed him."

"Luke," Sara and Tess said in unison.

"What's his problem?"

Tess and Joce looked at Sara.

"Don't look at me, I don't know. Yes, I grew up with him, sort of, but he's years older than I am, so I never really knew him. Big high school athletic superstars don't pay much attention to little cousins in elementary school. After high school he left town, and . . ." She trailed off with a shrug.

"And started a career mowing lawns. He seems intelligent, so why doesn't he have a proper job?" Joce asked.

Sara kept her head down and didn't answer.

"Why are you just a teaching assistant and now don't even have that job?" Tess asked. "If Miss Edi hadn't left you a fortune, where would you be now?"

"Is it really a fortune?" Joce asked, avoiding the question.

"I think that's a good question," Sara said, looking at Joce. "What **would** you be doing if Miss Edi hadn't been in your life?"

"I really and truly have no idea," Joce said. "And I can tell you that I've given it plenty of thought."

"What about you, Tess?" Sara asked. "You work for MAW, but you can't stand any of them, so what would you like to do?"

"Have an old lady leave me millions."

"That's not fair," Sara said. "You should—"

"No, let her talk," Jocelyn said. "Okay, so if you were left a big old house and a fortune, what would you do all day? Would you become a lady who lunches?"

"Lord no! That would make me insane. I'd . . ."

"You'd what?" Jocelyn asked. "I'd like to hear your ideas."

"I don't know. Start a business of my own?" Tess said.

"What kind of business?" Sara asked.

Jocelyn looked at Sara in speculation. "You have something you'd like to do, don't you? I can hear it in your voice."

Tess picked up an olive and sucked out the red pimento center. "Have you seen the clothes she designs?"

"You didn't tell me you design clothes," Joce said, and there was hurt in her voice.

"I've had one conversation with you. I couldn't tell you everything."

"A dress shop would be a business," Joce said thoughtfully. "Not a bad idea. What about you, Tess?"

"Don't look at me. I haven't a creative bone in my body. I'm good with numbers and organizing."

"You must be good with men," Joce said. "That's why so many of them visit you."

"Do they?" Tess asked, as though she'd never before thought of that.

"Tess," Sara said, "be fair. Both Ramsey and Luke were in your apartment yesterday."

"And how would you know that? They told you, didn't they? So what did Ramsey say about me?" Tess asked.

"Nothing. It was Luke who told me," Sara said.

"And when did you see him?"

"This morning. He was out there digging. He wants to put in an herb garden, but now he has to get the owner's permission before he can do anything."

"He told me that too," Tess said.

Both women looked at Jocelyn as though expecting an answer.

"He can put in any kind of garden he wants," Joce said. "What does it matter to me?"

"This house is now your responsibility," Tess said. "You owe it to the townspeople, the state, and most of all to your country to honor its long history and to cherish what it means to the American people. You should—"

Joce threw a piece of bread at her, and they all laughed.

H<small>I</small>," J<small>OCELYN</small> <small>SAID</small> to Luke as he lifted the shovel and threw the dirt onto the pile. He glanced at her but said nothing. "So what is this? You're not speaking to me?"

"I talk when I have something to say." He picked up a big bag of mulch and threw it on the back of his pickup.

She thought maybe he wanted her to leave him alone, but she didn't go. It was late Sunday afternoon, and she was exhausted from all that had happened in the last two days. "Did you see the food in my kitchen?"

"I haven't been in your house since you threw me out last night. And I haven't checked any door locks or windows."

"Thanks for not telling Sara that you and I were alone in the house late last night. I know you told her that you went to see Tess, but you didn't tell about me."

"So it's all right for Tess to get a bad reputation but not you?"

"I think that Tess could stand still and do nothing and she'd get a bad reputation. To look at her is to have carnal thoughts."

Luke turned away quickly, but she saw his smile. "I saw that! If you can smile at my jokes, you're not totally angry at me."

"See Rams at church?"

"He sat by me, asked me to marry him, and I accepted."

"I congratulate you. You two will make a fine couple. This time next year all you'll want to talk about are curtains."

"If you can see the future, would you ask it what I'm supposed to **do**?"

Luke began shoveling again. "What do you mean 'do'?"

Joce looked around for a place to sit, didn't see one, so she sat on the grass. "Miss Edi—" she began.

"What about her?"

"She was a very important person in my life."

"We all have important people in our lives."

"Yeah? So who's important to you?"

Luke held a shovelful of dirt for a moment. "The usual: parents, friends, relatives. My grandfather was very important to me until he passed away."

"He's not important now?" Joce asked softly.

Luke gave a bit of a smile. "Sometimes I think he's more important to me now than he was when I was growing up. I was a bit of a . . . Let's just say that as a kid I was a little bit obstinate."

"Bullheaded stubborn, had to do everything your own way or you wouldn't do it?"

"Were you my first grade teacher? The one who stood me in the corner half the day?"

"No, but I'm on her side," Joce said. "So what about your grandfather?"

"He was a solitary man, liked to do things by himself, and so do I."

"If that's a hint for me to go away and leave you alone, I'm not going to do it. That house is too big, too empty, and too . . . Anyway, it's nice out here. Tell me your story."

"There's nothing to tell. My grandfather and I were alike, that's all. He liked to be alone and so do I, so we were often alone together."

" 'Alone together.' That's the perfect description

of Miss Edi and me. The kids at school thought I was crazy to want to spend time with an old woman with scarred legs. They used to make up stories about how her legs got that way. They—"

"What happened to her legs?" Luke asked.

"World War II," Joce said. "She was in London in a car that was one of several hit by a bomb. Her side of the car exploded and she was . . ." Joce hesitated. "She was set on fire. There wasn't much of her legs left from about the knees down." Joce shrugged. "No one thought she'd live. She was moved from one hospital to another while they waited for her to die, but she didn't. By sheer force of will she not only lived, but she walked again, and after the war, she went to work for a doctor. They traveled the world together. After they returned, he used to visit her often, and he was a great storyteller. I used to listen to him for hours."

She paused for a moment as she thought. "Miss Edi had told me about Dr. Brenner and I'd seen him in countless photos, and I'd always had romantic thoughts about the two of them. I knew he was married and had two daughters, but still, I thought there was some great, unrequited love between them. But five minutes after I met him I knew there was nothing between them like what I thought. They were like a well-oiled machine in that he knew when her legs ached and he never even paused in his talking as he ushered her to the couch, covered her legs, and got her a cup of tea. And she did the same kinds of things for him. At the end, his heart had given out and she made sure he took his medication and didn't do too much."

Jocelyn paused as she tried to control her emotions. "But the kids didn't care about any of that. All they thought about was that her legs 'looked funny.' She used to wear thick black hose even in the summer, but you could still see the scars. And as she got older, she walked with two canes."

Luke paused in his digging to look hard at her.

"What's that look for?"

"You went to that little college and took a job as a teaching assistant to be near her, didn't you?"

"No, I liked the school and I liked my job. I did it—" She broke off when he kept looking at her. "Yes, I did, but I didn't tell her that."

"And I guess she didn't know. Too dumb to figure it out, huh?"

Jocelyn gave a little laugh. "She probably knew, but we didn't talk about it. I guess when you're Miss Edi's age you know that there's time after . . . After the people you love are gone, you have time to do things, like go to school and even to get a proper job." She looked at the house in the distance and thought about Miss Edi's ancestors living there. She could almost see Miss Edi as a child, running out the back door.

"So you got what you wanted from her, didn't you? She left you this house and lots of money."

"I did **not** stay with her because I wanted **anything** from her!" Jocelyn said as she came to her feet. "I stayed because I **loved** her. Maybe you don't understand that but I—" She glared at him. "Why are you smiling at me like that?"

"Got you away from the tears."

It took Jocelyn a few moments to calm herself, but then she saw what he'd done. "Sneaky."

"My middle name."

She sat back down and for a while watched him work. He seemed to have removed all the grass off a big rectangle of an area, piled it into a heap, and was now digging into the bare dirt. "Whatever are you doing?"

"This is called 'double digging' but, overall, I'm putting in an herb garden. I asked you about it, but you didn't say anything, so I went ahead with it. If you don't speak up, you don't get a say in its design."

"You didn't say a word to me about an herb garden. Last night you talked to me about Ramsey and . . . And, let's see, about Ramsey, but I never heard the word **herb** from you. For all I know, you don't even know the word."

"Are you telling me that you spent the whole day with Sara and Tess and not once did they give you my message?"

"Message?" Joce asked. "They said you'd told **them** you wanted to put in an herb garden. I didn't get the idea it was a message sent to **me.**"

"Who else would I be asking? You own the place."

"Do I?" Joce asked. "You dig up my backyard and I don't even get a say in what you're digging, so who owns this place?"

"All right," Luke said as he jammed the shovel in the earth, then leaned on it. "Do you like the idea of a reproduction eighteenth-century herb garden like I planned or not? Maybe you'd like something Victorian? Or maybe you'd like something with a chrome and glass fountain in the middle. That would go well with the house. Just let me know and I'll be sure to put it in. I'm just the gardener and I do what the mistress of the house tells me to."

Jocelyn opened her mouth to make a scathing reply but couldn't think of one. "Tell your mom thanks for all she did in my bedroom."

"I will," Luke said and again had to turn away to hide his smile.

"And thank you for putting the bed in."

"You're welcome," he said.

For a moment they were silent, with Jocelyn watching him. His muscles played under his T-shirt, and his jeans clung to his strong thighs. He had the body of a man used to working outdoors, and it showed.

She made herself take her eyes off of him. "You know what Sara and Tess and I did this afternoon?"

"From the sound of the laughter of you girls, I think you smoked some weed and ate chocolate."

"Think Sara's mom sells grass at her grocery store?"

"If she does, you can bet it's organic."

Joce smiled. "After we'd eaten until we could hardly walk, we packed all that food up and took it to a couple of churches in . . . I don't know where we were, but Tess drove us there at about sixty miles an hour and we loaded tables with food. It was quite nice. Tell me about Tess."

Luke gave a little snort. "I can tell you all I know about Tess in one word: nothing."

"But Sara said you visited her yesterday."

"I 'visited' you too, but that doesn't mean I know you. I keep beer in her fridge and I stop in when I want to talk to her about something."

"About gardens?"

"She knows less about gardens than you do. Usually, I talk to her about Ramsey."

"Right," Joce said. "Ramsey."

He gave her a sharp look. "You need to know that whatever you do with my cousin in the future, you'll have to share him with Tess."

"At the office," Joce said.

"No, everywhere. Rams . . ." Luke lifted his hand in dismissal. "I'm not going to talk about Ramsey and Tess. Ask them. Did you come out here to get the local gossip from me?"

"I wanted to see what you were doing in **my** garden."

Luke held his arms out. "What you see is right here."

"So why an herb garden?"

"Why not?"

Jocelyn groaned. "Did your lack of conversational skills come about because you were a loner as a child, or did your inability to answer a question make people stay away from you?"

"Some of both, I guess. What did Sara say about me?"

"What makes you think I asked her about you?"

He lifted an eyebrow at her.

"So maybe I did. She said you were much,

much older than she is, that you played high school sports, and that she knows nothing much about you."

"I genuinely love that girl," Luke said.

"So she lied?"

"Evaded. So what plants do you want to put in this thing?"

"Herbs," Jocelyn said quickly.

"I asked for that one. What kind of herbs?"

"I don't know," she said. "For pizza and spaghetti, I guess."

"They're the same ones. What else?"

"For . . ." Her head came up. "I know. I want lavender."

"What kind of lavender?"

"Would it make sense to say that I want the kind of lavender you can eat?"

"Perfect sense," Luke said, looking as though he was pleased with her. "**Intermedia** is usually considered the best for eating. It's better known as Provence lavender."

"Sounds wonderful. Can you put some in this garden?"

"It depends on how much of it you want to eat."

"I don't know . . . ," she said hesitantly.

"Do you want to graze lambs on it to make the

meat taste good, or do you want to make a few dozen cookies?" he asked without patience.

She narrowed her eyes at him. "I want to make a voodoo doll of you and stick lavender pins in it."

He laughed. "Come on, I'll show you where we can plant some lavender." He put the shovel down, took a towel off the bed of his truck, and wiped his sweaty face with it.

"I haven't seen much of the garden at all," she said, looking out through the big trees.

"You've been too busy—"

"Don't say it!" Joce ordered.

"What?" Luke asked with exaggerated innocence.

"That I've been too busy with Ramsey."

"I was going to say that you've been too busy getting to know people to spend much time in the garden, but if your mind goes to Ramsey and stays there, who am I to contradict you?"

"You can be a real pest, you know that?"

"I've never before had a woman tell me that. My mother, yes, my cousins often, and some of my uncles, but women never say I'm a pest."

"Spare me," Jocelyn said, but she was smiling. "You have dirt on your face."

"Yeah, so get it off."

He leaned down so his face was close to hers.

She lightly brushed her hand across his cheek, but the dirt didn't move. She brushed harder. "Is this stuff glued on?"

"Take your shirt off and wipe hard," he said without a hint of a smile.

Joce shook her head at him and stepped back. "Get it off yourself."

He wiped his forearm across his face and the dirt came off. "Better?"

For a moment Jocelyn just looked at him. He was a very good-looking man, with his dark hair and his green eyes. "When's the last time you shaved?"

"When House did."

It took her a moment to realize he meant Dr. House on TV. It was one of her favorite shows. Smiling, she followed him as he made his way through the trees.

As she looked at the land around her, she couldn't help thinking, All mine. Everything she saw belonged to her. "Could you show me the property lines?"

"Glad to," he said.

He took her around the eighteen acres she now owned, all that was left of the thousand acres the young man from Scotland had bought for his kidnapped bride. Luke knew the grounds well and pointed out where the old cabins used to be, the well house, the dovecote. He stopped at a treeless spot and said the blacksmith shop used to be there.

"When we were kids, we'd come over here and dig in this area and find pieces of hand-wrought iron. Charlie found three horseshoes."

"What about Sara? Did she find anything?"

"She was good at finding arrowheads. She said that the nineteenth century was too new for her to care about, so she didn't bother with horseshoes."

"Interesting that you know that about her, but she says she hardly knows anything about you."

Luke gave a little smile, then moved farther into the trees. "The old brick kilns used to be back here. Look." He pushed aside some bushes, and she saw a low brick wall. "I put these bricks back together so you could see the foundations." He spread his arms out. "We could put your lavender in here. The ground is sandy, and lavender likes that. And it gets a lot of sun."

"I can almost imagine what this place was like. Maybe I should restore it to what it once was."

"It would cost too much to do that, and besides, Colonial Williamsburg has done a better job than we could."

She liked that he said "we." It made her feel like she was part of something.

"This place likes having been here all these years," Luke said. "It likes the living, and likes the generations that have been here. I think the house breathed a sigh of relief when old Bertrand died."

"Maybe the house was glad he didn't get down to selling the doorknobs."

"He did, but Rams stopped him."

"Did you help?" Joce asked.

"I wasn't here then," Luke said quickly. "What do you think about this place for your lavender?"

"It looks great, but what do I know? Do you mean you were gone for that week or that you weren't living here in Edilean?"

"So tell me more about making love on top of blue corn chips."

"Point taken," she said. "No more personal questions. I wonder if Miss Edi let her brother sell so much because she was cleaning the house out for the next family."

"That's what Rams said, but I think she just wanted to be rid of the old junk. Of course the attic is still full of it. Have you been up there yet?"

"No. I went up the stairs but the door is locked and I don't have a key to it."

"Rams will give you one when he tells you about your inheritance." Luke started walking again and she followed him.

"So how much do you know about the deal with the house?"

"You stay, you get it all. You leave, the money stays with the house."

"Just what I heard," Jocelyn said, "but wasn't that supposed to be a secret?"

Luke shrugged. "Somebody took the dictation; somebody typed the document. Who knows how things get out?"

"It's my guess that you know exactly how it got out, but I also guess that you won't tell me."

"You're smart, aren't you?"

"Does that make a change from most of the women you know?"

Luke didn't answer but pointed to a long, low brick building in the distance. "I put that place back together."

"But it looks old."

"Thank you," Luke said. "That's a good compliment. I had to dig up old bricks, then clean them off before I could use them."

They had reached the building, and she saw the way Luke's hand touched the side wall. "It was a labor of love, wasn't it?" she said.

"More or less."

"Did you always want to be a gardener?"

He looked at her oddly and seemed to be about

to say something, but then changed his mind. "No, I came to it later in life. I decided that there was nothing like working with the earth. Nothing gives a man more pleasure and more satisfaction."

"Think it's an ancestral thing? Are you from generations of farmers tilling the soil?"

"Not that I know of," Luke said. "My dad ran offices full of salesmen and my grandfather was a doctor."

"Like Sara's father."

"Yeah," Luke said, obviously pleased that she knew that. "Uncle Henry worked with my grandfather for years before Gramps retired."

"To take you fishing," Joce said. "Just the two of you."

"That was the other grandfather."

"Oh," she said.

Luke opened the door to the brick building and Joce knew they were in his workshop. It was nice in there. Above the workbench with its tools was a round window. She stood on tiptoe to look out it and saw how close they were to the house. In fact, when she turned her head, she could see the entire back of the house and both apartment doors. She saw the little white table where she'd sat with Sara and talked.

She got off her toes and looked at Luke as he

studiously moved some tools around on top of an old cabinet on the opposite wall. "When you're in here, you can see everything that goes on at the back of the house."

"Can you?" he asked. "I guess I never noticed."

She glared at him until he turned to look at her, giving her a one-sided grin. Yet something else she'd learned about him. Now that Luke was looking a bit guilty at what could possibly be interpreted as spying, she thought she'd do what she could to get information out of him. "So who was Tess talking to on the phone today?"

Luke walked to the door of the shop. "About three?"

Jocelyn nodded.

"Her brother. She talks to him every Sunday afternoon no matter what. You could take her to a rock concert or have her hypnotized and if it was Sunday she'd call her brother."

"You sound almost jealous."

"You're an only child like I am, so aren't you jealous of people who have siblings to share their lives with?"

"Only child," Joce said. "What a lovely thought. I have—" She broke off. There was no way she was going to tell him who her stepsisters were. "Yeah, I've had a lot of fantasies about having sisters who were good and kind and who actually **liked** me."

He raised an eyebrow at her. "Did my remark open a can of worms?"

"If you did, let's have Ramsey make us a casserole," she said quickly, making Luke laugh.

"Pies. He made pies with a mud crust," he said. "When he was seven and Sara was barely a year old, he almost got her to eat one, but her mother caught him, and . . ." He looked around, as though to see if anyone was listening. "None of us ever knew what happened, but Aunt Ellie—that's Sara's mother—took Ramsey into her house, and when he came out, he looked downright green, and he never again made a worm pie."

"I don't know if I wish I'd grown up in this town or I'm glad I didn't."

"What was it like living with Miss Edi? Afternoon tea and concerts on weekends?"

"I didn't—" Jocelyn began, but closed her mouth. Let him think that she lived with Miss Edi full-time if he wanted to. It was too complicated to explain that her elegant mother fell in love with a man who thought what was painted on the gas tank of a Harley was high art. Too much trouble to explain her mother's death, her father's remarriage, and how Jocelyn had grown up with people who were so unlike her that she often felt as though she were from a different planet. Until she met Miss Edi, Jocelyn knew no other world.

"You didn't what?" he asked.

She started to make up something, but his cell phone rang.

He opened it and said "Yeah" four times, then handed it to her. "It's for you."

"Me? But who . . ." Luke's eyes told her. Ramsey.

"Hello," she said. "Everything okay?"

"So you're going through the garden with Luke," Ramsey said. "I wish I'd known you wanted to see it. I could have taken you."

"Or I could have gone myself," she said. "Luke works for me, remember?"

"How could I forget, since I sign his checks?"

"Do you?" Joce asked with interest. "I hate to pay bills. Could we continue this way?"

"Jocelyn, I'll continue with you any way you want. After church today all anyone could talk about was how pretty you looked in that pink dress. They liked the hat too."

Luke was staring at her as though he wanted to hear every word that was said. She turned her back to him.

"Can you come into the office tomorrow?"

Ramsey asked. "We can talk about the terms of the house."

"You mean you're planning to talk to **me** about **business**?"

"I most certainly am," he said, and she could hear his smile. "You wouldn't like to have lunch afterward, would you?"

"Are you asking me out?"

"Unless you want to go to my house and eat pasta again. By the way, I need to get Viv's chocolate pot."

"Did she have the baby?"

Ramsey hardly paused before he laughed. "No, she didn't have the baby and she isn't trying to make a new one. She wants it for some party for one of the kids she already has. Wanta go with me?"

"Sure. When is it?"

"Tuesday afternoon. One-ish. Can I pick you up? Or do you think that arriving at a party with me will make it look too much like we're a couple?"

"Maybe we should take Luke so it's not too obvious about **us.**"

"He hates kids and kids' parties. Better not take him. So how about coming to the office at eleven, then we'll go to lunch? Sound good?"

"Sounds delicious. I'll see you then."

She closed the phone and handed it back to Luke.

"Another date?"

"Business, then lunch, and on Tuesday, a party at his sister's house."

"What party?" Luke asked quickly.

"Ramsey said it was for one of his sister's children. A birthday party?"

"None of the kids has a birthday now. It's . . ." He trailed off, frowning for a moment, then he looked at her. "I think I better make an appointment if I want you to go to the nursery with me to pick out the herbs. How about tomorrow afternoon? If you can tear yourself away from Rams after lunch, that is."

"Why do you want me to go with you to buy herbs? I don't know one from the other."

"Okay, then, I'll plant some hemlock and henbane."

She thought Ramsey was kidding when he said Luke "hated" kids, but his remark made her unsure. "Nothing poisonous."

"Let's see, you told me you don't have any preference on the herbs, but so far you've told me you want lavender and nothing poisonous. What about mint?"

"I like mint," she said cautiously. He was up to something, but she didn't know what.

"Okay, you want the entire garden done in mint and nothing else."

"Not the whole thing, just some mint."

"For your information, mint is one of the most invasive plants known, so if you put mint in the herb garden, that's all you'll have. So do you want mint or not? Wait! Let me get a pad and paper, because this list of things that you do and do not want is getting too long for me to remember."

"All right!" she snapped. "Tomorrow afternoon I'll go with you to buy plants. I don't know what kind of plants, but whatever you tell me we need, we'll get. Why do you want me to go with you? Just to annoy Ramsey?"

"You don't have to go with me," he said, his voice lowering. "You could tell Rams that you can stay at lunch all afternoon because you have nothing else to do. Or you can tell him you have to leave because you're going with me to buy flowers."

Jocelyn blinked at him a few times, then smiled. "You have a brain under those whiskers, don't you?"

"My mom thinks so. My dad is less sure."

"What time do you want to leave?"

"Two. On the dot. I'll pick you up outside the restaurant."

"How do you know where he's taking me for lunch?"

Luke snorted. "The Trellis. That's where he always takes his women out on the second date—if there is one, that is. It's in Colonial Williamsburg. He'll order the special, then tell you you must share a piece of chocolate cake with him. It's great cake. The best. But it will take you until two-thirty to eat everything."

They were back at the new herb garden site and Luke's truck. "So I'm to tell him I have to leave at two?" she asked, thinking about what he was saying. All in all, she liked it. "If I were a less cynical person, I'd think you were trying to help me with Ramsey."

"He is my cousin," Luke said with a shrug, but he turned away so she couldn't see his smile.

"That's nice of you," she said, but her voice was hesitant. She slapped at a mosquito on her arm and decided it was time to go inside. "I think I'm done for the day." The light was fading. "Are you going to work much longer?"

"No, I'll just clean up, then go home."

She started to ask him where he lived but decided it was too personal a question.

"Tess let you keep enough food for tonight?" he

asked as he scraped dirt off a shovel with a trowel, then put it in the back of the pickup.

"Yes, but I need to buy some cookware for the kitchen," she said. "And I need to go to a grocery store."

"Easy enough," he said as he put a pitchfork into the truck. "Maybe tomorrow we can—"

"Just show me where things are and I'll find them," she said as she started for the house. "See you tomorrow at two."

In the next minute she was back in the house, and the stillness of it seemed almost eerie. It was a house that needed people. When there was one other person in it or several, the house came alive. It almost seemed to smile. But when Jocelyn was in it alone, she wanted to run upstairs and shut the bedroom door.

She went to the kitchen and picked up a couple of oranges out of a bowl. The table was covered with clean dishes that had contained the welcome food people had sent. Sara said that during the week the women would stop by to pick up their dishes and to have a chat. "People haven't been in this house in years and they're dying to see the inside of it," she said.

Jocelyn had groaned, dreading the constant tour guiding she'd have to do.

"Don't worry about it," Sara said. "They'll come in groups and save you from having to do too much."

Joce had smiled weakly. Now, she turned off the light, went into the big hallway, and checked both doors to make sure they were locked. She left a low-wattage light on in the hall and started up the stairs. Just as it was downstairs, there was a wide hall with rooms leading off of it. One side was the big master bedroom with an enormous bathroom, while the other side had been made into two bedrooms, each with its own bathroom.

She took a shower, moisturized her entire body, put on her nightgown, then walked toward the bed. On impulse, she looked out the window, parting the curtain just enough to see out. Luke's truck was in the driveway and the engine was running. Was he waiting for Tess? she wondered. Reaching over, she turned out the bedside lamp, and when the room was dark, Luke slowly drove through the gates. He'd been waiting for her to turn out the light.

Jocelyn meant to get into bed and wait a bit, then she'd turn the light back on and read a while, but the next thing she knew a ray of sunlight was coming through the curtains. It was morning.

8

JOCELYN LAY IN bed for a while, her hands behind her head, and looked at the ceiling of the bedroom. The house was hers, but since she'd arrived, she'd had very little time to herself.

She glanced at the bedside clock and saw that it wasn't even seven, and she didn't have to be anywhere until eleven. She'd use the time to look at the house thoroughly, not in the cursory way she had done.

She washed and dressed quickly, not bothering to blow-dry her hair, but pulling it back off her face. She glanced at her shiny skin, thought about putting on makeup, but didn't. Miss Edi was of the Estée Lauder school that believed a woman should wear full makeup at every moment. Even at the end, Miss Edi had dressed beautifully and always wore lightly applied cosmetics.

But this morning, Miss Edi's voice seemed farther off than usual, and Jocelyn didn't want to take the time to "put on war paint," as her father used to say.

She wandered through the upstairs, noting what was where. Her bedroom had the most furniture in it. The second bedroom had a bed and a little table by it, but nothing else, and the third bedroom was empty.

At the end of the hall was a window, with a door next to it. She'd already discovered it opened to a narrow, steep staircase that led up to another door that was locked. The attic. She remembered Ramsey telling her that it was full of trunks containing old clothes and diaries. As a researcher, she was looking forward to seeing those old diaries, and she wondered if the true story of Miss Edi's David was written down somewhere.

Downstairs, she went into the living room and looked at the familiar furniture, and for a moment she was lost in memory. She and Miss Edi had spent many an afternoon on that yellow couch. When it needed reupholstering, they'd had a good time looking at fabric samples and choosing one with honeybees on it. They'd talked and laughed together as they sat there, and—

Jocelyn had to leave the room, as the memories were too strong. The dining room needed a table and more chairs. There was a downstairs bath, a smaller parlor that had a cabinet with two lamps on it, but nothing else.

She went into the kitchen, sat down at the table, and looked around. She loved the big sink, loved the heavy pine table, but the stove was an eyesore. Holding up her hands, she formed a square with fingers and thumbs and imagined a big, stainless steel six-burner there. "With double ovens," she said out loud.

But it would be ridiculous to put in such an expensive stove, she thought. After all, she couldn't cook. That she'd often made cupcakes and cookies for Miss Edi's fund-raiser tea parties didn't count as actual cooking. But Luke's talk of an herb garden and Joce's memory of the lavender cookies she used to bake had made her think of a kitchen and a . . . well, of a home.

She looked in the refrigerator and saw that there were eggs, milk, orange juice, and bread in there. She frowned for a moment, then shook her head in wonder. It looked like while she'd been out with Luke yesterday evening, someone had put them in her refrigerator. Sara? Ramsey? Somehow, she didn't think it was Tess.

She used one of the pans from the day before to make herself scrambled eggs and toast and ate while looking about her. If she did have the money to remodel the kitchen, what would she do to it? Gut it and put in lots of granite and recessed lighting? The very thought made her shiver.

Before she knew it, it was after ten and she needed to get dressed to go meet Ramsey.

Jocelyn had heard of The Trellis restaurant and knew that it was quite upscale, so she put on her new oatmeal-colored linen trousers and her new pale pink knit top. Ramsey seemed to like her in conservative, feminine clothes.

Her suitcase was still on the floor, not yet fully unpacked. In the back, in the big zipper compartment, she pulled out a framed photo of her and Miss Edi. It was the only one she had. Bell had taken it one sunny day after she'd received a digital camera for her birthday. Of course the Steps hadn't been invited to Miss Edi's house, but both the Steps liked to show up unannounced—as though they hoped to see something they shouldn't. "What do you get out of staying over there all the time?" they used to ask. "The house is boring, and the old woman is mean. There's nothing to **do.**"

Jocelyn didn't bother to reply—which made them furious. Why try to explain to two girls who only thought of how they could decorate their bodies?

Jocelyn had known better than to ask for the photo—the Steps would never be so kind as to just plain give it to her. At best, they'd make her pay for it by doing something for them, such as writing a couple of school papers. At worst, they'd destroy the photo just for the pleasure of doing so.

In the end, she waited until the twins went out, then she'd taken the card from the camera, copied the photos onto her laptop, and put the card back. Later, the Steps taunted her with the picture, since they knew she'd want it, but Jocelyn just shrugged. As she knew they would, they erased the picture off the disk.

Now, she put it on her bedside table. She and Miss Edi were standing side by side in front of a Mr. Lincoln rosebush. The deep red of the rose contrasted nicely with Miss Edi's white linen dress. She was smiling at Jocelyn in a way that showed her love, and Joce was smiling back in the same way. When she first saw the picture, Jocelyn understood more of why the Steps were so jealous of her. Not even their doting mother looked at the twins like Miss Edi was looking at Jocelyn.

With another glance at the clock, she hurried to finish dressing, and was soon running down the steps to the front door. When she opened it, she gasped. Three women were standing on her doorstep, and she nearly ran into them.

"So sorry to have frightened you," said one woman.

"You're off to see Ramsey, aren't you?" asked the second. She had on jeans and a T-shirt and looked too young to have gray hair.

She'd seen them at church, had even been introduced to them, but she couldn't remember their names. For all she knew, one of them was Ramsey's mother. Or Luke's.

"I'm sorry but I can't stay. I'm late as it is," Joce said.

"That's all right, he'll wait for you," said the third woman. "We came to get our dishes and to see how you're doing. Did you like the squash casserole I made?"

"I, uh . . . ," Jocelyn began. She didn't know whose dish was what.

"Don't mind her," said the woman in jeans. "We all know what you did with the food. That was Tess's idea, wasn't it? And noble of you girls to do that."

"Yes," said the first woman. Her hair was dyed a

dark red that looked good on her, and by the roll around her middle, she didn't bother going to a gym. "We know how noble Tess is." She rolled her eyes when she said it and looked like she wanted to giggle.

The way they spoke of Tess made Joce give a silent thanks to Luke for not telling that he'd been in her house after Ramsey left. She didn't want these women rolling their eyes over her. "The dishes are on the table in the kitchen," she said as she went down the stairs to her car. "Help yourselves and thank you all so very much. You've made me feel very welcome. I can't possibly thank you enough." She opened her car door and got inside.

She put her hand out the window and waved as she went through the gates. The women were standing on her doorstep, watching her. "I'll probably be branded as the rudest Yankee ever to have moved to Edilean," she muttered under her breath.

Minutes later, she saw Ramsey's office—and he was sitting on the sidewalk in front. Beside him was a big picnic basket and under him was a folded quilt. When he saw her coming, he got up and put the quilt and the basket over his arm. She pulled to the curb, he opened the passenger side, got in, and put the items in the back.

"Bigger than it looks," he said, looking at the interior of the car.

"I bet you say that to all your dates."

"Only a few of them," he said in a husky way.

"So where are we going?" she asked even as she started to turn toward Williamsburg.

"No," Ramsey said. "Go right."

"But—"

"But what?" he asked.

"Nothing," she said. "I just assumed we were going into Williamsburg."

"I thought about it, but there's time to do that later. I thought we might spend some time alone together."

"'Alone together,'" she said under her breath.

"What?"

"It's just something I heard and I liked it. 'Alone together.'"

"Turn here," Ramsey said at a sign that said they were now leaving the State Wilderness Park. "Unless you want me to drive?"

"No, I'm fine."

"So how many ladies did you get this morning?" he asked.

"Surprisingly few. There were three of them on the doorstep as I left. I almost knocked them down."

"So who were they?"

She glanced at him.

"Right," he said, smiling. "You have no idea. Describe them."

"Dark red hair, not natural. Not athletic."

"'Not athletic.' How diplomatic of you. Ken's mother. You haven't met him, have you?"

"I thought I was going to meet him today, but you were outside waiting for me."

"Tess's idea. She said everyone would be staring at you, so if I actually wanted to talk to you, I should take you away."

"Ah," Jocelyn said.

"I'm not sure that's a good sound. What does 'ah' mean?"

"Luke said that Tess runs your life. In fact, everyone says that."

"And she does a good job of it too," Ramsey said. "Please tell me you're insanely jealous and you'd like to snatch her bald."

Joce laughed. "Sorry, but no. She's abrasive and has a chip on her shoulder the size of a mountain, but I almost like her."

"If you do, you're only the second woman in town who does. You and Sara. The girls in the office are terrified of her. They run into the restroom and talk about her so much that now if Tess is going in there, she yells 'incoming' then gives them three seconds to shut up."

"Why would they hate her for **that**?" Joce asked, wide eyed.

"Beats me," Ramsey said, smiling. "Turn here, down this dirt road. There! That's it. Park under that tree."

She pulled under a big oak tree and got out of the car. Ramsey got out, then pushed his seat back and removed the basket and quilt.

"Can you bear another picnic?" he asked.

It was beautiful where they were. Overhanging trees closed them in, and she could hear running water in the distance. "If this is where the picnics are, I can stand them every day."

"Come on, then," Ramsey said as he started walking. She followed him down a path until they came to a meadow that was covered in spring wild-flowers.

It was while they were crossing the meadow that Jocelyn got the idea that Ramsey had something important to tell her, something that he didn't want to say in a public place, like his office or a restaurant. She hoped it wasn't something that was guaranteed to make her cry.

When he looked back at her, she said, "It's beautiful here," and gave no hint as to what she was thinking.

"Virginia on a bad day is still the best there is."

"And this is a scientific observation?"

"Yes. Utterly without prejudice." He was walking backward in front of her, through the meadow, the sunlight glistening off his hair and his blue shirt. "Keep looking at me like that and we'll never get back to the office," he said, teasing.

"Why, whatever do you mean, Mr. McDowell?"

When he reached a row of trees, he slowed as he walked into them and waited for her to catch up. "My grandfather planted these trees," he said once they were in the shade.

"Does that mean you own this land?"

"My sister and I do. She and her husband are building a house on the other side of the meadow."

"Do you plan to build here?"

"Maybe," Ramsey said. They had come to a little creek, with willows hanging over the water. "Do you like this place?"

"Very much," she said. "Where would you put your house?"

He gave her a sharp glance. "You're worried that

I'll put in some concrete monstrosity in the middle of the meadow, aren't you?" He spread the quilt in the shade on a flat piece of land.

"It went through my mind."

"Farther up is a site where an old house burned down. The trees are gone and it's open land. I'd build there and keep all this exactly as it is." He motioned to the pretty little creek as he put the basket on the quilt and opened it. "I have no idea what's in here. Tess—" He broke off.

"Tess packed it," Jocelyn said. "I know. I'm getting the picture. I guess you heard what we did with all the welcome food that was left at my house."

"Yeah," Ramsey said, smiling. "Tess is like that. She thinks of people with less than she has."

As Jocelyn looked at him, she again wondered how much was between him and Tess.

"Don't you start too," he said as he pulled a loaf of bread out of the basket, and she knew he meant speculating on him and Tess. "If this is from Aunt Ellie's store, you can bet that it's half twigs and a quarter bark."

"You don't like it?"

"Love it!" he said loudly, then lowered his voice, "but sometimes when I'm out of town I order a tuna on white. Not whole wheat, but plain ol' white bread. Every time I do it, I expect Aunt Ellie to run through the door and lecture me on my digestive system."

"Tell her that white bread goes well with tequila."

At that, Ramsey gave a laugh. "You have picked up a lot about our residents, haven't you?"

"One or two things." She got on her knees, brushed his hands away, and began to unpack the basket. It was full of things that she loved: brie, crackers, olives, three kinds of berries, what looked to be homemade pâté, coleslaw, and bottles of juice. "Lovely."

"It's my guess that Tess watched what you ate yesterday, memorized it, and applied it to the basket."

"How scientific," Jocelyn said as she spread the meal on the quilt. There were plates in the bottom, and she put them out. She unscrewed the cap off a bottle of juice and started to pour some into a paper cup, but he took the bottle. She watched as he put it to his lips and drank. She liked that he didn't "swallow" the rim, but put his upper lip across the top.

She looked out at the stream and said, "Would you like to tell me whatever it is that you're dreading telling me?"

He gave her a look of astonishment and shook

his head. "Remind me never to play poker with you. What did I do to give myself away?"

"I don't know. There just seems to be something serious in your eyes today. And from what I gather, taking me out here on a second date is out of character for you."

"The curses of living in a town where people know me," he said, but he didn't smile. "I haven't been to bed all night. My father and I stayed up, and he told me what I've come to think of as the Great Family Secret."

"And now you have to share it with me? Is it as bad as all that?"

"Maybe," Ramsey said, looking away from her. "It depends on how you take it."

"So tell me," she said.

He filled a plate with food and took his time before saying anything. "Miss Edi and my grandfather were great friends, and they exchanged letters until he died. Even when I was a little kid, he read the letters to me, and as he got older, I read them to him. Miss Edi used to write a lot about you. She was proud of your intelligence, but she never mentioned what a good observer of people you are."

She was watching him intently. If he'd read letters written by Miss Edi, then he must know a lot about her, Jocelyn. That he knew so much about her was a shock. She tried to quieten her pounding heart. Did he have something truly awful to tell her? "I had to be nearly clairvoyant to survive the Steps."

Ramsey smiled. "My dad and I followed their career," he said. "From their first catalog work all the way to Milan. Are they as horrible as Miss Edi said they were?"

"Much worse," Jocelyn said impatiently. "Is what you have to tell me so bad that you can't get the words out?"

"There is no money," he said quickly.

"No money?"

"Last night my father told me that you get the house, but there is no money with it. None at all."

"I don't understand," she said. "I mean, I wasn't really expecting millions, but Miss Edi lived quite well. I can support myself, but that house will need maintenance."

"I know," Ramsey said softly, "and I—my family, that is—will help you with that. But there isn't any money. As for Miss Edi's expenses . . ." He shrugged.

"How long was she without funds?"

"She was self-supporting until she moved to Florida. After that, the house in Edilean and all the work she did for the town were paid for. And Bertrand's expenses."

"Who paid for her house in Florida and her charity work there?"

"My grandfather."

"And he would be . . . ?"

"Alexander McDowell."

Jocelyn looked at the stream for a while and thought about all she'd heard in the last few days. "Lissie's husband?" she asked softly.

"Did Miss Edi tell you about him?"

"Not a word. She didn't tell me about Edilean, much less anyone who lived here. I didn't know she owned a huge old house, didn't know—" She had to take a few breaths to calm herself. "Miss Edi mentioned Alex and Lissie McDowell in the letter she left me with her will, and Sara mentioned a Lissie who married the 'richest man in town' so I put it together."

"Her great-aunt," Ramsey said under his breath.

"What?"

"Lissie was Sara's great-aunt. She married my grandfather at the beginning of World War II, and from what I can piece together it all started just before then."

"What started?" Joce asked, looking at him, and she could see the strain on his face. He hated telling her all this. She smiled at him. "Come on, lighten up! I was poor yesterday and I'm still poor.

So what? I never expected any financial reward from Miss Edi, so there's no disappointment."

When he turned to her, he looked so relieved that she poured him a cup of juice and handed it to him. "I wish it were wine."

"Me too."

He lifted his cup to her. "To you, Miss Jocelyn, as much a lady as ever lived."

Jocelyn laughed. "What did you expect me to do? Throw a fit? Rage at a woman who left me no money in her will?"

"What would the Steps have done?"

"Did," Jocelyn said, then she told him about the pieces of coal that Miss Edi had cut into jewel shapes and left for them. "I was back at work when they found out and I wouldn't pick up the phone for their calls, but they left some blistering messages on my machine. I played them over and over. I don't think I've ever had such pleasure."

When Ramsey looked at her, she could see that he was still burdened by what he saw as terrible news.

"So tell me the whole story," Joce said. "Why did your grandfather support a woman he wasn't related to?"

"I don't know, and neither does my dad. All we know is that Miss Edi's family was the most prestigious in town, but Alex McDowell's family was the wealthiest. We know that something bad . . . awful happened in 1941, and Miss Edi helped my grandfather Alex, but we don't know the details. For most of her life, Miss Edi worked—"

"With burn patients all over the world," Jocelyn said.

"Right, and she supported her brother and paid for the upkeep of Edilean Manor. When she retired, she moved to Boca Raton."

"In a house near us." Jocelyn had her knees drawn up, her arms around them, and she was listening to him intently. "Owned by your grandfather."

"Yes. Between supporting her brother and keeping up the Manor, plus all she gave to people in need along the way, Miss Edi had nothing. My grandfather bought that house, and she lived in it rent free."

"Why didn't she go back to Edilean?" Joce asked.

"That's part of the Great Mystery," Rams said. "Dad said that Bertrand wanted to go to Florida to live with her, but Miss Edi said he had to stay in Edilean and look after the house. He had to keep it intact for the future. But neither of them married, and they left no heirs."

"So he didn't gamble the family fortune away?" Joce asked.

"No," Ramsey said. "My dad said that Bertrand liked that people thought he was a compulsive gambler who spent everything on the ponies. Bertrand said it was much better than being known to be just plain broke."

"So Miss Edi left me a white elephant."

"Pretty much, yes. But the good news is that the house is yours, free and clear, so you can sell it if you want. It would probably bring in a million or so."

"A million or so?" She sat still, hugging her knees to her chin, and looking at the water. "What about Luke? You said you pay his check. Weren't you to be reimbursed when I inherited the money?"

Ramsey shrugged. "He doesn't earn much, so I pay it out of . . ."

"Your own money," Joce said flatly.

"Look, don't worry about Luke. He's not poor by any means. He has . . . other income."

"What does that mean?"

"Telling you my cousin's business is not something I'll do. Let's just say that Luke hasn't had an easy life, but money isn't his problem."

She could tell that Ramsey wasn't going to say any more about that. "What I don't understand is how Miss Edi lived as she did if she had no money of her own. We went to the opera. She attended charity meetings, and I know she contributed. We did all this **together.** How could she do that if she had no money?"

"That was her job," Ramsey said. "My grandfather set up a trust, and Miss Edi administered it. He knew his son, my father, would hate having to deal with all those meetings, so he left it to Miss Edi to do."

"From a house in Boca?" Joce said. "Does that sound odd to you?"

"Yes and no. I think my grandfather trusted Miss Edi more than anyone else, and since she didn't want to return to Edilean, where people still talked about the fact that she was an 'old maid,' it worked out well. And Dad said he thought she didn't want to live with her brother."

"And the cold hurt her legs."

"I'm sure there were a thousand reasons for it all. I think my grandfather and Miss Edi worked it out so they were both happy with everything. My dad said she did a great job at administering the trust."

"She spent a lot of money on me," Joce said softly.

"Last night Dad told me that my grandfather

and your grandparents were friends. I think that's why he bought that house, so she could be near them."

Jocelyn gave a sigh. "Yet another lie. Or something that was hidden. Miss Edi never told me that my grandparents were friends of her friend." She took a breath. "So many secrets." She looked at him. "Does the whole town know that the Harcourt family was destitute?"

"No." Ramsey grimaced. "It was such a secret that until last night, even I didn't know. My dad said he used to go to Bertrand twice a year, and they'd drink fifty-year-old brandy and laugh about the poverty of the Harcourt family. Jocelyn, you have to understand that I knew nothing about this. I believed the papers I saw and thought you were inheriting about three million dollars plus the house. Before you even came here, you asked me on the phone about the money, and I told you the truth as I knew it. I would never have—"

She could hear the pleading in his voice, hear that he didn't want her to think badly of him. She didn't, but she thought she'd save him from humiliation by saying nothing. "Whatever did she do to make your grandfather take care of her and her brother for so many years?"

"I don't know. And neither does Dad. Last night

he told me that when his father turned the Harcourt account over to him, he asked him that very question, but Gramps wouldn't tell him. Dad said that over the years he asked a hundred times, but Gramps refused to confide in him. All Gramps would say was that Edi believed in him when no one else did, and if she hadn't, his life would have been hell. He said he owed everything he had to Miss Edi."

"What does that mean?" Joce asked. "Did she advise him to buy U.S. Steel at ten cents a share? He bought it, the stock went up, and voilà! He's rich. Maybe it was something like that."

"No, it couldn't have been that simple. If it was something like that, Gramps could have set up a trust for her in the open. It would have become a town legend, and everyone would have agreed that Gramps owed her. But this was something that was done in secrecy. Whatever Miss Edi did for my grandfather, it was done without the town knowing about it."

"In this town?! Two men visited Tess on a Saturday night and the next morning everyone knew about it."

"Exactly. But something happened, something big, and because of that, after Miss Edi retired, my grandfather took care of her and her brother."

"I'm beginning to think that everything she told me was a lie."

"She didn't lie when she said she loved you. She wrote Gramps that you were a gift from God, something for her old age. Jocelyn," Ramsey said as he reached out and put his hand on her arm. "I'll help you. I really will."

"You mean that you'll give me charity like your grandfather did? Your family are the true owners of Edilean Manor."

"Then Luke would work for **me**?" Ramsey said, and there was so much glee in his voice that Jocelyn laughed.

"What would he say if he knew you were paying him?"

"Probably hit me in the face. He has the meanest left hook I've ever seen. I think my eyes were black half my childhood."

"And what wounds did he carry?"

"None," Ramsey said. "I turned the other cheek."

She laughed again, only this time it was genuine. She looked back at the water. "Okay, so I have to find a job. Hey! I know. Why don't you fire Tess and let **me** work for you?"

When Ramsey looked at her with eyes wide with horror, she grinned.

"Why not? I'll wear dresses. They'll have skirts down to my knees, and there won't be any cowboy boots."

"If you don't quit saying these things I'm going to tell Tess on you."

Jocelyn put her hands up, as though to shield her face from blows. "Did I tell you what she said to me when I first met her?"

"No," he said, "but I heard what you said back to her. Something about honey catching more flies than a beautiful face?"

"Good synopsis." She began to pack up the basket, but Ramsey sat where he was.

"I have something else to tell you."

Jocelyn sat back down on the quilt. "What else could you have to say to me? That I'm in debt? Please don't tell me there's some debt I've inherited and I have to pay it or I'll be dragged off to debtors' prison."

He looked at her in astonishment. "Do you read the same books that Sara does?"

"Pretty much. So what else do you have to tell me?"

"I planned to keep this a secret." He took a breath. "The truth is that I arranged this, and I wasn't going to tell you, but last night when I found out the lies you'd been told . . . Well, I can't bring myself to tell you even the tiniest lie to add to all the others."

"That could be useful," she said, but he didn't smile.

"Look," Ramsey said, "there's going to be a trick played on you this afternoon."

"Yeah, I know."

"You know?"

"Luke told me. He's picking me up at two—or at least he's supposed to pick me up then. He said you always took women to The Trellis restaurant for the second date, so he said he'd pick me up there."

Ramsey snorted. "He's trying to make you think I'm a stick-in-the-mud and that I have a routine for 'my women.' The truth is that I don't have a set routine and I don't have many dates. But Luke isn't what I was talking about. A cupcake trick is going to be played on you."

"A cupcake trick? It that some Southern slang that I don't know about?"

"No, it's my big mouth. After I left you on Saturday evening I went next door to Tess's apartment."

"And talked about me," Jocelyn said. "You told me."

Ramsey gave her a quick look, as though trying

to figure out her tone. "I told her that . . ." He waved his hand in dismissal. "It doesn't matter what and why, but I told her that you mentioned that you can make cupcakes, and she said I should make a 'cupcake crisis.'"

"A cupcake crisis? What is that?"

"She meant I should get someone to pretend that he or she needs cupcakes more than life itself and you are the only one who can make them."

Joce looked at him in consternation. "I think I'm missing the point here. Why would someone **need** for me to make cupcakes?"

"The truth?"

"That would be nice."

"It started out as a way for me to get to know you better, a way for us to spend more time together. After our first date, I felt that we . . ."

"Ran out of things to talk about?"

"Exactly," he said.

"So after you left me, you went to Tess to ask her female opinion about what to do to get you and me more involved with each other?"

"Yes," he said sheepishly. "Sorry, I—"

She cut him off because she leaned across the quilt and kissed him on the lips. It wasn't a kiss of great passion, but it was a kiss that let him know she wasn't displeased with what he'd said.

"Wow," he said, blinking at her. "Was that for . . . I mean, was that because I told the truth?"

She didn't want to tell him why she'd kissed him. Maybe it was just relief that he really had gone to Tess to talk about her, Jocelyn. She knew it was stupid, but Miss Edi said that Ramsey was the perfect man for her, and in a way, she felt like he was hers.

She leaned back on the quilt and looked up at the leaves of the tree overhead. "So tell me about this cupcakes crisis."

Ramsey moved toward her. "I'd rather talk about kissing."

"No, not now," she said as she looked at him out of the corner of her eye. "I think I have other things in my life to resolve before serious kissing."

Ramsey gave an ostentatious sigh and lay back on the quilt, the picnic basket between them. "Tess took care of it. The cupcake crisis, that is."

"So even before she met me, she knew that I needed something to occupy myself."

"Yes," Ramsey said as he put his hands behind his head and looked at the tree leaves. "But she doesn't know the truth about the money. Joce, I know that everyone probably tells you that Tess—"

"**Warns** me that Tess—"

"Right, warns you that Tess takes care of my entire life, but it's not true. Yes, I've learned to play dumb so she does the work—she is a workhorse if there ever was one—but there are many aspects about me that she knows nothing about. And **you** are at the head of that list. I'm sure this has to do with my having heard about you since I was a kid, and I know this is early, but, Jocelyn, I like you a great deal. You're smart and funny, and I enjoy being with you. You make me feel good. Is that enough to base something between us on?"

"Yes." Every word he said made her feel better. She didn't want to think she'd been jealous of Tess, but it was nice to be reassured that there was no reason to be.

She sat up on the quilt and looked in the basket. "Did you eat all of that pâté?"

"Every bite of it." He turned onto his side, his head on his hand; his eyes on her were warm.

She had to make herself look away from him. Too soon, she thought. Much, much too soon. Miss Edi said that women who attached themselves to one man right away spent their lives regretting that there'd been no courtship. She said that David had courted her "ardently." "It was a long time before I agreed to . . . to be his girlfriend." When she said the word, she always blushed.

Jocelyn didn't like to think how that "ardent"

courtship had turned out. Miss Edi had come home from World War II, her legs a mass of scars, and found her beloved David married to another woman.

"So tell me about the cupcakes," Jocelyn said again as she spread cheese on a cracker.

"I don't know the details. You'll get a call from somebody, probably my sister and probably to-night, and she'll ask if you know how to make a cupcake."

"This will be the children's party you invited me to?"

Ramsey took the cracker she handed him. "Yes."

"Have you seen my kitchen?"

"Sure," he said, chewing. "It's—" He looked at her. "It's bare. So how do you make cupcakes with-out . . . without whatever it takes to make cup-cakes?"

"I thought you could cook."

"My sister taught me how to make that pasta dish. It's the only thing I can cook."

Jocelyn made a cheese cracker for herself and ate it while she thought. "I guess your sister's doing this to get her poor unmarried brother hitched with the woman she thinks is rich and lives in the biggest, oldest house in town."

"Sure. My mother has despaired of my ever marrying, and it looks like my sister is also about to give up on me."

"So I'm your last chance."

"**Very** last." He was smiling bigger by the minute. "I'm getting the idea that you have something in mind."

"Do you know what the latest thing in children's food is?"

"Dying it purple?"

"That's so old school," she said. "No, the latest thing is to dump a batch of puréed spinach in with the chocolate."

Ramsey gave her a look of such horror that she laughed. "It just sounds bad. Actually, it tastes good. You put squash in their mac and cheese, zucchini in their hot dogs. Of course the kids grow up never having actually eaten broccoli, but that's neither here nor there. The thing is to get them big and strong. When they go to college, they're on their own."

"A whole generation of children is going to grow up not knowing what real chocolate tastes like," Ramsey said, still looking as though this were the worst idea he'd ever heard.

"Does your sister have any money? If she's part of your family, then she must be rich."

"What?" Ramsey looked at her as though he couldn't believe what she was saying.

"If your sister had called me this morning and asked me to bake a few dozen cupcakes for a kids' party, I would have made them for her for free. But then, I'd been led to believe that I'd inherited a fortune with the house, not just a money pit that's going to take everything I earn just to keep the termites at bay. What I want to know is if your sister can afford to pay me for the cupcakes."

"Yeah, she can afford them. Her husband works at Busch, and he makes good money."

"And of course there's the trust fund from your grandfather."

"And there's the trust fund from my grandfather," Ramsey said, smiling. "What's going on in that pretty little mind of yours?"

"I don't think I want to spend my life making cupcakes, but for now, I can't think of anything else I can do. Sara said there weren't any good jobs in Edilean."

"None that I know of. People either work elsewhere or they open their own businesses. Maybe you and Sara could do something together."

"Open a dress shop where I serve the customers cupcakes? I don't think so. Besides, if I started doing this baking full-time and started making money at it—"

"You'd have the health inspector down your neck," Ramsey said.

"Right. Sometimes I almost forget that you're a lawyer."

"Is there a compliment in that?"

Jocelyn was looking at the stream and thinking hard. "Okay, so I'll have one chance to show the world, meaning Edilean and the surrounding area, what I can do. If I do a good enough job, maybe I can earn enough money to feed myself until . . . until . . ."

"This is making me feel bad," Ramsey said. "I'm the one who steamrollered you into quitting your job and coming here. I told you there was money with the house."

"Please hang on to that guilt. I may use it if I need a loan." In the distance, she heard a horn blow. "What time is it?"

Ramsey grimaced. "I don't need a watch to know it's two o'clock. Why are you going out with Luke?"

She was tossing things into the basket. "Plants. We have to buy lavender."

"What for?" He picked up one end of the quilt and Jocelyn the other.

"Cookies. I can make those too."

"You certainly don't seem upset to hear that you're broke."

"I think maybe someone just lit a fire under me." When the horn blew again, she looked at him.

"Go on," he said. "I'll get this."

"Thanks," she said as she turned toward the path, then looked back at him. "Three twenty-five."

"What?"

"That's what they charge in New York for super cupcakes. Three dollars and twenty-five cents each."

"Of course they do," he said, his face showing his shock at the price. "All right. I'll get my brother-in-law to agree to the price. I'll champion you, but if those cupcakes are awful, you'll make me look like a fool. And you won't get another job around town."

"I'll make you proud," she said as the horn blew again. "My car keys are in the basket." He nodded, and she took off running.

9

J OCELYN RAN THROUGH the meadow to Luke's truck, which was parked by her car under the oak tree. He didn't get out and open the door for her, just waited with the motor running. She opened the door of the big green truck, put her foot on the running board, and vaulted in. Luke was pulling away before she got the door closed.

"Are you angry because you were wrong?" she asked.

"I'm not angry and I'm not wrong, so what would I be angry about if I were?"

"About Ramsey not taking me into Williamsburg as you said he would."

Luke shrugged. "I guess Tess sent him somewhere else."

Jocelyn didn't say anything because that was too close to the truth. But Ramsey had wanted to tell her some important things, and she was glad they were alone when he told her. All in all, she thought she'd done well at hiding her shock at his words. The lack of money to care for the old house was bad, but not something she couldn't, somehow, deal with. Surely there were government programs to help with a house that old.

What bothered her was all the information about Miss Edi. It seemed that every hour she found out something else that wasn't true. Since she was a child, she'd spent as much time as possible with a woman who taught her everything that was important in life. Jocelyn had seen Miss Edi as the wisest person in the world. But now she was finding out Miss Edi hadn't been honest with her. She told herself that the woman had every right to keep huge parts of her life private, but it still hurt.

"Hey!" Luke said softly. "What's made you frown like that? You and Rams have a fight?"

"No," she said as she put her head against the side window and looked out at the road. "Have you ever believed in someone completely, then found out that that person wasn't at all what you thought?"

"Yes," he said. "You find out something about Ramsey?"

"No, I mean yes. He really cares about people, doesn't he?"

Luke gave her a glance as he turned a curve. "I guess so. What does he care about?"

"Everything. Everyone." She sat up straighter. "Where are we going?"

"Plants, remember?"

"I can't afford them," she said before she thought.

One minute Luke was driving straight ahead, and the next he'd done a U-turn and was heading back the way they came.

"What are you doing?"

"Taking you home, then we're going to sit down, and you're going to explain what you just said."

Ramsey hadn't said to keep what he'd told her a secret, but Jocelyn felt that it was just an oversight on his part. Whatever had gone on between Miss Edi and his grandfather had been kept quiet for so many years that she didn't think she should blab it now. "It's just some legal stuff," she said. "It's, uh, probate. It takes a long time to get the money Miss Edi left me to take care of the house, so I have to wait. Meanwhile, I have nothing but what I have in savings, which isn't much. But Ramsey got me a job at his sister's tomorrow. I'm going to bake some cupcakes even though I don't have so much as a baking pan, but if I can make the cupcakes, everything will be fine. I think. I hope."

Luke pulled into the driveway of Edilean Manor, turned off the engine, then went around to the other side and opened her door. "Out," he said when she just sat there. "Unless you want me to carry you, get out of the truck."

She got out, went to the front door, then fumbled in her pocket for the key. "The house key's with my car key, and Ramsey has it."

Luke reached across her and opened the door. "Who locks their front door in this town?"

"But you said—" She didn't bother to finish as he walked into the kitchen and she followed. He pulled out a chair at the big table and waited until she sat down, then he put a teakettle on the stove to boil.

"Where'd that come from?" she asked.

"My mother. I told her you liked tea, so she gave me a box of stuff for you. Okay, start talking."

"Probate," she said. "Ramsey said—"

"Ramsey said no such thing, and if you don't stop lying to me, I'm going to start shouting. I can be very loud when I want to be. All those years of sports."

"Don't shout," she said as she put her head on her hand. "Why are you doing this? I thought we were going to a nursery and . . ." She trailed off.

"You look like you got hit by a freight train," he said as he took the kettle off the burner and poured tea into a pretty teapot that Joce had never seen before. "I want to know what my cousin said to make you react like this."

"Nothing that you need to use your right hook on."

"Left."

"What?"

"Left hook. I'm not going to punch out Ramsey, but I will give him a piece of my mind. What was he thinking to let you leave looking as though you'd been drained by a vampire?"

"You're exaggerating. He just told me some legal stuff and—" His glare cut her off. "Okay, so I didn't let him see how much his words affected me. In fact, I let him think I was happy. Full of life. Nothing gets ol' Jocelyn down."

"But then you climbed into my truck and you looked like you'd—"

"I know," Joce said. "Hit by a freight train.

Drained of blood. You sure know how to make a girl feel good."

He set the pot in front of her with a matching cup and saucer, then went to the refrigerator to get milk. "So now that we have that settled, tell me what happened."

"I can't. It's . . . it's private."

"Everyone knows you're to get about three million dollars. Is that what's upset you? Overwhelmed by the money?"

"Not quite," she said as she sipped her tea. "This is good. You should have some."

"No thanks." He got a beer out of the refrigerator, then sat down in the chair beside her. "If you weren't overwhelmed, were you **under**whelmed? It wasn't as much money as you thought it was going to be?"

"It wasn't the money!" she nearly shouted. "There is no money to worry about!" She put her hand over her mouth. She hadn't meant to say that.

"Well," Luke said as he leaned back in the chair. "No money."

"Look, I can't say any more about this. I just need some time to think about everything, and I ask you to please tell no one what I said."

"You think I'm going to run out of here and tell

the town?" His brows were drawn together almost into a straight line.

Suddenly, she could take no more. She put her hands over her face and began to cry.

"Hush," Luke said as he drew her gently into his arms so her head was on his shoulder. "I didn't mean to upset you."

"You didn't. It was what Ramsey told me."

"That there is no money? Is that what he told you?"

"Yes, no," she said, still crying. "Everything was a lie. I'm finding out that everything I knew about a woman I loved so much was a lie. Who she was, where she came from, even who she loved, it was all a lie. Every word of it. Why did she lie so much? Did she not trust me? I don't understand."

Luke pulled a paper napkin from a holder on the table and handed it to her. Sitting up, she blew her nose as Luke got up. "Mind if I make myself a sandwich? I didn't have time for lunch."

"I'm sorry. I'm imposing on you. I never meant to do this. When I left Ramsey I felt great, but . . ."

"When you saw me, you broke down," he said, and there was amusement in his voice.

"It wasn't like that. Ramsey is . . . you know, so I didn't want to fall apart in front of him."

"I have no idea what 'you know' means. What is Ramsey?"

"A man I'm interested in," she said. "In 'that' way."

"I see," Luke said. "So when you're with him you keep your chin up, your eyes dry, and you don't let him see you with a snotty nose."

"Yes," Jocelyn said, blowing her nose again. "I didn't know I was feeling so bad until I got away from him. He's always so nice to me. He carries food around wherever he goes, and he's always complimenting me. He says I'm funny and smart and that he—" She blew again, only this time harder. "Sorry. What kind of sandwich is that?"

"Ham and cheese. You want one?"

"You have any pickles?"

"I don't know. It's your refrigerator."

"It's a magic refrigerator because I have yet to go to a grocery store but it's always full of food."

"I'm sure that'll end by this week. Everybody in town will be used to you and won't bother trying to get to know you. Especially not if they know you have no money."

"Ha ha," she said. "You aren't going to tell, are you?"

He paused in putting mustard on four slices of

bread. "You're worried that no one will like you if they know you aren't rich?"

"I don't want them to know that their beloved Miss Edi had no money! I don't want them to think bad about **her.**"

"So you don't care that they know **you** are poor." He had his back to her, but she knew he was smiling.

"No, of course not," she said as she took the plate with the thick sandwich on it. "This looks great."

"If you just had lunch with Ramsey, how come you're hungry now?"

"I couldn't very well stuff myself in front of him, could I?"

"Shades of Miss Scarlett," he said under his breath.

"What does that mean?"

"The barbecue," Luke said. "Ashley likes her with a healthy appetite."

"Oh, yeah, I think I remember that. This is good. What kind of mustard is that?"

"I don't know. Ask Aunt Ellie. I think you should tell me what Ramsey told you and if you even hint that I'm going to tell the world, I'll punish you as only a gardener can."

She smiled at his allusion to one of their first

conversations. "Where do I start? Before or after WWII?"

Luke's eyes widened. "Interesting. Start before."

"Ramsey told me that something terrible happened in 1941, just before we entered the war, that made Alexander McDowell so grateful to Miss Edi that after she retired, he set her up in an expensive house in Boca Raton and let her manage a lot of his money. I'm no financial genius, but even I can see that that's not the normal thing to do. Besides doing charity work, she used the money to add to my ordinary public school education and to support her lazy brother. So what happened to make him do that?"

"Why are you asking me?" Luke asked. "This is the first I've heard of any of it. Didn't Rams tell you what Miss Edi did for his grandfather?"

"He doesn't know, nor does his father. I think the story went to the grave with the people involved."

"What does this story have to do with the money?"

"Whatever happened, Alex McDowell spent a lot. I can't imagine why he paid so much. Did he give it freely?"

"Freely?" Luke asked as he finished his sandwich. "You don't think Miss Edi was blackmailing him, do you?"

"It did go through my mind," she said softly.

"Well, get the idea out of your devious little brain," Luke said as he picked up the two empty plates and put them in the sink. "You didn't know Alex McDowell, but I did. He scared all of us kids half to death and most of the adults. 'Gruff' didn't begin to describe him. He yelled at his employees and kept a tight rein on everything that he had a penny invested in. If somebody had tried to blackmail him, he would have picked him up by his neck and thrown him across the room."

"Yet he was married to a woman who looked as angelic as Sara."

"She was as sweet as he was sour. No one ever understood the two of them—except that ol' Alex adored her. Just plain adored her. It was close to worship."

"That would do it," Jocelyn said as she poured herself another cup of tea. It was no longer hot, but it was still good. "If a man adored me, that would go a long way to making me overlook his bad points."

"So marry Ramsey," Luke said. He was at the sink, with his back to her.

"Don't you think it's just an itty bit early to think of something like that? I only met him a few days ago."

"You lie to him about how you feel, about what upsets you, even about how much you eat. Sounds like the beginnings of love to me."

"I didn't lie to him!"

Turning, he looked at her.

"Okay, so maybe I put on a brave face in front of him, but it wasn't lying. I like him. He's everything I ever wanted in a man."

"So marry him. He's rich. Let him support you and this house. Your problems would be solved."

"For your information, Ramsey hasn't come close to asking me to marry him. Besides, if I married him now I'd always be grateful to him. When I got angry at him for something, I'd say nothing because I'd know I have a lifelong obligation to be grateful to him for saving me, so then I'd develop ulcers and probably die young when they all ruptured."

Luke took a moment to digest all this information. "I'm glad to see that the idea of marrying my cousin hasn't crossed your mind."

"I haven't had much time to think about anything. You know what the real irony of all this is? I didn't expect anything from Miss Edi after her death. Maybe a keepsake, but nothing else. She had a lot of charities, so I assumed everything would go to them. Why did she do this to me?"

"That's the most interesting question you've asked. She knew she had no money of her own, but she left you an old house that will—trust me on this—fall into decay if money isn't pumped into it about every six months."

"I'm not sure I can think about all this right now. Any minute Ramsey's sister is going to call and tell me she needs cupcakes and I have to figure out how to make them. Do you think the oven in that thing works?" She nodded toward the ugly white stove against the wall.

Luke blinked for a few moments as he realized that she wasn't going to talk about this subject anymore. But that was all right with him, as he had some questions of his own and he needed to work on them by himself. "I have no idea," he said as he turned the big knob to switch the oven on. "So what do you plan to make?"

"Chocolate with puréed spinach in it, and before you say a word, Ramsey has already told me what a bad idea he thinks this is. But I'll make them taste good, don't worry."

"Miss Edi leave you a magic wand?"

"I wish she had. I told Rams that I'd charge three twenty-five for each cupcake, so I have to live up to that, but I need equipment that I don't have. Is there a cookware store near here?"

Luke pulled the oven door open and stuck his hand in. "So far, it's cold. Why don't you borrow what you need?"

"Who's going to lend me a heavy-duty mixer and pastry tubes?" she asked.

"Did you forget that the church you went to was Baptist? Baptists love to eat. Whatever you need is in the kitchens of the women in this town. Make a list and I'll get Mom to find everything for you. Your kitchen can be fully stocked in about an hour and a half."

Jocelyn sat at the table, looking at him in wonder. "But I haven't had the call yet."

Luke pulled his cell phone out of the leather pouch on his belt and punched a button. "Mom?" he asked. "You think Dad would be willing to help Joce with a bunch of cupcakes?" He paused. "Yeah, I guess so. Sure, I could talk to her. Why don't **you** ask Viv?" As he listened, he smiled. "I think she'd like to do that, but she may charge you." His smile broadened. "Because a scheme like that could get Dad out of your hair for a whole week, that's why. Okay, but I'll tell her you said that. Do you want to tell him or do I? Coward! I'll be there in fifteen minutes." He listened some more, then his smile left him. "Yes, I'm behaving myself. You can ask her if you don't believe me."

Luke held the phone at arm's length toward Jocelyn. "My mom wants to know if I've made a pass at you."

"Not one man in this town has made a pass at me," she said loudly. "Not one suggestive word has been said to me. I've been fed until I'm bursting, but no passes have been made."

Luke looked at Jocelyn for a second, then he put the phone back to his ear. "Beats me," he said. "Ask Rams. Okay, I'll be there in a few minutes, but don't say a word to Dad. I'll tell him everything." He closed the phone and looked at Jocelyn. "So what was that all about?"

"Just girl stuff. So what did your mother say?"

"She already knew about the three twenty-five. I guess Rams told someone at the office because it's already all over town. Mom said that it was absurd to give a kids' party in the middle of the week and serve cupcakes like that. She wants to get my father involved and set up a major event and invite half of Williamsburg to it."

"Half of—" she said, wide-eyed. "What am I supposed to do? Set up a cupcake store?"

"If you want to find out about Miss Edi's life and answer some questions that seem to be tearing you apart, you need to get to know some people around here. I'll make sure Mom invites some of the old-timers who knew her. Sound like a good idea?"

"The best," she said, looking at him in gratitude.

"I'll ask you if you still think it's a good idea after you've dealt with my father for a week."

"Is he bad?" she asked softly, ready to play therapist to Luke.

"Horrible! He's retired."

"What does that mean?"

"You'll see," Luke said. "Give him a project and he'll think he's the ruler of the world. He'll boss you and the ladies around until you mutiny."

"Ladies? Who else will be baking cupcakes?"

"Welcome to Edilean," Luke said, grinning at her. "I have to go." He checked the oven again. "It's cold as a cave."

"I can't afford a new—"

Luke put his hand up. "Let my dad worry about this. He's going to love this whole project." He started for the door but stopped and looked back at her. "Just so you know," he said softly, "Ramsey is heading toward a proposal. He only takes women he wants to marry out to the land where he wants to build a house." Luke glanced around the hallway of Joce's house. "Or a weekend retreat."

"And that would be how many women?"

He smiled at her. "I'd like to say dozens, but it's only been one other woman."

"So why didn't he marry her?"

"That's not my business to tell," he said.

"That's just what Ramsey said about you."

"And what did you ask him about me?"

She opened her mouth to tell him, but closed it. If Luke didn't know that Ramsey paid his salary, she wasn't going to tell him. "Nothing."

"Good," Luke said as he looked her up and down. "Go take a shower and change those fancy clothes. I think you're going to be baking cupcakes for a few days."

She watched him drive away, then closed the door, and for a moment she leaned against it and thought about the last few days. So much had happened that it was a blur to her. In the next minute she was running up the stairs to her bathroom. When she glanced in the mirror, she saw that most of her eye makeup was under her eyes, and she realized she'd looked like that for most of the time she'd been with Luke. Smiling, she got in the shower and thought about what she'd said to his mother. Had it been Ramsey's mother, she would have been ladylike, but she could joke with Luke's mother.

She showered, then put on jeans and a T-shirt. By the time she was dressed, a car was pulling into her drive. She looked out the window and saw a man get out. Even from above she could see that he was an older version of Luke: handsome, gray haired, tall, and he looked like a man who was ready to do business. She ran down the stairs so fast she opened the door before he could knock.

"So you've come to organize me," she said, her face serious.

He didn't crack a smile. "Get out of line and I start shouting."

"And if I behave?"

"I'll make Luke put in that herb garden he conned you into for free."

With that, she gave him an elaborate bow. "Your wish is my command, oh master."

His eyes widened. "I've waited all my life to hear a woman say those words. Will you marry me?"

"I'll put you on my list," she said, smiling as she headed toward the kitchen. "Come and see my stove. It's so old I'm going to sell it on eBay for a million dollars."

"It's not too old, as I sold it to Miss Edi's brother about forty years ago."

Jocelyn stopped walking. "You sell appliances?"

"I did until about three years ago. I can get some killer discounts on most anything you want."

"Do you want sex or money?" she asked solemnly.

"Let me check with my wife on that." He was smiling as he followed her into the kitchen.

10

IT TOOK LUKE two hours to get everything under way with his parents. His mother took over the telephone lines, calling people in two counties to tell them about the party that Saturday. She made it sound as though Jocelyn had just arrived from Brussels and was an internationally renowned pastry chef.

Luke went to his father and said only half a dozen words before the man was out the door, ready to take over the organizing of anything, anytime, anywhere. He really was lost without a job to occupy fifty hours of his week. All Luke had to say was that Jocelyn's old stove was broken, and Jim Connor had his cell phone out. Luke wondered if Joce would get a Wolf or a Viking range within the next twenty-four hours.

As Luke left the house, he reminded his mother that she should call Rams's sister, Viv, and tell her about the party, being as it was going to be at her house. Since Viv hadn't even called Jocelyn yet, it was going to be a surprise to be told that on Saturday she was hosting a party for heaven only knew how many guests.

Luke went to his house, put on a freshly ironed shirt and khaki trousers, then got his BMW out of the garage. He was going to go see his grandfather David, and he knew that he'd get more information out of the man if he was dressed in something other than jeans and a dirty T-shirt.

Granpa Dave loved to tell Luke that he couldn't understand why, with all his education, he didn't dress in something clean. "If you have to be a gardener, at least look like a landscaper," he'd said a hundred times.

Nana Mary Alice would tell her husband to stop it, but it didn't matter. Granpa Dave was old school, and he believed in always looking one's best.

Luke always got along perfectly with his other grandfather, his father's father, a man who other people liked to stay away from. His never-ending bad temper put people off, but not Luke. He'd always been happiest with his grandfather as they fished together, watched sports on TV, or just rode together in a truck. It was Grandpa Joe who got him out of punishments when Luke got into trouble in high school. Luke had always been high-spirited and hated it when he was told what to do and how to do it. His teachers wanted him to obey without so much as a question, but Luke always had his own ideas about how things should be done.

One time Luke had a fight with the football coach that threatened to get him kicked off the team. His father had been so angry he'd sent Luke to his room at ten o'clock in the morning and told him to stay there until he could figure out what to do with him. At noon, Granpa Joe appeared at the window of Luke's second-floor bedroom. He was on a ladder. He didn't say a word, just lent Luke a hand as they went down the ladder, then to the lake to spend the rest of the day fishing. At six that evening, Luke was back in his room, and when his father came in, he didn't know that his own father had taken Luke out.

It had always been like that with Granpa Joe, but not with his mother's father. Besides being a doctor, Granpa Dave was a deacon at church, a Mason, and beloved by everyone.

But for Luke, there had never been the closeness that he'd had with his other grandfather.

Luke drove onto Highway 5, into Williams-burg, then into the Governor's Land at Two Rivers. It was an upscale country club community, with 60 percent of the land left open for its residents to use. Best of all, there was a huge golf course that his grandfather played on nearly every day. As he knew he would be, Luke found his grandfather on the course, at the fifth tee.

"I wondered when you were going to come see me," David Aldredge said as he looked down the green. "So how is she?"

"Who?" Luke asked. "Do you mean your daughter? My mother?"

David swung, and the ball went flying in ex-actly the direction he wanted it to. "If you want to play games, this is going to take a long time. Shall we start again? How is she?"

When his grandfather started walking, Luke hoisted the big golf bag. His grandfather didn't be-lieve in carts or caddies—but he did believe in young, healthy grandsons carrying the golf bag. "I guess you mean Jocelyn," Luke said.

"I heard that was her name, but not living in Edilean anymore, I don't get all the gossip I used to. However, I did hear that you've been spending pretty much all your time with her. Some people were saying you're even spending your nights there."

"People talk too much and they tell lies."

"So it's Ramsey who's been sleeping with her."

"He has not!" Luke said. "Rams has only been—" He broke off as he glanced at his grandfather. "I think there's an eleventh commandant that says grandparents aren't allowed to ridicule their grandkids."

"I'll tell you a little-known secret. On the day the first grandkid is born, we get a handbook that says we get to do whatever we want to the kid just to torture our own children."

"I can't wait to read the book."

"At your age, you may be too old to get children, much less grandchildren."

"Gramps, you're making me feel so much better."

"Always happy to oblige," David said as he stopped where his ball had landed. "So what's made you so gloomy today?"

Luke put his hands in his pants pockets. "Nothing. No one. Just thought I'd stop by and see you."

David hit the ball hard, sent it sailing, then looked at his grandson as they started walking. "Okay, so tell me what she's like."

"You mean Jocelyn?"

"Yeah, Rams's girlfriend. What's she like?"

"She's not—" Again, Luke took a breath. "Remind me to get you yet another tie for Christmas. Something really ugly. Jocelyn is nice."

"That's it? She's 'nice'? So where's the passion? You don't want to jump her bones?"

"Vulgar grandparents make me queasy."

"Oh, right. Your generation knows all about sex, but mine doesn't. For your information, your grandmother and I—"

Luke put his hand up. "Don't even think of recounting what you and Mary Alice Welsch did. That story is still being told fifty years later."

"Forty years," David said.

"Sixty-three, but who's counting?"

David leaned on his club and looked at his grandson. "Okay, so what's eating you so bad that you left tilling the soil to come all the way into Williamsburg?"

"It's just ten miles."

"Ten miles that you don't make very often," David said as he swung at the ball and hit it perfectly, then said quietly, "Has she asked about me yet?"

"No, not yet, but today she was pretty upset. Seems that Miss Edi left her no money."

"I know. Alex supported her. Or, rather, he subsidized Bertrand, and gave Edi money to give away."

"That's what Ramsey's dad told him. Rams handles the legal work, but he didn't know about there being no money."

"Yeah, well, we all agreed to lie to the second generation. Ben should have got the truth from his father before he died."

"I think he tried to, but Uncle Alex wouldn't tell." Luke gave his grandfather a hard look as they walked. "So what **is** the truth?"

"There are some things that I'm not about to tell. Some things are better left alone." He put up his hand when Luke started to speak. "What happened back then has nothing to do with today."

"Except that Jocelyn has no money."

"So? Who of us had at that age?"

"She has a monster of a house to take care of, and the thing eats greenbacks."

"So let her marry Ramsey. He's rich."

"But—" Luke broke off without finishing his sentence.

"But what?" his grandfather asked. "Don't you think they're a good match? Ramsey's money with the Harcourt house. It couldn't be better."

"I'm not sure she and Ramsey are good together."

"From what I hear, they were made for each other. Her pearls match his ties. They'll make that house into a showplace. It'll rival the best in Williamsburg for perfection."

"Perfection. Who wants that?" Luke put his hands in his pockets as his grandfather hit another ball. "They'll probably put a swimming pool in and never let their kids play in the pond."

"That pond always was a nasty, dirty thing," David said as he started walking. "The bottom three feet of it are probably all duck poop."

"Yeah? Maybe I'll dredge it and get some fertilizer."

"My point exactly. Who wants to let their kids swim around in manure?"

"It never hurt me," Luke said, sounding sulky even to himself.

"You were an oddity, my dear boy. You loved the outdoors."

"So did Ramsey when he was a kid."

"No, he tolerated it. Ramsey was always neat and clean. When you played in the mud you jumped in and wallowed. Ramsey—"

"Carefully made little mud pies."

"Just what I said. He and Jocelyn are perfect for each other. Their house will be beautiful, and their children will be clean and well mannered."

"Why does that sound so awful to me?" Luke mumbled.

"I have no idea."

Luke looked at his grandfather closely. "Are you laughing at me?"

"Great, huge horse laughs. I'm whooping it up at your expense. I'm not sure when I've had such a good time."

"Thanks, Gramps, you're a really great guy. You've made my day."

"You're welcome. Any time you want to make a fool of yourself, you let me know. I can always use a good laugh."

He put his club in the bag Luke was holding. "That's it. We're going to have lunch and talk."

"Talk? Any more of your 'talk' and you'll have to prescribe antidepressants for me. Besides, it's after four and too late for lunch."

David squinted his eyes at his grandson. "If you don't stop that attitude, I'll take you home to Mary Alice and tell her you're depressed and she'll pester you until you start telling her about your child-hood traumas **and** about Ingrid."

At that name, Luke turned several shades lighter and took a step backward.

A minute later, David had caught a ride with a fellow golfer, and they were on their way back to the clubhouse. Luke didn't say anything until they were at a table in the corner and his grandfather had ordered them a pot of tea, a plate of sandwiches, and a couple of Jack Daniel's.

"All right," David said, "so tell me what you **really** drove all the way here to ask me about."

"There seem to be some big differences from what people believe to be true about Miss Edi and what is real."

"Are you talking about the lack of money or the fact that she and I broke off our engagement before we both left for World War II?"

Luke looked at his grandfather with an open mouth. "Broke off your engagement?" he whispered.

"Why are young people so surprised to hear that people in the past also had secrets? Did you forget that I was the town doctor? Back in the sixties there was an outbreak of gonorrhea in town, and I knew who gave it to whom. I never said a word. And there was—"

"What was Miss Edi **really** like?" Luke asked, cutting his grandfather off. He didn't want to know more about people's private lives than he already did.

"Perfect," David said. "Never a hair out of place. Never a word spoken that she'd regret. She was strong, forceful, and knew what she wanted."

"You don't sound as though you liked her very much."

"I adored her. When we were toddlers Alex Mc-Dowell kept taking my toys—until Edi bashed him on the head with a wooden block, and he never bothered me again. She was a lady all her life. You do know, don't you, that she dedicated her life to helping burn victims?"

"I heard something about it."

"It was more than you can imagine. She hooked up with Dr. Nigel Brenner, and they traveled the world together. Edi handled everything. Twice she got them out of countries that had overnight become war zones. Both times, Nigel's nurses were hysterical, but Edi never lost her courage or her wit, and she got them to safety."

"But you married Nana Mary Alice," Luke said.

David smiled. "Feisty, funny, sexy Mary Alice Welsch. Until Edi left the country, I hadn't even noticed her. When I came back from the war with a wound in my shoulder that threatened to make me lose my arm, there she was. You know what her best medicine was?"

"If you tell me sex, I'm leaving," Luke said.

"Laughter. She made me laugh, especially at myself."

"To this day, the old-timers think—"

"That Mary Alice bewitched me and that she was little better than a harlot for seducing me away from Edi? She loves that. I wanted to tell people the truth, but Mary Alice said she liked being thought of as a man stealer. She said it made her seem sexy, like a movie star."

Luke had to laugh because that sounded just like something his grandmother would say. She was a cookie baker; she was always ready to help anyone who needed it, and she was as far from being a "man stealer" as could be. Yes, he could see his grandmother liking being thought of as a sexpot.

"Are you going to tell me what Edi's past has to do with you, or am I going to have to order more of these little sandwiches?" David asked.

"It's this girl . . ." Luke looked down at his drink. He'd hardly touched it.

"You like her, don't you?" David asked, his voice changing from teasing to serious.

"Yeah, I do. She went to a nothing college just so she could be near Miss Edi. Tess showed me some background on Joce, and with her grades she could have gone anywhere, but she didn't."

"At the end of her life, Edi had no one," David said softly. "Her brother was dead, but they'd never been close to begin with, so there was no one."

"Why did she live in Boca Raton? Why didn't she return to Edilean?"

"I'm not sure, but my guess would be that people here knew too much about her. She came back often and did a lot for the town—as I'm sure you know. But she preferred to live in Florida."

Luke looked at his grandfather. "What happened in 1941?"

David leaned back in his chair and his face closed as though a door had been shut. "There are some things that don't need to be talked about, and I don't care how many times you ask me, I'm not going to tell that story."

"But I think it has something to do with today. Miss Edi lied to Jocelyn, or rather concealed a lot from her. It's the kind of thing that wouldn't matter to me, but it's tearing Joce apart. As far as I can tell, Joce had a rotten life. I don't know much about it, but I think Miss Edi was the only good thing she had. But now the woman has played a bad joke on her by leaving her that old house and no money for its upkeep. Miss Edi could have used some of Alex McDowell's trust money to create an endowment for an historic house, but she didn't. And if Miss Edi worked hard to keep Joce from knowing about Edilean, why did she leave her the house? None of it makes sense."

David took his time answering. "The Edi I knew had a reason for everything she did, and I think she meant for your Jocelyn to find out what that reason was."

"Don't start on me again. She's not 'my' Jocelyn."

David ignored his grandson's angry tone. "Did you read Edi's letters to Alex?"

"Letters?" Luke asked, sounding as though he'd never heard of such a thing.

"Yes, letters. Alex and Edi corresponded all during the war and afterward. Ramsey must have them."

Luke thought about that for a moment. If there were letters between Edi and Alex, then Luke had no doubt that Ramsey had read them—and kept them a secret. No wonder Rams was pursuing Jocelyn with so much gusto. Picnic baskets, chocolate -covered strawberries, hassling Tess for advice . . . Suddenly, some things were making sense. Luke's mother used to visit Alex McDowell often. Had she read the letters? Had she colluded with him in some plan to hook up Rams and Jocelyn?

Luke looked at his grandfather. "What about you?"

David looked up at the waitress to signal for the check. "What about me what?"

"Letters," Luke said. "Did you and Miss Edi write each other?"

"For a while," David said, his voice barely audible.

Luke stared at his grandfather as he signed the check, and when he stood up to go, Luke stayed seated and kept staring.

Reluctantly, David sat back down. "Okay, yes, we exchanged a few letters, but . . ."

Luke studied his grandfather's face. "Nana Mary Alice doesn't know about them, does she?"

"Oh, she knew all right, but she made me swear to burn them, and I did."

Luke's face fell. "You didn't by chance burn some other letters, did you?"

"No. Your grandmother was forgiving of some things, but she got sick of being compared to Edi. She stood right beside me as I threw every one of those letters into the flames."

Luke looked at his plate, and for a moment David was silent.

"However . . . ," David said.

"However, what?"

"The truth is that those letters from Edi weren't very interesting. She just recounted where she was and what she was doing during the war. They were more perfunctory than enlightening. But the **sto-**

ries she sent to Alex . . . Well, they were a whole different kettle of fish."

"You mean the letters Ramsey has?"

"No, not those. I'm talking about the stories she wrote while she was recovering from her burns. She told Alex the **truth** about what she did during the war and she wrote down the story about the man named David who she fell in love with."

"Do you have those stories?" Luke asked, his eyes alight.

"Yes and no." David paused. "You know what Alex was like at the end. It was only by accident that I saw the stories, and I think some of them may have been destroyed. I kept all that I could find."

"Where are they?"

"In a safe-deposit box that my wife doesn't know I have."

"When can we get them?"

David looked at his grandson. "Meet me here tomorrow at ten A.M. and we'll drive to Richmond."

"You have to keep the safe-deposit box all the way in Richmond?"

"Be grateful I didn't open it in Nevada. Meet me here, and we'll drive there together."

"I look forward to it," Luke said.

"We won't go fishing, but maybe we can ride in a vehicle together," David said, and Luke knew he was making an allusion to Granpa Joe. It had never occurred to Luke that Granpa Dave could be jealous.

"So maybe you can give me some advice on how to get a feisty girl to think of me as something besides her best buddy," Luke said.

Just then two pretty girls walked by and when they saw Luke they started to giggle and batt their lashes at him.

"Now why do I think you'll have no problem with that on your own? Come on, I'll walk you to your truck."

"I brought the car."

"If I'd known you wanted information from me **that** much I would have made you pay the check. So, tell me, what's your father up to these days?"

Luke gave a low laugh. "He's solving a cupcake crisis."

When Luke started to say more, David put up his hand. "Save it for tomorrow and tell me on the drive. I may not sleep tonight from eager anticipation."

"And you can tell me about your broken engagement from Miss Edi."

They were in the parking lot now, and suddenly Luke looked at his grandfather with love. He knew from experience how quickly people could leave this life.

"Don't look at me like that. Go!" David ordered. "I'll see you tomorrow."

"Thanks," Luke said as he got into his car, but he put his hand on his grandfather's shoulder and gave it a squeeze.

11

"I F I NEVER see another cupcake in my life, it will be too soon," Sara muttered as she turned the little cake around in her hand and tried to make an icing rose on top of it.

"I would have thought you'd like this job," Tess said. She was making a big daisy on her cupcake.

"You just like it because it's better than working with lawyers," Sara said. "I don't like the mess. I don't like the smell, and I don't even like the sugar."

"You don't have to stay," Jocelyn said. She was at the huge, beautiful range that Jim, Luke's father, had put in for her four days ago. Already, it had been put through enough that it was a veteran.

"Go!" Jim said to Sara as he came in from the

hallway, his arms full of grocery bags. "Go sew your fancy clothes for ladies who eat too much."

Sara handed her cupcake to Tess and practically ran out of the room.

Jim surveyed the many cupcakes on the table and countertops as though he were a government inspector.

"Do we pass?" Joce asked.

"They look good to me, but I think Luke should yea or nay them. He knows more about flowers than I do."

Tess put down her big pastry tube and shook her arms. Few people knew how much muscle it took to squeeze the thick, heavy icing out of the big bags through tiny tubes to make the designs. "I'm going to write a murder mystery and the killer is a woman who is a professional cake decorator. No one suspects her because the murder took great strength to commit. Who would think that a lady who decorates cakes has the strength of ten men in her forearms?"

Jim picked up a cupcake that looked like a ladybug. The body of it was red with black spots, with a black face. Tess had added white eyes, a red nose, and a bright white smile. She'd also made a green turtle with Tootsie Roll legs and head. But her pièce de résistance was a bright yellow, smiling chick with closed eyes and happy little wings that made him look as though he was about to take off flying.

"You ought to go into business," Jim said as he picked up a cupcake covered in pink and yellow flowers with tiny white centers.

"No," Tess said slowly, "I'm just good at bossing lazy men around." She picked up an uniced cupcake and looked at it. "What do you think? Shall I try a bumblebee?"

"I think that whatever you attempt, it'll come out good," Jim said as he glanced at Jocelyn, who was straining a batch of spinach purée. They'd been working on the cupcakes for days now, and the biggest surprise to them all was how good Tess was at decorating them.

The first day, Jim had taken over. When he and Joce couldn't find Luke in the garden, Jim drove them to Luke's house to borrow his pickup. Jocelyn was curious to see where Luke lived, but all she saw was the outside. It wasn't a large house, but it had a deep porch across the front, and it was beautiful. She didn't know what she'd expected, but it didn't take an expert to see that the house had cost a lot. The windows were double paned and deeply trimmed with hardwood. The roof looked to be slate. When she peeked around the side, she could see what looked to be a fabulous garden in the back.

When she glanced at Jim, he was watching her. "I take it you haven't been here before," he said as he pushed some numbers on a keypad and the garage door opened.

"No. Is the town saying I have been?"

"This town says everything." When the garage door opened, he said, "He took the car."

"Luke has a truck **and** a car?"

Jim gave her a sharp look but didn't answer. "He must have gone into Williamsburg to see his grandfather."

"I thought his grandfather passed away."

"Told you that, did he?"

"Yes," Joce said cautiously as she got into the passenger side of the truck. Was there some secret about Luke's grandfather?

"My guess is he went to see the other one, my wife's father."

"Oh," Joce said but said no more. Just as she'd suspected, in front of the truck were three motorbikes: a muddy Honda dirt bike, an old Indian, and a sleek red Kawasaki made for the road. As she got into the truck, she wanted to ask more about Luke, but Jim didn't seem to want to say much about him. Actually, the man didn't seem to want to say much about anything, so they rode in silence for a while. "You wouldn't like to fill me in on what's going on with all these cakes, would you?"

"Beats me," Jim said. "Luke said he wanted me to organize a big party for Saturday where you sell cupcakes for twenty-five dollars each—or thereabouts. Sounds good to me. What kind of equipment do you need?"

"The kind that comes for free," she said without thinking.

"How about if I get you time payments that don't start for eighteen months?"

"To get terms like that you must have sold your soul to the devil."

Jim gave a little chuckle. "Worse than the devil, I owe my soul to the company store."

"Whadaya expect when you load sixteen tons?" Joce said without so much as a smile.

As Jim backed the truck out of the garage, he gave her a smile that almost cracked his face. "Anybody who can quote Tennessee Ernie Ford is my kinda gal. How does a forty-eight-inch six-burner with a grill and two ovens sound to you?"

"What are the BTUs?"

"At least sixteen thousand."

"I'd say that no wonder you were so good at your job. You talk porno to women."

He took her to a warehouse outside Richmond and introduced her to what seemed to be a hundred men, all of whom he'd trained, and all of whom were still in awe of him. Jim had been regional manager for the entire southeastern United States and had always topped his yearly sales quota by at least 4 percent.

What he was able to get for Jocelyn were damaged appliances. The huge range had a dent in the back of it that wouldn't be seen, but no customer paying top dollar would want it. He also got her a giant freezer that was in a discontinued color of pale yellow. "It looks like butter," she said.

"That's the problem," Jim said. "Today people don't even want to think about butter. They want to think about lettuce." The way he said it made her laugh.

By the time they got back to Edilean Manor, there were three cars in the driveway. "It looks like my wife is working hard to get rid of me," Jim said. "Maybe you and I should go into business together."

"Doing what?" Joce asked.

"I haven't figured that out yet, but if I come up with something, I'll let you know."

"What about Luke? Maybe you two could—"

"We'd kill each other in the first week. He likes to work alone."

"But he can't make much money at gardening. I'm no Realtor, but that house of his looked as though it cost a dollar or two."

"He just needs time to lick his wounds," Jim said as he got out of the truck. "He'll be fine. He likes you a lot, I know that. I haven't seen him less miserable in a long time."

Jocelyn sat in the truck and watched Jim as he went into her house. Miserable? What was Luke unhappy about? He'd never seemed "miserable" to her.

In the next minute the red-haired woman who'd been at her door the day before came out, opened the trunk of her car, and pulled out a huge mixer. Joce jumped out of Luke's pickup. "Let me help you with that." She slipped her arm under the top of it, then took the other box the woman handed her.

"I met you at church, but I'm sure you don't remember me. I'm Mavis—"

"Ken's mother."

"That's right," she said, pleased. "Where have you and Jim been?"

"Buying things. They should be here tomorrow."

"Ha! If I know Jim Connor, they'll be here any minute. There's a man in there disconnecting the gas lines already. Are you really going to open a cupcake store in Edilean and sell all over the U.S. by mail order?"

Jocelyn took a moment to digest that. "No. I can't think of anything I'd less like to do than bake cupcakes for the rest of my life. Actually, I'm thinking of writing a history of Edilean. I've heard so many delicious secrets that I thought I'd share them with the world."

Mavis gave Jocelyn a weak smile, then hurriedly started for the house. "If I were you, I wouldn't tell anyone that or you might find arsenic in your own cupcake," she said over her shoulder.

Joce followed her into the house. Interesting, she thought. She'd certainly hit a nerve with that remark.

Mavis was right, and the appliances showed up about two hours later. Jim was frowning and asking what the hell took them so long to do one simple job.

"Did they celebrate when he retired?" Joce whispered to Tess.

"Actually, they cried. He got the best out of them."

"Like you do with your lawyers."

Tess shrugged as she twirled a lazy Susan around. "You mind if I help on this? Sometimes I get sick of paperwork. It might be interesting to do something different."

"I don't know how big this thing is getting to be, but it's my guess that I'm going to need all the help I can get."

Later, she thought that truer words had never been spoken. At first, some of the women from church stopped by to see what was going on, and now and then one of them tried to decorate a cupcake, but between Tess and Jim giving orders, they soon left. "See what I have to put up with," Jocelyn heard Luke's mother say to one woman as they both left.

In the end, it was just Tess, Jim, and Jocelyn in the kitchen. Jocelyn baked and put the cakes in the freezer, then Tess decorated them. Jim made sure the women had everything they needed and he kept the bowls and bags clean. Tess soon learned that she didn't like parchment paper bags, so Jim got on the Internet and found huge canvas bags for her. They also ordered so many tubes, holders, paste colors, and rose nails that they arrived in a three-foot-square box. In the bottom was a DVD showing how to use the equipment. Tess used her portable player and caught on as though she'd done it all her life, and soon there were icing roses everywhere.

Late on the second day, Ramsey showed up with a briefcase full of papers and a list of questions for Tess. Most of them started with "Where is . . . ?"

Tess was piping butterfly wings on parchment paper. When they were dry, she'd peel them off, stick them together, and put them on top of the cupcakes. "I don't know," she said to Ramsey. "Ask one of the girls to look for whatever you can't find. Or have they finished their learn-to-read courses yet?"

"Tess, this is not funny. I'm due in court at nine tomorrow morning and I don't know what happened to the deposition."

"Did anyone type it?" Tess asked without looking up.

"Of course it was typed. When it was transcribed it was . . ." He trailed off. "Please tell me it's not still on tape."

"I didn't tell the girls to do it, so unless you did, my guess is that it **is** still on tape. And it's probably still in the recorder. I hope you checked the batteries. Did you make sure that the little wheels inside were going 'round and 'round?"

"I have to go," Ramsey said in a voice that

sounded like he was going to be sick. As he ran past Jocelyn he paused, as though he thought he should stop and say something.

"Go!" she said. "Check the recorder. Do what you have to do."

As he hurried through the hall, he yelled, "To-morrow, Tess. I want you in the office tomorrow morning. I want you in court with me." They heard the door close behind him.

Joce was stirring a pan and turned to look at Tess. "I'll hate to lose you, but if you're needed at work . . ."

"I have no intention of going back to that office until Ramsey McDowell and his partners offer me more money."

"And a car," Jim said from the doorway.

"And a new kitchen," Jocelyn said, then looked at Tess. "Okay, so no new kitchen. How about a company credit card and four weeks paid vaca-tion?"

"I like it," Tess said, smiling as she held up a cute little bumblebee cupcake. "Or maybe I'll quit and do this."

She was joking, but Jim and Jocelyn looked at each other with raised eyebrows.

It was at four o'clock on the day before the party, when Jocelyn was so tired she was swaying on her feet, that Jim said, "So what are the adults going to eat?"

"I thought there was going to be food for them."

"Yeah," Jim said, "there is. Viv's having it catered, but what about the cupcakes for them? Or cookies? They'll want something that doesn't have a five-inch-thick layer of icing on it."

"How about edible flowers?"

The three of them turned to see Luke standing in the doorway holding a big wooden box full of flowers.

"Where have you been?" Joce blurted out. "I haven't seen you in days. What have you been doing?"

Everyone looked from Luke to Jocelyn because she'd sounded almost angry.

"Glad to know I was missed," he said calmly as he put the wooden flat down on the edge of the table.

"Sorry, I, uh . . ." Jocelyn wasn't sure what to say, but she was certainly embarrassed by her outburst. "It's just that we could have used your help, that's all."

"From what I hear, the three of you are doing great. So, Dad, which ones did you decorate?"

"Humph!" Jim said. "I'm management. So where have you been? With my father-in-law in his fancy house in his fancy subdivision playing on his fancy golf course?"

Luke looked at Jocelyn. "Don't you just love families?"

"Yours, yes, mine, no," she said quickly, which made Jim chuckle.

"Could you get that dirty box away from the cupcakes?" Tess asked.

"It's not dirty," Luke said. "In fact . . ." He picked up a pretty nasturtium blossom and ate it. "These flowers are not only clean, they're edible."

When Jocelyn looked at him, her eyes widened. "Flowers," she whispered. "Like fried zucchini blossoms."

"Exactly," Luke said, smiling at her.

"Is that some Yankee thing? Fried flowers?" Jim asked. "And we Southerners are accused of frying too much."

"No frying," Luke said. "We're just going to stick them on top of adult cupcakes and cookies." He was looking hard at Jocelyn, as though silently transmitting something to her.

"You didn't!"

"I did. In the truck."

"Are we to guess what you two did in the truck?" Tess asked, but Jocelyn was already running out the door, Luke close behind her.

The four of them gathered around the back of Luke's truck as he untied a tarp. Under it were two bushel baskets, and in them were clear plastic bags full of some dried purple twigs.

For a moment Jocelyn was speechless, then she said, "I'll need a—"

Luke threw the tarp back farther and exposed a white marble mortar that was about fourteen inches across, with a big pestle inside.

Joce let out a squeal and spontaneously threw her arms around Luke's neck. "You did it! You're wonderful! Thank you, thank you, thank you!"

Tess and Jim stood back, watching the two of them. "Better start making out your guest list for the wedding," Tess whispered, but Jim made no reply. In fact, he was frowning deeply.

"All right," Jim said, "you two wanta tell me what this is? It looks like something Merlin would use. You gonna turn that stuff into gold?"

Suddenly, Joce felt embarrassed and abruptly let go of Luke, and stepped away. "He found lavender, and that's a mortar and pestle for grinding it. I can make my lavender cookies. They're perfect for ladies' tea parties."

"Sounds great!" Tess said with enthusiasm. "When do we—" She broke off at a look from Jim. "It does sound great, but I think I better go see what trouble Rams is having. If he can't find that tape he'll lose his case. I should see what I can do to help him."

"And I'm worn out," Jim said. "I'm too old for all this. I'll be here early tomorrow to help get everything to Viv's house, so don't sleep late." He gave a warning look to his son.

Jim pulled his car keys out of his pocket, went to his car, and drove away, and Tess went to her own apartment.

When they were alone, Luke asked, "Was it something we said? Maybe I should have showered."

"I gave up trying to understand this town after the first hour I was here. Come inside and tell me everything. And, by the way, you're putting in the herb garden for free. Or maybe your father is paying for it."

"That skinflint! Never. So what did he tell you to make my gardening free?"

"I behaved myself. Your father absolutely loves the word **yes.**"

"You didn't say that to him, did you?" Luke asked, his voice a groan. "When I was six months old, Mom and I made a pact that we'd never, never say that word to him, and we've kept our pledge. Please tell me you haven't ruined it."

"Six months old," she said, smiling as she went into the kitchen. Every surface was covered with the most beautiful cupcakes imaginable. There were flowers and insects and animals. About a dozen of them had drawings of high heels and dresses on them.

"Let me guess," Luke said. "Sara did these."

"Right on. She wanted me to make some cakes shaped like high heels, but it would take too much time."

"What about these? Did you do them?" He held up a cupcake with a puppy's face in brown and white.

"Tess did."

"Tess?" Luke asked. "Tess who works for Ramsey? Tess who disdains anything cute or sentimental?"

"The very one. I think your dad wants to open a business with her."

Luke sat down on a chair and stared at Jocelyn. "My father and Tess? But the two of them are bosses. They like to tell everyone what to do and how to do it. My father never gets along with anyone he isn't in charge of. And Tess isn't much better. She runs Rams's office like she's the captain of the ship."

Joce shrugged. "I have no idea how they work together, but they do. You should see them together. They're like a machine. If Tess runs out of blue icing, she doesn't say a word, but the next time she reaches for the blue, your dad has filled a tube for her."

"My dad? He made icing?"

"And filled the big pastry tubes. After the first day, he and Tess spent about two hours on the Internet and ordered a huge amount of tubes and bags and . . . well, everything."

"I wish I'd been here to see it."

"So where were you?" Joce asked as she poured batter into paper liners.

"Better let me do that," Luke said. "I don't want my dad to show me up." As he washed his hands he looked at the cakes on the counters. They really were beautiful and quite professional-looking.

"I'm waiting," Joce said.

"Sorry. I keep looking at everything."

"No, I mean I'm waiting for you to tell me where you've been."

"Well, Mom . . . ," he said, trying to make it sound as though Joce was his mother. But she didn't smile. "Show me how to do this."

Joce showed him how to use the bowl and a spatula to fill the liners, then how to put the pan into the oven and set the timer. "We have to get all these into the boxes your father ordered and you can talk while we work."

"Why do you think Miss Edi never told you about Edilean?"

"I don't know," Joce said, and she could hear the hurt in her own voice. "She told me so much about the rest of her life. I could write a book about her years with Dr. Brenner, but she left out everything about the town where she grew up."

"She said nothing about her childhood?"

"She told me she grew up in a little town in the South but that was all. She said her life didn't begin until she met David. And until I came here, I thought David was killed in World War II, but Sara said he jilted her. Miss Edi returned from the war with her legs a mass of scars and the man she loved had married some floozy he'd impregnated."

"That's one way of looking at it," Luke said as he filled a bakery box with a dozen cupcakes.

"What does that mean? You sound as though I've said something horrible. I'm just repeating what I was told."

"Good ol' Edilean gossip. Where do I put this?" He held up a box filled with cupcakes.

"I thought we'd stack them in the hallway. I need a place to put the big mortar so I can start grinding."

"You know that there are machines that can do that," Luke said.

"Sure, but who wants one? Not me."

She could see that Luke liked that answer as he took the box into the hallway and returned with the big mortar and pestle, then got the baskets of lavender.

"I think you have something to tell me, but you're hesitating," Joce said, "so out with it."

"If you could have any job in the world, what would it be?"

"Writing biographies," she said instantly.

Luke looked at her in surprise.

"When I was a junior in college, Miss Edi said that a friend of hers wanted to write a biography on her great-aunt who'd been a suffragette, but she didn't have any idea how to do the research. She didn't know a primary source from an encyclopedia."

"Primary source," Luke said as he packed more cakes in boxes. "Letters, unpublished documents, that sort of thing?"

"Exactly. I spent spring break with the woman, and we had a wonderful week going through old trunks and rummaging through the attics of some of her relatives."

"Did she write her book?"

"Yes and no," Joce said as the timer went off and she took the cupcakes out of the oven. "She wrote it, but she couldn't find a publisher, so it just made the rounds of her relatives, but that was beside the point. It was great to search and dig and find out about the life of a person. In her case she found out that her great-aunt had done nothing more than invite the suffragettes to tea at her house, but when her husband heard what she'd done, that was the end of that. But still, I loved doing it.

"Afterward, Miss Edi encouraged me to write letters to some editors, and I got a few jobs helping research some other books. It didn't pay much but I enjoyed it greatly."

"So who would you like to write about?"

"I . . ." Jocelyn hesitated, as though she was trying to get her courage up to tell him. "I thought about writing about Miss Edi's work with Dr. Brenner. He died a few years ago, but his wife has all the letters he wrote to her, and she said she'd be glad to lend them to me. But she thinks I want to write about her husband, not his assistant. That could cause problems."

"What if I told you that I have the beginning of a story that Miss Edi wrote about her war experiences and that I got it from the David you think jilted her?"

"You what?" Jocelyn looked up from the mortar at him. "Did the jerk write her a Dear John letter while she was in the hospital with her legs burned to a crisp?"

Luke had to swallow and wait a moment before he spoke. "Okay, we have to get something straight here. You have to stop quoting the lies that this town believes. The David who you think jilted Edilean Harcourt is my grandfather, and the 'floozy' he impregnated is my grandmother, and the resulting child is my mother."

"Oh," Jocelyn said as she sat down heavily on a chair. "Your grandfather courted her 'ardently' then he—"

"Before you say any more, I think you should know that there was another David and he was killed in World War II."

"Another David?" Jocelyn whispered. "Miss Edi was in love with **two** men named David?"

"I've spent the last couple of days with my grandfather and—"

"He's alive? Miss Edi's David is **alive**?"

"Very much so. And he's still married to Mary

Alice, and they're still mad about each other, and he gave me the first part of the story Miss Edi sent to a friend. I haven't read it, but Gramps says it tells what happened to her."

Jocelyn could only stare at him.

"If you don't get busy mashing that lavender up, we're going to be here all night and never get these cookies done."

"I want to see the story now," Joce whispered.

"No," Luke said firmly. "If I can delay reading it, so can you. We're going to finish all this, make some money off these things, then you're going to read it to me while I put in the herb garden."

Slowly, Jocelyn stood up and began on the lavender again. "I want to know every word that you know. You can't leave out even one detail."

"It's not much and I had to play golf with Granpa Dave to learn even what I was told. I hate golf."

"But you love fishing."

"Don't you start on me too!" Luke almost shouted, then said, "Sorry. I've had it for days. Grandparent jealousy."

"So what did you learn?"

Luke didn't say anything for a few moments. "Why is all this so important to you?"

"I don't know," she said slowly. "Sometimes I

think my whole life has been a lie. But even if it was the truth I don't understand it. Until I met Miss Edi, I had my grandparents, and Granpa used to spend hours telling me about my mother—but he didn't believe in whitewashing the stories. Granma used to chide him for talking to me as though I were an adult.

"Anyway, my mother spent her life in private schools. She could play the piano well enough to perform at concerts. She was beautiful, intelligent, and popular. She had dozens of suitors, but she turned down every marriage proposal, until my grandmother said she thought her daughter was never going to marry. But you know what she did?"

"I have no idea."

"She fell madly in love with the handyman who worked for the country club where my grandparents were members. He quit school in the tenth grade, and never opened a book. He lived in a one -bedroom shanty and spent every penny he had on motorcycles. My grandparents did everything they could think of to get her away from the man, but my mother said she'd run away from home if they didn't give her their blessing—and a place to live."

Jocelyn paused as she scooped out the crushed

lavender and began measuring ingredients for her cookies.

"By that time my mother was already thirty-three years old and her parents knew she had her own ideas. They gave in and pretended they were thrilled that their beautiful daughter was marrying the handyman. They even acted like they didn't mind when the newlyweds moved in with them. My granddad got my father a job at his insurance company, and my dad went to work every day, but he wasn't any good at it. But he certainly did love my mother."

"And that's what counted," Luke said.

"Yes, but still . . . My grandparents never said anything bad about my father, but I knew how they felt about him. Anyway, four years after my parents were married, I was born and five years later my mother died of an aneurism. When I was nine, my grandparents died in a car wreck and . . ."

"And that left you alone with your dad."

"Yeah," she said as she looked back at the cookies. "And he went back to what he had been. No more neckties for him. No more attempts at a nine-to-five job. My grandparents left the house to me, and what little money there was, was administered by the family lawyer. It was gone by the time I was twelve."

Jocelyn smiled. "But by then I'd met Miss Edi, and some of the loneliness of my life was relieved."

"All right," Luke said after a moment. "Can you cook and listen?"

"Are you asking me if I can make cookies and listen to Miss Edi's story? You have it with you?"

"I have chapter one."

"Is it in book form?"

"I think so." Luke gave a sigh. "I wasn't kidding when I said that about grandfather jealousy. Granpa Dave was the town doctor, so he knew everybody and he was always surrounded by people. If we went to a Christmas party, half the town would be lined up to show him a boil or a wart, hoping to get free medical advice."

"And you were a loner, so you stayed out of the middle of the crowd," Jocelyn said.

"Exactly. So now that Granpa Joe is dead and Granpa Dave is retired, he wants—"

"You to spend more time with him."

"Right," Luke said, "so that's why I haven't been around for a few days. Nana Mary Alice had some things to say to me as well, so . . ."

"So they blackmailed you into staying at their house, and how much weight did you gain?"

"None. I spent the days walking the damned

golf course and carrying Granpa Dave's bag. The thing must weigh a hundred and fifty pounds."

"So what did you get for it?"

Luke got up, went to his jacket that he'd tossed onto a chair, and pulled out a thick pile of paper, folded in the middle, from his pocket. The papers were old and yellow and worn around the edges.

Jocelyn sat down across from him, a big bowl of lavender-colored batter in her arms. "Is that the story?"

"The first chapter. It seems that when Miss Edi was in the hospital recovering from her burned legs, she wrote it all down and sent it to her friend Alexander McDowell."

"The man whose money Miss Edi managed. The man who owed her something but no one will tell us what. Have many people read the document?"

"I don't think so. Uncle Alex gave the papers to my grandfather a long time ago. Gramps read them and they've been in a safe-deposit box in Richmond ever since then."

She looked at the papers Luke was holding as she gave the lavender batter a stir. "Where's the rest of it?"

"My dear grandfather is going to give it to me

chapter by chapter. I think I have to play more golf with him."

"Or take him fishing with you," she said. "Or on a ride on one of your bikes."

"How did—? Oh, you and Dad borrowed my truck. Anytime you want a ride, let me know."

"Sure," she said, but he didn't seem to notice her hesitation.

"You read and I'll make cookies." As he opened his mouth, she said, "Wait a minute! I had this really horrible idea and I wanted to ask you about it."

"I like it already."

"One time I made something called Margarita Cupcakes for one of Miss Edi's charity events. They have a bit of tequila in the batter, and the icing has lime juice and tequila. Do you think I dare do something like that for Viv's party?"

"You have the ingredients?"

She opened a lower cabinet and pushed aside a stack of paper bags to reveal two bottles of tequila and a big sack of limes. "I didn't know how your father would take it, so I had Tess sneak them in for me."

"We won't tell them. We'll call them limeade cupcakes and leave it at that. You couldn't spare a bit for sipping, could you?"

Smiling, she poured two small glasses of tequila and handed him one.

"Ready?" he asked.

"I think so."

Luke opened the papers and began to read.

12

"CLARE!" CAPTAIN OWENS yelled at his sergeant, who was leaning against the jeep and staring into space. When he got no response, he waved his hand in front of his face but there was no reaction. "What the hell's wrong with him?" He looked to a corporal standing on the other side of the jeep.

"Her," Corporal Smith said as he reached up and took a cigarette from David Clare's lips. It was burning down and about to singe him.

"Who?" the captain asked impatiently. Sometimes these men didn't seem to realize there was a war going on.

The corporal took a last drag off Clare's cigarette, then nodded toward the big building in front of them. It had once been beautiful, but now a quarter of it was rubble. Standing on the steps was General Austin, a short bulldog of a man who seemed to believe all words should be uttered as quickly, as succinctly, and as loudly as possible. His orders had been known to put tears in grown men's eyes. The soldiers played a game they called "Worse than Austin." First line of battle or fifteen minutes alone with Austin? Torture or Austin? In the last year they'd developed a catchphrase. "Better than Austin." They used it when they were about to charge into gunfire. "This is Better than Austin," they'd say before attaching bayonets and charging.

The short, sturdy general was standing on the steps, bawling out three young officers, and Sergeant Clare was staring at him as though he were in a trance.

"Austin?" the captain said in disgust. "He's paralyzed by Austin? Oh hell! Get somebody else to drive the bastard. Clare! Come with me."

Sergeant Clare didn't move.

"Not him," Corporal Smith said. **"Her!"**

Captain Owens looked back just as "she" stepped from behind a pillar, and he smiled. Oh

yeah, **her.** Miss Edilean Harcourt, the general's secretary. The Untouchable One. The woman who it
sometimes seemed the entire military force lusted
after, but no man had been able to get near. There
was a rumor that her legs were three and a half feet
long and there was a lot of discussion of what a
man would do with legs like that.

Whatever their fantasies, no man had so much as
received a smile from Miss Edilean Harcourt—but
not for want of trying. Every type of man had tried
every method known to win her. From an Englishman with an accent so elegant it was whispered
he was royalty, to an American GI who'd grown up
in the LA slums, they all tried.

Flowers, candy, love poems, nylons, even a banner saying MISS EDI, I LOVE YOU strung across the
building during the night had elicited no response
from her.

It had been a great game for the men who'd
been there a while to watch the newcomers fall
apart when they first saw Edilean Harcourt. She
was a foot taller than the general and had a patrician beauty that the men couldn't take their eyes
off. The most common phrase uttered by new soldiers was, "She's a goddess."

When "that look" was seen in a new man's eyes,
money started changing hands. They bet on the

number of days it would take before he was given Miss Edi's "drop dead" look, and what the poor man would do to try to win her. They knew the general kept the chocolates sent to her, and he threw the flowers out the window. It was his hay fever. As for the nylons, all anyone knew was that **all** the girls in General Austin's office wore perfect nylons.

So now Captain Owens shook his head and closed his eyes for a moment. Another man had fallen under her spell. "How long has he been like this?" he asked the corporal.

"Since yesterday. I don't think he slept last night, just lay awake staring at the ceiling."

"Great," the captain said in sarcasm. "Just what I need. Clare was sent here specially to be Austin's driver. He drove another general straight through enemy fire, didn't blink an eye. He's up for some medal, and Austin wants him."

The corporal glanced at David Clare. He was a tall young man, dark blond hair, and blue eyes, and he was still standing in comatose silence as he stared at the woman on the porch. "From the look of him, he'd throw himself on a bomb for her."

"Yeah, well, so would we all, but she'd probably just step over his body."

"I see, sir," the corporal said, "you've chosen the Ice Queen route."

"Better that than to remember the roses I stole off a burned-out house and had tossed at my head by ol' Hardheart Austin."

"I understand, sir."

"How about you?" the captain asked as he leaned against the jeep, took out a cigarette, and offered the corporal one.

"Parachute silk," he said as he lit the captain's cigarette, then his own. "Stole it from the quartermaster. I could be court-martialed," he added, then shot a look at the captain.

"Don't worry. Nobody reports crimes concerning Miss Harcourt."

They smoked their cigarettes in silence, leaning against the jeep, the silent, staring Sergeant Clare between them. After a while, General Austin seemed to tire of bawling out the poor officers and started down the stairs. As always, close behind him was Miss Harcourt. They were an incongruous pair, she tall, thin, elegant; he short, thick, and common-looking. It was said that when he was sixteen a judge gave him a choice of jail or the army. It was also told that the general said the army was exactly like gang warfare except with better food, and that he'd bullied his way to the top. Whatever he'd done to achieve where he was, he was brilliant at warfare.

The corporal and the captain stood at attention as the general drew near, and the captain wished he'd dragged Sergeant Clare away. Austin would blame the nearest person for Clare's inability to function—and that meant Captain Owens.

But he'd underestimated Sergeant Clare. As the general approached, the sergeant snapped back into the world and opened the passenger door for him.

Whatever complaints there were about the general, he was courteous to Miss Harcourt. Before her, his secretaries had to be replaced every three months. A couple of the young women had been sent home, as their nerves were at the breaking point. The men said, "Bombs don't bother them, but Austin puts them in a hospital."

Miss Harcourt had been assigned to him nearly a year ago. There was a story the newcomers were told after their usual flowers and candy had been unsuccessful, about the first time the general yelled at Miss Edi. No one knew the full story, but she drew herself up to her full height, looked down her long nose at him, and said she'd like to see him in private. When the doors were closed, everyone pressed his or her ear up against them to hear, but Miss Harcourt's voice was low and quiet. They did manage to hear words like **bully** and **never again dare** and **respect.**

In the past year, those words had been greatly embellished and the story enhanced into legend status. It was rumored that when Mrs. Austin met Miss Harcourt, she hugged her much harder than she did her husband, and was much more concerned with Miss Harcourt's comfort than she was with that of her husband.

Whatever the truth was, General Austin treated Miss Harcourt with the utmost courtesy. He got in the back of the jeep, then waited patiently for her to take the passenger seat in front. While the sergeant got in, she handed General Austin a folder. "You might want to read that," she said.

The captain and the corporal watched the old man obediently take the folder and open it.

"Listen," the captain said so only Sergeant Clare could hear him, "you might as well give up now. You can't win her."

Sergeant David Clare gave the captain a look he'd seen many times before. It said that no one had won her because **he** hadn't tried.

Sergeant Clare started the jeep and maneuvered it through the many vehicles and people around them.

"So where are you from?" he asked Miss Harcourt.

"I think you should watch the road."

David gave a couple of twists to the steering wheel to miss a truck and went between a man on crutches and two pretty girls. That the tires almost ran over the man's foot and the side of the jeep grazed the women's skirts didn't bother him. The man raised a crutch and shouted at him and the two girls giggled. In the back, General Austin glanced up from the papers he was pretending to read and gave a little smirk. There was nothing he liked better than seeing a man make a fool of himself over his secretary.

"The South," David said. "I can hear it in your voice."

Edi didn't bother to answer him.

"So where in the South?" David persisted. "Louisiana? No, too far south." He looked her up and down as he jerked the vehicle around a deep pothole. "No, I can't see you sharing a table full of boiled crab. You're more the silver and china sort."

Edi pointed toward the road, then had to grab

the dashboard to keep from flying over it when David slammed on the brakes. In the back, the general dug his heels into the floorboard, but said nothing.

David waited while a truck drove across the road in front of them. "Georgia," he said. "Maybe Savannah." He looked at Edi for an answer, but she was silent.

"I'm from New York," he said as he pushed on the accelerator, leaving about an inch between the jeep and the side of the truck. "I drive a cab there and I have a little garage. I can fix most anything that has a motor."

David was looking at her and again almost hit another vehicle, this one as it unloaded four British officers. When he splashed water from a puddle on them, they shouted obscenities at him.

"Sergeant," Edi said with her back teeth clenched, "I must insist that you stop talking and watch where you're going. You have a very important passenger on board."

"I'll take care of you, don't you worry about a thing."

"Not **me**!" she snapped. "The general. You have General Austin on board."

"Him?" David said, glancing in the mirror as the general put the folder up to hide his face.

"He's from New York. We have worse traffic than this in Manhattan. But you seem to be nervous."

"I am not—" She broke off as she pointed to a big truck in front of them and another one coming toward them on the right.

"I see it. I'll fix it," David said as he gunned the jeep and went around the truck in front of them. For several long seconds, they were heading straight toward the oncoming truck. Edi grabbed the door and the top of the windshield. David swerved a second before they would have smashed into the oncoming truck, which was full of soldiers who cheered David's daring. He blew the horn and waved as he passed.

"See?" David said. "You're safe with me."

Edi gave him a look of contempt even as she heard a noise from the general that sounded suspiciously like a laugh. But when she turned to him, he had the open folder in front of his face.

"Virginia," David said. "You're from Virginia. 'Ol TJ's country. That's—"

"I know who TJ is," she said. "Thomas Jefferson."

"You teach school?"

"No, I barbecue New York cabdrivers in the back garden." She was sneering at him.

"Had a bad day, have you?"

"Not until I met you, I didn't."

"Me? So you're one of those snooty Virginians, are you? Overly proud to be from the land of our Founding Fathers, that sort of thing? Well, I don't blame you for being proud of your home state, but I don't think you should look down your nose at us poor Yankees. We—"

"Being from Virginia has nothing to do with my dislike of you. You are the worst driver I have ever seen."

"Bad driver?" he asked incredulously. "I've never had a wreck. A few dented fenders and maybe a smashed radiator or two, but nothing that I'd call a real wreck."

In the back of the jeep, General Austin put the folder down and started watching his secretary and his new driver as though he were at a drive-in movie theater.

"You nearly ran over a man on crutches, nearly hit a truck, nearly smashed into a car carrying four British officers, and nearly caused two trucks full of soldiers to crash into one another," she said, showing her anger.

"You sure use the word **nearly** a lot, don't you? You do know, don't you, that a miss is as good as a mile? So you **are** from Virginia. I was right!"

"Where I come from is none of your business. Your job is to watch the road!"

"I'd sure rather look at you. You have a boy-friend?"

"Yes!" she snapped. "I'm married and have two children."

"I may be a bit quick in my driving but you don't tell the truth. They told me about you when they said General Austin wanted me. Want to know what they said?"

Edi held on to the jeep, looked straight ahead, and said nothing.

David leaned so far toward her that his face was inches from hers. Even so, he maneuvered the jeep between two trucks and a motorcycle with a side-car. "They said that a dozen roses and a big box of chocolates would get anything a man wanted from you."

Such rage ran though Edi that she drew back her hand to slap him.

David held on to the wheel with his left hand, grabbed her hand with his right, and kissed her palm.

She jerked her hand away and looked like she wanted to shoot him.

"Naw," he said, "they didn't say that. But it doesn't feel good to be lied to, does it? Lies can hurt."

Edi turned her head from him for a moment, then looked back at the road. "Yes, I'm from Virginia and I have no boyfriend."

"Thank you, ma'am," he said, then glanced in the mirror at the general. He wasn't sure, but David thought maybe the old bulldog was smiling.

13

WELL," JOCELYN SAID as she cut Luke's sandwich diagonally, the way he liked it. She'd pulled the last batch of lavender cookies out of the oven, it was one o'clock in the morning, and she was jittery with fatigue, but she couldn't sit down. She knew without being told that Luke was hungry, so she made him a ham and cheese sandwich, put blue corn chips on the plate, and got him a beer.

He mumbled thanks as she put the plate in front of him. "So much for my grandfather being a monster. She was in love with David Clare."

"She couldn't stand him."

"Yeah, right," Luke said, his mouth full. "You make a mean sandwich, you know that?"

"At this time of the morning, anything I do is mean."

"Right," Luke said as he picked up the rest of his sandwich and his beer. "I better go. You need some sleep. Tomorrow's the big day."

When Jocelyn didn't say anything, he looked at her. "Are you okay?"

"No. Not really. It's all too much too fast."

Luke put his food down, then put his hands on her shoulders and sat her in a chair. "So tell me what's wrong."

"I think people want me to be Miss Edi, to be the Grand Dame, the Lady of the Manor. I think they have a future made up for me and I don't think I can live up to it."

"You're probably right."

She glared at him. "Shouldn't you be telling me that it's all my imagination? That no one expects anything of me?"

"I'd rather tell you the truth. Tomorrow everyone in Edilean will be at Viv's house, and they'll be looking you over, and comparing you, and—"

"You're making me feel worse."

"Would it make you less nervous if I tell you you're doing a great job?"

"How does anyone know that?"

"Do you know how scared this town was when

they heard that Miss Edi had left Edilean Manor to a stranger? Left this big, old house to a single woman with no husband, no kids, just herself. We were afraid you'd show up . . ." He waved his hand.

"With tattoos and piercings?"

"Worse than that, with ideas for 'improvements.'"

"Like chrome and glass fountains?"

"Yeah," he said with a one-sided grin, "like chrome and glass fountains. Listen." He took her hands in his. "You'll do great. Wear one of your little Alice outfits with a headband and they'll all think you're wonderful."

When Luke smiled at her that way, she could feel herself leaning toward him. She wished he'd take her in his arms, but when she moved toward him, he leaned back, away from her. Immediately, Jocelyn straightened.

"To bed!" he said. "Get some sleep so you'll be fresh tomorrow."

"Yeah, sure," she said hesitantly. "I'll have to ice the cookies, but that's all."

"I'm sure Dad will be here early to help with that."

As she got up, she yawned. "You'll be there, won't you?"

"Are you kidding? I have to drive into Williamsburg, pick up my grandparents, and drive them to the party. They're dying to meet you."

"Why?"

"The woman who's to fill Miss Edi's shoes? Of course they'll want to inspect you."

Jocelyn groaned.

"You'll do fine. Now go."

"But I need to—" She looked around the kitchen.

"The kitchen is fine. I'll close up the house. You just need to sleep."

She didn't realize how tired she was until she stepped onto the first stair step. When she got to the top, she smiled down at Luke, gave a little wave, then went into her bedroom.

Even as exhausted as she was, she took a shower, washed her hair, and put on a clean nightgown. As she climbed into bed, her mind seemed to be a kaleidoscope of thoughts and images. She could almost see Miss Edi as a beautiful young woman, pursued by an entire military force. But her icy exterior seemed to have been penetrated by only one man, a sergeant named David Clare. The David she'd come to love more than her own soul.

Jocelyn heard a noise downstairs and thought

that Luke was still down there, locking doors, maybe still boxing cookies.

Two gorgeous men, she thought. There were two beautiful men in her life and neither of them had so much as tried to kiss her. She'd kissed Ramsey, but **she** had initiated it. There was certainly no banner stretched across a building declaring love for **her.**

14

RAMSEY'S SISTER'S "BACKYARD" was about four acres of manicured garden, tended daily by four gardeners, only one of whom spoke English. There were tables set up under the trees, all with snowy white tablecloths and attended by uniformed staff. The guests were straight out of a Talbots catalog, the men in crisp blazers and even crisper trousers. The woman had on linen blouses and skirts, with hats with turned-up brims, and the children were as clean as their parents, with the girls wearing smocked cotton dresses. The place reeked of money and Old World etiquette.

"Having fun?" Sara whispered to Jocelyn.

"As opposed to being shipwrecked? Falling into

an ice crevasse?" she said out of the corner of her mouth.

"At least your cupcakes are giving me lots of work. Tomorrow I'll be called to let out a dozen dresses."

Smiling, Jocelyn handed a gray-haired man a cupcake with three nasturtium blossoms on top of it.

"Do you have any more of the lime cakes?" he asked.

"Sorry, they're all gone."

"Did you think no one would recognize the flavor of booze?" Sara whispered, making Jocelyn smile. "Come on, let's take a break. Have you seen Viv's house?"

"I haven't seen anything or been allowed to talk to anyone," Joce said with a groan. "In fact, every time a good-looking man approaches me, one of your thousands of cousins cuts me off from him. Ramsey's so busy talking to the Williamsburg big shots that I haven't said a word to him, and Luke seems to be stealing plants from the garden. Plus, the church women come up with something they just **have** to ask me whenever a man under fifty gets within ten feet of me."

"Come on inside, and let's talk," Sara said as she took Joce's hand and led her away from the tables, across the lawn, then the patio, and through French doors into a long, narrow garden room. It was furnished with white wicker and several patterns of blue and white fabric.

"Beautiful," Jocelyn said.

"This is what limitless taste and money can do. You know, don't you, that you've put Viv in seventh heaven today? Everyone is raving about the party."

"I was introduced to her and about a hundred people. If she weren't so pregnant, I'm not sure I'd recognize her if I saw her again."

"That's all right. She knows you and your cupcakes, and those purple cookies have so impressed the ladies who run the charities that they're going to ask you to cater another party next week."

"I do **not** want to become a caterer," Joce said firmly.

"I know that, but they don't. Come on, let's go upstairs and see the bedrooms."

"Shouldn't we ask permission before we go snooping?"

Sara glanced out the windows. "There are four old people headed this way and I think they're looking for **you.**"

"Let's go!" Jocelyn said as she ran out of the room. She followed Sara up the back stairs, where they hurried down the hallway.

"Kid, kid, kid," Sara said as she passed bedrooms. "Master." She opened a door. "Guest bedroom. Have a seat."

Gratefully, Jocelyn sat down in a big club chair while Sara stretched out on the bed. "So what's up with you and Rams?" Sara asked.

"Did you bring me up here to get the latest gossip?"

"Of course. Did you think I wanted your recipe for bourbon cupcakes?"

"I used tequila."

"Whatever. So? What about you and Ramsey?"

"I don't know. I told you that I've seen him today, but we haven't talked. He's a bit like a politician, isn't he?"

"He knows everyone and they know him. It's the way he gets business. So how late did Luke stay at your house last night?"

"I don't know. I went to bed," Joce said, watching Sara to see what she'd say, but she was silent. "Tell me, has this town already mated me to one of the men?"

"I think Rams has pretty much laid claim to you."

"How interesting," Joce said coldly.

"You don't like the idea?"

"I'm curious if the twenty-first century has

reached this town. Whatever happened to passion? To courtship? To men who make an effort to win you? Gifts? Banners? Dangerous driving just to get your attention?"

"I don't know what you've been reading but I want to borrow it."

"It's nothing," Jocelyn said, not wanting to tell what Luke had read to her. "So who's Luke seeing?"

"No one," Sara said tersely. "He lives alone and dates no one."

Jocelyn waited for Sara to say more, but she didn't. "That's it? Why is it that every time I mention Luke everyone clams up? Is he an escaped prisoner hiding from the law?"

"Sort of," Sara said as she looked down at her hands.

"You have something to tell me, don't you?"

"Nothing important, just . . ." Sara trailed off.

"You've met a man."

"Yes!" Sara said. "Joanne Langley introduced us."

"And she is?"

"The local Realtor. Sometime it's hard to remember that you haven't always lived here."

"That may be the greatest compliment I've ever received," Jocelyn said drily. "So tell me about him."

"He's tall, blond, and rich. Of course the rich doesn't matter, but—"

"You're not throwing him out because of it. So tell me everything."

"Greg Anders—that's his name—recently bought an old house just on the outskirts of town. Actually, the oldest part of the house was the overseer's cottage for Edilean Manor."

"That's not a good image—and don't you dare call me a Yankee!"

"Okay," Sara said, smiling.

"So what's he like?"

"So far, we've only been on one date, but he was charming and intelligent, and . . . and I felt a kind of loneliness coming from him that made me want to . . ."

"Adopt him?"

"Actually, to marry him, and have three kids. Yesterday I bought a copy of **Modern Bride.**"

"My goodness! That bad that fast?"

"Yeah, I think so. You know what? I think it was fate."

"How so?"

"You know Joanne . . . No, you don't know her, but she's the town matchmaker. If you're single and look at even an apartment through her she'll start looking for a companion for you. Her sister-in-law is a wedding planner, so it works out."

"So how did fate work with you?"

"Greg chose me. Joanne and he had a long lunch, and she told him about all the many single women around here, and—"

"Including me?"

"No," Sara said, then seemed to catch herself. "Sure, she must have."

Jocelyn decided to ignore that slip. "So Greg chose you from what? Photos? I can understand that." Today Sara had flowers in her long blonde hair, and her dress was of soft, cream-colored cotton with little rosebuds embroidered on the bodice.

"No. Joanne didn't have pictures. She just told him about some women. Since Greg is a business-man, she first suggested Tess, but Greg said he didn't think he'd like being around a woman who spent her life with lawyers."

"Maybe Joanne told him the truth about Tess having a . . . What can we say? A somewhat diffi-cult personality?"

Sara smiled. "You may be right. Whatever she said, I'm grateful to her, because he asked for my number and called me. We really did have a lovely time. We talked endlessly about everything. Don't laugh, but he was even interested in my sewing. He says I should open a shop." Sara took a breath. "I know it's early, but I really think maybe he's **the one**."

"How wonderful," Jocelyn said with a sigh. "Is he a good kisser?"

"The best." Sara looked at Joce. "I know he's my cousin, but how's Ramsey in that department?"

"Oh, fabulous," Joce said. "A truly great kisser. The man can't keep his hands off of me."

Joce's words seemed to please Sara a great deal and she started to say more, but a noise from downstairs distracted both of them. It sounded as though something had happened, as they could hear children shouting.

"What in the world is that?" Joce asked, jumping up and running to the window to look down at the garden.

If she'd awoken that morning and thought, What is the absolute **worst** thing that can happen to me today? the answer would have been for one or both of the Steps to show up. Below them, surrounded by every guest at the party, as though she were a queen and everyone had been waiting for her, was one of the Steps. As always, there were half a dozen hangers-on with phones stuck in their ears, and there was also a tall, emaciated woman with cut-glass cheekbones and a neck like a giraffe standing next to Bell.

"It's them," Sara said in a whisper. "Or one of them."

"Bell," Jocelyn said as she leaned back against the wall, and for a moment she banged her head against it. "I should have had Rams write them that I got no money, just a falling-down old house. I should have—"

"Who are all those people around her?" Sara asked.

"Her entourage. They spend her money faster than she can earn it."

"One of them looks like . . ." Sara's eyes widened as she stared harder at the scene below them. "Heaven help us! It **is**!" she said under her breath, then looked at Jocelyn. "I'm sorry," she said as she put her hand on Joce's arm. "Why don't we get out of here and not see them? We'll sneak out the garage door and make it to the cars and drive away. You'll never even have to see her."

"It sounds heavenly. Lead the way. I'll be right behind you," Joce said as she ran after Sara. "How'd she even know about this party?"

"There's an Edilean Web site. Haven't you seen it?"

"I guess I missed that section. Besides, I seem to see only what people are directing me to see, that is."

Jocelyn followed Sara down the front stairs at a pace that almost made her trip. "Come on!" Sara hissed as she crouched down, then ran behind the big kitchen island toward a door.

Never before had Jocelyn seen this reaction to the idea of meeting the Steps. Usually people shoved her aside to get to the models. But Sara was keeping Joce from a meeting that was guaranteed to be unpleasant. What a dear friend she was!

Still crouching, Sara reached up and turned the doorknob that led into the garage—and was faced with a little boy about five. He gave Sara a saucy little grin, then bellowed, "Mom! I found her!"

"Just wait until you see what you get for your next birthday, Jamie Barnes, you little snitch!" Sara said.

"Mom! Aunt Sara called me—"

Sara clamped her hand over the kid's mouth. "You tell and I'll make you sorry," she said into the child's ear.

"There you are!" said Vivian, Ramsey's tall, beautiful, and heavily pregnant sister.

"Mom! Aunt Sara said—"

"Yes, I know, dear, you ratted on her and she

threatened you. Since you and your brother are being babysat by her next Saturday I think you should think twice about tattling."

The boy looked pale for a moment. "Aunt Sara, I ate two of your shoe cupcakes and they were the best." With that, he ran through the garage and out of sight.

"Jocelyn," Viv said, "you and I have hardly had any time to speak, and I certainly haven't been able to thank you for this lovely party. And what a very pleasant surprise it's been to find out that your sister is—"

"Step!" Sara and Jocelyn said in unison.

"Sorry. To find out that your **step**sister is one of the famous modeling twins. She asked that we find you, as she can't stay long." Viv smiled as she held her arm back to make way for Sara and Jocelyn to go through the kitchen and out to the back garden. She wasn't about to let them escape.

"And Sara," Viv said as they left the house, "Ingrid came with her. I'm so glad. Maybe now things can be worked out."

Jocelyn was able to walk forward only because Sara and Viv were behind her. The crowd parted, all of them smiling fondly as they looked from the tall, very thin, heavily made-up Bell to Jocelyn. Bell had on a couple of big leather triangles that exposed the left side of her waist, and her right leg was bare from midthigh down. Her hair was a thick mass of extensions, and a child could have used her earrings as Hula-Hoops.

Compared to the conservatively dressed people around her, she was like a neon sign on a dark night. Some of the women tried to look scandalized, but Bell looked so radiant that no frown was genuine.

"Darling," Bell said when Jocelyn was near her, then she did an exaggerated bend, as though Joce were two feet shorter than she was. Bell gave double air kisses to Joce's cheeks, then pulled back and said, "How sweet you look. Really. I would have guessed you to be no more than fourteen years old. I love the no-makeup look."

Joce knew that to the wide-eyed observers Bell sounded like an adoring sister. Here she was, a superstar, flying all the way in from wherever just to attend her sister's little party. Joce didn't dare open her mouth because she knew that what would come out would be "What do you want?"

But neither Bell nor Ash had ever been at a loss for words. "You can imagine my surprise when Ingrid mentioned that her husband worked at Edilean Manor. Such a small world, isn't it? And when I saw a photo of him, I thought they truly

needed to be together. I'm **such** a romantic. When Ingrid said there was a big party in Edilean this weekend, and I saw that **you** were catering it with those purple cookies of yours, I just knew I **had** to come and give you my endorsement. Tell me," Bell said, batting her falsely thick lashes, "you don't still put that liquid marijuana in the chocolate cup-cakes, do you?"

Three people put the cupcakes down. One woman took a cake from her child.

Jocelyn could think of nothing to say that didn't involve profanity and physical blows.

"Well, darling Cindy," Bell said, "I must go, but Ingrid's staying on for a few days to be with her husband. I do hope you can spare him from work-ing in your garden. Oh, by the way, Ash and I had a gift made for you."

She held out a thin blue velvet box, but Jocelyn knew what was in it, so she kept her hands to her side. Sara took the box and opened it. The Steps had had the jewel-shaped pieces of coal from Miss Edi set in what was usually described as "pot metal" and made into a necklace and earrings. They were masterpieces of tawdriness.

"I hope you get as much enjoyment out of them as Ash and I did." With that, Bell gave two more air kisses to Jocelyn, then she floated away into a crowd of young girls who were barely able to control their squeals of delight.

When the crowd had departed, trailing behind Bell, Sara looked at the jewelry set she held. "Is that coal?"

But Jocelyn's attention was on the woman Bell had left behind, the woman she'd seen from upstairs. She wasn't as tall as Ash and Bell, and she didn't seem to have that air of believing herself to be the greatest thing that ever walked the earth, but just the way she held her shoulders gave it away that she was a model. Her beautiful face was made up to look devoid of makeup, and her clothes were simple but probably cost Jocelyn's last year's salary.

"You must be Ingrid," Jocelyn managed to say at last, and the woman smiled at her.

"I apologize about that introduction. Bell can sometimes be less than the nicest person on earth, but she did arrange for me to be here today. Your party looks lovely." She looked to the side of Jocelyn. "Hello, Vivian. Is he here?"

"If you break his heart again, I'll—" Viv said, but her husband put his arm around her shoulders and nodded toward the back fence.

"This is between them," he said. "Let Luke work it out with his wife. Come on, I saved you some of those purple cookies."

After they left, only Sara, Jocelyn, and Ingrid remained.

"I see him," Ingrid said, her pretty face melting into a smile, then she hurried toward the flowering trees that ran along the back of the property.

Turning, Jocelyn saw Luke staring at Ingrid, unmoving, his face unreadable. When Ingrid got to him, she put her long arms around his neck and kissed him on the mouth.

It took Jocelyn several moments to react, then she turned to Sara. "I understand everything now. Keep me occupied by married Luke so I see no man but the one chosen for me: Ramsey." Turning, she started toward the front of the house and her car.

"Joce!" Sara called after her. "Let me explain."

"There's nothing to explain," Jocelyn said when Sara caught up with her. "The town matched me up with Ramsey, and his married cousin Luke kept me occupied while Ramsey was busy drumming up law business. It worked perfectly. I've never seen a better plan. Did you guys choose my wedding dress for me?"

"Jocelyn, please," Sara called, but Joce didn't stop walking.

It took Jocelyn about ten minutes to get home. When she was inside, she locked the door, then went to the back and the side and locked those doors too. She even checked the windows to make sure they were all closed and latched. She didn't want anyone coming inside without her permission.

Her impulse was to pack a suitcase and leave, but she knew she had to remain calm and think about what she was going to do from now on. It was one thing to have a beloved friend leave her a letter saying that she knew of the perfect man for her, but it was another to find out that a town full of strangers had been planning her future.

Jocelyn hadn't been in the house for more than twenty minutes before there was a polite knock on the door. She glanced out the side window and wasn't surprised to see Ramsey and Luke standing there.

Her first thought was to tell them to go away and never return, but instead, she unlocked the door and opened it.

"We'd like to explain," Ramsey said.

"There's nothing to explain," Jocelyn said.

"Could we come in?"

"Of course," she said, standing to one side and letting them into the living room.

They sat side by side on Miss Edi's yellow couch while Jocelyn took the chair across from them. Ramsey was in his perfect party clothes, meant to show that he was an up-and-coming young businessman, while Luke was in jeans and a T-shirt.

"How is your wife?" Jocelyn asked Luke.

"Quite well," he said, smiling. "She loved your purple cookies."

"Did she eat an entire half of one?"

"More like a quarter."

"Would you two stop it!" Ramsey said. "Jocelyn, my cousin and I came here to explain some things that I think may have been misunderstood by you."

"Oh? And what would that be?"

"About our intentions."

"Intentions?" Jocelyn asked. "I have no idea what you mean."

"I told you she'd be mad," Luke said as he leaned back against the sofa.

"Because my cousin misrepresented himself," Ramsey said, and it was the voice of a lawyer, "doesn't mean that I have. I have never been anything but honest and clear about my intentions toward you."

"And they would be?"

"Would be . . . ?" Ramsey asked, not understanding her question.

"She wants to know what you intend to do with her," Luke said. "Marry her or set her up in a shop, as Sara's new boyfriend wants to do with her."

Ramsey turned to glare at Luke. "This whole thing is **your** fault. Why didn't you tell her you were married?"

"Never came up," Luke said, then looked at Joce. "You have any beer?"

"Not for you, I don't," Jocelyn said sweetly. "Why don't you ask your wife? Or does she just send you checks so you can live well but take on menial jobs?"

Luke's face turned red with anger, but Ramsey grinned. "She's got your number. Why don't you wait for us outside? Better yet, why don't you go home and leave us alone?"

Luke didn't say a word as he started to get up.

"Tell me, Ramsey," Jocelyn said, "was it me or my house you wanted so much?"

Luke blinked at her a few times, then sat back down.

"How can you say a thing like that? I've liked you since before we even met."

"And what a perfect match we'd be. McDowell money with the Harcourt land. I don't have the name, but I do have the house. I saw all those people you were courting today. Think of how you could entertain them in such style here. You aren't thinking of running for office, are you?"

Luke gave a sound in his throat like a chuckle. "She's got you there."

Jocelyn turned blazing eyes on him. "And **you** took up my time so I wouldn't meet another man while Ramsey was working. It was all so clever. So very well done."

"Joce, it wasn't like that," Ramsey began.

"No? At the second picnic you told me about the letters you'd read with your grandfather. What a touching story. You made it sound as though you've been in love with me since I was a child. But of course after that revelation, I didn't see you again for days."

"I think I'll leave you two alone," Luke said.

"Oh, no, you don't!" Joce said, and he sat back down.

"Look!" Luke said. "I never misrepresented myself. I'm your gardener, that's all. My personal life has never been an issue between us."

"I'm not even going to dignify that with a reply. Gardeners don't . . . don't take such an interest in their employers as you have in me. You're just like my father, with his slick talking, his Harleys, and his penchant for girls who don't know which side of a book to open."

"Your . . . ?" Luke said, aghast. "You think I'm like your **father**?"

"A photocopy if I ever saw one. And, by the way, your cousin pays your salary."

"I know," Luke said, his face still showing his shock over Jocelyn's words. "Every week I pad my bill by half."

"Why you—" Ramsey began.

"Out!" Jocelyn said. "I want both of you out of my house this instant, and I don't want to see either of you . . . maybe never."

"Jocelyn," Luke said as he tried to recover himself. "I apologize for whatever you think that I've done to you, but the garden needs—"

"Stay out of my garden," she said. "Don't come near it or me."

"But it needs care. It needs—"

"I'm sure I can find a high school boy who will mow the lawn."

"Jocelyn," Ramsey said, pleading, "you aren't being fair to me. I know that your stepsister was a real snake today, and I'm sure you're upset about it all, but I haven't done anything to deserve being told to get out of your life. Whatever Luke did to make you think that he was . . ." Ramsey looked at his cousin. "What the hell **have** you been doing to make her so angry to find out that you're married?

So help me, if you've touched her in any way, I'll—"

"I am not property!" Jocelyn shouted as she stood up and glared at both of them. "I am not a piece of land that you two can fight over and eventually win. Or in this case, that one can hold for the other. I am—"

"Joce, please," Ramsey said. "If Luke has been too familiar, it's not my fault, don't take it out on **me**."

"Why don't you go to Tess and tell **her** your problems?"

When Luke chuckled, Jocelyn glared at him. "And **you** can go to your **wife.** Now go! Both of you!"

15

J OCELYN LOOKED UP from her desk and stared vacantly out the window. The lawn needed cutting—again—and it looked like some bug was eating those . . . whatever those bushes were that ran around the side of the house. One morning she could have sworn she heard termites eating the wall, but it turned out to be only Sara and her boyfriend at it—again.

She looked back down at the slant-top drafting table she'd bought and at her papers. The desk wasn't what she someday hoped to be able to put in the house, but for now it was what she could afford.

She'd done a lot in the six weeks since she'd told Ramsey and Luke to get out of her life. First, she'd gone to a bank in Williamsburg and borrowed fifty grand on the house. She figured she needed that much to live on while she did her best to write a biography that she could sell to a publisher. She was tempted to write something about Thomas Jefferson, as all those books seemed to sell, but her heart wasn't in it. She wanted to write about Miss Edi.

Jocelyn knew from experience that no publishing house would give an advance to a writer who'd never written a book before, so she'd had to find other ways to support herself while she wrote. To repay the mortgage, she spent her days in Williamsburg researching the eighteenth century for a very successful novelist for a trilogy set during the American Revolutionary War.

During the evenings and into the night, Joce worked on the book about Miss Edi. Tess had told Joce she didn't know Luke was married. In fact, Tess said she and Ramsey had had a big fight about it. He told her that what went on in his **family** was his business.

Tess swore that if she'd known she would have told Joce. "I **hate** the way this town hides its dirty little secrets. Someone should have told me— you—**us** that he was married."

Tess's tone was so angry that Joce felt herself pulling back from her. But Tess got her the key to the attic and Joce had spent days going through every box and trunk. As far as she could tell, everything of value had been removed, and all that was left were thousands of account books. Perhaps someday she could do something with them, but she'd been hoping for a diary where someone admitted killing someone else, and after her bio she could write about it and make millions.

"So make up your own story," Tess said. "Kill someone, then figure out who did it and why."

It sounded so simple, but in the past whenever Joce had tried to do it, she couldn't. She liked to read about **real** events and **real** people, so that's what she wanted to write about.

"Miss Edi!" Tess said, putting her hands over her ears. "I've heard so much about that woman that if I saw her ghostly form standing in the doorway, I'd just tell her to go away."

"If you see her, please ask her to tell me what to do," Joce said gloomily.

It was yet another night that Tess was in Joce's kitchen making cupcakes. After the party at Viv's house—The Disaster, as Joce thought of it—Tess had agreed to do the next two catering jobs. Luke's father, Jim, said she was the best negotiator he'd ever seen. She didn't let anyone even suggest what was to be served at their own party. Tess told them what she'd show up with, and her manner was so authoritarian that they just agreed to whatever she said.

Since then, Tess, with Jim's help, had catered over a dozen kids' parties and ladies' teas. And all the cooking had been done in Joce's kitchen. While she worked on her book, she saw boxes of wonderously decorated cupcakes and cookies going out her front door.

As for Sara, a hundred percent of her time was taken up with her new boyfriend and the plans for the dress shop. All Sara talked about was what Greg said, did, thought. "Greg says we should—" seemed to start her every sentence.

During the day—morning, afternoon, or night—Joce and Tess would hear the sounds of their energetic lovemaking through the walls. At first it had been embarrassing, then laughable. After a couple of weeks it had become so commonplace that all they did was look at each other and say where it was happening. But that ended abruptly one night.

"Kitchen," Joce said.

"No, that's the pantry," Tess said.

Joce listened. "You're right. Oops. There they go into the living room."

"Sara really should let those carpet burns on her knees heal before she goes at it again in there. She—" Tess broke off because she'd looked up to see Jim standing in the doorway, a box of supplies in his hands. He didn't say anything, just put the box down and left the house.

Wide-eyed, the two women grabbed drinking glasses and held them to the wall. They knew Jim was going to Sara's apartment and they wanted to hear what he'd say. But, unfortunately, Jim kept his voice so low they couldn't make out a word. When he returned to the kitchen, Joce and Tess were busy at the table, their faces looking innocent. Whatever Jim said, they never again heard the sounds of lovemaking coming through the walls.

Later, Tess said, "I don't know whether I'm happy at the silence or miserable."

"Me either," Joce agreed.

For the first two weeks after The Disaster, while Tess baked, Joce wrote letters and e-mails, and made calls. Dr. Brenner's widow was so happy that Joce was going to write a biography of her husband—Joce gave up trying to tell her the truth—that she sent so many boxes of papers that they filled half a UPS truck. But as Joce went through them, she had to work to stay awake. Dr. Brenner may have been a great physician, but he was a horrible journalist. She would find entries of several deaths on one day, but there was no explanation of how or why. She began sending out more inquiries. She wrote the American embassies of countries where Dr. Brenner had worked. Twice she was told that the official word was that no American doctor had ever worked in their country.

While she waited, Joce wrote down all she could remember of Miss Edi's stories of her time with Dr. Brenner. Joce carried a notebook with her and wrote at every possible moment.

Through all the searching and recording, she thought of Luke. No! she told herself, she thought of the story Luke had read her while she was cooking. Joce had loved hearing about Miss Edi and her David, the jeep driver who she despised but came to love very much. But how did it happen? What put them together in a way that allowed them to fall in love? Joce hoped it wasn't just proximity and the passions of war. She hoped that they got to know each other, to really and truly **love** each other.

She very much wanted to contact Luke's grandfather and ask for the rest of the story, but she couldn't bring herself to do it. She couldn't believe he'd give her, a stranger, the stories, especially not after the way she'd thrown out his grandson.

Thinking of the story made Jocelyn Google General Austin. She saw that he'd been decorated many times, and there was mention of a son who'd received the last award for his father posthumously. Joce didn't think there was much hope that his family would remember a secretary from World War II, but she wrote them a polite inquiry to ask if they'd possibly heard of Miss Edilean Harcourt.

Four days later, Joce received an enthusiastic e-mail from William "Bill" Austin, the grandson of General Austin, saying that he was writing a biography on his grandfather, and, yes, he knew of Miss Harcourt, but not much. "I'll show you mine if you'll show me yours," he wrote.

The problem was that what she'd heard of General Austin was from a story written by Miss Edi and the portrait of the general was so unflattering that she wasn't sure the man's grandson would want to hear it. She told him that since what she had was from Miss Edi's life **after** the war, it would be of little help to Bill with his biography. However, she asked if she could please see whatever he had on Miss Edi.

Bill wrote back that there were some letters that mentioned Miss Harcourt, but they hadn't been transcribed yet so they were still in boxes—and he wasn't going to let the originals out of his hands.

"My transcriber was my ex-girlfriend and I'm either going to have to get a new transcriber—which I can't afford—or a new girlfriend who can type, or ask my ex to marry me. If I had a three-headed coin I'd flip it."

Joce bought some super glue and fastened three quarters—each from a different state—together to form a pyramid and mailed it to him without so much as a note. Two days later she got an e-mail from Bill saying that he and his ex-girlfriend could have bought a house for what her family was shelling out for a wedding. "It's going to take weeks of my time. And then there's the honeymoon. My work on the biography has been postponed indefinitely. I don't know whether to thank you or hate you."

"Me neither," Joce mumbled. She went back to what she could find out about Dr. Brenner. Twice, she hit pay dirt with people who remembered him and Miss Edi. When she found a nurse who'd worked for him, Joce drove to Ohio and spent three days recording what the woman could remember. But she'd only worked for Dr. Brenner for six months and she remembered Miss Edi as being "scary." "Coldest woman on earth. No heart at all," she said. Joce had to work hard not to tell the old woman off.

Now, as Joce looked up from her desk in the office she'd set up in the second parlor, she didn't know whether to give up or to keep butting her head against a wall.

"You miss him, don't you?"

Quickly, Joce looked down at her papers. "Miss Edi?" she said to Tess, who stood in the open doorway. "Yes, I miss her very much. I just wish people could have seen her as I did."

"Not her. **Him.**"

"Oh, you mean Ramsey. He's in Boston. I heard it was because he lost a big case here. I think the name was Berner, something like that, so he needed to drum up some business. But no, I can't say that I do miss him. We really didn't spend that much time together. Maybe when he gets back . . ." Jocelyn shrugged.

"If you want to lie to yourself, go ahead, but you can't lie to **me.** And stop leaving the door open in the hope he'll show up," she said as she shut it.

Joce put her head in her hands. Yes, she missed Luke. She missed him every single minute of every day. She did her best to pretend that she was working too hard to miss anyone, but she wasn't.

She missed his laugh, the way he listened, the way he understood whatever she was trying to tell him. The first thing she did in the morning and the last at night was to look out the window. She wanted to see his truck, his tools. She wanted to see **him.**

"He is **not** the man for you," she whispered. She was not going to be like her mother and run off with some man she'd end up waiting on hand and foot. She wanted a man like Ramsey who'd take care of **her.**

But reason didn't make her miss Luke any less. Even all that Sara told her about Luke and his . . . his . . . She could hardly think the word, much less say it. WIFE. Luke was with his **wife.** Ingrid had been in Edilean for nearly six weeks now, and Jocelyn assumed they were a happy couple. They were probably having a second honeymoon.

But no matter her good intentions, every time Joce got into her car, her thoughts went to Luke and Ingrid. She tried to direct herself to think about her book, but her mind went down its own path.

Obviously, Luke and his wife had been separated because of her job. Through some discreet questioning, Joce found out that, as far as anyone knew, Luke hadn't seen his wife in over a year until she showed up with Bell at that hideous party.

Whatever or however long it had been, it was

none of Joce's business. Luke Connor was just a man she'd known for a few days and had had a few conversations with. That's all. He was back with his wife now and was probably sublimely happy. She doubted if he even remembered her.

A noise to her right made her look to the door. Someone had slipped a cream-colored envelope under it. Getting up, she picked up the envelope and saw her name on it. When she opened it, she saw it was an invitation to lunch from Dr. David Aldredge.

"David Aldredge," she said out loud. Miss Edi's first love.

He was probably the man she most wanted to meet in the world. He'd been pointed out to her at Viv's party, but she hadn't had a chance to speak to him. Since the party, she hadn't had the courage to contact him. The truth was that she'd made an effort to stay away from the people of Edilean. They asked too many questions. They wanted to know what had happened between her and Ramsey, and they even asked about Joce and Luke. "All of you seemed like such good friends," they'd say, then wait for Jocelyn to tell them every detail of her private life. She'd just smile and walk away.

But now David Aldredge wanted to meet with

her. His e-mail address was on the note, and five minutes later she'd told him yes.

❧

In Williamsburg the next day, when she got to Dr. Aldredge's house, she was at first surprised to see that his home was rather small and very close to the one next to it. Maybe because she'd spent so much time in Edilean and Colonial Williamsburg, she'd expected something older, more historical.

She rang the doorbell, then tried to calm herself while she waited for him to answer. Would he be angry at her for throwing his grandson out of her house? Or was he more interested in the distant past? Would she have to hear some dreadful story about what Miss Edi did to him that made him jump into bed with another woman? He must be near ninety now, so would he be in a wheelchair with an oxygen tube in his nose?

When the door was opened by a handsome, gray-haired man, Jocelyn almost said she was there to see his father. "**You're** Miss Edi's David?" she blurted out, wonder in her voice.

He gave her a dazzling smile and said, "You have made my entire week. No, my whole year. I can hardly wait to tell Jim about you."

Jocelyn laughed. "I've heard all about the grandfather jealousy, Dr. Aldredge, but I didn't know it extended to the generation in between."

"Oh, yes. It goes all the way down—and back. I can't imagine what would happen if Luke had a child." At that he gave her a glance up and down.

"Shall I take that look as a fertility check?" she shot at him.

David blinked a moment, then smiled. "Jim said you had a saucy sense of humor, but it's better than he said. Won't you come in? My wife has made herself scarce for the afternoon, so we have the privacy to talk. And, by the way, call me Dave, or as the town does, Dr. Dave."

As soon as Joce stepped inside, she saw why he'd bought the house. The entire front of it was glass and it looked onto a small, storybook beautiful harbor. Sailboats and small motorboats and little docks led into the lovely James River.

"Wow!" was all she could say.

"We like it," Dr. Dave said, obviously pleased that she thought it was pretty.

The downstairs of the house was mostly one open room, with living, breakfast, and kitchen all in one area. To the side was a dining room that had been turned into a TV-library. Across the front of the house was a glassed-in porch with wicker furniture, and it looked like the place that got the most use.

She knew her guess was correct when she saw there was a little table set for two on the long porch. The dishes matched the napkins and the place mats, so she knew someone had gone to a lot of trouble.

"I guess I should have asked what you like to eat but—"

"Luke told you everything about me," she said.

"No." Dr. Dave looked surprised. "My grandson would probably hit me over the head with one of my own golf clubs if he knew I'd invited you here. He has a true belief that he can solve all his own problems all by himself."

"And you don't think he can?"

"I don't believe anyone can solve their problems all by themselves. What about you?"

"I don't know," she said cautiously. "I don't think I ever thought about it before, but I guess not. I know that I grew up being very attached to Miss Edi, and she helped me with whatever problems I had."

"Ah, yes, now we get down to it," Dr. Dave said as he removed the cover off the big soup tureen in the center of the table. "Do you like cold vichyssoise?"

"Love it. But only if it's from organic potatoes."

Dr. Dave chuckled. "You've spent some time around Ellie."

"No, just her daughter and all the other relatives." At the thought of Sara, Jocelyn couldn't keep her face from turning red.

"So Sara has a new boyfriend, does she? Bit noisy, are they?"

Jocelyn took a sip of the soup. Delicious. "Jim stopped that."

"So I was told, and my wife made me leave the room when I started to laugh. Jim always was a bit of a prude. I can't imagine why my daughter married him."

Joce knew he was teasing, but she didn't like it. Jim Connor had been very good to her. "Maybe because he's the kind of man who looks after people and cares about them and helps whenever he's needed."

"I see," Dr. Dave said, sitting down and taking a sip of his soup. "Like father, like son."

"What does that mean?"

"Just that Luke and his father are very much alike. That's why Luke got along with the other grandfather so well. I'd offer Luke a trip to Disney World and Joe would offer him two days on a smelly boat. I always lost out."

"Were you disappointed that Luke didn't become a doctor?" she asked.

"Why, no," Dr. Dave said, as though he'd never thought of the idea before. He got up to get some rolls out of the oven. "Mary Alice would skin me if I forgot these. Only Henry, Sara's father, wanted to be a doctor. The rest of them did what they wanted to."

Jocelyn broke a roll, buttered it, and took a bite. She'd had enough of chitchat. "So what happened between you and Miss Edi?"

"People don't know this, but we broke up before we left for war."

Jocelyn could only blink at him. "But I thought . . ."

"Everyone, including us, thought we were going to get married. I asked her, she said yes, and I slipped the ring on her finger. But a few weeks after that, Pearl Harbor was bombed and everything changed."

"Or did things change because of what happened earlier in that year?"

It was Dr. Dave's turn to look surprised. "You do your research, don't you."

"I know that Alexander McDowell supported Miss Edi after her retirement, and I assume it was probably his money that sent me to college. Now why would he do something like that?"

"Would you like some more soup?"

"Love some."

"And I have sandwiches. Cucumber, tuna, chicken salad, and egg salad. Help yourself," he said as he put the big plate on the table.

"Okay," Jocelyn said as she took a tuna salad sandwich and bit into it. "Something happened in Edilean about the time of the attack on Pearl Harbor on the seventh of December 1941, and because of it, a whole lot of things changed."

"Please tell me you aren't going to dig and snoop until you find out what happened."

"I'm afraid I am."

Dr. Dave gave a sigh. "Young people always want to know family secrets."

"From people who already know them," Jocelyn said.

Dr. Dave chuckled. "I knew I was right in asking Mary Alice to get us a chocolate cake from The Trellis."

"You mean one of those nine-layer Death by Chocolate things? They aren't an urban legend?"

"They're real, and I have one. Now what is it you most want to know?"

"Right now, I'm interested in 1944."

"Edi's story," Dr. Dave said as he took the empty bowls off the table. He waved to Jocelyn to stay where she was. "So you read the story I gave Luke."

"Sort of. Actually, he read it to me."

Dr. Dave put the dishes down on the kitchen island, then turned to her slowly. "What do you mean? He read it to you?"

Joce stood up and wandered around a bit, looking at the pictures on the walls. Unless she missed her guess, they were original works gathered from around the United States. "Just that. I was baking cupcakes for that . . . that **party** and he read to me." She said the word with so much anger that she had to take a couple of breaths. Where had Bell flown in from? Milan? London? Paris? All just to ruin Jocelyn's first venture into society where she now lived. Between working that day and Bell's hateful little stunt, Joce hadn't talked to even one person about Miss Edi—which had been her main objective of the day. That and earning money.

"Who else was in the house?" Dr. Dave asked.

"Just us," Joce said, then gave him a sharp look. "Have people been saying that Luke and I—"

"No, I've heard nothing, and thanks to e-mail, texting, and the telephone, my wife and I hear pretty much everything that goes on in that town.

So you and my grandson were alone in your house, you were baking cupcakes, and he was reading to you?"

"Yes," she said, giving him a puzzled look. "Am I missing something here? Did I commit some Southern taboo? Sara keeps telling me I'm a Yankee, and Tess . . . Well, who knows what Tess thinks?"

"No," Dr. Dave said softly, "you did nothing wrong. It's just not a way I've seen my grandson before. He's pretty much of a loner."

"Loner?" Joce said. "He's married. Did you forget that?"

Dr. Dave took his time as he removed the cover off a big cake holder, and under it was the wonderful chocolate cake. "You wouldn't like to hear the truth about Luke's marriage, would you?"

"It's not any of my business," Joce said tightly. "I know that I overreacted when I found out, and by the state of my garden now I should have kept my mouth shut, but in the last few months of my life I've had more betrayal than I can handle. Even if they aren't interested in you as other than a friend, married men don't usually sit in your kitchen night after night and—" She took a breath. "Whatever. You don't by chance need a job mowing lawns, do you? We pay in cupcakes."

"No," Dr. Dave said, smiling. "Night after night, huh?" He handed her a plate with a three-inch-thick piece of cake on it. "Maybe this will last you while I tell you about my grandson's marriage."

"Does he know you tell people this?"

"Luke doesn't even know some of what I'm about to tell you."

"Ah, well, then," she said as she took her first bite of the divine cake. "I'm all ears."

"Luke was living and working in . . ." Dr. Dave waved his hand. "Up north. It doesn't matter. What does matter is that he met a tall, skinny, pretty waitress and one thing led to another. Six weeks later, she told him she was pregnant. Old story, huh?"

"The oldest," Jocelyn said.

"The difference is that my grandson was involved. Luke the Good. Luke the Honorable. He married her. He told me that he liked her and he figured that love would come. More importantly, he said he wasn't going to desert the child she carried."

Dr. Dave looked down at his cake. "I was the only one who had the nerve to suggest that he wait and get a paternity test." He looked back at Jocelyn. "Luke almost kicked me out of his life after that. I make jokes about it, but it hurt."

He took a breath. "Anyway, after the wedding, they honeymooned in New York. It's where Ingrid wanted to go, and Luke would have done anything for the woman carrying his child. They were there only a day when a photographer handed her his card and asked her to come by to have some pictures made. Ingrid thought it was a joke, but Luke had heard of the man, so he encouraged her to go. Of course Luke went with her to the photo session."

Dr. Dave paused to take a bite of his cake. "The pictures were so good that the photographer asked to show them to some people, so Luke and Ingrid ended up staying in New York for two weeks. To make a long story short, Ingrid was pretty much an overnight success. You know how it is. They want the girls as young as they can get them."

"I know more about the modeling world than I want to," Jocelyn said.

"Luke needed to get back to his job, but Ingrid begged him to stay with her. I think that to Luke's mind it had all been a lark. I think he thought that someday she'd show her model photos to their children."

"Did she refuse to go back with him?" Jocelyn asked.

Dr. Dave jammed his fork into the cake. "No. I

wish she had, but she didn't. She may be a stupid girl, but when it comes to herself, she is exceedingly clever. She packed her bags and said she was going with him, that she loved him enough to give up everything for him. She just wanted one last assignment, so of course Luke said yes. How could he refuse? So she went to her last photo shoot while Luke stayed at the hotel and changed all the flights back home.

"The next time Luke saw Ingrid, she was in a hospital. She'd miscarried and she was saying that she was so unhappy that she wanted to kill herself. Of course Luke couldn't leave her there alone, and she was in so much pain that he couldn't drag her onto a plane."

"What happened?" Joce asked.

"In the end, Luke stayed in New York with her. He lived and worked in the city."

"Gardening in New York?"

"My grandson can do a lot of things, but whatever he does, he hates doing it in a city, but they lived there together for about eighteen months. Then, one day, quite by accident, Luke found out that Ingrid hadn't miscarried. Her 'last assignment' in New York had been to get an abortion."

"Luke must have been . . ." Joce was unable to think of words.

"He was devastated about the child, the loss of . . . the loss of everything in his life. He returned to Edilean and started taking on gardening jobs. His paternal grandfather had left him an old house, and Luke fixed it up, then he turned his hand to Edilean Manor."

He looked at Jocelyn. "As far as I know, my grandson hadn't seen or heard from Ingrid in nearly two years."

"Why didn't he get a divorce?"

"If she filed papers, I'm sure Luke would have happily signed them, but he's not the kind of man to present a woman with divorce papers."

"But now they're back together."

"Can I trust you?" Dr. Dave asked.

"Do you mean will I tell the entire town whatever you say to me?"

"That's exactly what I mean. Sometimes it's good to be surrounded by people who've known you all your life, but sometimes it's horrible. From the beginning Luke has refused to talk to anyone about his disastrous marriage. I think he feels he was just plain dumb to have fallen for someone with so little . . ." He shrugged.

"Soul? Lack of self-interest? I know what she's like. I lived with two of them."

"What you don't know is what **I** am like."

"You mean about you and Mary Alice Welsch?"

At that Dr. Dave smiled, and she could see Luke in forty-plus years. "No, I don't mean that. I mean that I hired a private investigator to find out about Ingrid's very convenient 'miscarriage.' It took months, but he found the clinic she went to to have the abortion, then I made sure my grandson 'accidently' found the papers."

"If Luke found out you did that . . . ," Joce whispered.

"I guess you can see how much I'm trusting you."

She leaned back in her chair. "You're telling me this because you've found out something else, haven't you?"

"Yes." Getting up, he opened a drawer in a table, pulled out a thick folder, then removed a big envelope. "Yesterday I received this from the same PI who found out about the abortion. It tells why Ingrid has come back."

She took the envelope, but she didn't open it. "I really hope you're not asking **me** to tell Luke about whatever is in here."

"No, I'm not. It'll all come out in the newspapers soon enough. What I want to say is that when Luke was spending time with you—" He put up his hand when she started to speak. "Yes, I know it was just a few days, but he was the happiest I've seen him in years. He even played golf with me."

"You do know, don't you, that he hates golf."

"Yeah," Dr. Dave said with a chuckle. "And he's really, really **bad** at it."

"Then why—?"

"It's just a family joke. He used to spend so much time with his other grandfather . . . Oh, well. It'll all work out." He pulled an old, yellowed stack of papers from inside the folder, and Joce's eyes lit up. "You know what this is?"

Like a cobra hypnotized by a flute, she leaned toward the papers, both of her hands out to take them.

Dr. Dave pulled them away and put them back into the folder. "You make my grandson smile again and I'll give you part two."

"Have you read them?" Her voice was little more than a whisper.

"Oh, yeah. I especially liked the part where they slid into a river in an overturned car. Edi has to— Oh well, maybe you're not interested."

"I am, but—"

"But what?"

"Ramsey. I told both him **and** Luke to get away from me."

"Funny you should mention Ramsey, but some

new cases have come up in Massachusetts, and it looks like they're going to take weeks."

"Heaven help me!" she said, aghast. "**You** sent him there, didn't you? I really **am** being used as a piece of property. You want me for **your** grandson, don't you?"

"I'm too old to think that far ahead. Right now I want to use whatever I can to get my grandson away from that grasping little gold digger he married. And I want you to add these stories to the book you're writing on Edi."

"How do you know—? Never mind."

"Post office," he said. "Return addresses, an Internet search, and it was easy to figure out what you were doing."

"For the life of me I can't understand why Miss Edi wanted to get away from that town," she said in sarcasm.

"From what I hear, you're fitting right in. You like people knowing who you are and you like living in the Big House."

"What kind of doctor are you? A shrink?"

"GP," he said as he searched inside the folder.

"Please tell me you don't have something else for me to read? A new Dead Sea Scroll maybe?"

"Better. Ah, here it is. It's my daughter's pot roast recipe."

"Pot roast?"

"That's right. Make some, freeze it, and have it ready so when I make Luke so miserable that he goes back to digging holes at your house, you'll be able to feed him."

"It's called double digging and . . . Why are you looking at me like that?"

"You miss him, don't you?"

"Actually, I've been so busy that I haven't had time to even—" She cut off when he was smiling at her. "You know something? You're as annoying as he is."

"I take that as a great compliment. Remember. Freeze the pot roast and have it ready."

16

JOCELYN AWOKE LATE the next morning. Between Dr. Dave's stories and the chocolate cake, she'd been in a stupor for the rest of the day, and had fallen asleep early.

Part of her wanted to deny some of the things the man had said, but another part knew that he was right. She'd missed Luke—and she was oh, so very, very glad to hear that he was miserable.

She showered and dressed, then looked at the big envelope that Dr. Dave had given her yesterday. She'd read it last night while she was in bed, and not a word of it had surprised her. Ingrid had been having an affair with a rich, prominent, married New York man and some reporter had found out about it. If the man's wife discovered the affair and

filed for divorce, it would cost him everything because the money was hers and the prenup he'd
signed was not a pretty thing.

Ingrid had run back to her husband in the hope
that the New York man could pacify his rich, angry
wife.

"Poor Luke," Jocelyn said as she pulled her hair
back into a pony-tail, but she couldn't keep the grin
off her face. She could say the words, but she didn't
feel that there was anything "poor" about him at
all. Maybe he'd visit today. Maybe he could—

She paused because she thought she heard
something outside. Maybe it was a truck, but when
she looked out the window, it was only Greg, Sara's
boyfriend. No doubt they were going to work on
the dress shop today. True to what Sara had told
them about him, he seemed to have a bottomless
bank account, and he'd bought the used-furniture
store on the corner McDowell Street and Lairdton,
diagonally from the Great Oak, as Joce had found
out that it was called.

As she looked down at Sara and Greg from her
bedroom window, Joce had to work not to envy
them—and to wonder if she'd been an idiot. When
she'd arrived in town, two men had come into her
life, but she'd thrown them both out—and they'd
made no effort to get back into her good graces.

"So much for an 'ardent courtship,'" she said aloud.

Downstairs, the kitchen was empty, as it was Monday morning and Tess wasn't catering a party. Joce didn't know how she did it. She was working full-time plus catering as many as four parties on the weekends. Of course Jim was there helping her, but it was still a lot to do.

Joce had some milk and a bran muffin, then went to her desk to start work, although it was becoming more frustrating with each day. She was tempted to e-mail Bill Austin and ask if she could visit him and make photocopies of the letters his grandfather had sent about Miss Edi. She'd take one of those tiny photocopy machines with her so the letters would never leave the premises. She'd promise him that she . . . As often happened lately, her mind wandered off into thinking what she could do, wanted to do, but it always came back to the fact that she'd pretty much hit a brick wall in her biography of Miss Edi.

She remembered the story that Dr. Dave had dangled before her eyes. An upside-down car. A rescue. What happened?

Jocelyn went back upstairs and got the little double-framed picture that had been Miss Edi's prize possession. On the day she passed away, Jocelyn had surreptitiously slipped it off the bedside table and hidden it inside her shirt. At the time, she'd assumed that everything would go to charity, but she wanted that one thing to remember her friend by.

Jocelyn well remembered the first time she asked Miss Edi about the hair in the braid. She'd been about ten years old and curious about everything in the world.

"It's hard to imagine it now," Miss Edi said, "what with men today having hair down to their waists, but back then the sides of men's heads were shaved with a buzz cutter. But David hadn't had a haircut in a few weeks, so I was able to get a few strands of it and I wove the braid of his hair and mine."

"What color were his eyes?" Joce asked, looking at the black-and-white photo.

"As blue as yours," Miss Edi said, smiling. "And he had a chin with a dimple in it like you do."

"Like my mother's," Jocelyn said.

"Chins like yours are a hereditary trait."

"My grandfather said his chin was just like ours, but that his four other chins covered it."

Miss Edi smiled. "I wish I'd been here then and could have known your mother and her parents."

"I'm glad you came to rescue me," Jocelyn said.

"I'm like one of your burn patients except that my scars are on the inside."

Miss Edi shook her head in wonder at Jocelyn. "Sometimes you say things of extraordinary wisdom." As they often did, they smiled at each other in perfect understanding.

Jocelyn glanced up from the photo and her memories to the window, then did a double take. She put the frame down, then leaned closer to the window. She could just see what she thought was the end of the bed of a truck. Luke's truck, and it was parked where he was working on the herb garden.

Slowly, Jocelyn stood up and looked down at herself. Miss Edi would be appalled, but she had on a new pair of jeans—Sara had sold them to her from the wholesale clothes she was buying by the truckload—and a dark pink shirt. Was her shirt too formal? Should she change? Into what? A halter top? Something with spangles and tassels?

Laughing at herself, she ran down the stairs and into the kitchen to go out the back door, but she paused, then ran to the freezer, grabbed a pack of pot roast, and tossed it into the microwave. "Might as well be prepared," she said as she went out the door.

"Hi," she said as Luke rammed the shovel into the ground and pulled up a huge hunk of dirt.

"This place is a mess," he said. "Look at the weeds growing here. They've probably established themselves until I'll have to burn them out."

"With your bad temper?" she asked without a hint of a smile.

"Flamethrower breath," he said, still frowning, then he jammed the shovel in the ground and glared at her. "Look! I'm married. I'm sorry I didn't ask if that was all right with you. For some stupid reason I thought I was your gardener, not your boyfriend. The whole town thought you were coming here to marry Ramsey. You were going to at last connect the families of McDowell and Harcourt.

"I don't know what was wrong with my not knowing that I couldn't talk to you because I was married. And if I may remind you, that's **all** I did. I apologize. I live alone. Sometimes it seems like every person who lives in this town is related to me, so what's to talk about? Our childhoods? How we used to skinny-dip in your pond?

"So put me up against a wall and shoot me, but I talked to a woman who was **not** my wife. Who, by the way, I haven't seen in so long that I hardly recognized her.

"So now everyone in town is angry at me. My father's half in love with you; my mother is so mad that she won't invite me over for dinner even once a week, so right now I'm at the mercy of Ingrid and a microwave. And the church sent the pastor over to have a talk with me about infidelity and about corrupting minors. Maybe he means Ingrid, but thanks to enough Botox to give her the plague, she only **looks** fourteen.

"So I came over here to dig. Nobody else in town will let me near their gardens, but I **need** to work with the earth. You have any problem with that?"

"You like pot roast?"

"Pot roast?" he asked dumbly.

"With carrots and Worcestershire sauce. I have your mom's recipe." She put her hand up. "If you start crying, you can't have any."

Luke pulled the shovel out of the dirt and tossed it onto the back of his truck. "Why do I feel like I'm the object of some plot?"

"Join the club," Joce said. "Your grandfather is using me to get you away from the . . . I want to quote him exactly . . . 'that grasping little gold digger he married.' Yeah, that was it."

"Shouldn't you be keeping this a secret between you and my grandfather?"

"Are secrets allowed in this town?" she asked as they neared the house. "I thought there was a law against them. Keep a secret and get put in jail. On the other hand, your cousins kept the secret of your being married so well that not even Tess knew about it. I hear she yelled at Ramsey so long and loud that they had to repaint his office."

He blinked at her. "I think you've lived in Edilean too long."

"But you came back to it from wherever you were, doing whatever you were doing . . ." She looked around to see if there was anyone near, then lowered her voice. "Up north."

"What in the world are you talking about?"

"Did you know that your right eyebrow twitches on the tip when you lie?"

"No, that's hunger."

"Whatever it is, you and everyone else have again jumped over some big secret about you. I mean, other than the fact that you're married, that is."

"About to be unmarried," he said as he opened the door and let her go in first.

"Don't tell me you at last had the courage to file for a divorce."

"Annulment. We haven't spent enough time together to call it a marriage."

"And she committed fraud," Joce said softly. "You thought you were getting one kind of woman and she turned out to be something else." Joce politely left out the truth, that she'd used her pregnancy to get him to marry her, then had an abortion.

"Yeah," Luke said, "but maybe I should have tried harder. Maybe I should have . . ."

"So she came back to see if you two could get back together?"

"More or less," he said as she handed him a beer.

"And how's that working?"

Luke gave a one-sided grin. "Not so good. How come you aren't still mad at me?"

"Your grandfather said that if I talk to you he'll let us have part two of Miss Edi's story."

"That the only reason?"

"Only one. As I'm sure you know, I'm trying to write a book about Miss Edi, but I can't find a lot of information. I need those stories."

"So it's just work, is it?"

"Just work," she said, but she was smiling.

"I guess you just want to read what must be a very romantic story."

"Of course I want to hear what Miss Edi did. I always assumed she was a virgin."

"Why'd you think that? Her David get wounded in the wrong place?"

"I couldn't exactly ask her that, now could I? Did you wash your hands?"

"No. Is that really my mother's pot roast?" he asked as he washed his hands.

"It is if she makes it by the recipe, but maybe she left a secret ingredient out of it. Maybe I should have put a few borage flowers on top."

"Getting sick of the cupcakes?"

Joce rolled her eyes. "Your dad and Tess are starting to talk about opening a store in town. Between Sara's upscale dress shop and Tess's bakery, Edilean is going to turn into SoHo."

"That is a very unfunny joke."

"Maybe the Steps and Ingrid could do some photo shoots here. They could languish in the back of your pickup wearing Armani. It would be a great setting. Why are you looking at me like that?"

"Could you stop it with Ingrid? That's over."

"No it's not. You're still married until you have the paper saying you aren't."

"Does that matter to you?" he asked.

"No, of course not," she said quickly as she used a pot holder to remove the big pouch of pot roast from the microwave and put it in a bowl.

"Have you ever kissed Ramsey?"

"I really and truly don't think that's any of your business," Joce said.

"I have a reason for asking."

"Yes, I've kissed him at least a thousand times. Truly a magnificent experience."

Luke was leaning against the sink, the beer in his hand. He set it down, then walked toward her without saying a word.

"Let me get some silverware and—"

He put his hand under her chin and tipped her face up to his, then he kissed her. It was a gentle, sweet kiss, but it made her knees start to buckle.

When he pulled back, her heart was racing, and she wanted to put her arms around his neck and continue.

"Do you understand now?" he asked as he stepped away, not touching her.

"Understand what?" she asked.

"About you and me. About why my grandfather had you to his house for lunch, why Ramsey was sent out of town, why Ingrid was brought back into my life."

"You want to stay with her?"

"I need to end it legally between her and me. She can fight her own battles with the big shot in New York."

"You know about him?"

"Did you think I thought she came back here

out of **love** for me? I married her because she was carrying my child and she—" He looked away. "I don't want to relive that. As soon as MAW can get the paperwork through, the marriage will be annulled, then I plan to do some 'ardent courting.'"

"Ardent, huh?" she asked, grinning. "And how would that start?" She stepped toward him.

"It's going to start out with no touching until I'm no longer married. And until you realize that I'm not like your father."

"What?"

"You said I was like your father."

"I know," Joce said, and she stood up straighter, no longer leaning toward him. "But—"

"No buts. We'll start over. So what devious plan did you and Gramps come up with to get me to do what he wants me to do?"

"First, you have to take golf lessons," she said as she put a huge helping of pot roast and vegetables on a plate and served it to him.

"What?" Luke asked in horror.

"Just a few. Twenty or so, then he'll give us the second part of the story."

"And what do **you** have to do?"

"Pass muster of **all** your many relatives, make the town believe I'm worthy of a house they think is theirs, live up to comparisons of Miss Edi, be—"

"Okay, I get the idea. How are you doing so far?"

"What do **you** think?"

He gave her a look of such lust that Jocelyn could feel her hair roots becoming warm.

"What's going on in here?" Tess asked from the doorway. "You two planning on giving Sara a run for her money? Watch out for carpet burns and splinters."

"Are you talking about what I think you are?" Luke asked, sounding very prudish.

"Whatever fits your imagination," Tess said as she smiled at Jocelyn.

"Do you need the kitchen?" Joce asked. Luke was halfway through the plate of food.

"No," Tess said, "I came by to deliver a gift to the two of you."

"So who knows we're in my kitchen together?" Joce asked.

"Everyone who saw Luke drive his truck down Edilean Road heading for here knows."

"Which means the entire town," Luke said, but he seemed to expect it.

"So what's the gift?" Joce asked.

"Oh, yeah." Tess stepped back into the hallway for a moment, then returned with a big picnic basket with a bow on the handle.

"Did you and Jim do that?" Joce asked, smiling.

"Why would we?" Tess asked.

"Because you two use **her** kitchen, dumping all the expenses onto Joce, but you and that tightwad father of mine keep all the profits."

"Oh, that," Tess said as she shrugged. "But, no, it's from Dr. Dave." She put her hand on the back of Luke's chair. "So how come Jim and his father-in-law can't stand each other? Jim is so sweet. I can't understand—" Pausing, she patted Luke's back. "Are you all right?"

"No one's ever called his father 'sweet' before," Jocelyn said. "Luke and his mother team up against the dear man."

Luke groaned as he kept eating. "My grandfather—"

In the next second, Luke and Jocelyn looked at each other, their eyes wide as it hit them who had sent the picnic basket. Instantly, they made a dash toward Tess. Luke got up so fast the chair fell backward and hit the floor.

Tess's eyes widened, then she started running toward the front door, afraid they were going to stampede her.

"The basket!" Jocelyn yelled. "Leave it!"

Tess bent as she kept running, put the basket on

the floor, then went out the front door, slamming it behind her.

Joce and Luke attacked the basket with both hands. Packets of cheese, a slim loaf of French bread, containers of salad, and a thermos were hurriedly put on the floor. In the bottom, wrapped protectively in a plastic bag, were the yellowed pages that Joce had seen at Dr. Dave's house.

She and Luke grabbed them at the same time, lifted them, then looked at each other.

"We have to be sane about this," Luke said.

"I agree," Joce said, nodding, but not releasing the pages.

"Food. Outside. You read. I dig."

"Perfect," she said as she kept one hand on the pages, the other putting the food back in the basket.

When everything was back in place, Luke narrowed his eyes at her. "You have to let go."

"No, **you** have to let go."

"So when will your book be finished?" Luke asked, sounding as though he were just making conversation and meant to stay there all day, never releasing his side of the manuscript.

"As soon as you let me go so we can read this!"

Luke couldn't repress his smile as he let go of his

end of the manuscript. "Okay, but you don't get out of my sight."

"I think I can handle that," she said suggestively, and Luke's smile grew broader. He took the basket in one hand, and as they went through the kitchen he got the plate of his mother's pot roast, which he hadn't finished.

Ten minutes later, they were outside and the food was spread around them. Luke sat on one side of the red and white cloth his grandfather had included in the picnic and ate while Joce reverently opened the old pages.

"Ready?" she asked Luke.

He nodded. "Stop talking and read!"

She looked down at the pages and began.

17

"SIR, I RESPECTIVELY decline this assignment," Edi said, her eyes straight ahead, her spine rigid as she stood in front of General Austin's desk.

"Harcourt," he said in a voice of patient intolerance, "this is a war and you'll do what you're told to do—as we all have to. If I send two soldiers to Dr. Jellicoe's house, people will see them and suspect him. His cover will be blown. Therefore, I want you, a woman, to go with my driver and deliver this magazine to Dr. Jellie. Do I make myself clear?"

"Perfectly clear," Edi said. "But I disagree with

your decision about who to send. One of the other women, Delores perhaps, would be better at this job than I would be."

"Delores is an idiot. A flat tire would send her into hysterics. I need someone who can be cool under stress."

"Perhaps you could mail the magazine to him."

General Austin leaned back in his chair, his hands together. "Exactly what is it that you object to about this particular assignment? Are you afraid? Are you too cowardly to do something that our American boys do every day?"

Edi didn't answer him. She'd proven her lack of fear at every bombing raid. She was always the last one to go to the shelter, as she made sure that all the other women in the office were safe.

"What is it?" General Austin barked.

"Perhaps, sir, you could send me with another driver, or I could go by myself. You know that I often travel about the English countryside alone."

"A different driver? Are you saying that your objection to going on this mission is that you don't **like** Sergeant Clare?"

Again, Edi said nothing.

General Austin got up from his desk, went to the window, then turned back and looked at her as though he couldn't believe what she'd just said.

"**Like,** Harcourt? All those men out there who run into enemy fire shouting 'Better than Austin,' do you think they **like** me? Hell! My own wife doesn't **like** me. I don't think like and dislike have a place in a war." By the time he finished, his voice was so loud it was a wonder the glass didn't break.

"No, sir," Edi said.

"All right, Harcourt, I want you to pack an overnight bag and take something pretty. You're a girl going off into the country with her soldier boyfriend, and you're going to stop to see an old friend of a friend, Dr. Sebastian Jellicoe, and you're going to give him a magazine. That won't be the story that's given out around here, but that's what you're going to do. Do you have any questions? Anything you don't **like** about this assignment?"

Edi kept her rigid stance, but she wasn't going to be intimidated by him. "Yes, sir, I do have a question. What is this **really** about?"

General Austin took a moment to answer. "In normal circumstances I'd not tell you, but Dr. Jellie is a retired professor—Oxford, I think—and he knows more about words than anyone else on this planet. We send him top secret documents that need to be decoded. The problem now is that we think he may have been found out. He's good at playing the absentminded old man who's too senile to even know a war's going on, but someone has found out his lie, and we fear for his life. The magazine carries a coded message, so he'll know it's from me, and it tells him to leave with you and Clare. And as soon as you two get him back here, Jellie will be sent to the U.S.

"Does that answer your question? Do you think Delores could handle this?"

"Yes, sir, and Delores would be useless."

"All right, now go. Clare will pick you up at 0900 tomorrow morning. Be here at 0700 and I'll brief you more."

Fifteen minutes later, Edi was in her tiny apartment and packing. Tomorrow she planned to wear a suit so severely cut it made her uniform look casual. The other women talked endlessly about getting out of the stiff uniforms and into pretty dresses, but Edi thought that the men didn't need any more encouragement, so she stayed covered up.

She had other clothes, some pretty civilian dresses, but she wouldn't put them on until they—she and the odious Sergeant Clare—were out of sight of the soldiers.

After she put the dresses and her underwear in a small case she was ready to go. If she overlooked the fact that she was going to be with the detestable David Clare for this assignment, Edi would have admitted that she was . . . well, excited about it. Getting out of that smoky office, away from the general's never-ending bad temper . . . To go into the country! To see trees! She almost looked forward to it.

On her rare days off, she wasn't like the other girls, running to the nearest place where they sold drinks and played loud music. No, Edi hopped a ride with anyone she could and went into the English countryside and spent the day. Or if she was lucky enough to get away from the general, she'd stay for days. She walked, she sat under trees, and she watched the cows graze. To Edi's mind, she wanted to be reminded why a war was being fought, to see what they were trying to preserve.

Sometimes she'd spend the night at a farmhouse. She'd soon learned to lie and say she was a war widow and that her husband had been English. People were suspicious of a tall, pretty American woman roaming about alone, but a widow who wanted to see the country of her dead husband opened doors and made friends. When Edi returned to General Austin's office after a weekend away, she'd have a list of names people had given her. They wanted to know the whereabouts of their sons and daughters. Illegally, but without guilt, Edi used General Austin's contacts and his credentials to find out about the names on her list. Within an hour of her first misuse of her closeness to him, General Austin knew what she was doing. Nothing ever escaped his attention. But he just grunted— his own personal way of approving—then piled even more work on her. But it was a small price to pay for being able to help the people who'd been so kind to her. Twice, when she couldn't find the sons of people she'd met, she handed the names to the general. Both times he found the answer. One young man had been killed in Italy, but the other was wounded and in a French hospital.

After she was packed, Edi boiled herself an egg and heated some toast on the little electric hot plate in her room and tried to read the documents she'd brought from the office. But her mind kept going back to the assignment. If General Austin wanted a man with her then there was a lot more danger to the job than he was telling her.

❧

"So what did you do to PO Austin so much that he made you wear this thing?" the medic asked David Clare as he tightened the inset screws on the long leg brace.

David was sitting on top of a surgical table, wearing only his shirt and his underwear, and the medic was fastening a hideous-looking steel cage onto his left leg. "You didn't hear that I'm going with Harcourt?"

The medic paused, and for a moment his mouth was open in awe, but then he closed it. "It won't work. You'll never get her. Especially not with this thing on."

Looking at the steel strips wrapped around his leg, David grimaced. He'd been told Austin was a bastard, but he hadn't realized how much until early this morning. Last night a lieutenant told him he was to drive Edilean Harcourt into the English countryside to visit the wife of a friend of the general. Her husband had just been killed, and the general wanted to offer his personal condolences to the widow—"personal" meaning that he was sending his secretary.

"Oh, wait," the lieutenant said. "I was told to give you this." He held out a white envelope, the kind that held an invitation.

"What is it?" David asked.

"I'm not sure, but I think it's an invitation to the officers' ball next month. You come back alive and you get to go. Last year Miss Harcourt wore a dress in an electric blue that . . ." The man shook his head to clear it. "If I were you, I'd hold on to that. You can't get in without it."

"I'll treasure it," David said as he slipped it inside his shirt.

David and Edi were to spend the night, then return the next day. David only hoped Heaven would be as good as his vision of those two delicious days.

But this morning a smart-ass lieutenant had told him he was to report to a Captain Gilman, a doctor, on the double. Of course by that time everyone in London and probably half of France knew Sergeant Clare was going to be alone with Miss Harcourt for two whole days.

David should have known there'd be a catch. The doctor told him the general said that an able-bodied soldier traveling around the country would engender too many questions. Why wasn't he fighting?

"I could be on leave," David said. "Did he think of **that**?"

The doctor looked at him incredulously. "Are you asking **me** to explain the inner workings of Bulldog Austin's mind?" He went on to say that General Austin thought it would be better if Sergeant Clare were seen as unfit to fight, therefore he was to be fitted with a steel leg brace that went from his upper thigh down to his ankle. At the knee was a four-inch round hinge that could be loosened or tightened with the use of an Allen wrench with an odd screw pattern.

Ten minutes later, David was on the table, and a medic was clamping the torturous brace onto his leg.

"Don't lose this," the medic said, holding up the little L-shaped tool. "Lose this and the only way that thing comes off is with a hacksaw."

There was some padding between his skin and the steel of the brace, but the fabric was worn and frayed, the cotton batting sticking out in places. "You couldn't find a worse one than this?" David asked. "Maybe something a little older, a little more beat up?"

"Naw," the medic said, grinning, "that's the worst one we had. It was left over from the last war."

"Would that be the Civil War or the French and Indian?"

"War of the Roses," said an English soldier passing through. "That thing was probably handmade over a forge. I bet there's chain mail under there."

"I'll donate it to one of your museums," David called out after the man. "One of them we've saved for you guys."

The Englishman's laugher floated back to him.

"All right," the medic said, "let's see how well you can walk in it."

David turned on the table and gingerly put one foot on the floor, then the other. As he took a couple of steps in the brace, it was worse than he thought. It was heavy, confining, and the hinge moved only half as much as his knee did. "What the hell—!" David said as he lifted his leg. He could bend his knee only a few inches.

"Sorry about that," the medic said, but he was smiling. No soldier felt sorry for the man who was going to get to spend two days with Miss Harcourt. The medic inserted the Allen key into three inset screws on the hinge and rotated them about a quarter of an inch. The hinge loosened and David could bend his knee.

"I hate this thing," David said as he tried walking in it.

"Be glad you don't need it for real," said a voice behind him.

"Lord deliver me from do-gooders. **You** want to put this damned thing on—Oh! Sorry, Reverend," David said. "I didn't mean—" He didn't know what to say.

The reverend was smiling. "I've been called worse than a 'do-gooder.' I believe there's a car waiting for you outside and a young lady you're to pick up."

"Yeah," David muttered, wanting to curse the

brace and especially General Austin for making him wear the damned thing. One of the men said it was a chastity belt, that David had to wear it to make sure he didn't touch the general's precious secretary.

They'd all waited for David to make a smart reply to that, something about his leg not being the part he planned to use, but David said nothing. He didn't want anything bad he said to get back to Miss Harcourt.

It was impossible to wrestle himself into the trousers of his uniform, so the medic got him a pair that were two sizes larger. To hold them up, his belt made deep wrinkles in the waistband. So much for looking good to impress the most beautiful woman in the world, he thought.

David was further dismayed when he saw the car the general had sent for their use. It was an old Chrysler, and by the sound of the engine, worn out. He wondered if it was made the same year as the leg brace.

It took several tries to get the car started, and he wished he had half a day to work on the engine, but he didn't. When he got it started, he found that even the steering was off. To make matters worse, the car was English right-hand drive, so that everything was on the opposite side of what he was used to. All in all, the car was a danger to drive.

She was waiting for him, standing on the curb, and he could feel the eyes of the men around them on him.

If possible, Miss Harcourt looked even more rigid than she usually did. Her dark hair was pulled back so tight it looked as though it were painted on, and her wool suit was stiff enough to have been carved out of wood. At her feet was a small brown suitcase, and from her shoulder hung her handbag and a black leather case that she was clasping as though it were a safe full of jewels.

"Beautiful day, isn't it, Miss Harcourt?" he said as he opened the front passenger door for her.

When she opened the back door and got in, David heard the laughter of what sounded like a hundred men, but he didn't look up.

It was hard to drive with the long brace on his leg. Pushing a clutch in as he shifted gears caused him pain at every move. Already, the padding had slipped to one side, and he could feel the steel rubbing his skin raw. If he had any sense, he'd pull the car to the side of the road and adjust the padding. But he glanced at Miss Harcourt in the rearview mirror, saw that her beautiful face was set, as though she knew he was about to do something awful, so he grit his teeth and tried to ignore the pain.

"I was told you know the way," he said, glancing at her in the mirror.

She gave a brief nod, but that was her only acknowledgment that she heard him.

"Do you think you could share those directions with me?"

"When necessary, I will."

In the back of the car, Edi sat straight up. Just this morning she'd again suggested to General Austin that she go alone to Dr. Jellicoe's house. She said she could do her usual pretend of being a war widow and she could make her way around the country by herself. But the general's answer had been a single word: "No." He hadn't shouted or explained, but there was something in the way he spoke that made her know for sure that there was more to the assignment than he was telling her. Again, she knew that if he wanted a man with her, then that meant there was danger involved. The general had casually told her, as though it didn't matter, that under the backseat of the old car were half a dozen M1 rifles and enough ammo to hold off most of a battalion.

After that, General Austin handed her **the** magazine. It was a **Time** magazine, May 15, 1944, with Dr. Alexander Fleming's portrait on the cover. It was a few weeks old but she hadn't seen the issue.

"Get it to Jellie," General Austin said, then handed her a packet of English money and a map. If she was going to find Dr. Jellicoe, a map was essential. The English roads had been laid out in medieval times by wagons and animals. If a tree was in the path, or a hill, or someone's house, the wagon went around it. Property lines were based on waterways or rock outcroppings or whatever a person could use for identification.

In modern times, those roads were still used, and they rambled about as they twisted and turned around landmarks that had long ago disappeared. In peacetime, there were signs posted everywhere. If a person came to a meeting of eight roads, the signs were the only way to know what led where. But in wartime, as a precautionary measure, most of the signs around England had been removed. Without a map or a knowledgeable guide, no one could find anything.

Edi tried to study the map—and to keep her mind off Clare's driving. However, today he seemed to be more cautious. He wasn't speeding, wasn't darting in and out of traffic, and, best of all, he wasn't smart-mouthing about everything.

She spent an hour on the map and twice sketched it from memory. If it were lost, she didn't want to not know where to go.

As for the magazine, she was almost afraid to open it. Treating it with the reverence she'd have used if she were holding a Gutenberg Bible, she went through it page by page, reading that Dr. Fleming's penicillin was going to be made available to the public, and that an American, Kathleen Kennedy, had married a man who was going to become the duke of Devonshire.

What she was most interested in seeing was some mark made in the magazine, something in the text or in the margins, but as far as she would see, there was nothing.

"Interesting magazine?" he asked, looking at her in the rearview mirror, but Edi was silent.

"It's going to be a long ride if nobody talks," Sergeant Clare said from the front seat.

"I see no reason for idle conversation," Edi said. She could see the side of his face, and he was frowning. Let him, she thought. Let him frown all he wants. She just needed to get the magazine to Dr. Jellicoe, then on the ride back, the doctor would be with them. That would put a further barrier between her and the obnoxious David Clare.

They rode in silence, and at about 1 P.M. it began to sprinkle rain. Sergeant Clare pulled the car off the road and started down a gravel lane.

"What are you doing?" Edi asked, alarmed. Was something wrong?

He stopped the car in front of a little cottage that had a sign that said HOME COOKED LUNCHES AND TEAS. David put his arm across the back of the seat and turned to look at her. "Miss Harcourt, you may be so disciplined that you've trained yourself not to eat, but I'm human and I need food."

"Yes, of course," she said, but she didn't meet his eyes. By her reckoning, they should reach Dr. Jellicoe's by eight tonight. General Austin said the doctor didn't know they were coming. "If he knows, he'll hide," the general said. "The element of surprise is important." Even though she asked, he didn't tell Edi how she was going to persuade Dr. Jellicoe to leave with her and Sergeant Clare— but then, wasn't the magazine supposed to do that?

As they got out of the car, Edi could see that something was wrong with Sergeant Clare, but she wasn't about to ask him why he was limping and seemed to be in pain. If he'd been injured in an action, she would have known about it through the general's office, so if he was hurt, it was because he'd tripped over something, or, more likely, banged a vehicle into something.

She held on to her satchel and handbag as they entered the restaurant, which was actually the living room of a rose-covered cottage that was being used as a tearoom.

"Oh, dearie," said a plump, pleasant-looking woman as soon as she saw Sergeant Clare limping. "You've been wounded. You just sit down here and let me get whatever you need. Here's a menu, and I'm Mrs. Pettigrew, and you two just take your time with whatever you want." She left the room, leaving Edi and David sitting at one of the four tables. They were the only customers.

Edi had a moment of feeling guilty. Perhaps the reason General Austin had sent Sergeant Clare with her was because the young man had been injured.

"You were wounded?" she asked from behind her menu.

"Yeah, by your damned general!" David muttered. "Think the potatoes are any good here?"

Since the menu was mostly dishes made with potatoes, Edi didn't bother answering him. She looked for the woman to take their orders but she was nowhere to be seen. "I think I'll . . ." Edi broke off, not wanting to say that she was going to the restroom.

"Go on, I'll order for you," he said in a way that

was nearly a growl. "Unless you want something other than potatoes."

Edi had been around General Austin enough to know when a man was looking for a rousing good argument, and if Sergeant Clare didn't stop speaking to her in that tone, she was going to give it to him. It was enough that she was in charge of seeing that they got to their destination and that the magazine was delivered; she didn't need to put up with a surly man. From her observation, if Sergeant Clare wasn't dangerously cocky, he was angry. When she got back to General Austin, she planned to tell him in detail what she thought of this man he'd sent with her.

Edi got up from her chair, picked up her handbag, and started to reach for her satchel, but thought that carrying it to the restroom would draw too much attention to it. She didn't think that Sergeant Clare had been told anything and she wanted it to stay that way.

She took a while in the restroom. It was a home bathroom, with rose-printed curtains and pretty little soaps in a glass jar. This room, so very lovely, was why she got away from London and the soldiers and everything that reminded her of war as often as she could. She took her time washing her face, applying fresh lipstick, then taking her hair down, recombing it, and pulling it back again.

When she got back to the table, the food was there, and it was delicious. There were huge, fluffy potatoes slathered in homemade butter, some beef that had been cooked for hours so it was tender, and some green beans that had probably been taken from the garden that morning.

Neither she nor the sergeant spoke much, just a couple of comments on the rain, which seemed to be about to stop.

After lunch, as Sergeant Clare limped back to the car and again held open the front passenger door for her, he said, "It would be nice if you sat in front so you could give me directions." Again she ignored him as she opened the back door and got in. "One thing I can say about you is that you don't give in easily, do you?" he said as he got into the car, again struggling with his left leg, which seemed to be stiff.

"Would you please get back on the road? We need to make a turn in about three miles."

"Are you ready to tell me where we're going and what we're doing?"

"General Austin wants me to offer my condolences to the widow of a friend of his."

"Yeah, I heard all that," he said. Just then, the

sky seemed to open up and the rain started coming down hard. David turned on the windshield wipers, but they didn't work very well. The rain was so loud that he had to shout to be heard. "Do you know this road where we're supposed to turn?"

She started to say that she didn't, but she wouldn't give him the satisfaction. "I have a map and it—"

"So you know nothing," he said loudly as he used his shirtsleeve to wipe the fog off the inside of the window. "Maybe we should pull over and wait this out. This car isn't the best for these roads."

"No," Edi said from the backseat. "We need to get to—" She almost said "Dr. Jellicoe's" but caught herself. The car lurched as it hit a pothole, then slipped a few feet.

"I really think we should pull over," David said. "I can't see where I'm going."

"Then we'll walk if we have to," Edi snapped. What was wrong with the man if he let a little rain bother him? She picked up her leather satchel off the seat and opened it to reassure herself about the magazine. If anything happened, she didn't want it to get wet. Whatever was inside it had to be preserved at all costs.

But when she opened the case, there was nothing in it but her notebook, two pencils, a pen, and the folded map. In disbelief, she pulled everything out onto her lap. There was no magazine. She put the contents back, then started searching the seat. Did the magazine fall out? She got down on her hands and knees and looked under the front seat, on the floor, in the rack in the back.

"What the hell are you doing?" Sergeant Clare yelled over the sound of the rain.

She leaned forward, her mouth close to his ear. "Where is the magazine?"

"What magazine?"

"The **Time** magazine!" she shouted at him. "Where is it?"

"What's wrong with you?" he yelled back, his hand over his ear. "I don't know what happened to your magazine. You took so long in the bathroom I got bored, so I started reading it. Maybe I left it on the chair, I don't know. I'll buy you a new one."

In all her life, Edi had never panicked, but now she did. "We have to go back!" she screamed. "Now! This minute. Turn this car around and go back. We have to get that magazine!"

"Calm down—" David began, but then he saw her face and muttered an obscenity under his breath. "Why the hell didn't you tell me it was important?"

"It's not your job to know anything!" she screamed at him. If he weren't driving the car, she would have put her hands around his neck and squeezed. "I knew you were incompetent. I begged the general to give me someone else, but, no, he had to send me with **you.** So help me, when we get out of this—if we do—I'm going to recommend that you be court-martialed."

"You want to sit back and hold on?" David said in a voice that let her know he was as angry as she was. In the next minute he slammed the car around in a circle that sent them skidding on the muddy, slick road. The old car almost conked out, but it gave a couple of coughs, then kept moving. David gunned it and it slid from one side of the road to the next, but he kept it under control and finally straightened it out.

In the back, Edi was slammed against one side of the car, then the other. She tried to grab on to the armrests, but when she'd get near one, the car would turn the other way and she'd miss it. Her head hit the door twice, and half the bobby pins in her hair came out then flew about the car, one of them just missing her eye.

In a tidal wave of gravel, David stopped the car in front of the little cottage where they'd eaten lunch. "Wait here and I'll—"

"Go to hell!" she said as she got out of the car into the driving rain.

There was a CLOSED sign on the window and the door was locked, but Edi started pounding and yelling over the rain. David started to say something to her, but then hobbled toward the back of the house to find another door. He was back minutes later.

"Anything?" she shouted, the rain running down her face; her clothes were drenched, her hair straggling about her face.

"Nothing. The place is locked up."

"There has to be something we can do," Edi said. "Break the window."

"What?"

"Break it down. Get inside. Look for the bloody magazine!"

"If this is supposed to be a secret," he shouted, "that will expose it."

"Do you have a better idea?" she yelled back.

"Yeah, we could—"

David didn't say anything more because the front door opened, and Mrs. Pettigrew peeped out.

"Come in," she said. "You're soaking."

Edi practically pushed David aside as she went into the restaurant. "Did you see a magazine?" she blurted out.

"Oh, yes, the **Time.** We don't see them much around here. It was nice to see about the Cavendishes and the—"

"Where is it?" Edi asked, her question a demand.

David stepped in front of her. "What she means is that she promised the magazine to her uncle and it was my fault it was left behind. Do you have it?"

"Sorry, but I don't," Mrs. Pettigrew said, smiling. "But I have some very nice issues of **Country Life.** Maybe your uncle would like a couple of those."

"No," David said before Edi could speak. "That magazine has an article in it about her cousin and she needs **that** issue."

"Oh, well, then, I think that Mr. Farquar has some old **Time** magazines. Maybe he has that issue."

"We want **that** magazine," Edi said, her teeth clenched. "What happened to it?"

"Aggie took it."

"Aggie took it," Edi said in barely a whisper.

"Aggie Trumbull. She works for me two days a week. I can't afford to pay her much, but I let her keep bits and pieces that the guests leave behind." She looked at Edi in reproach. "Like old magazines. Usually, people don't mind."

David put his arm out, as though to keep Edi from attacking the woman. "So where can we find this Aggie?"

"She goes home where she lives with her grandfather. If you come back in three days, she'll be here and we can ask her about the magazine. I'm sure she took it for her old grandfather. He loves to read."

"Three days," Edi said. "Three days?"

"Maybe we could go to her grandfather and get the magazine ourselves," David said. "Could you tell us where he lives?"

"Three villages over," Mrs. Pettigrew said, "but in this rain you'll never make it in a car. The bridge goes out at half this much rain, and at this time of year the river will be flooded. No, you'd better stay here for a couple of nights and wait. I could put you up. Do you want one room or two?"

Again, David stepped between Edi and the woman. "No, we won't be needing any rooms, but maybe you could draw us a map of the way to Aggie's grandfather's house. And if it wouldn't be too much trouble maybe you could pack some lunches for us."

"It's past time for lunch," she said, looking as though she wasn't going to move.

"Tea, supper, and something for breakfast," Edi

said coldly. "We'll buy all the food you have. Now will you draw us a map?"

"I'd be happy to," Mrs. Pettigrew said. "And it'll just take me a minute or two to fix you a few boxed meals." She left the room.

Edi gave David a look like she wanted to murder him.

"Don't look at me like that. This is your fault for not telling me what was going on," he said under his breath so he wouldn't be heard. "If you'd told me that that blasted magazine held some kind of secret, I would have—"

"What, Sergeant Clare? Not gone snooping in my bag and stolen it, then left my private property on a chair so someone else could steal it? If the safety of our countries depended on **you** we'd have lost this war years ago."

"If you weren't such an uptight snob who thought she knew everything and no one else in the world had a brain, we wouldn't be here now."

"Snob? You call taking care of Top Secret information snobbery? Is that what you're labeling it?"

"Top Secret? Since when does a secretary have Top Secret security clearance?"

"When it is necessary."

"To console some widow? There are thousands of widows right now and they—" Halting, he looked at her. "There is no widow, is there? This is something altogether different, and neither you nor that loudmouthed general you kiss up to told **me** anything. Damn you!" he said. "You're talking something dangerous, aren't you?"

"It's none of your business what's going on. You're just the driver."

"And you're just the secretary!" he said, his face nearly touching hers.

"Oh, dear," came the woman's voice from the doorway. "I'm afraid I've caused a bit of a tiff between you two. That'll be ten pounds six," she said.

"Ten pounds?" Edi said, aghast. It was an enormous amount of money. "I don't think—"

"I think that's fine," David said, getting out his wallet. "Could I have the map now?"

"Of course, dear," she said, not looking at Edi. She handed him a folded piece of paper, and he took it without looking at it.

"I'd help you out with the boxes but it's a bit damp out there, so . . ." She trailed off, then left the room.

On one of the tables were six large white boxes, each tied with string for handles. "I think she did this on purpose," Edi said, "and I think she had these ready and waiting for dumb Americans to come back and pay a king's ransom for them. Give me the map."

"Not in this lifetime," David said as he picked up four of the boxes. He reached for the other two, but Edi took them.

"I want the map now."

"No," he said as he opened the front door and ran out. He tossed the boxes in the backseat of the car, then held open the front passenger door for Edi. It was raining so hard she could barely see the car and she didn't want to take the time to fight with him. Besides, she wanted that map.

She got into the passenger seat, put the boxes in the back, then waited for him to get in the car. He put his stiff left leg in, then had to twist his whole body to get his other leg in.

She pulled a handkerchief from her handbag and wiped her face. "What happened to your leg? Did you shoot yourself?"

"You know, if you weren't a girl, I'd—"

"You'd what?" she asked, her eyes narrowed at him.

"Don't use that tone with me and don't tempt me." He slammed the door, then spent the next ten minutes trying to get the old car to start.

"I thought you could fix any mechanical engine."

"I was given this piece of junk this morning. I didn't even get to see the motor." When it started, he gave a sigh of relief and turned out of the parking lot.

"So let me see the map," Edi said, and David reached inside his shirt and pulled it out. It was damp, but the ink hadn't run.

"Ten pounds for this," she said in disgust. "It says you go to the church, turn right, then keep going until you reach Hamish Trumbulls's farm. That seems easy enough that even you can do it."

David gave her a look that told her she was treading on thin ice with him and she'd better watch out.

18

"WELL," JOCELYN SAID when she'd finished reading. Between them, she and Luke had eaten nearly everything in the basket, plus Luke had eaten a large serving of pot roast. "Not a great way for love to start, is it?"

"Sounds all right to me," Luke said. He was stretched out on the cloth, his hands behind his head. "What else do you want?"

"I don't know, a meeting of the minds. I guess I thought that Miss Edi and her David looked across a room, their eyes met, and they were in love. Instant and without any doubt to it. I thought that they'd go out to dinner and talk, and find out that they were exactly alike in everything. But this man . . ."

"This man, what?"

"He doesn't sound like her . . . I don't know how to say it without sounding like a snob. He doesn't seem like her type. She's educated, from a long lineage of, well, society, but this man is . . ."

"What? Like the gardener and the lady of the manor?"

"Are you going to start on me again?"

"I'd like to," he said softly as he gave her a look up and down.

She couldn't help herself as she moved toward him, but he rolled away and got to his feet.

"There's something bothering me about this story," Luke said as he picked up his shovel again.

"Like what?"

"I don't know, but something about all of it is puzzling me. Uncle Alex and Miss Edi, you meeting Miss Edi, everything. Something about it keeps going 'round and 'round in my head, and it always seems like we're missing something."

"I don't see any mystery," Joce said. "My grandparents and Alexander McDowell were friends, that's why he bought that house in Boca and that's why Miss Edi moved there.

"I guess," Luke said, "but there's something odd about it all. Alex McDowell didn't make friends. He was grumpy and he liked to work. And you know what Edilean is like. Everybody knows every-thing. The last time I had to play golf with my grandfather I asked him when and where Uncle Alex had made friends with your grandparents, and Gramps said that to his knowledge Alex rarely left town."

"What about World War II?" Joce asked. "My grandfather manufactured helmets and he traveled to Europe several times. Maybe they met then."

"Uncle Alex didn't go to the war. He had some disability that kept him out of it, so he stayed in the U.S. and moved money around."

"He was a banker?" Joce said, but Luke didn't answer her. He was concentrating on his digging. She began to clean up the picnic, and she put the precious story on top of the basket. "I'm going to type this."

"Computer got a battery?" Luke asked.

"Sure, it—" She smiled. "Okay, I'll bring it out here." As she stood up, she noticed that there were some plants in a cardboard box in the back of Luke's truck. "What are those?"

"Some things I dug up here and there. There used to be a lot of cultivated gardens around here, and some of the plants have survived."

To her, all of them looked like weeds. "So if you're just walking around and you see a plant, you know what it is and how to dig it up so you don't kill it?"

"Yeah," he said, seeming to be amused by her question.

"I'll be back in a few minutes," she said, smiling, but he seemed to be so preoccupied that he didn't notice.

The minute Jocelyn got to the house and closed the door behind her, Luke opened his cell phone and called his grandfather.

"Hey! Luke!" Dr. Dave said, "I just made a hole in one."

"Congratulations," Luke said quickly. "Mind if I come over tonight? I want to talk to you about something."

"About my lie to Jocelyn about part two having the car wreck in it?"

"No," Luke said slowly, "she didn't mention that particular lie to me. This is about something else. Who knows the most about what Uncle Alex was up to?"

"I'd say his wife."

"Someone who is alive."

"I guess that would be me."

"Did Uncle Alex leave any diaries?"

"Diaries are made of paper, and paper costs money," Dr. Dave said. "Why don't you come over now and we can play a few rounds together and talk?"

"As much as I'd like to do that, Joce is bringing her computer outside and she's going to type the story while I work."

"Good. I like that."

"Me too," Luke said. "Listen, I have to go. She's coming."

"So whatever you want to talk to me about tonight is to be kept secret from her?"

"Add it to the secrets you told her about me and you should have a full load."

Dr. Dave was laughing as Luke hung up the phone.

"You're frowning," Joce said, "so whoever you were talking to wasn't a friend?"

"Just my grandfather. He and I argue all the time."

"Your grandfather who no one got along with was your best buddy, but Dr. Dave, who is beloved by everyone, drives you crazy."

"You got it."

"So," she said, "do you think that's you or them?"

"Them."

"Now why did I know that answer before I asked?" she said as she sat down on the ground and opened her laptop.

"So how fast do you type?"

"Very fast, then I spend two hours with the speller as I correct every word because they all have typos. What about you? Can you type?"

He gave her one of his looks that said he found her amusing, then looked back at the dirt.

"So what did you talk to your grandfather about?"

"Nothing important. He wants me to go to their house for dinner tonight."

"That sounds nice," Joce said, then stared at him hard, but he bent his head over the shovel and didn't look at her. "I haven't met your grandmother."

"Haven't you?" He went to the truck and got out a digging fork.

"Is she nice?"

"Very nice."

"I guess she's a lot different from Miss Edi, isn't she?"

"From what I saw, she is, but then I only met Miss Edi once."

"Really?" Jocelyn said. "I would have thought that you'd have met her more often than that. Since your grandfather chose another woman over her, I would have thought you would have been very curious about Miss Edi. If it had been me I would have wanted to see—"

Luke stopped digging. "I can't ask you to go with me," he said in exasperation. "I have some . . . business to talk to my grandfather about and I can't take you."

"I understand," Jocelyn said, "and I certainly wasn't hinting that you should take me. I would never in my life think of inviting myself to someone else's house. I was merely asking about your grandparents. It's just that I know your father so well and have spent time with your mother, and she's been so very nice to me, and your grandfather has been wonderful. Did I tell you that he went to The Trellis and got a chocolate cake for our lunch? He—"

"Seven!" Luke half yelled. "I'll pick you up at seven. Now will you type and quit nagging me?"

"Gladly," Jocelyn said as she put her head down so he wouldn't see her smile. She had really and truly missed him!

❧

"What do you think the men are up to?" Mary Alice asked Jocelyn when, after dessert, Luke and his grandfather disappeared into Dr. Dave's study and were still in there.

Since she and Luke had arrived, she'd been fascinated with this woman who had married the man Miss Edi had once been engaged to. To Jocelyn's mind, no one was as great as Miss Edi, but Joce could see the attraction between Dr. Dave and Mary Alice. She was sweet and loving, and it seemed that all she wanted to do in the world was please her husband and grandson. All during dinner, she'd jumped up and down, going to the kitchen often to make sure that everyone had the best she had to offer.

Physically, she was as different as she could be from Miss Edi. Mary Alice was short, plump, and homey. Miss Edi had been tall, thin, and elegant. Miss Edi looked at home in pearls; Mary Alice would look comfortable in a reindeer sweater.

"I have no idea," Jocelyn said. "Luke was strange from—" She broke off from saying that Luke had been acting oddly since she'd read him part two of Miss Edi's story. It was Joce's experience that nothing in Edilean faded with age. The people's faces and bodies might age, but the stories, the secrets, seemed as fresh today as they did fifty years ago. With this in mind, she thought it was better not to mention Miss Edi.

Instead, she started talking about Luke's gardening, but when Mary Alice kept darting her eyes away, Jocelyn gave up on that subject as well. Was there some Edilean secret about his **gardening**? she wondered.

Later, when they were in Luke's truck and driving home, Joce asked him what he and his grandfather had talked about for so long.

"Sorry about leaving you alone, but we had things we needed to talk about."

"That's what I just said. I want to know **what** you were talking about."

"Plants," Luke said quickly. "He wants to put in a garden and he wants me to do it."

"Sure," she said slowly. "That's why it was all done in secrecy, because I know nothing about plants so you have to hide it all from me."

"We didn't want to bore you. How'd you get on with my grandmother?"

"We had absolutely nothing to say to one another and your eyebrow is twitching."

Luke put his hand up to his eyebrow, then down again. "All right," he said with a sigh, "I wanted to talk to Gramps about my doubts about this whole thing. For reasons that you can imagine, I don't talk to him about Miss Edi in front of Nana. And before you tell me that I could talk to him during the day, might I remind you that I've been working and I don't want to have to spend my days hauling a golf bag around?"

Jocelyn noticed that the tip of his eyebrow was

still twitching. If he was telling the truth, he certainly wasn't telling all of it.

❧

Luke and Jocelyn were on a trail into the nature preserve that surrounded Edilean. He was leading; she was following. They both wore day packs that Luke had carefully filled with supplies they would need in case of an emergency, which included a rainstorm.

It had been two days since they'd been to his grandparents' house, and they had spent most of each day together. The first day had been for Joce, as she went over everything she'd done with the biography and told Luke how disappointed she was over the boring letters of Dr. Brenner. "I can't get much out of them. Even on the days when I know that they were shot at, he wrote nothing but a record of how far they traveled that day. He didn't mention any danger."

"Then how do you know they were being shot at?"

"History and what Miss Edi told me," Joce said. "And checking dates with the name of the country at that time."

"You need to dig deeper," Luke said. "Someone somewhere knows about this. Have you checked the names of the other people mentioned in the letters?"

Joce had pulled a piece of paper from the pile on her desk and showed him the names mentioned in Dr. Brenner's journals.

"Did they have a guide?"

"I don't know," Joce said, her eyes opening wider. "You know, I think Miss Edi once mentioned a guide. Charles something."

"There you go," Luke said. "Find him. Or find his relatives. There are people who know about them."

The next day, she'd spent with him on the herb garden. They had at last gone to the nursery to get the plants, and Luke said he was sending the bill to Ramsey. "Don't worry, he's going to deduct every penny off his taxes because it's an historical garden."

"How is he?" Jocelyn asked.

"You mean the IRS or his accountant?"

"My husband-to-be, since you're taken."

"Not for long," Luke said, smiling at her.

She wanted to ask him about Ingrid and the annulment and about a lot of personal things, but she didn't. Instead, she just smiled back and said, "This is pretty. Let's get some of these."

"Modern hybrids. What we want is over there."

The plants that Luke liked looked as much like weeds as they did flowers. "Smell this," he said, holding some gray-green, fuzzy-looking plant in front of her nose.

"Heavenly."

"Your modern hybrids don't keep the smell. They're for looks alone, and you can eat few of them."

"Not roses. You can smell them and eat them." She was proud of herself for knowing that.

"That reminds me. We need to get some species roses."

She didn't know what that meant, but she was learning that if it was a plant that Luke liked, it was sure to have more leaves than flowers. "Species roses."

"Yeah. They have great hips in the fall, and you can make jelly from them."

"Oh, goody," Joce muttered as she followed him. "I get to make jelly. I can hardly wait."

Today, they were in the preserve, walking along trails that Luke seemed to know well. She'd wanted to get a map of the hiking trails, but he'd told her that he'd been on the trails so often that he could draw a map for her. He was taking her to a place he loved, and there they were going to picnic and read part three of Miss Edi's story.

All during the last days, Luke had been on his cell phone often, and he rarely told her who he was talking to. After their evening at his grandparents' house, Luke seemed to have made some resolve that he wasn't going to tell Joce anything more, no matter what she did to get information out of him.

But she could see that something was bothering him and she wanted to know what it was.

"I don't know what I want to know, exactly, except that all of this has my radar up," he said. "Something about it doesn't ring true, that's all."

"I don't get what you mean. Miss Edi fell in love with a man who was killed in World War II. What's so strange about that?"

"That's not the strange part," Luke said. "It's what happened so many years later. Alex McDowell said he owed Miss Edi for something and wanted to pay her back."

"Owed her for what?" Joce asked.

"It's no use trying to get **that** secret out of me because I don't know it, and no one will tell it to me. Last night I again tried to get Gramps to tell me but he wouldn't. He said that all I needed to know was that Alex felt that he owed Miss Edi."

"So when she retired and had nothing but a small pension to live on, he gave her a house in a warm climate and a job that she was good at. It sounds like he was an honorable man. He repaid the debt."

"But why Boca?" Luke asked. "Why not Miami? Or Sarasota? Or somewhere in Arizona?"

"Why not Weeki Wachee and she could go see the mermaids every day? Why **not** Boca Raton? It's a wonderful place. And Alex had friends there."

"Yes, your grandparents. I called Ramsey and he said he'd never heard his grandfather mention anyone named Scovill, but then he never heard him mention Miss Edi, so he was no help."

"Did he ask about me?"

Luke gave a little half grin. "I believe he did. And he mentioned my grandfather too, then he said he was coming after both of us with weapons if we—Well, I can't repeat what he said in front of a lady."

"Yet again, I am considered property. From the way people act you'd think that I was to marry Ramsey to fulfill some kind of prophecy."

"Maybe just righting what some people see as wrongs. Everyone has always thought that the richest family should marry the one with the oldest name."

"But I'm not related to Miss Edi," Joce said. "I got the house because she had no one else to leave it to."

When Luke said nothing, Joce looked at him. "You have something on your mind, don't you?"

"I want to see those letters from General Austin to his wife."

"Bill Austin's on his honeymoon, or maybe he's not even married yet, I don't know. I do know that he won't let the letters off the premises."

Luke turned around and started walking backward on the trail. "But then the grandson doesn't own them, does he?"

"Sure he does. He—" Joce looked up at him. "No, he doesn't. General Austin's wife is still alive so she owns them. Do you think you could talk her into sending them?"

"No, not me, but my grandfather could. He could turn on that bedside manner of his and charm her into anything he wants."

"It would certainly be interesting to see what's in them," Joce said. "Maybe it's nothing, but maybe he mentions when Miss Edi came back from her time with David Clare. Hey! Is that water I hear?"

"Yes. A waterfall and a lake. Icy cold and beautiful." Luke turned around and kept walking.

"You know this place well, don't you."

"I spent a lot of time walking here when I was growing up. I think it's what first made me interested in plants. I used to wander along the trails with a guide to wildflowers in my hand and try to learn the names of all the plants."

"What's this one?" she asked, bending down to a weedy-looking plant with red flowers.

"Penstemon—and that's the last I'm doing of that. I'm not a tour guide."

"No, you're a gardener who I'm told doesn't have to worry about money. You didn't really take earnings from your model wife, did you?"

"What do you think?"

"That you'd live on the street before you did that."

"You do know something about me, don't you?"

"I'm learning," she said.

"And what have you learned so far?" he asked.

He said it lightly, as though it didn't matter, but Joce could see the way his shoulders tightened. "That if anyone wants anything from you they have to draw it out. You don't just sit down and spill your guts to people."

"Is that good or bad?" he asked.

"Good for me," she said, "because I'm learning how to get 'round you to find out your secrets."

He stopped walking and turned to look at her. "You think so, do you?"

"Oh, yeah. I already know everything there is to

know about you. Except for a few small things, that is, like why you've never let me see the inside of your house, why you and Ramsey are so competitive, why you didn't tell me you were married, and what you and your grandfather are really cooking up. Other than those things, I know everything."

"And I know that you can nag a man to death to find out what you want to know," he said, but she could hear the smile in his voice. When he turned off the trail, she followed him. They came to a small waterfall that fed into a stream that went into a lake. It was beautiful and peaceful and it felt as though no one else in the world had ever been there before, but Luke knew just where to put their packs in a little alcove behind some rocks.

"Been here often, have you?"

"A million times," Luke said. "When I was a kid I came here to get away from my father's expectations and my mother's constant watchfulness."

"You and Ingrid came here?"

"Never," he said.

"Couldn't find designer boots?"

"She couldn't find anyone who wanted to be alone with her on a wilderness trail," he said softly, looking at Jocelyn.

It was natural to slip into his arms and to share

a kiss. His mouth came down on hers slowly and tentatively at first, then deeper. As his arms tightened on her and his body came closer, she knew that he wanted her. If it had been up to Jocelyn she would have made love there in that beautiful spot, but he pushed her away.

"I can't," he said.

"That's not what your body says," she said, her voice husky.

"No, I mean, I don't feel that I have a right. This thing about the . . . the marriage. I have to straighten that out first. And us. I want us to know about each other. I want—"

"Not to make a mistake again," she said.

He didn't say anything, but she knew that's what he meant. Minutes later, they were stretched out on the ground, the water before them, and he pulled the next part of Miss Edi's story out of his pack. His grandfather had given it to him last night.

"Shall I read or you?" he asked.

She liked his voice and liked that he'd said **shall.** "You read." She put her hands behind her head and prepared to listen.

19

WITH THE RAIN coming down so hard, it was difficult to even see the bridge. When they did, they both drew in their breaths. The river was high and already running over a bridge that didn't look like it could hold a bicycle, much less a heavy car.

"That thing is pre-Columbian art," David said as he slowed down, wiped the windshield, and stared ahead.

"Late medieval," Edi said. "Look at the stone pillars on the side. They—"

"So help me, if you start giving me a history lecture, I'll throw you out."

She thought he was lying for effect, but she wasn't absolutely sure, so she said nothing more.

David put his hand over the back of the seat and reversed the old car. "I'm going to hit that bridge at a run. We'll either get across it or we'll skid and go over the side, probably upside down. Are you ready?"

Edi braced herself and nodded.

"On second thought, why don't you get out and wait for me?"

"If another man impugns my courage I'll take one of the rifles out of the back and shoot him."

David blinked at her. "Rifles in the back," he said under his breath. "I'm driving an antique tank. I bet this thing was used in Sarajevo."

In spite of the situation, Edi gave a bit of a smile. In 1914, World War I was started when Archduke Francis Ferdinand of Austria and his wife were assassinated in Sarajevo. It looked like that, in contrast to his seeming crassness, Sergeant Clare knew a bit about history.

She held her breath as he got to the top of a little hill and gunned the motor, then he moved the shift down to low, let up on the clutch while his foot was on the brake, and in the next minute they went toward the old bridge in a dense flurry of mud and water. Edi could see nothing. The windshield was covered in seconds and the wiper blades refused to even try to cut into the mud.

The only way she knew they'd reached the bridge was when she heard the bottom of the car hit the wood. There was a hollow sound that incongruously made her think of **The Three Billy Goats Gruff.**

When they hit the road again and the bridge was behind them, they both yelled in triumph.

And that was when they saw the cow. The rain had washed enough of the mud off the windshield that they could see, and lazily walking across the road, as though she had all the time in the world, was a huge black and white cow.

"Hold on!" David yelled as he tried to move the heavy car to the side and not hit the cow. At the moment, he wouldn't have cared if he smashed the thing, but a cow that big would make them crash.

But they crashed anyway. The car hit the hedgerow at the side of the road, went into a spin, then turned around twice before heading back toward the bridge. David fought the big steering wheel with all his might, but then the leg brace tightened up on him and he couldn't move his knee. While turning the wheel, he had to lean toward Edi as he fought to get the clutch all the way to the floor so he could downshift and try to slow the car. But the clutch, the brake, and the mud were all too much for him and the old car.

The car flipped over, Edi tumbled upside down, and the big car slipped on its top down into the river, beside the bridge that they'd just successfully crossed.

For a few seconds both of them were stunned, not able to realize what had just happened. There was blood on the side of David's head and Edi's right arm hurt.

"You have to get out," David said, reaching for her.

She'd been thrown, so she was on the roof of the overturned car, but David was still behind the wheel and hanging with his head down. She followed his eyes and saw that the water was rising around them. The only thing keeping the water out was the closed windows of the car—but that wouldn't last long.

"Yes," she managed to say. She was dazed, not sure what was happening. "I'll open the window and we'll swim out." She was pleased that she'd been able to see what needed to be done.

"Can you swim?" he asked.

"Yes, quite well," she answered. Her head was clearing with each second. "What about you?"

"High school swim team," he said and gave her his little grin that she'd seen several times.

"Okay, then," she said. "Are you ready? We need to go as soon as I get the window down."

"Hey, Harcourt," he said softly. "A favor? How about a kiss before you go?"

"A kiss? You think that now is the time to—" She broke off when she realized what he'd said repeatedly. When **she** went, not him, just her. "What's wrong with you?"

"It's this damned brace," he said. "Bad luck on my part. It's steel and it's stuck. I can't get out."

Edi gave a look out at the water surrounding them and the rain still coming down hard. In minutes they were going to be completely underwater and the pressure would probably burst the windows and they'd drown.

It wasn't easy to get her long legs and arms twisted around so she was upright and she could get to his legs, but she did it. His foot was trapped under the crushed pedals of the car, and there was another piece of metal that had stopped at his calf.

"Just move your leg, bend at the knee, and take it out. Is your leg broken?"

"I don't think so, but it's encased in a steel brace. You need to go. There isn't time to waste. You have to—"

"Shut up," she said. "How do I get you out of this thing?"

"You can't. You aren't strong enough. My leg is trapped under some steel and—"

"Just for once in your life stop talking!" she shouted. "How do I move the brace?"

"In my pocket there's an Allen wrench. It's—"

"I know what an Allen wrench is." For the first time, she saw that his right arm was bleeding. He couldn't get inside his own pocket. She moved so she was lying across him, then stuck her hand down deep into his pocket and found the little piece of metal.

The second she had it, the window in the back of the car cracked and the interior started filling with water.

"Three screws in the round hinge at the knee," David said. "You should go. Give me the wrench and get out of here."

Because the car was upside down, the last place to be filled was where David's feet were trapped, but his head was near the roof. Even if she got him loose, he might still drown before she could get him out of the car.

Edi half stood, half knelt on the roof as she reached up and pushed David's trouser leg back and tried to find the screws on the hinge to loosen them. She found one, twisted, and it moved. But she could feel the water around her legs.

She looked down and David's head was almost underwater. He was bending as far forward as he could, but he couldn't move much because of the huge steering wheel across the front of him.

Edi took a deep breath, went under the water, looked at David, and touched his lips. It took him a full second to realize what she meant. She kissed him all right: she released air into his mouth, then went back up to the brace.

She got the second screw loose, then took another breath and went under to give air to David.

The third screw stuck, and she thought she wasn't going to get it loosened. There were only inches of air space in the car now. She went under again to give him more oxygen and he motioned for her to get out. She didn't waste her time shaking her head no.

She had to put her face up against the roof to get a breath of air, then she went under to loosen the last screw. When the hinge gave way, she gave a hard push on his leg and it moved. He was free!

Edi went downward, toward David's face to tell him to help her get him out, but his eyes were closed, and he was limp. She pushed out with her legs to get to the roof for more air, but the car was full of water. There was no air to be had.

Already, her lungs were hurting. She reached across David to the big handle that turned the window and cranked it. It was difficult to move and she could feel her arms giving out and her head was feeling light. But she got the big window down enough that she thought she could get him out.

The water made him lighter, so she was able to maneuver him toward the window enough that the current of the river seemed to suck him away. Edi nearly panicked when David's body disappeared, but in the next second the current grabbed her too and she went flying upward.

When she came to the surface she took a deep breath, then was pulled down again. The next time she came up, she looked for David, and saw him entangled in the roots of a tree just a few feet away. His eyes were closed, but at least his head wasn't under water.

She tried to swim to him, but the current was pulling her in the opposite direction.

"Grab this," came a voice, and she turned to see a long pole just inches from her head. It seemed to be attached to something but she couldn't see what, nor could she see who had spoken. She had to lunge at the pole twice before she caught it, then she held on with both arms.

"Him!" she yelled to the unseen person who'd saved her. "In the trees. There!"

Edi held on to the pole with her arms and swiped the water out of her eyes as she saw someone in a green coat on the bank. From the shape of him, with his hunched back, he looked to be an old man. But he was obviously strong as he pulled David by his collar and dragged him out of the water as though he were a big fish he'd just caught.

Edi was battling hair and rain to see what was going on, but she didn't dare let go of the pole. Turning to her left, she saw that it was part of the bridge, maybe something used to ferry barges across the river. Slowly, she began to use her arms to pull herself along to try to reach the end of the bridge and the land.

As she moved, she wondered what the man was doing with Sergeant Clare. Would the old man think he was dead and make no attempt to save him? If Edi could get to him she thought maybe she could apply some modern lifesaving techniques, and maybe she could get the water out of Sergeant Clare's lungs so he wouldn't die.

"Come on!" she heard a man shout. "Only another foot and you're home."

Her arms were killing her and she was shaking with cold and fatigue, but she looked up and saw Sergeant Clare standing there. The rain was so hard and the mist so dense that she thought maybe she was seeing a ghost. Had he died and his spirit come back to help her across the raging river?

"Come on, Harcourt!" he shouted. "Get your back into it. I'd come out there and save you but I'm too beat up. You'll have to do something for yourself this time. You can't always depend on **me** to save you."

"You?" she managed to say. "Why you—" As anger surged through her, she began to kick with her long legs and she pulled harder on the pole. But even with her anger and her renewed energy, she was giving out. Instead of coming closer, the bridge seemed to be going farther away.

She blinked hard to clear the water out of her eyes, but things were going hazy.

In the next minute, she felt a strong arm around her. "I have you now," she heard in her ear. "You're safe now. Let go of that thing and let me have you."

She obeyed the voice. Her arms fell away from the metal and went around his neck, and her head collapsed against him. She felt him carry her out of the water, and she felt someone else's hands on her.

"She dead?" she heard a man ask.

"No," she heard Sergeant Clare say. He was carrying her and she could feel the drag of his leg from the brace that he still wore. All she'd done was loosen the knee hinge; she hadn't removed it.

"Your arm?" she managed to whisper as she remembered that it had been bleeding.

"I can't figure out if my arm hurts more or my leg. The dilemma is keeping me from fainting."

"Good," she said as she snuggled closer to him. She closed her eyes and went to sleep.

❧

When Edi awoke, she was in a bed on a soft mattress and there was sunlight coming through the window. Her head ached and her arm was sore, but she didn't feel too bad. She looked about the room. It was small, with flowered wallpaper, and two beds. The bed beside hers was made up with an old quilt and fat pillows. There was a big old wardrobe against one wall and a dressing table along the other. The facing wall had a window with lace curtains.

When she tried to sit up, she was a bit dizzy, but her head cleared in a minute. She heard a soft knock on the door, then Sergeant Clare came in carrying a tray with one arm. His right arm was in a sling.

"You're awake," he said, smiling, then gave his concentration back to the tray when it nearly un-balanced.

"Let me—" Edi began as she started to get out of bed, but then she realized she was wearing only her peach rayon teddy. She hastily pulled the covers back over her. "Where are my clothes?"

"In the kitchen, dry and waiting for you," David said as he set the tray down on the end of her bed, then stood up and flexed his arm. "You can stop looking at me like I'm about to attack you. It's too late for modesty."

Edi didn't drop the covers from around her neck. "What does that mean?"

He sat down on the opposite bed, picked up a toast wedge, and began to eat it. "If you don't want that food, I'll take it."

"I need something to put on," she said.

Reluctantly, he got up, went to the wardrobe, and pulled out a man's shirt. It was huge and nearly worn out, but Edi took it and put her arms in the sleeves. When she was covered, she bent toward the tray and poured herself a cup of tea. "Tell me what happened," she said. "Where are we? How soon can we get out of here and get the magazine?"

"Which answer do you want first?"

"All of them," she said.

"The accident happened yesterday and we're now at the home of Hamish Trumbull."

Edi stopped with a piece of toast to her mouth.

"It seems that Mrs. Pettigrew was so sure we wouldn't make it over the bridge that she called a neighbor who told ol' Hamish to get down to the river to save us."

"But you did make it over the bridge," Edi said, sounding affronted. "If it hadn't been for that cow—"

"Who, by the way, belongs to Hamish."

"If it hadn't been for **his cow,** we would have made it."

"Thank you," David said. "That's just what I told Hamish, but he didn't believe me. He says we missed the bridge and went into the river upside down. He says I'm the worst driver he's ever seen."

"You should have hit his cow," Edi said, her mouth full.

"My sentiments exactly. Here, let me pour that for you." David used his left arm and his right hand to maneuver the teapot, his leg held stiffly out from his body.

"So what's the story on the magazine?" Edi asked.

"The granddaughter Aggie has it and no one knows where she is."

Edi groaned. "How old is she to be out unsupervised?"

"Sixteen and her goose is cooked. She told Mrs. Pettigrew that she was going home to Gramps, and told Gramps she had to work. Poor kid. When she does show up, she's in for it."

"So how long do we have to wait for her to return from wherever she is?"

"Us," David said as he got up off the bed and walked to the window. "About that 'us.' You see, Hamish is a bit old-fashioned, and I had to tell him some fibs."

When he didn't say anything else, just kept looking out the window, Edi started to piece things together. "You told him we were married, didn't you?"

"It was either that or I had to sleep in the barn. Sorry, but the feather mattress won over the straw."

She thought about the way he'd pulled her from the water yesterday and she couldn't begrudge him a bed. "All right, so we're married and . . . what?"

David turned to her with sparkling eyes.

"In your dreams, soldier," she said.

"If wishes were horses . . ." David said, then

dragged his leg as he crossed the room to sit back down on the other bed. "It seems that Aggie the Missing is due back here day after tomorrow. All we can hope is that she shows up with the magazine."

"You didn't tell Hamish—?"

"I didn't tell that old man anything. Mrs. Pettigrew made up a great whopping lie about the magazine being some sort of spy vehicle and the entire fate of the war resting on our getting it back. She— Why are you looking at me like that? Please tell me that isn't true."

"I don't know," she mumbled, eating the last piece of toast.

"I want you to tell me every word that you do know and don't even think about not telling me all of it."

It took her about four minutes to tell him all that she knew. It wasn't much.

"So you're to give the magazine to this man . . ."

"Dr. Sebastian Jellicoe."

"Then we're to get him to London so he can be sent back to the safety of Minnesota—or someplace in the U.S. Is that right?" David asked.

"That's what I was told."

"But where he lives and the map to get there is inside the car, which is now at the bottom of an overflowing river."

Edi leaned back against the headboard. "I memorized the map."

"You did what?"

"While you were in the front of the car, whining that nobody would talk to you, I was in the back memorizing the map. I was hoping to find the marks in the magazine and memorize them too, but I couldn't find anything."

"Whining?" David said, picking up on the one word. "If you were in as much pain as I was you'd be complaining too."

"What happened to your leg?" Edi asked, and as she said it she remembered how she'd gone underwater and loosened the screws, and how she'd kissed him to give him air.

For a moment their eyes met, as he seemed to be thinking about the same thing, but he broke away and pulled up the leg of his trousers. "Your general, that Satan you work for, decided that an uninjured man traveling around England would rouse too many suspicions, so he had me disabled."

Edi looked at the bottom half of the brace and at the round hinge she knew well, and she couldn't help it, but she started to laugh.

"I don't see anything funny about this," David said. "I have blisters all over my leg where it rubs against me and— Will you please stop laughing?"

"I think he did it to protect me," Edi said, still laughing. "He's like an old sultan, and he thinks of all of us women who work for him as his vestal virgins."

David stopped frowning. "Yeah, he does have the most beautiful of all the women."

"Half of them are idiots," Edi said. "I hired a woman who could type a hundred words a minute without an error, but that old bulldog fired her because she was ugly. He said he wasn't going to survive bombs **and** ugly women."

David laughed. "She isn't the one who works for Colonel Osborne, is she?"

Edi nodded. "She can do more work than three of Austin's girls."

"Except you."

"Except me," Edi agreed, "but I get stuck with trying to deal with all of them. One day I almost got hit by a falling roof when one of the girls ran back to get her lipstick. I told her that gunpowder was the best eye shadow there was and she was going to get plenty of it if she didn't get moving. And you know what? She believed me!"

"You're kidding."

"Not at all. You know Lenny . . . ?"

"Escobar?" David's eyes widened. "I saw him taking the powder out of some shells. It wasn't for—?"

"It was."

Laughing, David moved back on the bed and lifted his leg onto it. "Okay, so now all we can do is wait until Aggie shows up and hope she has the magazine. In the meantime, I think Hamish means for you and me to stay busy."

"What does that mean?"

"He had me in the barn this morning . . ." He looked away, and Edi thought maybe his face was red.

"In the barn doing what?"

"Remember the cow?"

"I will go to my grave remembering that cow," Edi said. "What about her?"

" 'Her' is the key word."

"Oh," Edi said, smiling. "He had you milking."

"And mucking. I think that's the proper term for using a pitchfork to remove manure."

She looked at him. "How did you do that with an arm in a sling and your leg like that? Can you move it?"

"Not at all. I think the hinge rusted."

"We'll have to get it off you," Edi said. "Maybe this man has an Allen wrench."

"No," David said sadly. "No Allen wrench that will fit, no anything that will fit. I was in the barn at four A.M. this morning because it seems that that's when cows want to be milked and horses have to have their floors swabbed. I tried every tool the old man has, but nothing worked. The screws are set deep into the steel, they're rusted, and nothing will touch them. You didn't by chance . . . you know . . ."

"Know what?"

"Hold on to the little Allen wrench after you . . ."

"Saved your life? No," Edi said, "I didn't think to hold on to it. I guess I was a bit busy with the window and the water and all that."

"Just thought I'd ask."

From outside the room came a loud voice. "Clare! You in there?"

David rolled his eyes. "I'd rather go back to the front lines than deal with that old man. I'm telling you that Austin is a sweetheart compared to him."

"I'll get up and see what I can do to help," Edi said.

"I better warn you that I think he expects you to cook."

At that Edi's face turned pale, and she put the cover back over her. "I don't know how to cook."

"You don't know how to cook?"

"Don't give me that!" she snapped. "I grew up in a house with a cook. I don't know anything about it. Food was served to me on a plate. I can't even make a pot of tea."

"Really?" David said, his smile becoming broader by the minute.

"What is so very amusing about that, Sergeant Clare?"

"Because I **can** cook."

"**You** can cook?" she said in astonishment.

"So now who's stereotyping? My mother is Italian. I can cook. Look, why don't we tell him that you're injured and have to stay in bed so I'll do the cooking?"

"And who will milk the cow?"

"Let ol' Hamish do it. He does it when we're not here."

"So you're saying that I'm just a poor, feeble woman who can't pull her own weight. Is that it? I'm to stay in bed and do nothing?"

"Unless you can milk a cow and clean up after horses, I don't think there's anything you **can** do."

"As it so happens, I nearly grew up on a horse."

"Of course," David said. "Rich girl. The kitchen is beneath you, but you're a stable lad in the barn."

"You really are the most obnoxious man I have ever met in my life," Edi said.

He stood up and looked down at her as he walked to the door. "And you, Miss Edilean Harcourt, are the most beautiful, intelligent, resourceful, courageous woman I have ever met. And, by the way, I plan to marry you." He left the room, leaving Edi with her mouth open in astonishment.

⌘

"You're a mess, you know that?" David said as he pried Edi's hands open and looked at the blisters. "What got into you to do all that work?"

"I don't know," she said, shrugging. "It felt good. I get so tired of being inside and listening to typewriters all day. I liked being outside."

They were in the kitchen of Hamish Trumbull's house and there was a night-and-day difference between the way it was now and how it had looked that morning. For all his complaining that Edi had worked too hard, David had spent the day scrubbing the kitchen, inside every cabinet and every pan. He'd filled the wood box and kept the old stove going all day as he cooked. The room was warm and smelled wonderful.

"You haven't exactly sat around," she said, wincing as he examined her hands.

"No, but I had help," he said without a smile,

and the absurdity of that made them both start to laugh, then they quietened.

"Where is he?" Edi asked, referring to Hamish.

"I wore him out with churning butter," David said as he got some and slathered it on her blisters.

"Butter? You can **make** butter?"

"Of course. How did you think you got it?"

"By pumping the cow's tail up and down," she said.

David laughed. "Okay, so I'm no farmer, but I know what to do once the stuff's in the kitchen. Taste this." He dipped a wooden spoon into a pan bubbling on the stove and held it to her lips. When she started to take it from him, he pulled back.

"Delicious," she said. "I've never tasted anything like it. What is it?"

"Alfredo sauce to go on the pasta."

"The what?"

"Spaghetti," he said. "You Americans call all pasta spaghetti. Are you ready to eat?"

She stood up slowly. This morning she'd raided the wardrobe in the bedroom they shared and found a pair of men's trousers that almost fit her. They were long enough, but they were so big around the waist that she'd had to make a new hole in an old leather belt to hold the pants up. She and

David had shared a laugh over both of them wearing trousers that were too big.

Edi had spent the day outside, and David had stayed in. Both of them had soon seen that the little farm was nearly falling down. With all the young, strong men at war, most of the farms were neglected, but this one seemed worse than usual.

That morning, Edi had met Hamish for the first time, and instead of seeing a gruff old man as David described, she saw sadness. "Don't ask him anything," she whispered to David. "I can't bear to hear the answer." So many people had horror stories about the loss of loved ones that Edi couldn't take any more.

"Agreed," David said.

She found the falling-down old shed that served as a henhouse and got a few eggs. After breakfast, she started on cleaning up the outside. As David said, she'd not had much to do with the kitchen when she was growing up, but she loved the barn and the henhouse and all the things that had made Edilean Manor nearly self-sufficient.

When she went into the house for lunch, the kitchen was sparkling, and David had just pulled bread out of the oven. That he'd done all that with one arm in a sling and his unbending leg made her smile in appreciation.

After lunch, she tackled the chicken coop. One of the fence posts around the yard had fallen over, pulling the fence down with it. If any foxes decided to enter, nothing would stop them. The wind was picking up, and Edi wanted to get the post back up before it started to rain again.

She was digging the hole and trying to hold the post at the same time when David came running, with his odd gait, and took over. She held the post while he stamped it in. Then, together, they put stones around the edge of the fence.

"I have to get back," he said loudly over the wind that was getting stronger. "Don't stay out here too long."

"I won't," she called back, but once he was inside, she got a pitchfork and started cleaning out the inside of the henhouse. From the look of it, it hadn't been cleaned in a couple of years. It wasn't good for the chickens or the people eating them.

She didn't realize her hands were blistered until she'd finished. She had a tall pile of manure outside the fence, and she'd dragged two fresh bales of straw from the barn into the chicken coop. She looked in the barn for some gloves but couldn't find any, so she went on with the chores barehanded. By sundown, she'd made headway on the barn, both in repairing and mucking out.

She didn't realize how tired she was until she went inside and sat down. David took one look at her and took over. He opened her hands, washed them, then slathered them with butter to help with the pain of the blisters.

"Oh, no, you don't," he said when she nearly fell asleep in the chair. "You need to eat."

"You sound like my mother."

"I'll take that as a compliment," David said as he set a huge plate of homemade pasta with a cream-based sauce in front of her. "I want you to eat every bite of that and drink all the milk. You need your strength."

"Yes, sir," she said. She was so tired that she couldn't even keep her rigid posture of sitting upright as she ate, and she smiled as she thought of what her mother would say if she saw her daughter now.

"Want to share the reason for that smile?" David asked as he filled a plate for himself.

"I was just thinking about my family."

"Tell me about them," he said. "Rich farmers, right?"

"Used to be," she said, "but the rich part is gone. We used to own an entire town, but . . ."

"But what?"

"It doesn't matter. That seems like a lifetime

ago. This is really good. Ever think of opening a restaurant?"

"Did you ever think about visiting New York? There's an Italian restaurant on every corner."

"Is he okay, do you think?" Edi whispered, nodding toward Hamish's closed bedroom door.

"Based on the sound of his snoring, I think he's been sleeping all day. Or else someone's been throwing grenades into that room."

"You're awful," Edi said, smiling. "Poor man is worn out. Don't forget that he saved both our lives."

"Humph!" David said. "Do you know how he revived me?"

"I saw him pull you out of the water and I remember hoping that you weren't dead."

"He slammed his foot on my stomach."

"He what?"

"Like this," David said, and he hit the floor with his unbraced leg. "Pow! I nearly choked as I started to vomit up water and Mrs. Pettigrew's lunch."

Edi tried not to laugh, but couldn't help it. "And we wondered why Aggie didn't want to come home."

"If I lived with him, I'd join the army—even if I were a sixteen-year-old girl."

"Come on, he's not that bad."

"You didn't spend the day inside with him. You should have heard him complain about the way you were working on that chicken house."

"Coop."

"What?"

"Henhouse or chicken coop, but never mind," Edi said. "What did he say about me?"

David shook his head in disbelief. "He said . . ." He lowered his voice. "He said that if he had a wife with legs like yours he wouldn't be in the house washing the floor—at least not with a mop."

"He didn't."

"Cross my heart," David said and made the gesture. "He wanted to go out there and help you, but I talked him out of it."

"And how did you do that?"

"I showed him my fist, then looked at his scrawny old face."

Edi laughed hard, putting her hand over her mouth to hold the sound in. "So who's worse? You or him?"

"I hope I am, but he's learned a lot in his many years." When David saw Edi's eyes begin to blink slowly, he took her hands in his and pulled her upright. For a moment they were standing very near each other. Instantly, the relaxed attitude was gone and they were both tense.

"I have hot water for you," David said, breaking the tension as he turned toward the sink. "You can wash what you can reach. Or you can strip naked and I'll hold a towel for you."

Edi laughed again, the tension gone. "No, thank you. I think I'll just wash my face and hands and leave the rest to when I have a tub. I'm too tired to care how dirty I am."

"I like earthy women."

"I think, David Clare, that you like **any** kind of woman."

"Think so, do you? Then that's where you're very, very wrong. Okay, you wash and I'll check the clothesline. Take your time."

Edi didn't take much time washing. She was telling the truth when she said she didn't care how dirty she was. She gave her face, neck, and armpits a bit of a dash, then she went into their bedroom and shut the door.

As she began to undress, she looked at the two beds. It was extraordinary what ten or so hours of hard, physical labor could do to a person. Two days ago, if she'd been told that she had to spend the night in the same room with a soldier, she would have said she'd rather sleep on a stone pallet in the rain. But now it seemed natural for David—not Sergeant Clare, but "David"—to sleep in the same room.

On the chair at the end of the bed was a clean nightgown, and Edi knew David had put it there for her. It was probably Aggie's, and it was so clean and Edi was so dirty that she almost didn't put it on, but she did. She slipped it over her dirty body, pulled back the sheets and covers on the bed nearer the door, and was asleep in an instant.

When she awoke, the room was dark and something had jolted the bed. At first she panicked. She had to get to the air raid shelter! Had to find the girls and get them there first!

"Ssssh," David said. "It's only me. Go back to sleep."

She sat up on her elbows, trying to see in the dark. "Turn on the light."

"There is no light," he said. "Remember? No electricity."

"Oh, right," she said, lying back down. "Hamish."

"That's right," he said soothingly. "Just go back to sleep."

She did, but was awakened again when something again hit the bed and she sat up.

"Sorry," David said. "It's this damned brace,

and the beds are close together. As soon as I can turn around I'll quit hitting your bed. Now go back to sleep."

This time she was more fully awake. "Would you get a lantern?"

"What for?" he asked.

"I want to see your leg."

There was a moment of silence before David spoke. "As enticing as that sounds, my leg is fine."

Edi sat up straighter. "I think that tomorrow I should do the cooking, and you should milk the cow and gather the eggs."

"You win," he said, and a moment later he came back into the room, holding the lantern. He was shirtless, shoeless, and wearing only the trousers that were too big for him.

He put the lantern down on the table between the beds and said, "Now what?"

"Off with them," Edi said as she got out of bed, went to the wardrobe, and took out the old shirt she'd worn that morning over her underwear. Judging by the fit of her clothes, Aggie was shorter and plumper than Edi, which made the nightgown much too short, and the top fell away whenever she moved.

"I love that gown," David said as he unbuckled his trousers.

"Be quiet or I'll tell Hamish the truth about us and you'll have to sleep in the kitchen. On the floor."

"You're threatening to punish me if I don't take off my trousers while I'm alone in a room with the most beautiful woman in the world? The woman I plan to—"

"Stop it," she said, but she was smiling.

When David struggled to get his trousers down over the heavy brace, she took the cuffs and pulled. He tried to make jokes, but she was too horrified by what she saw to smile. His leg was raw from the steel. The old padding had nearly all fallen away, and the straps of the big, cagelike thing had scraped and cut until his leg was a mass of blisters and bleeding sores.

"I love General Austin," David said.

"He'll hear about this from me, you can be sure of that," she said, her mouth clenched into a line of anger. "Stay here and I'm going to see what I can do to clean this up."

"I'm all yours, baby," he said as he leaned back on the pillows—and went to sleep immediately. When he awoke, Edi was sitting on a kitchen chair, a bowl of hot water on the bedside table, and she was trying to wash some of the wounds and bandage them.

"This hurts, doesn't it?" she asked softly.

"Not too much," he said, but she knew he was lying. She'd thought that her hands were bad, but she couldn't imagine what he'd gone through today with those sharp edges cutting into him.

She went to the wardrobe, pulled out another old shirt, and began to tear it into strips. "Your blisters and those cuts have stuck to the steel, so this is going to hurt, but I'm going to wrap cloth around the metal so it doesn't gouge you so much. Think you can stand it?"

"I'll do my best."

As she started, she saw the way his jaw was working, saw the pain he was in, and she wanted to distract him.

"So tell me about your family. Any brothers or sisters?"

"Eight of them. I'm the second one, but . . ." He took a breath against the pain. "Bannerman. One year older than me. Takes care of all of us. The best there is. He . . ." David broke off as some of his skin came away with the steel.

Edi thought it would be better if she talked. "My brother Bertrand is the laziest person in the world," she said.

"Oh, yeah? And how lazy is that?"

"When he was three and saw all his gifts under

the Christmas tree, he said, 'Who's going to open them for me?'"

David gave a little snort of laughter. "I've heard worse."

"When he was six, my father bought him a bicycle and took him out to teach him to ride it."

"And?"

"Bertrand did very well. My father ran along behind him, holding on, and my brother balanced perfectly. But when my father let go and the bicycle stopped, Bertrand asked why. When my father said he had to **push** on the pedals, my brother left it lying there in the street, and he never got on a bicycle again."

David was still wincing when she cleaned one of the cuts, but less so. "Not bad, but I've heard worse."

"When he was twelve, my parents took us out to a restaurant, the first one we'd ever been to, and my father ordered steaks for each of us. When my brother's came, he looked at it and asked how he was to eat it. My father showed him how to cut the steak, then how to chew it. My brother called the waiter back and ordered a bowl of mashed potatoes."

"Okay," David said, "that's getting up there, but I have heard a few worse."

"When he was sixteen, my mother arranged for her beloved son to go to a dance with a very nice young girl. He was to pick her up at six P.M. At six-thirty Bertrand was sitting in the living room and my father asked him why he hadn't gone on his date. My brother said, 'Because she hasn't come to get me yet.'"

David laughed. "All this is a lie, isn't it?"

"Not a word."

"But how did he survive? What does he do with himself? How'd he get through school?"

"My brother is a brilliant young man. In school he'd get someone to tell him what a book was about, and five minutes later he could discuss it. Debate it. He loves to sit and talk." Edi wrung out a piece of cloth. "And gossip. He knows everyone in town, and they all tell him their secrets."

"I guess he didn't go to war."

"Four-F. Flat feet." When Edi gently pushed at another piece of cloth, David gave a little groan of pain. "Want to hear more?"

"Yes," he said through clenched teeth. "Got any about Austin? Something mean and juicy?"

"No, just Bertrand stories. Want to hear why he didn't go to his own wedding?"

David opened his eyes wide and looked at her. "Tell me."

"My mother arranged everything. Bertrand saw the girl, said she was suitable, and that was enough for both my mother and the girl."

"Marrying money and an old name, right?"

"I already told you there was no money. But, yes, there was the name," Edi said. "My mother was thrilled and spent months planning the most elaborate wedding the town had ever seen. My father had to mortgage our old house. The evening before the wedding, my father went into his son's room to have a talk with him about the wedding night."

"The wedding night," David whispered. "I like this story the best of any you've told. Maybe of any I've ever heard in my whole life."

"No one knows exactly what was said by my father, but everyone heard Bertrand shout for the one and only time in his life. He yelled, 'I have to do **what**?'"

David started laughing. "Now you have me. That **is** the worst story I've ever heard. What happened?"

"Bertrand stayed home the next day and nothing anyone said or did could get him to move."

"And his bride?"

"She showed up for the wedding that never happened. Poor dear. Her family was so humiliated, six months later they moved to Atlanta."

"What did your brother say to explain?"

"Nothing. To my knowledge he's never mentioned that day. The work other people do has never concerned him."

"And your mother?"

"After that, she stopped trying to manage her son's life, and my father said that that was almost worth the expense of the wedding."

David was really laughing now, and Edi had finished with the bandages. She could tell by his eyes that he was at last comfortable enough to sleep. She pulled a quilt over him, then went to her own bed.

When he whispered, "Good night," she smiled and went back to sleep.

20

JOCELYN WAS LAUGHING when Luke finished reading. "I've heard so much about Bertrand that I wish I'd met him."

"He would have loved you."

"Really?" she asked, feeling flattered.

"You leave your door open and people walk in and out all day. You feed anybody who stops by, and you always have time to listen to anyone. Yeah, I think you and Bertrand would have made great housemates."

"I'm not like that," Jocelyn said. "I'm . . ."

"You're what? More like Miss Edi? Like the way that nurse described her, as cold and heartless?"

"I ought to send that woman a copy of this story and see if she still thinks Edi is without a heart." For a moment Joce was quiet as she sat up and looked at the water, hugging her knees to her chest. "To think that Miss Edi lost him. There she was in the war, surrounded by men who were making fools of themselves over her, but she saved herself for True Love, but when she found it . . ."

"He was killed," Luke said softly. "And later Miss Edi was injured severely. I wonder if that accident is why she didn't marry and have children."

"You mean you think she **couldn't** have children?"

"I don't know. How bad were her burns?"

"Toward the end, I helped her dress, and the scars were from her knees down. I don't think the fire went higher. She told me it was very cold that day, so everyone was bundled up, and two soldiers threw themselves on her with their heavy coats on. If they hadn't done that, the fire would have spread, because she had gasoline all over her."

"Threw themselves on her," Luke said, shaking his head. "And David was dead by then."

"Yes. She said that she called out for him in the hospital. They kept moving her from one hospital to another while they waited for her to die."

"They didn't expect her to live?"

"No," Joce said. "The gasoline and the fire and even the wool of the men's burned coats all caused her to develop a serious infection. She ran a high fever for weeks. I think General Austin stepped in and had her sent back to the States, even though she wasn't working for him then."

"Did she quit him? Do you think she told him she couldn't take his bad temper anymore?"

"I don't know. I didn't ask because she never even hinted that he was a difficult man. She just said that when she was burned she was still in England, but she was no longer working for General Austin. I don't know what she was doing. I assume she was still in the military or she would have gone home to Edilean."

"Would she?" Luke asked.

"Why do you say that?"

"Why would she go home to Edilean? What was waiting for her? An old house that costs a lot to keep in repair and a brother who set standards for laziness?"

"And your very happy grandfather," Joce said.

"Yes, my happy grandfather, who had broken up with Edi the day after Pearl Harbor was hit."

"Did your grandfather ever tell you why they broke off their engagement?"

"Yes. When we went to Richmond he told me that it was because they realized that there was nothing to find out about each other," Luke said. "Gramps said that when he and Edi saw that they were excited to go off to war, they knew that their perfect lives weren't so perfect after all. Miss Edi told Gramps that they should have been devastated that the future they'd always looked forward to was going to be changed, but they weren't. Gramps said she gave back his ring, they shook hands, and laughed together, both of them quite happy for the engagement to be over."

"But they never told anyone."

"The whole town would have been sad. War was enough, but it was far away. Edi and David had been together all their lives."

Joce turned to look at him, stretched out on the blanket they'd brought, his head on his hands. "I'm glad I haven't known you all my life."

He moved as though he were going to take her hand in his, but he didn't. "Jocelyn, I think . . . ," he began, but cut himself off, then lay back on the blanket. "You still think I'm like your father?"

"Why has that statement bothered you so much?"

"Who wants to be like his girl's father?"

The old-fashioned term "his girl" made a little shiver run through her body. "The more I hear of

Miss Edi's story, the more I think she and I are alike. And like my mother. We seem to like only men who . . ." She didn't know what else to say.

"Who aren't lawyers?" Luke said. "Your mother fell for a handyman and Miss Edi loved a car mechanic, and now you like the gardener."

She could feel the anger under his voice. "Luke, I didn't mean it like that."

"You ready to leave?" he said as he got up.

She stood up. "Are you angry at me?"

"For telling me that you . . . what? That you like me in spite of who and what I am? What if I'd become a doctor like my grandfather? Would you like me better then?"

"No, but I could afford some furniture for that big house," she said, smiling.

Luke didn't smile. "So this is about money? As soon as Rams gets back in town are you planning to run to him because he's rich?"

"I was just making a joke," Joce said. "I would **never** marry a man just for money."

"Are you sure? Maybe you want my cousin for the life you think he can give you. Vacations to the Orient, nannies for the kids, silver for the table. Is that what's important to you?"

When he started to move away, she put her hand on his arm. "None of that is important to me," she said. "If it were up to me I'd live in a two-bedroom ranch and write while the kids take naps. But Miss Edi left me that house, so I—"

"Miss Edi!" Luke said. "Is she all you think about? Her life, not yours?"

"Of course not! I think about my own life, but Miss Edi said Ramsey was perfect for me." As soon as she said it, Jocelyn put her hand over her mouth.

"She said what?"

Joce picked up her pack and began to put things inside it.

Luke caught her arm and turned her to face him. "I want to know what you're talking about. When did she tell you about Ramsey?"

"In the letter she left me with her will. You didn't know her, but she was great at judging couples who'd stay together or not, and she said that there was a man in Edilean who was perfect for me."

Luke dropped her arm and stepped back. "And that was my cousin Ramsey?"

"Yes," she said. "But she didn't know **you.** She—"

"She sure as hell didn't know Ramsey either," Luke nearly shouted. "All she knew about him is his money and his ancestry. Did you ever think that **you** were part of the bargain between Alexander McDowell and Miss Edi? Maybe she tried to thank Uncle Alex by giving his descendant the old manor that he'd coveted all his life."

"That's a ridiculous idea."

"You've lived here a while now. Do you really think it's not possible?"

"I don't know." Joce put her hands over her ears. "I don't want to hear any more of this." When he said nothing else, she took her hands down and looked at him. He seemed to be waiting for her to say something, but she could think of nothing to reply to his accusations.

"Are you going to live your entire life for Miss Edi?" Luke asked. "You live in her house, and you've given your life over to writing about her, reading about her. She seems to be all you think about. Are you going to marry some man you don't love because she told you that you should?"

"No," Joce said. "You're twisting this all around. Besides, no one has asked me to marry him."

"But he's going to," Luke said, "and you know it. You ready to leave?"

"Yes," she said, but she didn't want to go. She wanted to stay and argue this thing out with Luke. It had been such a wonderful day, with more of the love story revealed, but it had all ended in a fight, and she wasn't even sure how it had begun.

She started to say that she didn't want to leave, but there was a flash of lightning and a crack of thunder and the next second they were hit with a downpour of rain. Instinctively, Jocelyn looked for shelter, but Luke grabbed their packs and pulled out their plastic ponchos. He helped Joce into hers with one hand while pulling his over his own head.

"We need to get out of here," he said over the rain. "Can you walk?"

"Sure."

"Stay close to me."

His long legs set a pace that was difficult for her to keep up with, but she managed it. When they reached the truck, he threw open the door, and she got in, then he quickly raced around to the other side.

"Will you listen to me?" she asked as he started the engine. "I'm not marrying anyone. I'm sorry I talk about Miss Edi so much and I wish I hadn't told you what she wrote to me."

He didn't look at her, but he gave a quick nod, then drove out of the parking lot, and minutes later he pulled into the driveway at Edilean Manor.

"How long are you going to stay angry at me?" she asked, feeling close to tears.

Suddenly, Luke reached across the seat, put his hand behind her head, and kissed her hard and long, and with more passion than Jocelyn had ever felt before.

When he released her, her head fell back against the window and her eyes stayed shut.

"Forget about Ramsey," Luke said. "He's too much like you and you'd come to hate each other."

When she felt him reach across her, she opened her eyes, ready to kiss him again, but he opened the truck door. "Go inside and take a hot bath. I have to go out of town for a few days, but when I get back we'll get the next part of the story from Gramps."

"Okay," she said as she got out of the truck. She closed the door behind her, then went into the house.

21

THE NEXT MORNING was Friday, and Jocelyn was sitting in her kitchen finishing off a pot of tea when Tess walked in and let out an exclamation.

"You scared me," Tess said as she went to the refrigerator. "What are you doing here?"

"Last I heard, I live here."

"Oh, my, we are surly this morning. You and Luke have a fight?"

"No, of course not," Joce said, but her head was aching from a sleepless night. Luke's words, his anger, even his unexplained trip out of town were all bothering her.

"Ramsey gets back today," Tess said. "His plane lands in Richmond at ten this morning, so I figure he'll show up here for lunch. Last night he called me and asked all about you and Luke."

"Why couldn't he have called **me**?" Joce asked. "If he wanted to know about me he should have asked **me**."

"You're in a bad mood this morning. So what did you and Luke fight about?"

"Ramsey, probably," Sara said from the doorway. "Luke and Ramsey have bickered with each other since they were born. Now they have Joce to fight over."

"I'm not a—" Jocelyn had said the words so many times that she couldn't get them out again.

Sara went to the refrigerator and got a carton of eggs from her family's farm. "I'm going to scramble some eggs. Anyone want some?"

"Yeah, sure," Tess said. "You better make extra because Jim will be here any minute. You know how he eats."

Jocelyn sat in the middle of her own kitchen, watching the two other women moving about, and she remembered what Luke had said about her house always being open. So what was wrong with that? she wondered. Just because his house was as closed as a prison didn't mean hers had to be.

"Why are you looking so gloomy?" Sara asked. "And where is Luke?"

"Why is it that since the first moment I set foot in this town that I've been connected with either Ramsey or Luke? Why can't I just be myself?"

Tess and Sara exchanged looks, as though some understanding had passed between them.

"Why don't you go into town with me today and see my new shop?" Sara asked. "You've been so busy with your book that you haven't even seen it."

"You've been pretty busy yourself," Jocelyn said. "What with a man you love, and a new business, and everything wonderful that's happening to you, you must be very happy."

"Come and spend some time with Greg and me today," Sara urged. "You really haven't got to know him, and he's a great guy."

"That's not Joce's fault," Tess said. "You two spend all your time in bed or at the new store. Neither of you has time for anything or anyone else."

"Your jealousy is showing," Sara said, barely looking at Tess.

"Ha!" Tess said. "I'm not jealous of anyone. Just because you two—"

"Girls!" came a voice from the doorway as Jim walked in, his arms full of grocery bags.

It was too much for Jocelyn: too much company, too much of everything. She set her cup down and went upstairs to her bedroom. At least the top floor of the house seemed to be off limits to people who wandered in and out.

She sat down on the edge of her bed and picked up the double frame, Miss Edi's David on one side, a young, beautiful Edilean Harcourt on the other. She envied her for knowing the man she wanted.

When a soft knock sounded on her open door, she looked up to see Sara. "Hi. Mind if I come in?"

"No," Joce said. "I was just . . ." She couldn't think of anything to explain what she was doing.

"Would you like someone to talk to?"

"Yes. No. I don't know," Joce said. "It's just . . ."

"Men," Sara said. "That's what it always is and always will be. Men."

"You met a man, fell madly in love with him instantly, so what do you know about men problems?"

"More than I can tell, and in spite of what Tess says, there's more between Greg and me than just sex and business."

"I'd settle for that."

Sara leaned back on her elbows on the bed. "So tell me what my rotten cousins have done to you and I'll tell you the answers. If there's one thing I know it's my cousins."

"Didn't you tell me that Luke was so much older than you that you hardly knew him at all?"

"That's what I tell strangers," Sara said. "But I hope that by now we're friends. That day at Viv's house proved that."

Jocelyn groaned. "Don't remind me. Bell showing up wearing next to nothing, you and me running through the kitchen like escaping thieves, and Luke's . . ."

"Yeah," Sara said. "Luke's you-know-what. I hope he told you that that's over. He's been working with Ken at MAW to get his marriage annulled."

"He told me," Joce said.

"So soon he won't be married. Legally, he'll never have been married, so what's the problem?"

Jocelyn put her hand to her head. "Me! I am the problem. As far as I can tell, I have a choice between two fabulous men, but I'm not sure if either of them wants **me** or if it's just some male one-upmanship between them."

"So who makes your heart beat faster when you see him?"

"Luke."

"Who do you want to spend every minute of every day with?"

"Luke."

"Who do you see when you imagine a home and kids?"

"Ramsey."

"Oh, my," Sara said. "You do have a problem. I think you need to make up your mind and stick with one of them. You can't bounce back and forth."

"It's not as though either of them has asked me to . . . what do you call it as an adult? Go steady."

"Luke wouldn't say anything until the annulment is final."

"And Ramsey?"

"He could possibly return with an engagement ring. He likes grand gestures."

"But I hardly know him!"

"Interesting," Sara said. "I wonder what you would have said if I'd told you Luke was returning with a gift for you."

"Where is he? Where did he go? He left town, and I don't even know where he is."

Sara sat up on the bed and looked at Jocelyn. "You may think you can't decide between the men, but I think you have decided. Didn't Luke take you hiking?"

"Yes."

"Up to some lake?"

"Yes. We stayed up there and ate sandwiches while we took turns reading Miss Edi's story. Sara, you should read it! It's the most romantic thing I've ever read in my life."

She stood up. "You know what **I** think is romantic? The way you've made my cousin smile. Luke may act tough and as though nothing ever bothers him, but underneath he has a very soft soul. He married a woman he didn't love because she was carrying his child. How sweet is that? He's the one who helped her get started in modeling and she repaid him by—" She stopped talking.

"I know," Jocelyn said, "with an abortion."

"Who told you that?"

"Dr. Dave."

"My goodness, but you do get around. Dr. Dave told you about his grandson's problems in his personal life?"

"Yes. What's wrong with that?"

Sara stood there, looking at Jocelyn for a moment. "You know what I think? I think it's possible that you're so in love with Luke that when he's gone for even a few days you're down in the dumps."

"The last thing I am is in love with any man on this earth. I've known Luke what? Two months?"

"How long did your precious Miss Edi know the man she loved?"

"Days."

"There you have it. I want you to put on some makeup, pull your hair back with one of your headbands, and I want you to spend the day with Greg and me at the new shop. You need to get away from this house, from the story you're so involved in, and you need to talk to people other than my cousins."

"Is that possible in this town?"

"Funny," Sara said, "but jokes won't help you." Reaching out, she took Joce's hands in hers and pulled her to stand. "Now fix yourself up and let's go. I have so much work to do that I don't know where to begin."

❧

"No, not there," Greg Anders said to Sara. "It should go over here, not there."

Jocelyn was sitting on the floor, her legs crossed as she painted the bottom of one wall of the store. She'd been with Sara and Greg for hours now, watching them, and all she could say was that Greg made her want to find Luke and run to him with open arms. How in the world sweet Sara could like such a bossy man was beyond Jocelyn's ability to understand.

The store they were refurbishing was going to be beautiful. It had been full of old furniture for many years, and Sara told Joce that the owner had been so old that the store was rarely open, and when it was, he was asleep. "People used to leave checks and money on the counter, then take what they wanted to buy. When my mom saw tourists go in the shop, she'd send one of her delivery boys over to watch the place, and make sure they didn't steal anything."

"So now you've bought it," Jocelyn said, looking around. It was quite large, and when it was painted and the floors refinished, it was going to be exquisite.

Soon after they'd arrived, Greg had come in, grabbed Sara about the waist, and bent her over to give her a kiss that Jocelyn thought should have been done in private. But Sara didn't seem to mind. "Jocelyn has come to help us today," she said when they finally finished kissing.

As Greg held on to Sara's waist tightly, as though he wanted to let people know she "belonged" to him, he looked Joce up and down in such an appraising way that she had to work not to frown. "So you're the owner of the town mansion," he said. "Would you like to sell it?"

"Stop it!" Sara said, smiling. "She'll think you're serious."

"I am serious," Greg said, looking at Jocelyn. "Sell it to me and Sara and I'll make it into a showplace."

"Will you stop it?" Sara said, but in a giggling sort of way, as though she found what Greg was saying highly amusing.

"I think I'll hold on to the house," Joce said, forcing a smile.

"So, Jocelyn," Greg said as he let go of Sara, "how about if I give you some painting to do? That is, if being the lady of the big manor doesn't mean you're too good to do a little painting."

"Greg!" Sara said.

"It's okay, Jocelyn knows I'm just teasing, don't you, Joce, ol' girl?"

"Yeah, sure," Joce mumbled. "Very funny jokes."

Now, she'd spent about three hours in the new shop, and Greg had worked both her and Sara half to death—while he disappeared often. He wandered in and out of the shop at will, never telling anyone where he was going or when he'd return, and doing no real work at all.

During his second disappearance, Sara went to where Joce was painting. Sara was holding an electric drill, as she was putting together some big oak frames that Greg had ordered. Joce thought that if Greg was as rich as he seemed to be, why couldn't he hire a carpenter and not dump that work on Sara?

"I know he's a little rough," Sara said as she looked down at Joce, "but Greg makes me feel so alive. I spend most of my life with a needle in my hand or at a sewing machine, and my only excitement is whatever I have on DVD. But Greg is full of ideas and he wants to do everything **now.** If I had approached one of my cousins about putting in a clothing store, he would have spent months researching whether it was a good idea or not. But Greg and I talked about it over dinner one night and the next day he told me he'd bought the old furniture store."

"That was fast," Joce said. "But maybe a little thought would have been good. How are you going to get customers to come out here?"

"Greg has that all planned. He's hired an advertising firm to let all of Richmond know that we're here."

"Wow," Joce said. "Richmond. What about Williamsburg?"

"Greg says Williamsburg is too small for us. We have to look at the big picture. He wants us to go to New York a couple of times a year to buy designer clothes, then bring them back here and sell them for twice what we paid for them. He really is a great businessman."

Or a dreamer, Joce thought, but said nothing.

"Uh oh, there he is. I better get back to work."

"Did I see you two ladies goofing off while my back was turned?" Greg said as soon as he was in the store. "I'll have to dock your pay for that."

"I wasn't aware that we were being paid," Jocelyn said, and more animosity than she meant to reveal came out in her voice.

"Now, now," Greg said, "ladies need to keep their tempers in check. Hey, Joce, maybe you'd like a job working here. It might help support that big house of yours."

Jocelyn could feel the blood leaving her face. It looked like the news that Miss Edi had left her no money for the upkeep of the house was out.

"Greg!" Sara said in exasperation. "I told you that in confidence."

"Oh, right. Sorry, Joce."

Joce stood up. "Listen, it's almost lunchtime, and I need to go. Tess said that Ramsey would be back today, and I need to see him about some legal things."

"Sure," Greg said. "So I hear you have two boyfriends and can't make up your mind which one you want."

"Okay," Joce said. "I better go. I . . ." She looked down at her dirty brush and knew she should clean it, but she didn't want to stay there a minute longer. "I'll see you later, Sara, and your store is going to be beautiful."

"I'll see you tonight," Sara called as Joce went out the door.

Joce heard Greg say, "What did I do? I was just teasing her."

When she was outside, Joce breathed a sigh of relief, and she practically ran to Ramsey's office.

"I figured I'd see you today," Tess said as soon as Joce entered. "Did you come to see Ramsey or to get away from Greg the Obnoxious?"

"To get away," Joce said. "I feel like I could use a shot of tequila. What a jerk he is. How can Sara like him?"

"I don't think anyone has lived long enough to answer the question of why someone likes someone else. She laughs at his jokes and thinks his grandiose plans are great."

"Do you think that people from Richmond are going to drive all the way to Edilean to go shopping?"

"No," Tess said. "Why don't you come into my office?"

Joce looked around her and realized she'd never been inside Ramsey's office before. She'd walked and driven past it many times, but had never been inside. It was an old house, probably built in the early

1900s, that had been remodeled into a comfortable but elegant office space. In the front was a waiting room furnished in reproduction eighteenth-century pieces.

"From Colonial Williamsburg?" Joce asked.

"Of course," Tess said as they went to the back of the building. They passed two desks with women behind them, and they looked up curiously when Joce walked by.

"They're shocked that I have any women friends," Tess said as she closed the door to her office. It was beautiful but in a stark way that Joce couldn't have stood for long. There were no photos on the desk, nothing personal anywhere. Just like her apartment, Joce thought. It's as though she doesn't want anyone to know about her life.

"So what was he up to today?" Tess asked as she sat down behind her desk, leaving Joce to take one of the seats in front.

Joce didn't like the desk between them, but she said nothing. "You mean Greg?"

"Yes, of course. I was so involved in the catering and you were so wrapped up in your book, that neither of us paid any attention to Sara's new boyfriend. It'll be more difficult now."

"True," Joce said, but her voice was cautious. "You aren't suggesting that we do anything about it, are you? And, besides, as far as I can tell, Sara likes him. She doesn't need anything to be done."

"After I met him, I talked her into letting MAW handle the legal aspects of the store."

"Meaning?"

"That I reminded her that she has no money, so she shouldn't sign any papers. Let him pay for everything, and let it be on his head when the thing fails."

"You're sure the store will fail?" Joce asked.

"I think that if Sara opened a little place with her own creations and did a lot of altering for a select clientele, she'd do well. Sara is good one-on-one, but I can't see her getting involved in Fashion Week in New York. Can you?"

Jocelyn narrowed her eyes at Tess. "I can't see that either you or I know what's best for Sara and that we should let her live her own life."

"That's a thought," Tess said, then she glanced up at the window by her door. "Rams is back."

For a moment, Jocelyn just sat there, staring at Tess. It had only been a flash, maybe a sixty-fourth of a second, but there had been a light in Tess's eyes when she saw Ramsey, that . . . Joce wasn't sure what it meant, but she knew that Tess was glad to see him.

Turning in her seat, Joce watched Ramsey

stride through the building and straight to Tess's office. He didn't slow down to set his briefcase down, or acknowledge the greetings of the many people who said hello to him. He ignored the pink telephone notices that the two secretaries tried to hand to him. Instead, he raced across the long room to get to Tess. He threw her door open so hard he nearly hit Joce with it—but he didn't notice.

"What's happened while I was away?" Ramsey asked her.

Joce sat in her chair, half hidden by the door, and looked from one to the other, and noted the way their eyes saw only each other—and Jocelyn wanted to do a dance of joy. It was almost as though she could hear bagpipe music in her head and she wanted to put her arms above her head and do a Highland reel.

Smiling so wide she was showing her back teeth, Joce said, "Hi, Ramsey. Have a nice time in Boston?"

When Ramsey turned to look at her, there was a second when his eyes didn't register who she was. "Jocelyn!" he cried, sounding as though she were the person he most wanted to see in the whole world. In the next second he had his arms around her and was hugging her.

"Did you miss me? Did my horrible cousin try to run off with you?"

"Which one of your cousins would that be? You have so many."

"Luke," Ramsey said as he put his face in her neck, as though he meant to start kissing her.

Joce stole a look at Tess and saw that she had sat back down at her desk and was studiously looking at some papers. Joce pushed Ramsey away from her. "How can anyone run off with me when I'm anchored to that house? I was just about to tell Tess that Greg Anders offered to buy it from me. He knows I have no money to support the place, so he volunteered to take it off my hands."

"Who the hell is Greg Anders?" Ramsey asked Tess.

"Sara's new boyfriend," Tess said. "Bought a house here, has lots of money, and they're opening a designer dress shop in the old furniture store."

Ramsey's eyes widened. "This all happened in the short time I was away?"

"Mmmm," Joce said. "Lots has happened since you were away."

He turned a serious face to her. "Such as?"

"I think I'll let Tess tell you," Joce said. She was trying to get her smile under control, but she couldn't. "I need to go."

"You aren't going to do more painting, are you?" Tess asked.

"You're painting Edilean Manor?" Ramsey asked, his voice full of horror.

"Lavender," Joce said. "My favorite color. Think about the morning sun hitting that lavender house. The image boggles the mind, doesn't it?"

"You can't—" Ramsey began as Jocelyn closed the door, and she heard Tess say, "She was making a joke, so try to find your sense of humor and don't make a fool of yourself."

Laughing, Joce left the office, aware that the secretaries were staring at her in disbelief. Joce was probably the only person to ever leave Tess's office and be laughing.

22

LUKE WAS GONE for nearly two weeks. During that time, he didn't call her or contact her in any way. But Jocelyn was fine. She now knew where she wanted to go and what she wanted to do. She thought it had a lot to do with the way Sara looked at Greg, and that flash of light in Tess's eyes when she first saw Ramsey. Love didn't have room for the word **should** in it. She **should** be interested in Ramsey because Miss Edi told her he was the perfect man for her, and with that great house to care for, she **should** share it with Ramsey. He'd know how to decorate it and care for it. Luke would probably put weeds in empty mayonnaise jars and think they looked great.

But none of that mattered. Jocelyn knew where her heart lay, and that made her at peace.

She spent most of the time he was away in Williamsburg researching. One day she idly looked up the name of Angus Harcourt and found that he'd been part of the founding of the country. He'd never been a politician, but he'd been there and he'd had a lot to say about breaking away from England.

Joce hadn't thought much about the man, just smiling at the story that Miss Edi had included in her letter in her will. It was romantic to think of a young Scotsman kidnapping the laird's daughter and running away with her and a wagon full of gold, but she hadn't thought about what they did afterward.

Jocelyn had joked about writing a history of Edilean, but finding Angus Harcourt's name mentioned along with that of Thomas Jefferson made her see the possibilities of such a book.

Joce organized all she'd been able to find out about Miss Edi's time with Dr. Brenner, typed it, then went over the earlier stories written by Miss Edi. Again, Joce laughed about Bertrand, marveled at the love between Edi and David, then, as always, tears came to her eyes when she thought of David's death. If only they could have had a **life** together! she thought.

23

WHEN THE PHONE rang and the caller ID showed that it was Luke, Joce put her hand over her heart to quieten it.

"Did you miss me?" he asked without preamble, "or did you not even notice I was gone?"

What she wanted to ask him was if his annulment was finished, was he free, and she thought maybe she wanted to tell him that she loved him. "Yes and no," she said. "I kept really busy. I met Sara's new boyfriend and helped them paint the new shop."

"Nice guy, huh?"

Jocelyn's grip on her emotions left her. "You talked to someone here before **me,**" she half shouted.

Luke's chuckle let her know that he heard her jealousy. "Not like you mean. Nana met the boy-friend, and she told Gramps, who told me. That make you feel better?"

"Not much. So your grandfather talked to you while you were away." She knew she was sounding like a sulky little girl, but she couldn't stop herself.

"Sort of," Luke said, and she could hear how much he was enjoying all this. "He was with me part of the way, then I dropped him off and flew on. It was while we were together that he talked to Nana and she told him."

"Is this supposed to make me feel better? Where have you been?! And don't you dare call me 'Mom.'"

"New Hampshire, then London. I left Gramps in New Hampshire, then I flew to London. I just got back an hour ago."

"London?" she asked softly. "You did something about Miss Edi, didn't you?"

"Yes. Oh! And I stopped in New York too. Gramps has some friends there. Does that answer all your questions?"

"Yeah, and now I'm completely content. When are you coming over here to explain what you and your sly grandfather have been up to?"

"He is sly, isn't he? Good observation."

"Why don't I meet you at **your** house? That would make a nice change. I'd like to see how you've decorated it. Do you grow orchids in the shower?"

"Only if I haven't had a bath in a couple of weeks. Then I get them in my left ear. I don't know why it's always the left and not the right one. And my belly button—"

"Stop it! Leave the bad jokes to me. I want to know what you and your grandfather have been up to these past weeks."

"Snooping and spying in a big way."

"Luke," she said, and her voice was half warning, half pleading.

"Gramps went to New Hampshire to meet General Austin's widow and sweet-talk her out of the letters."

Jocelyn drew in her breath. "Did he get them?"

"Yes," Luke said, but he was hesitant. "Listen, Joce, we found out some things that . . ."

"That what?"

"That I think might upset you a bit."

"Oh, Lord, what now?"

"It's nothing bad," he said. "It's just . . . I swore to Gramps that I wouldn't tell you, so I have to keep my mouth shut. If it were up to me I'd be over there right now with a stack of papers that—"

"What kind of papers?"

"History," Luke said quickly. "Gramps has to rest today. He can't take all this traveling, so how about if I pick you up at four and we go to his house?"

"And he's going to be there when I see all these papers?"

"That was part of the deal with him. Besides, he's a doctor."

"What does that mean?"

"Nothing," Luke said quickly. "Forget that I said it. Is four all right with you or are you going to be one of the slaves Sara's boyfriend uses on the new shop?"

"Ramsey and I have an appointment to get a marriage license at one, so I guess we can make it."

"Joce?" Luke said. "I'm curious if you've ever made one of those marrying-Ramsey jokes around Tess."

"Let me see . . . My head is still on my shoulders, I have both arms, and even my feet are still on. No, I don't think I have."

"Finally, at last, you see it."

"You could have **told** me."

"Then have you tell Ramsey and Tess? No, let them find out all by themselves."

"You could come over here before four, you know. I think that garden of yours looks pretty bad and it needs some work."

"Don't try to entice me. If I spent ten minutes with you, you'd get everything out of me, and Gramps said that if I told you when he wasn't there, he'd make me play golf with him every day for a month. He even threatened to use that ol' I-won't-be-here-much-longer bit that always gets me."

"I hope you didn't inherit his cruelty."

"I probably did, since I haven't let you see the inside of my house."

That threw Joce for a moment. She'd teased him about not seeing inside his house, but she hadn't thought there was actually anything bad in there. Or maybe not bad but strange. "What's, uh . . . what's in your house?"

"Pictures of other girls," Luke said. "I have to go. I need a couple of hours of sleep, then I have some things to do. I'll pick you up at four. By the way, Nana is copping out of this, so it'll just be the three of us."

After they said good-bye, Jocelyn held the phone a while and thought about what Luke had told her. The letters from General Austin, then

Luke went to London to . . . to do what? Was there something in the letters that made him go to London?

Joce called Tess. "I want to get my hair . . . I don't know . . . looking great. Where do I go?"

"So Luke's back," Tess said. "Let me make a call and I'll call you back."

Ten minutes later, Joce was in her car and heading into Williamsburg for what Tess called an "emergency appointment." "I'm not that bad," Joce had mumbled, but she didn't care. She just wanted to look good for this evening.

When Luke came to pick her up, he was in his car, a dark blue BMW sedan. He got out and came around to open the door for her. "Wow! This is great," she said as she slid onto the leather seat. "You said you wanted your grandfather there because he's a doctor. Are you being nice because you're planning to tell me that I have only six months to live?"

When he didn't answer, she looked at him sharply. "Luke?"

"People's lives change," he said solemnly. "Sometimes for good, sometimes for bad."

"Now you're scaring me."

He reached out and took her hand in his. "Sorry for all the mystery, but it's what I promised Gramps.

Right now I think he's the happiest person on earth. We talked on the plane, and he told me how much he truly loved Miss Edi. He can never say that around Nana, of course, but he did love her. Gramps said he and Edi spent their entire childhoods together and it's because of her that he became a doctor. After he saw her legs, he went back to school on the GI bill, and . . ." Luke squeezed Joce's hand harder. "You look different."

"Tess sent me to a salon where I got plucked and dyed and buffed. It took hours and I was so nervous I could hardly sit in the chair."

"No, it's not that, although I do like that pink polish. I've seen peonies just that color."

He dropped her hand and put his back on the steering wheel. "There's something else different."

"I, uh, decided that I like you better than Ramsey."

"Did you?" Luke said, sounding as though that meant nothing, but she could see the tip of his eyebrow begin to twitch. So it wasn't just lying that caused that, but also great emotion.

"I like you better than Ramsey too," he said softly.

"Let's ask him to be our ring bearer."

Luke laughed. "That's a deal. But only if he wears a powder blue velvet jacket."

Jocelyn's heart was pounding in her throat so hard that she could hardly breathe. She wasn't sure, but she may have just been proposed to. Or proposed to him. Whatever it was, she didn't think she'd ever felt happier.

When they arrived at Dr. Dave's house, every light seemed to be on, but the brightest thing was his face. He looked as though he'd found the Secret to Life.

"I really wish you two would tell me what's going on."

"I thought we'd have some tea first," Dr. Dave said.

"You have got to be kidding," Luke and Joce said in unison, then broke into laughter.

"I'd be embarrassed to know where you two have been all afternoon."

"In a hair salon," Joce said.

"Taking a nap," Luke said.

Dr. Dave looked from one to the other. "Well, something has happened." He put up his hand. "Don't tell me. My old brain can't take any more information."

He turned to Jocelyn. "My grandson and I know most of what we're about to tell you, but some of it we can't do until you know what we do. If you don't want to wait until after tea, then I suggest that we have tea while my grandson reads us the last part of Miss Edi's story. Are you ready, Jocelyn?"

"Is the tea hot?"

"Steaming."

"Then I'm ready."

24

I AM FEELING A bit peckish," Hamish said at breakfast, and both Edi and David had to hide smiles.
"Peckish" was English slang for hungry, and if there
was anything the man could do, it was eat. At first
he'd made some comments on David being a trai-
tor because it was Italian food and Italy was on the
German side.

"If you don't want to eat it . . . ," David said as
he started to take the plate away, but Hamish
reached for it.

"I guess it won't hurt the world to eat one plate
of spaghetti."

"That's—" David began, but stopped. Why bother to tell the man the difference between pizza and spaghetti and pasta in general? He was glad when the old man disappeared into his room right after breakfast.

That morning Edi had found a broken-down old greenhouse at the back of the barn. It had been nearly covered with dead vines, and when she'd hacked through them, she'd found the glass house, and inside were tomatoes that had reseeded themselves. The vines had kept the soil warm through the winter, and their lack of leaves in the spring had let the sunlight in.

"I could kiss you for these," David said, picking up one of the precious globes from the little basket Edi held out to him. "In fact, I could kiss you for anything at all."

She backed away so the table was between them, but she was smiling. "Don't you know that I'm the Untouchable One?"

"I heard that," David said in a husky voice as he moved toward her, but this time Edi didn't move away.

But David's stiff leg caught on the corner of a chair and he went into a spin that almost made him fall. He caught himself on the edge of the table, then sat down heavily. "I hope Austin rots in hell," he muttered as he rubbed at his sore leg. "How can a man do any courting with this thing on?"

When Edi said nothing, he turned to look at her, and she had a strange look in her eye.

"What's going on in that little mind of yours?"

She scratched at her head. Today she hadn't bothered with trying to style it. She'd just let it hang loose about her shoulders, and when it got in her way she shoved a couple of Aggie's barrettes at the sides. Between her too-big shirt and her too-big trousers that were belted at her waist, and her dark hair about her shoulders, David thought she looked magnificent. If it weren't for his leg he would have made a move toward her before now.

"I need a bath," Edi said. "I think I got something from the chickens in my hair."

"I saw some kerosene in the barn. Should we use that?"

"No," Edi said, smiling. "I'm going to take a bath in the river."

"That's not a good idea. It's still swollen, and the current is—"

He didn't say any more because he heard the door close behind Edi. When he went to look out the window, he saw that she was running. Obviously, she was on a mission, but he wondered what

it was. When she came out of the barn a few minutes later and she was carrying two coils of rope,
he knew exactly what she was thinking of doing.

"No," he said when she came into the kitchen.
"No, no, double no. If you try that I'll hike out of
here and find a telephone and tell Austin what
you're planning to do."

"Can you tie good knots?"

"No," David said firmly as he sat down on a
chair.

"Okay, then we'll have to make do with my
knots." She put the end of one of the ropes around
her waist and tied it. "There. Nice and strong,
isn't it?"

David reached up, grabbed one end of the knot,
and pulled. It came loose easily.

"Maybe I should tie it in three loops."

"Please don't do this," David said, his voice almost tears. "It's not worth it. We have one more
day, then Aggie will be back, we'll get the magazine, then—"

"What about this knot?"

David pulled both ends, and they were tight.

"Perfect," she said. "We'll use that one."

"And what if you get caught down there and
want to get out?" he asked, his voice low. "Do you
take a knife with you and saw at the rope?"

"Then **you** fix it," she said, "and I don't want any lectures about why I shouldn't do this. I'm a great swimmer."

"Edi," he began, refusing to get up from the chair. "This is very noble of you, but I don't want you to do this."

Bending, she put her lips to his and kissed him. "We have very little time left," she said, "and how can you make love to me with that thing on your leg? I'm going to do this no matter what you say, but I'd very much appreciate your help with it all."

David was so stunned by what she'd said that it took him a moment to react. When she started to walk away, he caught her wrist and pulled her to him so she landed on his lap.

He kissed her. Gently, then with increasing passion, his kiss deepening. "I fell in love with you the moment I first saw you," he whispered. "It was like I knew you from somewhere. Heaven, maybe. I knew you were mine and always will be."

She ran her hand along his cheek. "I detested you."

David chuckled. "You sure know how to make love to a man."

"Sorry, but I know nothing in that department, but I've been told that I'm a fast learner."

He kissed her some more, his hands in her hair.

Then the spell was broken when Edi moved away to claw at her scalp. "There's something crawling in my hair, so I'm going to jump in the river to wash it, and I might as well get that Allen wrench. Are you ready?"

When he frowned and looked as though he was about to again ask her not to go, she put a fingertip over his lips. "Think on the bright side. I might not find it. It could be in the Thames by now and you'll be in that brace for the rest of the war."

David put his hand on the kitchen table and heaved himself up. "Lead the way." He was trying to sound jovial, but she could hear the fear in his voice.

"Come on," she said, teasing, "I have the buggy already hitched."

"Buggy," he said, smiling as he followed her out the door. Maybe ol' Hamish had a car buried under that mess in the barn and Edi'd found it. Maybe—

All good thoughts stopped when he saw Edi drive out of the barn in a contraption that looked like it was made in the 1890s. It was a horse carriage with two big wheels in back and two smaller ones in the front. There was a frayed and worn padded seat in the front and what looked to be a standing area in the back. Hamish's old horse was tied to it with lots of leather straps, and Hamish himself was standing to the side, looking so pleased he was almost smiling.

"You know how to use it, do you?" he asked Edi, who looked as though she'd been born sitting on a buggy.

She had a long whip in her hand and she gave it a snap over the horse's head, then a few clicks, and the animal moved quickly in a perfect circle.

"Oh, aye," Hamish said, "you know how to drive."

"I have about a hundred ribbons and trophies at home," she said. "Oh, but look at him, how he loves it."

She was referring to the horse—certainly not David, who was already backing toward the house.

"That he does," Hamish said as he lovingly stroked the horse's nose. "He won many a race in his time, and he remembers them. The war people said he was too old to be of any use to them, but he's got a lot in him yet."

"We won't be long," Edi said. "David's going to tie me to the bridge and I'm going back into the car to get some things. Maybe we can get that horrible contraption off his leg."

"Don't need it, do he?" Hamish said.

Edi smiled at the top of the man's head. He may be old, but he saw a lot. "Come on," she called to David. "Hamish will help you get up on the back. You'll need to hold on when we go downhill, but I think you'll be all right."

"Think we should tie him on?" Hamish asked.

"No, I do not need to be tied on," David said, making Edi and Hamish smile at each other. It was easy to see that David thought the buggy might as well have been a mastodon. To his eyes, it was old and dangerous.

Since the old horse was dancing about, remembering the days when he was young and fast, it took Hamish's help to get David up on the buggy. The back of it was flat and open, so it couldn't be used for carrying things. There were a couple of handles, but it was difficult for David to sit, his leg out straight, and hold on to them. "What good is this thing? You can't carry anything with it."

"What good is a race car?" Edi asked, and Hamish nodded.

"All right, girl, take her down. But be careful. He pulls to the right."

"Don't worry, I won't let him," she said, then clicked to the horse, who took off as though someone had fired a starting pistol.

In the back, David hung on with both arms and the jarring made the steel cut into his skin, and his teeth were rattling together. "Do you have to go this fast?" he yelled up at Edi, but all he heard was her laughter.

To David, it seemed about three hours before they reached the river, but it was only a few minutes. They could have walked through the woods, but with David's leg that would have been torture.

He could see that the water had receded enough that it no longer went over the bridge, and to one side he could see the bottom of the tires of the car. If the water kept going down, within a day or two half of the wheels would be visible.

By the time he got down from the buggy, Edi was already tying a rope about her waist. He brushed her hands away and redid it. "Listen to me," he said softly. "If anything goes wrong and you want me to pull you up, jerk on the rope twice. If the rope tangles and you need to get it off of you, pull this end. See?" He gave it a firm jerk and the rope fell away. "I'm going to count, and if you stay longer than fifty-eight seconds, I'm going in after you. Do you understand?"

"Perfectly," she said as she kicked off the big old boots she'd been wearing for two days. Then she pulled on the cord and let the rope fall to the bridge. The water had receded and the wood was dry, but it still didn't look safe.

"What are you doing?" David asked.

"I can't swim in all these clothes. Do you mind if I strip down?"

"I don't even know how to answer that," he said in a whisper, then stepped back to watch her unbutton her shirt, then slip out of it. She was wearing the peach-colored teddy that she'd had on when he undressed her the first night—and he'd never seen anything more beautiful than she.

She dropped the old shirt on the bridge, then went to her belt, but the horse began to act up and Edi started to go to him.

"Shut up!" David said to the horse, and it instantly became still.

Smiling, Edi unfastened her belt buckle and let the trousers fall to the bridge.

"They were wrong," David whispered.

"About what?" Edi asked.

"Your legs. They have to be **four** feet long."

"I don't know. I've never measured them. Would you tie the rope around me?"

"Yes," he said, but he took his time, looking at every inch of her while he slowly walked toward her.

He put the rope around her waist, tied the end

to the side of the bridge, then nodded toward the other rope in the back of the buggy. "What's that for?"

"If there's anything still in the car, I'm going to get it out."

"Meaning your suitcase?"

"Yes, my own clothes," she said, as she glanced down at the big trousers he wore. "Did you bring anything that would fit without the brace?"

"Yes, but I don't want you to bother with getting it. If you can find the Allen wrench, fine, if not, then nothing else is important. You understand me?"

"You're going to make a great father," she said, "but I already have one. I think if the car is hidden, then the water is deep enough for a dive, don't you?"

"No!" David half shouted. "We'll go to the edge and you can walk in. You don't know—" He broke off because she climbed onto the railing and did a perfect swan dive into the river. He held his breath as he waited for her to come up and every terror went through his head. Had she hit bottom? Was she unconscious? He was halfway over the railing when she came up.

"It's cold!" she said.

"What did you think it would be? Tropical?" he said, doing his best to hide his fear. "Are you all right?"

"Fine. It feels great. I'm going to wash my hair. Throw me that soap off the seat, will you?"

"Soap!" he said, mumbling. He just wanted her to get this done and get out of there. With his leg held stiffly, he half ran, half hobbled to the buggy and got a bar of soap off the seat, then tossed it to her. "Good catch," he said.

"I was the best batter on my school baseball team," she said. "I could hit the ball just ten feet and still outrun them all." She was soaping her hair while treading water. Turning, she looked at the car, then swam to it and climbed on top.

"Look at me," she yelled.

"Yeah, look at you." She had on a clinging teddy that was wet and transparent, and she was standing on top of an upside-down car that couldn't be seen above the water. She looked like she was standing on the water. "My kingdom for a camera," he whispered, but he had none.

"Be careful on that thing," he called. "The bottom of a car isn't as smooth as a mattress."

She kept rubbing her hair with the soap, then threw the bar back to him. To his shame, he missed it and had to chase it across the bridge. When he looked back, she was gone, and for a moment his heart seemed to stop beating.

He waited what seemed to be minutes but there was no sign of her. He gave a tug on the rope, but she didn't tug back, and she hadn't released it. "I knew this was a bad idea," he said. "I knew it. I should have stopped her. I should have forced her to—"

"To what?" she said and she was below him, her hand on a pillar of the bridge.

"Forced you not to do this."

"I'd like to have seen you try," she said in a suggestive way. "Can you reach my hand?"

David got down on his stomach and reached down until he touched her hand—and she passed him the Allen wrench. He clasped it tightly, then rolled onto his back and for a moment held it to his chest. Such a little thing, but so very important.

"I got it," he said, "so now you can come up." But when he looked, she was already gone. With lightning speed, David unbuckled his trousers and pushed them off, then he gave one last look of hatred to the steel brace and began loosening screws. For the sake of comfort, all the screws were recessed so the protruding heads wouldn't chafe a person's skin, but that made it necessary to use an unusual tool to remove the cage.

Half of the screws were too tight from water and rust, and one of them broke as he twisted. But with David's determination and just plain anger—not to mention the desire he had for Miss Edilean Harcourt—he kept working.

He broke blisters and made some new cuts as he wrenched the thing off his leg, but he managed to tear it away from his skin, then he threw it toward the far end of the bridge.

When he was free of it, he had trouble standing, but he made it. He had to bend his knee half a dozen times before it began working again. His leg was a mess, with blisters and bloody patches and bits of cloth stuck to raw places, but to him it looked great. "I'm out of it," he yelled as he looked back at the river, but Edi didn't answer him.

He unbuttoned his shirt, threw it on the bridge, climbed on the rail, and dove in.

"What took you so long?" she asked as she swam into his arms.

25

T HAT'S IT," David Aldredge said.

"What do you mean that that's it?" Joce asked.

"That's all the story Edi wrote, or at least it's all that I have. Alex McDowell left the papers to me in his will, and I don't know if that's all he had, or if Edi wrote more and it was lost. At the end, Alex was pretty bad."

"Bad?" Jocelyn asked. "What do you mean?"

"Alzheimer's. He couldn't remember who he was, much less anything about a story sent to him many years ago. However . . ." Dr. Dave paused, as though for a drumroll, "I found something interesting just a few years ago. You know how it is, boring day, playing on the Internet, and I typed in Dr. Jellie's name.

"This is an excerpt from a series of books about World War II. As far as I know, it's the only place Dr. Jellicoe's name is mentioned. Would you like me to read it to you?"

"Yes, please," said both Luke and Jocelyn.

Dr. Sebastian Jellicoe's contributions to WWII were never acknowledged during his lifetime, or even afterward. Anyone who met him didn't come away talking about his great brain or how he could look at a scrambled-up jumble of words and tell at a glance what it said. What people always remembered about him was his great storytelling. He could go to the grocery and come back with a story worthy of being published.

For myself, at the time a young and eager student wanting to learn at the feet of a master, the story I remember best was about the young couple who probably saved his life. It was near D-day in 1944, and Dr. Jellie told that he was sitting by his fire on a cold, rainy night, half asleep in his chair, when he heard the noise of a horse and a man shouting curse words. He said that for a moment he was so befuddled that he thought it was Father Christmas and the fat man had just collided with his roof.

Instead, it was two tall, strikingly good-looking young Americans, and they'd come tearing across the countryside in the middle of the night in the ancient racing carriage of his old, grumpy neighbor named Hamish. Dr. Jellie said the man couldn't get along with anyone and as a result he was left alone. It was told around the village that he'd once been a driver of carriages in races and that he'd won nearly everything until an accident made him quit. He retired to his father's farm and spent the rest of his life complaining to his long-suffering wife and children.

But on that cold, drizzly night, here came one of Hamish's buggies being pulled by a horse nearly as old as Hamish, and driven by a girl so tall and beautiful that Dr. Jellie said he thought maybe he'd died and was about to enter Heaven. She looked like Boadicea riding into battle.

In the back of the buggy was a young man who was taller than she was, just as handsome, but a man who obviously hated carriage riding as much as he adored the young woman.

"You certainly paid me back," he said to her when he got down and after he'd lost his dinner in the bushes.

"I don't like your driving and you don't like mine. We're even," she said as she smiled at Dr. Jellie and introduced herself as Eddie, and he was David. Over the years Dr. Jellie had forgotten their last names and I've often wondered who they were and what happened to them.

He invited them into his house to have some tea. Young David followed him inside the house, but Eddie, like the good horsewoman she was, put the horse and buggy in the barn first. When she came in, her dark hair was wet, her clothes stuck to her, and both men stared at her, speechless, for a while.

She was the one to break the silence. "Here, I have this for you." She then handed him a copy of **Time** magazine that was a few weeks old.

"And what am I to do with it?" Dr. Jellie asked.

"There's a message in it from General Austin," she said. "I'm his secretary."

"Ol' Bulldog Austin. My goodness but I haven't seen him in a long time. You mean no one's shot him by now?"

"Everybody wants to," David said, "but no one's done it yet."

"I think you should look at the message," Eddie encouraged. "I think it's important. You're to go back to London with us."

"Am I?"

"It seems that someone knows what you're doing for the war effort," David said.

"Oh, everyone knows that. Mrs. Pettigrew delivers the envelopes with my lunch. They're all marked Top Secret."

David and Eddie looked at each other with their mouths open.

"But—" David began.

"I thought—"

Dr. Jellie looked at the **Time** magazine. "I've seen this issue. Is it the one Aggie took? Are you two the Americans who were searching for it?"

"We had no idea you were so close," Eddie said. "But we couldn't have come anyway because we didn't have the magazine and we needed it. I really must insist that you look at it. I think that what's in there is very important."

"Oh poppycock!" he said. "They never mark anything that's valuable as important. Those envelopes that say Top Secret on them? Seed catalogs. It's the letters from my daughter that hold the secrets."

"Your daughter works in London?" David asked.

"I don't have a daughter."

"Oh," Eddie said.

In the next second, Dr. Jellie threw the magazine on the fire, and both David and Eddie jumped. "Only thing it's good for," he said. "I'm sure everyone in the village has seen it by now. You two caused quite a stir, what with missing the bridge and putting your car in the river."

"We did **not**—" David began, but stopped as he stared at the magazine burning in the fire. "I'm afraid we've come here for nothing," he said, but as the words came out, he gave a look at beautiful young Eddie that nearly set the house ablaze.

"Did Austin give either of you anything else?" Dr. Jellie asked.

"Nothing to me," Eddie said. "He gave me a map which I don't think was accurate, and a packet of money. I left them back at Hamish's farm. Should I go get them?"

Just then a clap of thunder came, and Dr. Jellie said, "No, dear, I think it can wait." He looked at David. "What about you? Did you receive any paper?"

"No. Austin had a steel brace put on my leg that was like a medieval torture and he—"

"But no paper?"

David shook his head. "Except for the invitation, there was nothing."

"Let me see it," Dr. Jellie said.

"What invitation?" Eddie asked David.

"To a dance where you wore an electric blue gown."

"The Officers' Ball," Eddie said, "but that wouldn't have anything to do with this. Those invitations go out to a lot of people directly from the printer." She watched as David got his wallet out of his back pocket and removed the envelope. It didn't appear to have even been wet, but she knew it must have been underwater.

"How in the world did you keep that dry?" she asked him.

"You take care of things that are important to you," Dr. Jellie said as he looked at David, smiling.

"Yes, sir, you do."

"Waxed cloth? Courier's packet?"

"Yes," David said, grinning back at him. "We fished our suitcases from out of the car in the river and that was inside mine and as dry as when I put it in there."

"Good boy," Dr. Jellie said, getting out of his chair. He took the invitation over to a table and opened a box that contained glass jars of what looked to be alcoholic beverages.

"I could use some of that," David said, putting out his hand.

"Drink one of these and your tongue will dissolve in a very unpleasant fizz."

David drew his hand back.

"Now let me see," Dr. Jellie said, "which one should I try?"

David put his hand on Eddie's arm and

drew her toward the fire to give Dr. Jellie some privacy. A couple of awful smells came from his direction but at last he said, "There, now, I have it. I'm to go to London with you two and Austin is going to send me to the U.S."

David was the first to recover. "That's it? But we already knew that. We **told** you that."

"Spies have a rather frequent habit of disappearing, so they find that paper is better."

"But that paper ended up on the bottom of a river."

"Ah, but even then it was protected. My guess is that Austin knew it would be so precious to you that you'd take care of it."

"Yes," David said, looking at Eddie and smiling. "Very precious."

"Well now that that's done, I suggest we all get a good night's sleep and start off to London tomorrow. Do you require one room or two?"

"One!" Eddie said quickly, and held up her left hand to show the ring she wore on her trip around the country. "We're married."

"So you are," Dr. Jellie said, smiling.

He said that the next morning the beautiful Boadicea rode off in the carriage to return it to Hamish and an hour later came running down the hill. He said he'd never in his life seen a more beautiful sight than that tall girl running down the hill toward her lover. Dr. Jellie said he always wondered how different his life would have been if there had been a woman who looked at him like that, but, alas, there never was.

He told how the three of them took the train back to London and he said that he'd never seen any two people more in love than they were. They had eyes only for each other, only wanted to be with one another. There was someone waiting for Dr. Jellie when they got to London, and the beautiful Eddie and her love, David, were swept away. He never saw or heard about them ever again.

26

JOCE WAS SITTING quietly in Dr. Dave's study and she was thinking about Miss Edi and her beloved David. She knew what happened next. He was killed and she was burned.

"That's only the beginning of the story," Luke said softly.

"The beginning? That was the end of it."

"No," Dr. Dave said. "Right after you told me about General Austin I wanted to go to New Hampshire and see if I could get the letters."

Joce looked at Luke. "That's what you two were talking about that night at dinner."

"Yes," he said, "and that's why I didn't want you to go with me, but you nagged until I couldn't stand it anymore, so I let you go, then you got your feelings hurt because—"

"You two already sound like an old married couple," Dr. Dave said. "Save it for later. Show her the letters."

Luke pulled a single piece of paper out of his grandfather's briefcase and handed it to her. She dreaded reading the letters, as she was sure they'd be full of the accident and what Miss Edi had gone through in the two years it took her to recover.

6 October 1944

Remember Harcourt, the best secretary I
ever had? I sent her on assignment with
my driver, and it looks like they did more
than I asked of them. She's four months
pregnant. I got so mad I would have made
them get married, but he was sent to another unit and even I can't find him. Harcourt wanted to transfer out but I won't
let her.

18 December 1944

Remember Harcourt? That guy she married got killed. Her kid's due in the spring,
so I'll have to send her away after Christ-

mas. Thank God she hasn't grown a big
belly yet so nobody knows. Without her
my office will fall apart.

21 April 1945

Remember Harcourt? I just heard she was
in a horrible accident where she was badly
burned. She's not expected to live. The
nurse I talked to said the kid was stillborn. I
don't think any loss in this war has hurt me
as much as this one. I had her transferred
stateside so she can die at home.

Jocelyn read the excerpts three times before she
looked up at Luke and Dr. Dave. "Baby?" she
whispered, and tears came to her eyes. "That poor,
poor woman. She lost more than even I thought
she did."

"No," Dr. Dave said as he took Jocelyn's hands
in his own. "You have my grandson to thank for all
of this, as he was the one who was suspicious."

"Suspicious of what?" she asked as Luke handed
her a tissue.

"That nothing rang true," Luke said. "If you'd
known Uncle Alex you would have understood.
He said he owed Edilean Harcourt his entire **life,**
and he wanted to pay her back. Giving her a job,

letting her live for free in a house, that meant nothing to him. He'd done that for several people who'd worked for him all their lives."

"Luke, what are you trying to tell me?"

"With Gramps's help, I hired an entire team of researchers in England and we went back through a lot of World War II records."

"To find out where the baby was . . . was buried?" Joce asked softly.

"Yes and no." He sat down on an ottoman in front of her. "It was the name Clare that did it for me. Remember in the section where Miss Edi said she kept calling for David when everyone thought she was going to die?"

"Yes."

"David **Clare.**"

Joce looked at Dr. Dave. "I'm not getting the point here. What am I missing?"

"Who else do you know is named Clare?"

"No one I know has that last name."

The two men kept looking at her.

"My mother is named Claire."

Dr. Dave and Luke smiled at each other.

"Wait a minute!" Joce said. "You're not trying to tell me that my mother—"

"Was the daughter of Edilean Harcourt and David Clare. Yes, she was. Show her," Luke said.

Dr. Dave handed Joce some charts such as she'd often seen on TV. DNA charts. She looked at them blankly.

"Sorry for all the secrecy, but if what we suspected hadn't been true, we didn't want you to be hurt," Dr. Dave said. "It was easy to get DNA from you, and not so difficult to get it for Edi. She was a great letter writer and she'd licked a lot of envelopes."

"Miss Edi was my grandmother?" Joce asked in a faint whisper.

"She didn't know," Dr. Dave said. "If she'd known, I'm sure she would have told you. I think that Alex knew about her pregnancy, but no one else did. She stayed in London where no one knew her so she wouldn't have to answer questions. She was burned just a couple of weeks before she was due to deliver."

"But the general said the child was stillborn."

"We figure that's what he was told. We have no paper proof, but it looks like Alfred Scovill was in Europe at the time, making contracts for helmets, and there was a dying woman who'd just given birth to a baby. As far as we could find out, the birth certificate was made out with Alfred and Frances Scovill as the parents—which, of course, wasn't true because his wife was back home in the

States. But it was wartime, and there were a lot of orphans, a lot of tragedies. No one asked many questions. I think Mr. Scovill took the baby home to his wife in the U.S., moved down to Boca Raton, where no one knew them, and never told anyone the truth. His only concession was to name the child 'Claire' from what the dying mother kept saying."

When Jocelyn tried to stand up, her legs were so weak that she wobbled. Luke put his arms around her to steady her, and held her against him for a few minutes. But Joce pushed away and looked at him.

"This is why you said I might need a doctor here." She was trying to make a joke, but neither man smiled. They were looking at her hard.

"Are you okay?" Luke asked.

"Just in a state of shock, that's all. How I wish she'd known. Wish I'd known when she was alive. To share that bond!"

"But you did," Dr. Dave said, taking her hand. "Alex found out about your mother, about the people who'd adopted her, and he bought a house close to them. He set it all up for her to administer the trust, but then he began to lose his memory."

"Alzheimer's," Jocelyn said.

"Yes. He set everything up through MAW and

he concocted that story about knowing the people who adopted you. We figure Alex meant to let Edi spend some time getting to know you, then he'd tell her the truth. But Alex . . . he simply **forgot.**"

Luke went to a side table and mixed her a drink. "I think you need this," he said as he looked at his grandfather.

Jocelyn took the drink and sipped it. "I can feel that you two have something more to tell me. Better get it out before I faint from what you've already told me.".

"We found David Clare's relatives."

She looked up at the two tall men, both of them hovering over her, watching her as though she might collapse at any moment. But their words made her feel less like collapsing than anything they'd said. It would take her a long time to deal with the fact that Miss Edi never knew what they were to each other, but the idea of relatives was startling.

"You mean I might have relatives who have an IQ over seventy, who don't make it their life's work to belittle me and make me feel bad?"

"Actually, I think that's what all relatives do," Luke said. "My cousins— Ow!" he said when his grandfather punched him on the arm.

"You have the telephone number?" Dr. Dave asked Luke.

"Sure. Right here with me. I thought I'd call, then Joce could—"

She snatched the paper out of his hands. "They're my relatives; I'm calling." She went to the big phone on Dr. Dave's desk. "Shall I put it on speaker?"

Both men nodded.

Joce took a couple of deep breaths, then called the number in upstate New York. Immediately, a man's voice answered. "I'm sorry to disturb you, sir, but I'm looking for anyone connected to a man named David Clare, who fought in World War II."

"Speaking."

Jocelyn shrugged in puzzlement to the two men. "Are you related to him?"

"I guess I am," the man said, chuckling.

"You know about Sergeant David Clare who served with General Austin, **that** David Clare?"

"Young lady, I don't know how else to tell you that I **am** David Clare and that **I** served with old Bulldog Austin."

"You," Jocelyn began, but her voice dropped to a whisper. "But you were killed."

"I was reported dead, but actually, I was held

prisoner until the war was over. I can assure you that I am alive, not particularly healthy, but alive."

"Did you know Edilean Harcourt?"

There was a long pause from him. "Yes. She was . . . killed in 1944."

"No. Miss Edi died only last year."

The man's voice rose in anger. "I don't appreciate this. Edilean Harcourt was killed in a fire when a jeep exploded."

"She wasn't," Jocelyn said, near to tears. Was she really talking to Miss Edi's David—to her own grandfather? "She lived. Her legs were horribly burned, but she lived. I met her when I was ten years old and she was my guide, my foster mother—I don't know what you call her. When she died, she left me her old house—"

"Edilean Manor," he whispered.

"Yes. Miss Edi never married. She spent most of her life traveling all over the world with a Dr. Brenner and helping him with disasters. They—" Joce broke off and looked at Luke. "I think he's crying." But then Joce could no longer hold back her tears.

Luke took the phone from her, and by that time a man was yelling. "I don't know who the hell you are to make Uncle Dave cry, but—"

In the background, Luke could hear, "No, no, no. It's about Edi. They knew Edi."

The angry young man stopped shouting. "You know something about Miss Edi?"

"You've heard of her?" Luke asked.

"Are you kidding? I grew up hearing that name. The Lost Love, the only woman Uncle Dave ever loved. You know something about her? Like where she's buried? Wait! Uncle Dave wants the phone back."

Luke put the phone back on speaker so they could all hear.

"Who are you?" David Clare asked.

"I think I'm your granddaughter," Joce said before she started crying again, then David also gave way to tears.

The young man took the phone over again. "Holy hell! What is up with you people?"

In the background David was saying, "Come here. Now. Today. I want to see you **now.**"

The young man said, "It looks like he wants you to come here. If you do, should I have a defibrillator on standby?"

"We may need one for both of them," Luke said, then took the phone off speaker and quickly told the story of Miss Edi being pregnant and delivering the baby, but no one thought she'd live, so a man named Scovill adopted the baby.

"You mean Uncle Dave had a kid?"

"A daughter named Claire."

"Claire Clare," the young man said, amused.

"Yeah," Luke said, looking at Joce, who was crying hard. "Claire Clare. Could we visit? Would that be all right?"

"What I'm wondering is why the hell you're still on the telephone. Can you take a red-eye?"

"I don't know," Luke said, looking at Joce. "Can we be there tomorrow?"

She nodded.

"Listen, uh . . ." He didn't know the man's name.

"Eddie," the man said, then paused. "My name is Edward Harcourt Clare. I was the last of the litter, so they let Uncle Dave name me. If I'd been a girl I'd have been named Edilean."

Luke looked at Jocelyn. "His name is Edward Harcourt Clare."

Joce started laughing and crying at the same time.

"Okay," Luke said, "let me check flights, and I'll call you back in an hour and tell you when we'll be there."

"When you get here, we'll never get the lot of

them to stop crying." Pausing, he lowered his voice. "I just want to say that this is great of you. Uncle Dave has been like a second father to all of us kids. I can't begin to tell you all that he's done in our little town. He's not well and he doesn't have long, but to get to see his own granddaughter . . . Well, thanks. All I can say is thanks a lot."

27

IN THE END, after much discussion, David Clare decided that he'd rather go to Edilean than for them to come to him. "I don't have much time," he said, "and I want to at last see her home." He told how he'd tried to force himself to go many times before, even once buying plane tickets, but he couldn't do it. He knew he'd be reminded of her too strongly and the pain would be more than he could bear.

Luke and Jocelyn spent a frantic two days getting the house ready. The women of Edilean Baptist Church lent beds, linen, and even furniture, and Luke's mother made all the complicated arrangements for transportation. She'd worked for her father off and on for most of her life, so she knew about medical transport. David Clare was driven from the airport in Richmond to Edilean in an ambulance, and he'd made the two EMTs in the back with him laugh through the entire journey.

"Your granddaughter is just like you," Luke told him. "She makes the world's worst jokes at every possible opportunity."

"Go away," Dr. Dave said, "or you'll make them start crying again."

The first meeting between Joce and her grandfather had been so fraught with emotion that neither could say a word. They'd just stared at each other, holding hands as he was lowered from the emergency vehicle and taken into Edilean Manor.

The downstairs parlor, where Joce had done all her research, had been made into a bedroom for Sergeant Clare. After he'd rested for twenty-four hours, he could walk about on two canes—just as Edi did at the end. And the first place he wanted to see was where she was resting.

"But before we go," he said, "is there room beside her for me?"

"Yes," Jocelyn said, holding his old hand on her arm.

Everyone—meaning most of the town—marveled at how much alike Joce and David looked. Their square chins with a dimple, their pale skin, their dark blue eyes. They were even built alike.

"More like me than Edi," David said, looking with love at his granddaughter. "Too bad you didn't get her legs."

"That's all right," Luke said. "Anyway, I like the parts that stick out better."

"Luke!" Joce said, and David laughed so hard he nearly choked.

"She's built just like my mother, and my dad liked her too, as I had eight brothers and sisters."

"We read that." Joce's eyes widened. "That means I have cousins."

"Hundreds," David said.

"Just so I have more than **he** does," she said, looking at Luke.

"A true marriage already," David said.

The stone for Miss Edi's grave was small. "We'll fix that," David said, then looked around her at Luke. "I bet you, college boy, know where I can get a sculptor."

"I can find one."

"'College boy'?" Joce said, smiling. "Luke works for me. I can't afford to pay him, but he's my gardener. And he works for other people too."

David looked at Luke, shaking his head. "I may be old, but my mind still works. One of my grand-nieces stood in line to get a book autographed by you, and she came home wanting you more than the book. She downloaded a photo of you and hung it over her desk. I recognized you the minute I saw you."

Jocelyn stopped walking, glared at Luke, then dropped her grandfather's arm and started walking back to the house.

"Uh, oh," David said, "did I say something wrong?" He turned on his canes when Luke went after Joce.

"You bastard!" she said when he caught up with her.

"I didn't mean to lie to you, but—"

"Why not? Everyone else has. Are there no more honest people in the world?"

"I wanted you to see me as me," Luke said. "I'm sorry I didn't tell you that I write books, and sorry I didn't tell you I was married, but Ingrid's major interest in me was my royalty checks."

"Everyone in this town knew about your marriage and your occupation but they didn't tell me."

"I asked them not to."

"And that's it? You just told them not to menton your writing and they obeyed?"

"Yes," Luke said simply.

"Well, isn't it just lovely that you have people who love you so completely? Personally, that's never happened to me." She turned and started back to the house.

"Yes, you have," Luke said. "Me. I love you that much. I've loved you since that first night when I dumped mustard all over you."

"That was an accident," she said over her shoulder.

Luke moved to stand in front of her. "Yeah, it was, and I liked that you were honest and told Ramsey the truth."

"Honest? Do you know the meaning of the word?"

"I'm learning it," he said. "But then, I've had some master teachers of how to hide the truth. You, Ingrid, my family, Ramsey, even Miss Edi."

Jocelyn tried to get past him, but he kept moving to block her way. Finally, she put her arms across her chest. "All right, so what do you write?"

"Thomas Canon," he said.

Joce's mouth dropped open. Thomas Canon was the main character in a series of books that were very popular. They were set in the eighteenth century, just before the American Revolution. Thomas had been in love with a beautiful young woman named Bathsheba since they were children, but her parents made her marry a rich man she didn't love. Heartbroken, Thomas spent book after book traveling around the newly forming country, meeting people and getting into one scrape after another.

"Luke Adams," Joce said, for that was the name of the author.

"That's me."

"So the gardening—?"

"My degree is in botany and after Ingrid I was . . ." He shrugged.

"Who gets a degree in **botany**?" Joce said. "How can you make a living with a degree in botany? You should have—" She broke off because he pulled her into his arms and kissed her.

"Jocelyn, I love you. I apologize that it took me so long to say it and that I kept so many things from you, but I had to be sure. Do you think you can ever forgive me?"

"Sure she can!" David Clare said from behind them. "If Edi could forgive me for being an uneducated lout, she can forgive you for pretending to be one."

Luke and Jocelyn smiled at him because they'd learned that since the war he'd built his little garage into a franchise that was all over the Northeast. He was a multimillionaire. And he'd put all his businesses under the name of his beloved brother, Bannerman, who'd perished in the war.

The switching of the names was why Edi had never found out her David was still alive.

"Can you forgive me?" Luke asked.

How could she not? she thought. But she wasn't about to let him off so easily. "On one condition. You have to tell me if Thomas Canon is ever going to get Bathsheba."

"Not you too," Luke groaned. "I have a huge box full of letters in my house, all from readers asking me the same damned question. I don't know."

"Who do you mean you don't know? You created those people. You control them."

"Sort of."

"What does that mean?" Joce asked.

David was laughing. "You'd better give up now," he said to Luke. "She may look like me, but she's just like Edi."

"I'm not at all like her," Joce said, her eyes wide.

"Identical," David said. "Did she tell you about the time—"

"Wait right there," Joce said. "I'm going to get a tape recorder. Unlike some people, I don't make up characters."

When Luke and David were alone, the older man was still chuckling. "You have your hands full there, boy."

"Yes, I do," Luke said, grinning.

It was later, after dinner, when David was asleep, that Luke and Joce sat alone in the kitchen and talked. She was still feeling a bit distant toward him about his concealing his occupation from her, but Luke was wearing her down.

"Last night my mother told me the oddest story," he said, then watched Joce's ears perk up at the word **story.** "She went to Miss Edi's house about six months before she died."

"Why?" Joce asked.

"I'm not sure," Luke said. "My mother's never been a good liar, but—"

"Unlike you?"

"Yeah," Luke said, grinning. "She said something about a secret that needed to be repaired."

"A secret about what?"

"I don't know. She wouldn't tell me, but it's my guess that my mother knows why Alex McDowell felt like he owed Miss Edi for his whole life."

"**That** secret?" Joce asked. "And your mother knows what it is?"

"Maybe. Why don't you ask her?"

"I think I will."

"Anyway," Luke said, "she said that she and Miss Edi talked a lot about me, about my writing, my dead marriage, about how I used to spend so much time alone with her grumpy ol' father-in law. You know what? That time Grampa Joe sneaked me out of the house to go fishing? Mom knew all about it. She said I always got along better with old people."

"Me too," Jocelyn said. "My mother's . . ." She hadn't had time to think about the people she'd loved so much but who had never told her about the adoption. "Those grandparents, then Miss Edi." Joce looked at him. "What about Ramsey?"

"Everyone knows he and Tess—"

"No! I mean in her will." Joce put her head in her hands. "Now I understand. Miss Edi knew I hated being told who to date. She fixed me up with some really nice men, but I went out with them with the idea that I'd hate them. I was awful! I refused to laugh at their jokes. Everything they said or did, I didn't like . . ." She looked back at Luke. "I think maybe Miss Edi told me Ramsey was the man for me because she didn't want me to have him."

Luke looked at her in wonder. "And my mother told me to stay away from you. She knows I can't resist the forbidden."

"Do you think they were working **together**? Is it possible that you and I have been manipulated?"

They looked at each other. "No," Luke said.

"Too diabolical," Joce said.

"Too conniving. Too—"

"Right," Joce said.

"Certainly not," he agreed.

After a moment, Luke said, "You can have Ramsey if you want him."

"No," she said, smiling as she reached across the table and put her hand on his. "I've decided that I'll follow the tradition of my female ancestors and stick with men who work with their hands."

Luke's eyes warmed. "Why don't you come over here, sit on my lap, and let me show you how well I can work with my hands?"

"Yes, please," Jocelyn said as she got up and walked into his open arms.